S0-ASL-142

PRAISE FOR *TEARS OF TIME*

"Nancy Asire follows in the Tolkien tradition of epic high fantasy; she has a gift for storytelling on the monumental scale.

"*Tears of Time* continues the saga of the rise and fall of an entire world, the clash of two cultures who embody the opposing forces of Good and Evil, yet whose individuals are forced to make the impossible choices of whether to fall, or use the tools of evil for the purpose of good and suffer the possibility of being corrupted by those tools.

"Nancy Asire has created the archetypal hero, forced to choose the chancy path *between* good and evil, a hero who is willing to face corruption of his own soul in order to save his people and his world.

"This is an action-packed and thrilling saga of the kind that the old Norse heroes would recognize and applaud, the fans of Tolkien will cheer, the kind of epic that is seen all too rarely, and is seldom handled with this kind of skill."

—MERCEDES LACKEY

TEARS of TIME

NANCY ASIRE

Annie's Book Stop
Freeport Outlet RT 1
Freeport, ME 04032
(207) 865-3406

TEARS OF TIME

This is a work of fiction. All the characters and events portrayed in this book are fictional, and any resemblance to real people or incidents is purely coincidental.

Copyright © 1993 by Nancy Asire

All rights reserved, including the right to reproduce this book or portions thereof in any form.

A Baen Books Original

Baen Publishing Enterprises
P.O. Box 1403
Riverdale, N.Y. 10471

ISBN: 0-671-72191-7

Cover art by Nancy Asire, Larry Dixon and C.W. Kelly
Map by David Cherry

First printing, October 1993

Distributed by
SIMON & SCHUSTER
1230 Avenue of the Americas
New York, N.Y. 10020

Typeset by Windhaven Press, Auburn, N.H.
Printed in the United States of America

FOR:

Jack and Evelyn Asire,
Mom and Dad, with Love

Susie—another one for you

Marty, Christopher, Brett and Erisa

Sally, Jeff, Janet, Chris and Pat,
for motivation

Ehuika and Aeko;
just because

and

all my various and sundry cats
who have assisted my writing

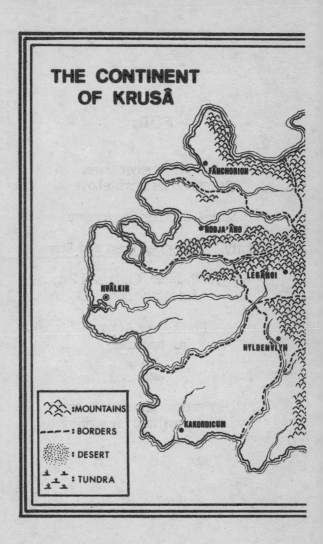

THE CONTINENT
OF KRUSÂ

FANCHORION

NODJA'ÅNG

LEGANGI

HVÅLKIR

HYLDENVLYN

KAKORDICUM

⛰ :MOUNTAINS

---- : BORDERS

⣿ : DESERT

🌲 : TUNDRA

CHAPTER 1

RODJA'ÂNO—
THE NORTHERN FRONTIER

Tsingar reined in his horse at the foot of the stone stairway, in the last patch of afternoon sunlight that fell into the courtyard. Dismounting, he threw the reins to one of the waiting guards and hurried up the stairs. The opened doorway of the palace loomed up before him and he swallowed heavily. Gods! Why had he been summoned? And by Queen Aeschu herself! He paused a moment, nearly losing his nerve, then drew a deep breath and stepped inside.

The high-ceilinged hall was crowded, yet not one thought leaked out from tightly shielded minds. Darkly clad men stood clustered together, a shaft of sunlight glinting off chainmail and weapons. Tsingar passed them by, these men who bore his own rank or higher. Sweat broke out on his forehead. Did *they* know why the Queen had called for him? He bit his lower lip and hurried on, glancing only once out a window as he walked.

Rodja'âno lay below the citadel height, fire-gutted and haunted by shadows, rebuilt only enough so that the warlord Ssenkahdavic and his Queen could have

1

their highest ranking warriors nearby. The rest of the vast army lay camped around the walls, this side and the other of the River Lhanic.

Tsingar felt the presence of the other men in the room again, heavy and overpowering. They were as responsible as he to the warlord for what went on in the captured city. And as far as he knew, no one had betrayed that trust.

Two of the warlord's honor guard stood beside the closed doorway at the end of the hall. Tsingar increased his pace, licked his lips nervously, and stopped a few steps short of that door.

"Tsingar of the Clan of Higulen," he said, "reporting as commanded."

One of the guards nodded, turned and opened the heavy wood doors. Tsingar shivered, ran his fingers down the long scar that marred the side of his face, and stepped into the room beyond.

The doors shut behind: for a moment he stood in darkness, gathering courage to go forward. Only four lamps shone, their light nearly lost in the dark hangings of the room. Three shadowy figures waited at the far end of the chamber, one seated on a raised dais, the other two standing nearby.

Tsingar's bootheels sounded loud on the floor. *Gods! Why am I so nervous? This is an honor for me, for my Clan. There's nothing to fear.* He cringed inwardly. He had much to fear, here at the center of darkness.

He stood at last before the raised chair, his eyes downcast. In a ritual old as his Leishoranya people, he slowly removed his weapons, kissed them each, and laid them in submission before the man who sat in that chair. Then, he fell to his knees, lifted both hands as if shackled above his head, and bowed forward until his forehead touched the cold stone floor.

"I exist only to serve you, Dark Lord."

"Rise, Tsingar." A woman's voice—soft, and full of icy power: Aeschu, the Queen. "Behold, your Lord."

He rocked back on his heels, and stood, his knees gone weak. Then, but only because he was compelled, did he look directly at the man seated before him.

Though Ssenkahdavic sat with closed eyes, Tsingar knew himself watched; for a moment, he felt pulled into the darkness of the warlord's mind, his soul shredded away, his life a brief nothing. Shadowed by lamplight, Ssenkahdavic's perfect face seemed beautiful beyond all imagining. Custom decreed that only children of sufficient strength and beauty be allowed to survive, yet even so, Ssenkahdavic put all others to shame. He would have stood out from other men, however, despite his handsomeness: down the left side of the warlord's hair ran a streak of pure white, startling against the surrounding blackness.

Tsingar stirred uneasily, burrowed even deeper behind his shields, and tore his eyes away from Ssenkahdavic. *Marked—he's marked by the Gods for the death of the Light.*

"Don't be afraid, Tsingar." Once again, it was the woman who spoke. "You've not been summoned for punishment."

Tsingar let loose his pent-up breath, trying not to stare at the Queen. Tall, raven-haired, her face sculpted by the Gods for its beauty, she represented every physical characteristic his people found desirable in a woman. Gold jewelry caught the lamplight. Her dress of rich, blood-red velvet lent the room its only color.

And now, his eyes grown used to the dimness, Tsingar recognized the second person who stood in the shadows by the high-seat, dressed, like the warlord, in rich black and gold.

Mehdaiy.

Tsingar caught back the grimace before it reached his face. Mehdaiy: brother to Dhumaric, his old commander. One of the Great Lords, Dhumaric had died in that hilltop battle a year ago fighting against three

Krotànya princes, the deadliest of whom were Kahsir dàn Ahzur and Lorhaiden dàn Hrudharic.

Queen Aeschu spoke again, her voice quiet in the room's quietness. "You've been summoned here for reward. Your performance hasn't gone unnoticed, in the year since we took Rodja'âno. Even Dhumaric thought highly of you."

Dhumaric? Tsingar struggled to keep expressionless. He sensed something more to all this than he could see.

"I know what's happened to you, Tsingar," Aeschu said, moving closer to her husband's side. "All of it. How you disposed of Chaagut when he challenged your power. How you left Girdun to die after he tried to kill you." A smile colder than death touched the Queen's beautiful face. "You're clever—clever and intelligent. And you know your bounds. My lord husband likes that in his commanders."

Tsingar bowed at the compliment, his heart tightening.

"The Krotànya are fighting hard in defense of the last of their kingdoms." A shadow touched Aeschu's eyes. "A great battle took place to the south of Elyâsai, near the River Mijhàda. The Lord Chiyuksai was killed there by none other than the Krotànya Throne Prince, Kahsir. It was a defeat for us, Tsingar . . . a grave defeat. I'm sending Mehdaiy south to take over Chiyuksai's command."

Tsingar glanced quickly at the tall man who stood at Ssenkahdavic's side. The resemblance between Mehdaiy and his late brother Dhumaric was amazing; here lay coldness and cunning only Dhumaric had rivaled. A thin tickle of sweat ran down Tsingar's cheek, but he kept his eyes level with the Queen's.

"A word of caution." The merest hint of a smile touched Aeschu's face, though her eyes held no expression. "Don't be deluded as Dhumaric was. That delusion cost us a commander we greatly miss. Search for Kahsir and Lorhaiden—fight and harry them well.

If you can, take them or kill them. But don't let revenge cloud your mind, as it did Dhumaric's."

Tsingar sensed more than saw a stirring on the throne: Ssenkahdavic sat motionless, wrapped in some somnolent communion with the Shadow he served, yet totally aware of what took place before him. A touch on Tsingar's mind: though thin, its power made him flinch behind shields he knew to be useless.

—*They'll be mine at last,* came the whisper of Ssenkahdavic's mind-touch. *The Gods have promised it.*

Tsingar shivered before the wave of icy power that swept out through the room.

"Go," Aeschu said. "Bring honor to your weapons and your Clan."

"My life is yours," Tsingar whispered. He bowed again, once to the Great Lord and once to the Queen. But to Ssenkahdavic he gave full obeisance, kneeling, forehead to floor. One by one, he picked up his weapons, offered them to the shadowy figure in the high-seat, then kissed them and returned them to their sheaths. Eyes lowered, he rose and backed away from the dais into the darkness behind. And only when he sensed himself dismissed, did he turn and walk hastily toward the opening double doors.

HVÂLKIR—CAPITAL OF THE KINGDOMS OF VYJENOR

Kahsir looked at the game board, hesitated briefly, then set his tile in place. He glanced up: Ahndrej stared at the developing game, darted a quick look up from the board, then drew a game tile from the table. For a long moment, Ahndrej looked at the tile; Kahsir watched him closely, but Ahndrej gave no hint of what he thought. Slowly, deliberately, Ahndrej placed his newly drawn tile at the end of one of the patterns he was constructing.

The game pieces lay in a heap to Kahsir's left. He reached out and drew one from the far side: another continuation tile. Looking at his own patterns, he found the weakest, and added the new tile to the end of the line.

Kahsir glanced up at Ahndrej, whose dark face gave no indication how this affected things. Ahndrej rubbed his jaw, looked a moment longer at the board, then reached out for another tile.

This time, Ahndrej's expression cracked: he lifted one eyebrow and stared at the tile in his hand. Enough pieces had been played that Kahsir could guess what his sister's lover had drawn by the patterns already established on the board.

"Why do I do this to myself?" Ahndrej asked in a weary voice. "I've never been lucky at this game. Yet every time you ask me to play, I agree." He tapped his head with the game tile. "Stupid, don't you think?"

Kahsir shrugged and leaned back in his chair. Never been lucky? As much as Ahndrej complained, he played better than most people.

"Is Grandfather still down in the garden with Tebehrren?" asked Iowyn.

Kahsir's eyes traveled from his sister, who stood behind Ahndrej's chair, to the window overlooking the garden. "Probably. When those two start arguing, there's little can stop them."

"Huhn. I'd think your wedding might slow them down. Grandfather's in the midst of the plans."

Kahsir laughed. "The rest of the family's not here yet. Be patient. You'd think *you* were getting married."

Iowyn smiled slightly and glanced at her lover. Ahndrej snorted something unheard, concentrating on the board, the pattern he was building, and the tile he held. Kahsir smothered a grin and reviewed his own positions: his tiles marched in three steady lines down the squares of the game board toward its far edge, forming patterns of inevitability. Ahndrej would take his time before making his next move.

Kahsir stood and walked to the window that overlooked the garden: new spring leaves and budding flowers ran along a gravel path. The distant murmur of voices rose from his right—his grandfather and Tebehrren. He set one hand on the windowsill and leaned outward, but could not see them or hear what they said. *It's probably best. I've heard all their arguments before.*

He ran his fingertips across the smooth wood of the windowsill. Suddenly, he was a child again, a child who could barely see over that sill. The towering silverleaf tree that stood in the center of the garden was a sapling so small he could encircle its trunk with both hands. From out of his memories, the laughter of his brothers and sister rang through that garden.

He looked at the tree again, at the stub of one missing branch: centuries past a lightning bolt had scarred the tree. His ancestors had brought the silverleaf with them in their flight to the continent of Krusâ—it lived nearly as long as the people who prized it. By contrast, the other trees in the garden died and were replaced after only a few hundred years.

He willed himself to remember more, forced the partitions burying the Old Memories, and called up sights and sounds of long ago.

Time shifted—present became past again. A slender dark-haired girl stepped from behind that growing tree. Another playmate of his own age, daughter of one of his father's friends.

Eltàrim—his coming marriage. For the first time in his life he would become responsible for her happiness and safety. He smiled briefly. Responsible for her? She had always been capable; her strength had attracted him from the first. He saw her as if she stood beside the silverleaf again, only grown now: her sureness, her quiet competent movements, her soft laugh.

Fully back in the present, he looked at the tree again,

then turned away. Sunlight streamed in through the other window, on the west. A gnarled miniature tree stood on that sill, a tree his grandfather had carefully cultivated over the past two centuries. *Patience, that's what trees are about. And Grandfather's more patient than most.* A brief pang of envy tightened his heart. *Lords! To be that patient! Will I ever be old enough?*

He glanced at Ahndrej, who sat in one of the chairs grouped before the High-King's desk. The low game table was made of the same warm wood as the rest of the furniture in the room, and was just as old. Iowyn leaned over Ahndrej's shoulder, the sunlight touching her long dark hair.

Ahndrej: eldest of the House of dàn Herahlu. Short, black-haired, hazel-eyed, dusky complexion darkened further by time spent overseeing his lands; he laughed easily and often, and loved the land he worked with a fierce, consuming passion. Though head of an immense steading, Ahndrej was Land-Born and held no title of his own. Iowyn had been courted by princes, many of whom could not understand her love for this simple man of the south. Kahsir snorted softly: *they* did not know Ahndrej as he did.

Iowyn murmured something soft in Ahndrej's ear and straightened. She stood taller than Ahndrej, tall even for a woman of a Star-Born House. To Kahsir's eyes, it was only a matter of time before his sister and Ahndrej declared themselves Chosen, their wedding in these troubled days hastened as his own.

Ahndrej made a small noise of disgust; Kahsir left the window and stood beside his own chair, waiting for the next move.

After a moment, Ahndrej looked up, frowned and waved a weary hand. "Will you go away and let me think in peace? I'm having a hard enough time as it is without you staring at me."

Kahsir lifted one eyebrow as his opponent looked back at the game board. Something was obviously bothering Ahndrej, though he had not spoken about it and had his shields tightly closed. If Ahndrej had been a warrior, he could have taken no more care with his strategies. *Don't think about the war. Don't think of it!* He walked across the room. *Your wedding's almost here. Darkness and war have no place in it.*

The large map hung at the far wall of the study: sunlight brightened the red marks Vlàdor had made on it, inked indications of encroaching enemy armies. Cities lay broken and burning . . . battles turned open meadows to scenes of slaughter. For nearly fifteen hundred years—unending warfare against the invaders of the continent of Krusâ. Kahsir shuddered, but the memories remained.

Suddenly, his sister's mind touched his and he saw himself through her eyes: tall, broad-shouldered, dressed in a house tunic of supple suede; long, dark hair, prominent jaw below shadowed eyes; hands clenched into fists, stance at odds with the peace of the quiet room. Random thoughts spilled from Iowyn's and Ahndrej's minds.

—*Why am I even bothering to play this game, Io? He's always been better at it than I have.*

—*Luckier, too.*

—*Is it luck? Lords know he's got one of the most powerful minds in your family.*

—*Ah, Dreja. He wouldn't cheat and Read you. Not Kahs. He's far too honorable.*

—*I know, I know. Sometimes he's too honorable for his own good.*

—*And you're worrying about your family. . . . You can't keep your mind on the game.*

Kahsir stirred and sensed Iowyn's attention turn in his direction.

—*Quit thinking about the war, Kahs. You've been fighting too long without a rest as it is.* And aloud: "Forget the map. There's time for that later. Worrying about the war won't win it."

He turned to face his sister. She stared back, then dropped her eyes.

"Alàric's certainly been asleep for a long time," she said.

"Aye." Kahsir thought of his youngest brother, walked to his chair and sat down. "That wound needs it."

"When did you say Haskon's due home? This afternoon?"

"Any time now. He's taking the mind-road straight from the eastern front. With all those leagues to travel and little time, he doesn't have much choice. He fought in battle only yesterday and—"

"He'll be all right." Iowyn smiled slightly. "He has enough energy for all of us." She glanced at the opened northern window. "What *are* Grandfather and Tebehrren talking about? They've been out there for over an hour."

"Lords only know," Kahsir replied. "As for me, I'm not sure I want to." Chief of all the Mind-Born, the *Aisomàk-Wehàrya*, Tebehrren was more: scholar, teacher, and Advisor to the High-King. Kahsir stretched his legs out, crossed one booted foot on the other and stared at his opponent. "Would you move, Ahndrej? We'll be here all day if you don't do something."

Ahndrej scowled at the game tile he held. "That's easy for *you* to say."

"Oh, just set it down." Iowyn gestured at the two rows of Ahndrej's tiles he was struggling to turn from the center of the board to its edge. "It won't make any difference which row you choose."

Ahndrej frowned again. "I wanted to ask you something," he said, looking up at Kahsir. "My family's making plans to leave Vharcwal. It's only a matter of time before the enemy crosses our borders. Some folk have already fled Tutuljad, and that's four days' ride southeast of Vharcwal. You're in charge of the southern border. How urgent are things?"

Kahsir stared. Though Ahndrej had finally brought up what bothered him, something remained unsaid, something barely below the surface of his mind, hidden by his shields. *Why don't you come out and say it, Ahndrej? We all know who's defending Tutuljad.*

Iowyn shifted from one foot to the other behind Ahndrej's chair. "Don't trust Lorhaiden," she said in a rush. "Don't, Kahs. He'll let you down."

Kahsir sighed quietly, intensely aware of Ahndrej's stare.

"Let me finish before you cut me off." Iowyn flipped a long strand of hair over her shoulder. "We've been over this before, you and I, times without number. Hard days are coming in the south. Ahndrej doesn't have to tell you that. The *last* thing you need is a captain blinded by a killing-oath. Lorhaiden sees things only in black and white, never gray."

He stared at her for a long moment. "There are times when you see in black and white, too. And Lorhaiden—"

"He's crazy! And I don't want you hurt because you're oathed to him." She gestured sharply. "It's not that I *dislike* Lorhaiden. Lords of Light! He's grown up right under my nose, near a brother to me. But—"

"Lorhaiden's changed. He has a command. The responsibility has done him a world of good."

She glanced away. "I can see I'm not going to change your mind." The hint of a smile tugged at the corners of her mouth as she looked back. "Not that I have in the past, either." All humor left her face. "If you won't listen to me, then listen to Alàric, to Haskon. Listen to any number of people who'll tell you the same thing."

"Ahndrej?" Kahsir asked. "You know Lorhaiden. Do *you* think he's crazy?"

Ahndrej smiled slightly. "I think I'm going to make my move and stay out of family fights." He reached out and set his game tile down on the board.

Iowyn drew a deep breath and some of the tension drained from the room.

"You would have been smarter to move over there," she said to Ahndrej, pointing at the board and his other line of tiles. "See how Kahs is setting himself up to—"

"Who's playing this game anyway?" Kahsir asked. "Ahndrej or you?"

Ahndrej glanced over his shoulder, his smile brilliant against his dark face. "You can take my place if you want to, Io. Then *you'll* lose."

Iowyn frowned and walked away from the game table.

Kahsir stared at the board a moment and drew another tile from those spread out along the edge of the game board. He carefully placed it at the end of one of his game rows. Ahndrej groaned in despair.

"You never did tell me, Kahs," Iowyn said from across the room, "now that Lorhaiden's commanding his own army, who acts as your shieldman?"

Kahsir glared at his sister. "You can't let it alone, can you?"

"Well?" She set her chin stubbornly. "Who is it?"

"I don't have one."

"What? No shieldman? How do you think you can—"

"I've sworn not to take another shieldman while Lorhaiden's alive. You know that. If I did—if I took another, I don't think he'd understand."

"Because he's stiff-necked, narrow-minded—"

"He's also my sword-brother, my *baràdor*," Kahsir said softly, "and *that* oath I can't break." He lifted his hands helplessly. "It's all too tangled. One oath runs from the other."

"And both bound up in Lorhaiden's revenge."

"There's that. But I'm protected. Pohlàntyr—he's my new second-in-command—serves as shieldman now that I'm separated from Lorhaiden. I trust him."

Ahndrej drew another tile and the hint of a smile crossed his face. "Io. Come look at this."

Kahsir turned slightly as his sister took up her position again behind Ahndrej's chair. "Am I to play both of you together," he asked, "or just one at a time?"

Iowyn grinned. "Dreja needs all the help he can get."

Ahndrej snorted loudly and reached out to place his tile on the board. Iowyn pushed his hand aside.

"Not there, Dreja," she said in a pained voice. "Can't you see where Kahs is trying to go?"

Suddenly, the swift touch of his grandfather's mind brushed Kahsir's awareness . . . quick and heavily shielded.

"Io," he said, standing. "Since you're being so helpful, take my place, will you? Grandfather wants to see me."

Iowyn met his eyes, her face gone serious. "Why—?"

"Probably more wedding plans," Kahsir answered, keeping his voice light. "I'll be back. See that you don't lose my advantage."

Iowyn watched her brother leave the room, waited until the door had shut behind him, then turned to Ahndrej.

"What's that all about?" he asked.

She shrugged her shoulders, came around from behind his chair, and sat down in Kahsir's place. "I don't know. But I don't think it's as innocent as Kahs made it out to be."

Ahndrej's eyes met hers. "You don't think—"

"—it concerns the southern border?" she finished his thought for him. "It might."

"But things have been quiet now . . . ever since Kahs won at Mijhàda."

Iowyn picked up a game piece, sat idly dropping it from hand to hand. "You were the one who asked Kahs how things were going to the south, Dreja. Of course what Grandfather wants to talk about could concern the war. Doesn't everything these days?"

"I know." Ahndrej sighed softly. "Dammit, Io! I don't trust this lack of action to the south. I'm afraid for my family. If anything should happen to them . . ."

"They should be safe. With our armies strung out all across the southern border, we shouldn't be surprised by the enemy."

"Shouldn't." He chewed on his lower lip a moment. "That's no certitude."

She set the game piece down unplayed. "I know. But will they listen to us? No. I'm just the baby sister."

"Kahs listens."

"Aye, but he's one of the few. He's more suspicious of the enemy than I am." She threw up one hand. "If the Leishoranya are quiet over here—" a quick gesture to her right "—then beware of what they're doing over there. By the Light, Dreja! Can't they understand? I'm tired to death of staying home, of not putting my talents to use in the field." Her back straightened. "I'm a warrior and a commander, but *they* won't let me fight or lead."

"Then come home with me," Ahndrej said, reaching across the table and taking her hand. "Marry me now, Io. We might not have much time left."

"We're not even Chosen," she murmured, keeping her eyes lowered, unwilling to meet his. "There's—"

His hand tightened. "Dammit, Io! That's all I ever hear from you! 'We're not Chosen.' I *love* you . . . can't you understand that?"

"And I love you," she replied, looking up from the game board and holding his gaze. "But . . ."

"What's holding you back? I know I have no title—"

"Dreja! I don't care spit about your lack of title or possession of one, and you know it!" She drew her hand from his and stood. "I want to fight the enemy. I want to *do* something, instead of sit around and worry about what other people are doing!"

He rose from his chair and came to her side. "You're working against tradition, Io. Women have fought only recently alongside men. For thousands of years, we've had peace. . . ."

"Until the Leishoranya found us again!" she snapped. "Don't tell me what I already know. I realize I'm not physically as strong as you are, but I've got my mind! So has every other woman alive! At the very least, we could use them to help our cause!"

"We can't use mental power save for defense, Io."

"What do you *think* I'm proposing, Dreja? If women can't fight in battle, we could help defend against the enemy!"

Ahndrej made as if to put his arm around her shoulders, but she moved from his side and walked across the room to the opened window.

"Io," he said, trailing her. "Eltàrim commands bush fighters to the north. Perhaps . . ."

"Eltàrim's Eltàrim. I'm me. I don't want to sit here in the capital, moving little pins around on a map and having secret discussions with spies and scouts!"

"That's not fair. Eltàrim's helping our cause more than—"

She closed her eyes briefly. "I know. More than I am. But I want to *be* there, Dreja! I don't have Eltàrim's patience, and I know it. I have to *see* the results of my actions!"

"Then marry me, Io . . . come home with me. You could command the defense of Vharcwal and the steadings that lie close to my own. You could—"

She turned around so she faced him, struggling to keep her voice even. "I can't marry you now, Dreja. I want to, but I can't. Try to understand. If I *did* marry you, I couldn't keep my mind on the military situation at hand. I couldn't trust my judgment. I'd be afraid that any decision I made might be colored by that love."

"Kahsir's not worried that *his* marriage will cloud his vision," Ahndrej replied stiffly.

Iowyn's heart tightened. "Kahs has been leading

armies for the entire length of this war. If nothing else, *he* has experience. I've got none. And nobody seems willing to let me get any!" She reached out and touched his cheek. "Let's drop the subject, Dreja . . . leave it alone for awhile. I'm of two minds concerning everything lately. Give me a chance to go one way or the other."

He turned away. She saw his shoulders tense with either emotion or anger, but he was so heavily shielded, she had trouble Reading him.

"Well, then, Io," he said at last, waving toward the red-inked map across the room. "Make up your mind soon, *tahvah*. We may be running out of time."

CHAPTER 2

Kahsir took the back stairs down to the garden, his heart thudding in his chest. His grandfather's brief mind-touch was not responsible for this reaction, but Kahsir sensed something apart from the brief Sending—something, perhaps, his grandfather did not know.

Vlàdor waited in the garden, seated under one of the *melenor* trees. Nothing in his expression hinted as to what he thought: the darkly bearded face was calm, the gray eyes hooded. Kahsir coughed politely and stepped out from the shadows.

"You wanted to see me?" he asked softly.

Vlàdor lifted his head. Looking up into Kahsir's eyes, he gestured to the empty end of the stone bench. "Aye. Sit, Kahs."

"What's wrong?"

"Nothing. Everything." Vlàdor's laugh was brittle. "With the military situation the way it is, you ask what's wrong?"

Kahsir leaned forward on the bench, resting his arms across his knees, and met his grandfather's gaze. "The southern front?"

"Aye." The High-King looked up at the sky, then down again. "I'm beginning to believe you, Kahs, though I don't want to. The enemy's up to their tricks

17

again. This period of inactivity has gone on too long without them taking *some* action."

"You'd hoped that after Mijhàda we might end up with a few years to regroup and rebuild—"

"I wasn't the only one who hoped that. Your father . . ." Kahsir looked away.

"Kahs." Vlàdor's voice commanded his attention. "You and your father are going to have to come to some kind of agreement. Even since Rodja'âno fell, you've been terse and all business around him."

"Why shouldn't I be? He's fighting to the north, and I'm stationed in the south. We seldom cross paths."

"That's not what I'm talking about, and you know it."

Kahsir grimaced. Rodja'âno. Because of his decision to disobey his father's orders—and his grandfather's— he stood mainly responsible for the great loss of life in that city's fall. No matter that his holding out against Ssenkahdavic had weakened the Dark Lord to the extent that he had gone dormant, leaving the command of his vast armies to his wife and his generals. The fact still remained: thousands of good men had died, men who might have lived to face the enemy elsewhere. In addition, most of the Mind-Born in Rodja'âno had fallen beneath Ssenkahdavic's mental attack, their loss as keenly felt as that of the warriors.

And Nhavari? His good friend, Nhavari, King of Tumâs? Dead, also, because he had trusted Kahsir's plan of defense. Kahsir's fists clenched. He could no more disassociate himself from those deaths than he could take the mind-road to one of the moons.

"Kahs. Don't." Vlàdor's voice was gentle. "You did what you thought was right and, for the most part, it turned out to be. Nhavari could have left Rodja'âno before you arrived with your plan of defense."

Kahsir tightened his shields. "I know. But it still hurts—hurts deeply. And the way Father's treated me since—"

"You haven't helped things by your attitude."

"*My* attitude? He's been cold as ice to me ever since he found out I'd disobeyed him." Kahsir gestured briefly. "I've tried to stay out of his way, to keep my mouth shut and my thoughts to myself. That hasn't changed things."

"He incorporated your plans for defending Tumâs," Vlàdor pointed out.

"And then sent me home like a misbehaving dog!" Kahsir straightened and turned on the bench so he faced his grandfather. "We'll never see eye to eye on strategy, but, by the Lords! Can't he see what's going on? We can only defend so long until we don't have anything left to defend! He keeps falling back, trusting the land and nature to be his allies. One of these days, he'll—"

"You're still upset because we didn't allow you to keep attacking to the south, aren't you?"

Kahsir drew a long breath, tried to put his unruly thoughts in order. "Upset is stating it mildly. If we could have organized ourselves and gone after the enemy while they were leaderless and disorganized, we might have been able to push them back from the border. Now, we've given them the time to reorganize *and* for the high command in Rodja'âno to find someone new to lead them!"

"I know."

Kahsir met his grandfather's eyes, saw the shadows there, and knew how much that answer had cost.

"I had hoped, as you pointed out, that the very decisiveness of your victory at Mijhàda would give us time to regroup. To let wounded men heal. To strengthen our defenses." Vlàdor rubbed his bearded chin. "And now I'm beginning to think otherwise. The enemy *is* up to something, Kahs. The Mind-Born can't Read them, but I've fought the Leishoranya long enough to know they'll never do exactly what you expect."

"So. What were you and Tebehrren talking about?"

"The usual things. Offense as opposed to defense. Using our minds to retaliate against the enemy. I know . . . I know. The Law. We can't disobey the Law or the Shadow will grow stronger. But it's a fine line that divides offensive and defensive attacks."

"In other words, you're saying that once we've been attacked mentally by the enemy, if we strike back in kind, it could be considered a defense."

"Aye. But Tebehrren said it's still the same thing. Our minds should not be used for destruction."

Kahsir looked away, off into the garden. Rodja'âno. His own futile mental attempt to attack Ssenkahdavic. Willing to damn himself to save the city's defenders, he had withdrawn at the last moment, sickened not only by what he was doing, but by the brief contact he made with the Leishoranya warlord. No one knew what he had tried, and he had buried memories of it so deep he hoped no one would ever find out.

"Ah, forget Tebehrren," the High-King said, dismissing the Mind-Born with a flick of his fingers. "I don't think our arguments will make a difference in the outcome of this war."

"Probably not."

"At least your victory gave you time to come home and be married. Lords know *that's* been put off long enough."

Kahsir frowned. "And that's another thing . . . if Father doesn't stop telling me how much we need a child of mine to be heir, I swear I'll—"

"It's true, Kahs. We *do* need an heir. Neither you, nor your brothers or sister have given any indication you would ever marry. Don't you see? What happens should I die . . . should your father, you and your brothers and sister die? What then? Who will lead our people?"

"I'm *getting* married, dammit!" Kahsir replied. "Isn't that enough for you?"

"It is . . . it is. Forgive your father for pushing. He's thinking about the future."

"Well, he can—"

"My Lords."

Kahsir turned; Tebehrren stood on the graveled walkway, his white robe brilliant against the shadows and the green of the garden.

Vlàdor stood. "What's happened?"

"I've had word from Lorhaiden," Tebehrren said, his voice never altering from its usual calm.

"Lorhaiden?" Kahsir was on his feet in an instant. He glanced at his grandfather, his mouth gone dry. "Why—?"

"He didn't Send to you, Lord," Tebehrren explained, "because of the situation. Tutuljad's been attacked. It's close to falling. The enemy was blocking any Sending he tried to make for help. I was lucky that I could receive. He's facing ten thousand men or more, and he's lost around a third of his forces."

For a long moment, it seemed no one breathed, that the world itself hung motionless. Kahsir's heart lurched and he closed his eyes. It had happened at last: a Leishoranya army, obviously well-trained and well-led, had crossed the border into Elyâsai.

O Lords of Light! Could this be it? The final push? If it is, we're doomed! As things stand, we'll lose it all . . . everything we've managed to hold until this moment. And suddenly, Eltàrim's face formed in his mind, along with his longing for her, his love. He clenched his hands at his sides. *Not now . . . of all times, not now! We've waited too long to get married—far too long! With the enemy across the borders . . .*

"Does anyone else know?" Kahsir asked finally, his voice trembling.

"No. Not yet." Tebehrren's level gaze never wavered. "I just learned."

"Dammit to Darkness! Tutuljad's lost if Lorhaiden's suffered those kind of casualties." Kahsir turned to his grandfather. "Do you know what this will mean?"

"Aye." Vlàdor's voice was steady, as controlled as his

face. "I'm all too aware of it. But I can't see any way of saving the city. We don't have enough time or men."

"What of Ahndrej?" Kahsir asked. "He should know about this as soon as possible. His family—"

"I'll tell him," Vlàdor said. This time, Kahsir noticed a faint tremor in his grandfather's voice.

Kahsir fell silent. Ahndrej would Send to his family and, if he thought it necessary, go south himself, though his brother was a capable man, well able to coordinate the family's evacuation.

But Lorhaiden . . . a third of his army lost? "Lorhaiden . . ." Kahsir's voice broke momentarily. "Is he all right?"

"Aye," Tebehrren answered. "Only his pride's been wounded."

"I've got to go to him, Grandfather. He had five thousand men with him at Tutuljad. Even if the enemy's lost the same number that he has—"

Vlàdor snorted. "Knowing Lorhaiden, increased odds will make the fight more enjoyable." He held up a hand. "Wait, Kahs. Lorhaiden's too thoroughly outnumbered. He might be able to hold another day or two, but Tutuljad's all but gone. I'm going to call for a council meeting of sorts and I think you ought to be present for that."

"Lorhaiden's still going to need reinforcements. He'll have to regroup."

"Eltàrim. Your wedding."

Kahsir stood silent for a long moment. His Chosen Woman, soon to be his wife, weighed against his sword-brother, his *baràdor*, dearer than any friend.

"Wait awhile," Vlàdor said, setting a hand on his shoulder. "At least until after council."

Kahsir nodded wordlessly. He turned, walked to the edge of the garden, and stared at the blooming flowers. Drawing a deep breath, he commanded his heart to beat slower.

"I'll wait, Grandfather," he said at last. "But I'm leaving tonight, no matter how late."

While Vlàdor reported the enemy invasion, Kahsir looked around the study, lit now after sunset by hanging lamps and candles. Most of the commanders who usually attended such meetings were gone from the capital, leading armies on Elyâsai's troubled borders. But those present were men his grandfather loved, his most trusted commanders—men he could depend on for advice and loyalty.

Here also sat three generations of the House of dàn Ahzur: himself, his grandfather, his father, his two brothers, and his sister Iowyn. The other men sat with easy familiarity in the study: Lord Devàn dàn Chivondeth, Rhudhyàri dàn Vijhalis, and Tamien dàn Khondaven. And seated slightly to one side—Lord Tebehrren, Chief of all the Mind-Born.

Kahsir glanced at Iowyn: pale-faced, she looked back. Ahndrej had indeed Sent to his family, telling them of Tutuljad's peril. Then, despite the late hour, he had taken the mind-road those thousand and more leagues to be with them in person. If Ahndrej felt things were under control, he would return the following day.

"So." Vlàdor leaned back in his chair, clearly relieved at having reached the end of his tale. "There you have it: Tutuljad's plight, Lorhaiden's defense, and the Leishoranya in Elyâsai."

"Who will you send south with reinforcements?" Lord Devàn asked.

Kahsir sat up straighter in his chair. "I'll be taking them. Lorhaiden's my sword-brother. I'm bound to go."

"I won't be able to give you many men," Vlàdor said. "Right now, I can only spare five hundred."

"No more? I'd hoped for at least a thousand. Lorhaiden's probably lost nearly twice that number by now." Kahsir rubbed his chin and looked at his grandfather. "I'll go to my own army first and gather enough warriors to give me another five hundred. I've got a lot of wounded, or I'd take more. Then there's the loss of time. Tutuljad's a hard two days' ride west of my army. That might be two days too long."

"What of your wedding, Lord?" This from Rhudhyàri, who sat at Vlàdor's right hand. "It's only five days away."

"I'm oathed to aid Lorhaiden. Eltàrim will understand." He drew his shields tighter. *She must understand. We've survived too many other delays, each unavoidable as this.* He looked around the room, his eyes briefly resting on each face there. "I don't have a choice. I've *got* to go."

Alàric muttered something and shook his blond head. "Lorhaiden will resent your interfering, Kahs."

"Perhaps." Kahsir squared his shoulders and met his youngest brother's eyes. "I know you think he's crazy, Ahri—you and everyone else in this room. But he's not."

"At least *sometimes* not," Haskon said.

Kahsir looked at his middle brother, seeking a hint of humor, but found none. *Dammit, Lorj. If you weren't so caught up by that* fihrkken *Oath of yours. . . .*

"Go to him, then," Vlàdor said. Kahsir saw a brief flash of sympathy cross his grandfather's face. "But don't overextend yourself."

Kahsir turned to Tebehrren. "He *did* ask for reinforcements, didn't he?"

"No, Lord."

"No?"

"That sounds like him, Kahs," Vlàdor said. "He didn't ask, but I'm sure he won't turn them down."

"How many did Lorhaiden say he's facing?" Tamien asked Tebehrren.

"Close to ten thousand."

"Ten thousand?" Tamien echoed. "Until now, we've faced armies of less than five thousand. Save for the one that Kahsir met and defeated, we haven't seen forces this large since last spring."

"The Leishoranya I fought recently numbered well over five thousand," Alàric said, absently touching the binding on his wounded leg. "Each new army has been larger than the last."

"Tebehrren." Vlàdor turned to the white-robed man. "Save for brief answers, you've been uncommonly silent. Don't you have anything to add?"

"Nothing, Lord. One doesn't have to be Mind-Born to see what faces us."

"It's plain enough to me," Rhudhyàri said. "Elyâsai's threatened on all three borders. There's only one thing the enemy *can* be doing. They're consolidating for a major invasion."

Tamien cursed softly. "I wouldn't be surprised. We've been fearing that for years now. But the coordination necessary to accomplish such a thing staggers my mind."

Kahsir stirred impatiently in his chair. "That skill's been used against us in the past. If anyone can do it, it's Ssenkahdavic."

"Lords of Light!" Devàn's face went pale. "You don't think he's—"

"Awakened only a year after taking Rodja'âno?" Kahsir shook his head. "I don't know."

"It *could* be Ssenkahdavic's wife," Vlàdor said. "She's equal to any of their generals."

The silence that followed was stifling. Kahsir longed to say something, anything, that sounded cheerful. *We're still alive. There's always that.*

"There are times," Xeredir said, the first words he had spoken since the council convened, "when it seems madness to go on."

"What choice do we have?" Tebehrren leaned forward in his chair. "In ages past, so long ago that even we have forgotten, we faced the enemy in another place, another time. Long before we came to this continent, we opposed them. For every one of us who falls in defense of the Light, the Light grows stronger. When this universe dies and is reborn, how strong the Light is in opposition to the Shadow depends on what we do today."

Lord Devàn snorted. "That's so far off in the future, none of us—and, I suspect, not even *you*—could guess *how* far off. We're fighting a life and death war now, Tebehrren. Not in the future. *Now!*"

Tebehrren met Devàn's angry look with his usual coolness. "Very well. You want to talk about now? We have two choices, my Lord. We can surrender to the Shadow and ensure our deaths and the destruction of all we are. Or we can fight, hoping that one day some of us will live to push that Darkness back."

"Hjshraiel," murmured Alàric into the quiet that followed.

Kahsir glanced up at his brother. *Hjshraiel*. The one foretold. The one who would stand against Ssenkahdavic, to become a channel for the Powers of Light as the Leishoranya warlord was for those of Darkness.

"He hasn't come, Ahri," Vlàdor said bitterly. "We're facing the Shadow alone. And, if Hjshraiel *does* come, if he's *not* some comforting myth, may the Light grant him living Krotànya to lead."

Tebehrren stirred in his chair again, his white robe rustling in the silence. "He'll come, Lord," he said, his voice full of certainty. "He's the Man of All Possible Futures. When the times have converged upon his moment, he'll come. And when he does . . ."

"When, when, when," Devàn snapped. "That's all you can talk about, isn't it, Tebehrren? Why don't you tell us something useful, like *when* the enemy will attack us next? How many warriors have they massed at key positions? What are—"

"Devà," Vlàdor said, lifting a hand. "Leave off. All Tebehrren could tell us is what he Sees in a myriad of futures. We'd still be left to speculate."

Kahsir rubbed his nose, hiding his expression. There was no love lost between the cavalry commander and Tebehrren, and everyone in the room knew it.

"So." Vlàdor stood and Kahsir and the others rose with him. "We go on. We fight on. As always." He squared his shoulders. "Kahs will go south with Lorhaiden's reinforcements, and with luck, he'll return in several days. Then," he said, coming around from behind his desk, "we can get down to the business of seeing him married."

Rhudhyàri and Tamien smiled, but Devàn still glowered in Lord Tebehrren's direction. Vlàdor caught Devàn's eyes and motioned toward the door with a slight movement of his head. The cavalry commander muttered something, turned and walked stiff-legged to where Rhudhyàri and Tamien waited. Tebehrren lifted one eyebrow, threw Vlàdor an unreadable look, and was the first to leave the room, followed by the three men who stood aside to let him pass.

"Devà's certainly no fonder of Tebehrren than the last time they met, is he?" Kahsir asked.

Vlàdor shrugged and shook his head. "For all his posturing, I think he knows Tebehrren's doing the best he can. And I'm guilty of the same intolerance. This afternoon, Tebehrren and I—" He gestured briefly. "Maddening as the Mind-Born can be, I still trust them."

Kahsir nodded in agreement, then caught Alàric looking across the room at the large map of the Kingdoms of Vyjenor—or what was left of them. Vlàdor's custom of using red ink to mark off territory lost to the enemy made the situation painfully clear: scarlet dominated the map.

Tension filled the room as other eyes followed Alàric's.

"Things are worse than we've been told, aren't they?" Alàric said softly, turning to Vlàdor. "Despite Kahs' victory. Am I right?"

Kahsir cringed inwardly at the look of sorrow that crossed his grandfather's face.

Alàric motioned toward the map. "Look at what we've lost! How little we have left. We Krotànya walk the edge of a void so vast my mind reels."

"Ahri," Vlàdor said. "Ssenkahdavic's power may be vast, but he's ruled by the same physical laws as we are. He can't be everywhere at once. And where he's not, we still have a chance of winning."

Alàric nodded slowly. "It's our *only* chance, unless Hjshraiel comes to lead us."

"He'll come, Ahri," Kahsir said. *Lords! Those are Tebehrren's words!* His heart quivered suddenly, and his sight blurred. "We may not see it, but he'll come. He *will* come."

For a long moment utter stillness held the room. Kahsir shook free from his Seeing, looked around, then suddenly remembered what he had said.

"I'm sorry to be so gloomy," Alàric murmured. "I'm tired and my leg's bothering me. I'm going to my room and rest."

Kahsir started to speak, but his grandfather signaled for silence. He watched his brother limp carefully out of the room.

"Xerej," Vlàdor said, nodding toward the doorway.

Xeredir rose and, with Haskon a few steps behind, went after his youngest son.

Kahsir sat staring at the wall. His grandfather and sister were heavily shielded, so it was impossible to know what they were thinking.

"I suppose," he said at last, "I'd better tell Eltàrim what's going on. I'm not looking forward to giving her the news."

"Kahs."

He turned in his chair, caught by his sister's voice.

"Now that Tutuljad's been attacked, Ahndrej's family—" Her voice faded and she gestured helplessly. "I know you aren't stationed close to Vharcwal, but please

keep watch over Ahndrej's steading if you can. Maybe
you can talk to Mannishteh: that's his area to patrol."

"I'll talk to him. And don't give up on Lorhaiden
yet. He's still a force to be reckoned with, especially if
I can get him reinforcements." He looked at his
grandfather. "If Tutuljad falls, we'll be vulnerable on
that part of the border. Will you send more warriors
south after I leave?"

Vlàdor shook his head. "Not immediately. We've suffered more wounded in the spring fighting to the
north and the east than I could have foreseen. But I'll
send what men I can when I'm able."

"You know more about Mannishteh than I do,
Kahs," Iowyn said. "Can you count on him to keep
close watch on Vharcwal?"

Kahsir nodded. "He's an excellent commander. I'd
trust him. I've never fought with him, but all reports
concerning him are good. I still think you're not giving
Ahndrej or his family enough credit. They'll know when
to leave." He called into mind Vharcwal's location: over
one hundred leagues from Tutuljad. Unless the enemy
had made a simultaneous attack along the entire length
of the southern border, Vharcwal would not be in
immediate danger. Yet. "If Tutuljad falls, the Leishoranya
will need time to consolidate. They'll try to move north
then, but I don't think anyone should be caught by
surprise. Rumor's still faster than any army I know of."

"Go see Eltàrim, Kahs," his grandfather said. "You'd
better tell her."

Kahsir stood, looked from Vlàdor to Iowyn, and
nodded. "Wish me luck. I think I'm going to need it."

Eltàrim stood beneath one of the hanging lamps in
her room, its golden light shadowing her eyes so that
Kahsir could not see them. Her mind lay shielded
from his, so hidden he could not tell what she might
be thinking. He shifted his weight uneasily, glanced
down at his feet, then up again.

She focused her attention entirely on the map before her. It was similar to the one that hung in Vlàdor's study, but she used it for other purposes than marking off territory lost to the enemy. Ever since her family had been slain in defense of their lands, she had led the bush fighting against the Leishoranya, mainly by Land-Born farmers and others who had no warrior training but who could raid and ambush as well as any. Coordinating her movements with those of the regular army, she and those she directed had done more damage to the enemy than Kahsir had guessed until the battle for Rodja'âno.

"So," she said finally, her voice trembling. She dropped her pen on the desk and looked up, her face unreadable. "What do you want me to do, Kahs? Scream? Rant and rave and say, No! You're not going!" Her mouth thinned into a frown. "I *could* throw something if it would make you happier."

"Tahra—"

She lifted a hand. "I know. I've done that before and if it didn't work then, it won't work now." She looked down again. "And I was so certain this time we'd be married at last. Lords know it took us long enough to make up our minds."

He nodded: it was all too true. They had been Chosen well over seventy years now, pledged to marry, but unable—either because of circumstances beyond their control, or their own reservations—to finalize the act. They loved each other, and had loved each other for centuries, but she demanded the same independence that he cherished . . . the same freedom to come and go at her own wish. It seemed that whenever one of them was ready to make the binding final, the other hesitated.

"I suppose it's no one's fault—our waiting, that is." He reached out, took her hand, and drew her closer. "Old habits, old patterns of thinking take long to die. Seventy years. What's that? Not long at all. But everyone's had to learn to do things differently since the enemy invaded Krusâ. Time has suddenly become important to us. We no longer have the luxury of acting otherwise."

She bent her head, and when she spoke, her voice was very quiet. "There should be at least *one* thing left in this world that the Shadow hasn't touched. Now even love must hurry."

He drew her into his embrace. "So you do see why I've got to go south to aid Lorhaiden?"

"Aye. You're not one to take your oaths lightly." She tensed in his arms. "But sometimes I wish you hadn't oathed with Lorhaiden. He's always getting himself into trouble only you can get him out of."

He closed his eyes wearily. "Just once—just once I'd like to hear someone say *something* good about Lorhaiden. It's as if he's—"

"Kahs." She lifted her head from his chest and looked up into his eyes. "It's not Lorhaiden I object to, it's that Oath of his. It's warped him. I remember what he was like before his family was killed. The two Lorhaidens—the one before the massacre and the one we know now—are as different as night and day." She sighed quietly, and he felt her sadness as if it were his own. "Go to him, *tahvah*, dearest," she whispered. "Only come back to me soon."

Kahsir stood next to his horse in the courtyard in front of the palace. Lamps lit many of its windows, a rarity for such a late hour. Most of the retainers were already abed, but those still awake went about their duties at a daytime pace.

The five hundred men his grandfather had promised waited mounted in orderly ranks, silent in the darkness. Their numbers prevented all of them from assembling in the courtyard, but their companions had gathered behind, outside the gate.

Leading his horse by the reins, Kahsir stopped at the front of those ranks.

"The enemy has attacked Tutuljad, and that's where

we're going. So far, Lorhaiden's lost a third of his men. This isn't common knowledge, so don't talk about it. We'll stop at my army first and gather another five hundred to ride with us. With luck, we'll reach Tutuljad in time to keep Lorhaiden from being routed." He looked from face to shadowed face. "This won't be easy; we'll take the mind-road tonight and then again tomorrow morning. When we get to my army, rest—all of you. I don't care *how* good you feel. I want you ready to ride again tomorrow and to fight afterward. And believe me, come morning, I'll send back anyone who's *not* rested. Questions?"

Nothing. A slight stir had run through the ranks when he had mentioned Tutuljad and the Leishoranya attack, but the warriors were quiet now, statues seated on statue horses. He nodded in their direction and turned to his horse.

Footsteps grated on the stairs: Kahsir looked up from tightening the last of his gear as his family and Eltàrim walked down into the courtyard.

"You're ready to leave, Kahs?" his grandfather asked.

"Aye. Has Tebehrren heard anything more from Lorj?"

"No." Vlàdor's face was shadowed despite the many torches held aloft by attentive retainers. "Don't wear yourself out, Kahs. Two trips that close together down the mind-road are enough to exhaust anyone."

Kahsir's eyes strayed to Eltàrim. "I know. I'd like to take the world's roads from my army to Tutuljad. If I could surprise the enemy by not using mental power, I'd do more damage to them than if they sensed me coming."

"Time's against you on that. I'm not sure how much longer Lorhaiden can hold."

Kahsir shrugged. "My plans aren't set in stone. I'll take the mind-road into battle if I have to."

"Whatever." Vlàdor reached out. "Stay well. Come back to us soon."

Kahsir embraced his grandfather, his father, his brothers and sister, then turned to Eltàrim.

"Tahra," he said, and held her longest. "I'll be home sooner than you think, *tahvah*."

"Soon or late," she whispered through a kiss. "Just come home."

He straightened, reluctantly releasing her from his arms. Biting back words he would have said if they had been alone, he touched her mind, kissed her again, then walked to his horse.

"Kahs."

He paused, one foot in the stirrup and glanced toward his sister's voice.

"Remember Vharcwal," she said, her voice clear in the darkness.

He nodded, swung up into the saddle, and turned for one last time to look at his family. Their thoughts spilled out unshielded: their concern for his safety, for what he must do. He briefly brushed their minds with his, and then faced his men.

They sat in silence—for all the torchlight, shadows awaiting his command. Sensing each man's readiness, he visualized his destination, remembering what it felt like to *be* there . . . the noises of his camp, the sights, the smells. Holding the vision firm, he transferred the image to the waiting warriors. Their minds touched his, gathering strength for this riding—linked, their power augmented his own.

Now, to help maintain the gate to the mind-road for the passage of so many men, he sought the minds of Tebehrren and several other Mind-Born. Grounded in their power, he reached out with his mind and began constructing the gate.

Suddenly the glowing arc to the mind-road shimmered into existence, his destination waiting behind it.

"Forward!" He motioned for his men to follow, and urged his horse into the shadows that lay on the other side of the opened gate.

CHAPTER 3

Lorhaiden blinked at the blood in his eyes, winced with pain, and lashed out at the Leishoran warrior he fought. Behind him and to the right, Tutuljad burned: the dark pillar of smoke that rose from within its breached walls blotted out the sunlight. Lorhaiden blinked again. He had missed his opponent and only had time enough to shift his shield to take the enemy's swordstroke. Squinting through half-shut eyelids, he saw enough of the enemy warrior to strike out again. This time, his sword bit through leathers and chainmail to flesh. The Leishoran cried out and, grabbing at his side, toppled heavily to the ground.

Lifting his swordarm, Lorhaiden quickly wiped the blood from his eyes. He had lost his helmet to the enemy swordstroke that had cut open his forehead and, with his head unprotected, stood as an easy target. He looked for his helmet, but it likely lay buried beneath the bodies at his feet. Cursing, he glanced over his shoulder at the burning city.

All morning long, he and his army had fought in defense of Tutuljad: now, everywhere he looked he saw the enemy. Mounted and on foot, they had gained advantage on the battlefield.

Another Leishoran ran forward, and Lorhaiden met him with a flurry of swordstrokes. Blood from his wound began trickling into his eyes again. He caught a quick breath—half-blind, he had no hope of beating this fellow. The Leishoran was too damned good.

See with your mind, idiot! he snarled at himself. *Quick! You can tell where he is!*

Lorhaiden shut his eyes, Saw his enemy, ducked and cut up under the warrior's shield. His sword caught momentarily on the Leishoran's chainmail. Heart in his throat, he yanked the blade away as the enemy warrior fell.

"Sahmdja!" Lorhaiden bellowed. His second-in-command fought close by. "For the Light's sake! Give me some relief if you can!"

"Where's your shieldman?" Sammàndhir shouted back.

"Hairon's hurt." Lorhaiden ducked another foeman's stroke, lashed out and felt his blow connect. "Get over here!"

Time slowed down. Lorhaiden fought in a battle of patchy darkness, brightened only when he blinked the blood away. He glanced to one side: Sammàndhir had engaged another Leishoran. *O Lords! I can't fight much longer like this! Hurry, dammit! Hurry!*

Suddenly Sammàndhir was there, ready to meet the blows of any enemy who might approach. Lorhaiden blinked the blood from his eyes again, grabbed at his cloak, and slashed a long strip of fabric from its edge. Quickly driving his sword point-down into the grass, he bound the cloth around his head.

Wiping the blood from his eyes, he snatched up his sword. Sammàndhir fought another opponent now; one more rushed from the right. Lorhaiden lifted his shield, took the swordstroke, and stabbed out at the enemy. A familiar red haze tinged his vision, a distortion separate from oozing blood. *Die, you motherless scum! My father, mother, my sisters! Slaughtered before my eyes! Death to all Leishoranya!*

And suddenly he found no one left to fight; the tide

of battle had momentarily shifted. Lorhaiden looked around. Sometime during the darkest part of night, reinforcements had swelled the enemy force. Out-flanked to the right and pushed to the east of the city, Lorhaiden had been unable to keep the enemy from Tutuljad itself. More than a third of his warriors slain, he now faced an army that outnumbered his nearly four to one. And since the Leishoranya held control of the city, he ran the risk of being attacked from behind. Only foolishness would keep his army here much longer.

What? he asked himself. *You're leaving? With all these enemy slime still alive? What about your Oath? The blood of your family? Have you forgotten all that?*

He bared his teeth in a snarl. *Dammit! I'm a commander now. What of my army? Will they die for my Oath?*

Lorhaiden flinched; a wave a shame followed, doubly powerful. *It's up to me now. I can betray my Oath or betray my warriors.*

"Sahmdja!" he called, speaking in their private battle language. "Pass the word! Withdraw to the hills!" Another Leishoran ran in his direction—he ducked the enemy's wild stroke, thrust quickly up under the warrior's shield. Jerking the weapon free from the falling body, he glanced sidelong at Sammàndhir. "Retreat in groups of fifty. We'll join forces when we've reached the hills."

Sammàndhir nodded: his coded mental command flashed out across the Krotànya army. Lorhaiden Sent his own message to the men who fought beyond Sammàndhir's ability to reach. He risked another look around: the plains to the north stood between his army and safety. His men's superior knowledge of the land could increase their chances for survival—the only hope they had.

He fought in detached violence now—the pain from his cut, the weight of his chainmail, receded into an annoying aggravation. If the Leishoranya followed patterns he had seen at the fall of other cities, they would consolidate their forces in and around Tutuljad. Then, from that base, they would send out squadrons to pursue the fleeing Krotànya.

The warriors at the rear of the defending army began to slip away into the fields of tall grass north of Tutuljad. Lorhaiden sensed them going and began to fight with increased ferocity. His swordarm ached with exertion and his shield dragged heavily at his arm, but the enemy seemed to be tiring as quickly as his own men. If he and his comrades could hold out awhile longer, the wearied Leishoranya might not pursue any who fled the battlefield.

And if such pursuit did come, it would likely be on foot. Part of Lorhaiden's strategy had been to kill or cripple all the enemy horses he and his men could find.

He dropped his opponent, glanced to either side, then behind. Most of his men had fled into the grass—he and a ragged few still held the front line. The time had come to stand and die, or to retreat and fight again.

—Krotànya! he Sent, again coding the message. *Now, brothers, now! To the hills and safety!*

He turned and ran across the battlefield, leaping over bodies of the slain, Sammàndhir at his left side in the position of shieldman. With no time to search for any living Krotànya, he had ordered his men not to look, though the shame of leaving the wounded burned in his heart.

He glanced behind as he and the others entered the tall grass. *Horses, dammit! To make the hills quickly, we need our horses.* But they had lost what horses they had brought to the battlefield to death or panicked escape—the rest stood tethered on the other side of the city and might as well have been on one of the moons. Thank the Lords that infantry comprised a majority of the enemy army. Lorhaiden hurdled another body and nearly tripped. Regaining his balance, he ran on, death at his back.

Hairon! His shieldman—where the Void was Hairon? He cursed and nearly missed his stride. *You fihrkken idiot! How could you have left him when—*

—I be here, Lord. Hairon's thoughts came edged with pain and fatigue. *Behind.*

One of the knots in Lorhaiden's stomach dissolved. Hairon might be cantankerous, dour, and disapproving, but he had proved himself more than once in battle.

—How's your arm? Are you in much pain? Can you last?

—Got to, Lord, the farmer replied. *Don't got a choice, do I?*

Lorhaiden looked ahead. The fields stretched off into the distance, new spring grass a brilliant green against the hard blue sky. The afternoon sun shone warm on his left side, nearly too warm; heat would slow the pace. The hills lay before him: darker green, touched with browns and gray, they held the horizon— a distant refuge.

The waist-high grass whipped at his legs, stinging even through his trousers. The enemy still came in pursuit, but only a few of them, and those on foot. He grinned inwardly; he had managed to judge the enemy's weariness to an astounding degree. The major objective of taking Tutuljad accomplished, most of the Leishoranya had stayed behind. There would always be time to hunt down the fleeing Krotànya later.

For all their warcraft, they're still fools. Lorhaiden altered his stride, seeking an even run. *Huhn. Fools reap what fools sow. Let them catch us now.*

The sun had just set when Lorhaiden finally raised his hand in a signal to halt. His men staggered to a stop, several of them crumpling exhausted down into the grass.

Knees weakened to the point they shook uncontrollably, Lorhaiden stood panting in the dimming light, his ears ringing and his heart pounding in his chest. His mail shirt dragged heavily on his shoulders, and the sword cut on his forehead hurt abominably. Sweat ran down his face, sides and back, though the evening was cool. He snorted a laugh. *If the enemy's downwind, they'll smell us before they see us.*

"Lord." Sammàndhir's voice, thin with weariness, came from alongside. "Are they following us?"

Lorhaiden faced his second-in-command. "No." He drew a deep, ragged breath, turned and faced south. "Not yet."

"Not yet?" echoed a warrior sprawled out in the grass close by. The man struggled to sit up, then sank down again. "Do you think they'll keep hunting for us today, Lord?"

Lorhaiden looked down at the young man. "Aye." He wiped the sweat from his face. Taking several more slow, deep breaths, he willed his body calm. "We've got to keep going."

"Damn them!" This from another warrior off to Lorhaiden's right. "Those motherless *fihrkken* bastards! Damn them to—"

Hairon glared, his broad face slick with sweat. "Oh, shut up and let the rest of us die peaceable."

Lorhaiden grinned; he had stopped panting and his heart had settled to an even beat. He looked at the fifty men who lay in the thick grass close by; squinting in the twilight, he glanced south, then back to the north, to the hills he hoped to reach before dawn. The land rose gently as it ran to those hills. The prairie grass still stood waist-high; if any of the enemy came near, it would afford some cover. Yet the tracks he and his men had left behind them stood out painfully clear. A moonless night would obscure those tracks, but if the enemy came close before visibility was utterly gone, they would be able to follow easily enough.

He looked at his men again. *Damn! How much longer can I let them rest? We can't wait too long, but if we leave too soon, nobody will be in any condition to fight if the enemy finds us.* He glanced north again. The Leishoranya might have sent patrols out a fair distance from the city to run down survivors, but it would take some doing to reorganize an army of the size that had attacked Tutuljad. Even the enemy did not have an inexhaustible store of energy.

He shrugged; he still could not detect immediate pursuit. Weariness descended in a flood. He hunkered down on his heels, closed his eyes, and carefully shielded his mind.

It had happened at last: the invasion of Elyâsai. As far as he knew, Tutuljad was the first city within that kingdom to fall. A city of no great size, it had stood at the border between Elyâsai and the fallen Kingdom of Bynjâlved. Hardly an important place until its destruction gave it importance: the gateway the enemy chose to Elyâsai.

He sat in the deep cover of the grass and kneaded the calves of his legs to ease their cramping. *Kahsir knows. He's got to know what's happened.* He glanced up at the dusky sky, his face gone hot with embarrassment. He had Sent a second message north to the capital, telling of Tutuljad's fall, hoping to breach the enemy's mind-block. Once again, Tebehrren, Chief of the Mind-Born, had received the Sending, and had said Kahsir was already on the way with reinforcements. Damned little good that would do now. Tutuljad had fallen, and Tebehrren had certainly relayed that news to Kahsir. Lorhaiden flushed again: what would Kahsir say about Tutuljad's loss?

He glanced at the other men, the few he could see, but no one seemed aware of his discomfort. *By the Light! I fought as well as I could. I've only lost a city, not Kahsir's confidence.*

Only lost a city. . . . He closed his eyes in agony. To be remembered as the first commander to have lost a city within Elyâsai. It could not be . . . it *must* not be. Somehow, he would redeem himself. *Lorhaiden,* he heard the ghostly voices whisper. *Lorhaiden. Ah* . . . *he's the one who lost Tutuljad.*

He spat off into the grass. Kahsir would be coming with aid despite his forthcoming marriage, but coming too late to save Tutuljad. Too late to save the lives lost in retreat. Too late to . . . He cursed softly. Perhaps he should Send to Kahsir, telling him to turn back.

"Lord?" Sammàndhir came crouched to Lorhaiden's side through the tall grass, his expression hard to read in the fading light. "Most of the men think they've rested long enough to go on."

"Good." Lorhaiden reached up to touch the improvised bandage wound about his head. His hand came away dry—he had stopped bleeding. "Dusk should give us some cover, but keep away from any heights. No mind-speech, either. It's a long way to those hills— twenty leagues or more. The enemy will be mounted. None of us has bows or arrows, and they'll probably have archers with them."

Mind opened to any sign of pursuit, Lorhaiden walked in the center of his warriors, holding their course to the far side of any hills or ridges. Few of those existed—though generally rising, the land lay fairly flat. Several of his band glanced now and then behind, keeping watch over the darkened land, but he trusted more to his own senses.

For the better part of four hours he had kept the pace steady, though not to the all-out run he had held his men to when they fled the battlefield. Alternating between a fast walk and a loping trot, he had tried to minimize the strain on already exhausted legs and lungs. If he could keep up this pace, he and his band would reach the hills before dawn.

He looked at the way they had come, the path they must take. He had kept their course due north, only deviating from it when forced by the land itself. Now that all three moons had risen, he went with even greater caution. Though only the smallest was half full and the others mere crescents, their light added to the starlight made it easier to see.

Suddenly Lorhaiden froze—his men came to a dead stop close by. A coldness touched his mind, slithered across it with nightmare slowness. He shuddered, whirled around, and faced south.

"Chuht!" His hissed oath was loud in the silence. Still a considerable distance behind rode a squad of Leishoranya, their course aimed straight at his men. He could not see them yet, but he felt their coming, sensed their numbers . . . forty-five mounted men. They rode fanned out in a long line, leaving only a few paces between their horses, common enough practice used by hunters to drive out prey. He had too little time to avoid their coming—they were mounted, his men were not. And weary as he and his men had become, taking the mind-road offered no escape.

"Lords!" he whispered. "Those *fihrkken* bastards have seen our tracks for sure!" He turned to his second-in-command. "Your family lived near Tutuljad, Sahmdja. You're more familiar with these plains than I am. Is there any place close where we could take cover?"

Sammàndhir shifted his weight uneasily, a creak of leather clothing in the dark. "None, my Lord. As I remember it, the land's unbroken between us and the hills."

Lorhaiden cursed again and glanced behind: he could see the enemy horsemen now. The fools were still using mind-speech; they must have thought themselves far enough behind their quarry to risk such communication. He shrugged. What happened next would depend entirely on the strength and skill of his warriors.

"Listen to me," he said to his men who had gathered around. "I don't think they've spotted us clearly." He gestured off to a dim, shadowed bulk in the darkness. "There's a low rise there, off to the northwest. Make for it fast as you can. Try to set yourselves between the enemy's horses. If we're lucky, they'll miss us. If they don't, kill quickly and in silence if you can. Now go!"

The grass grew shorter on top of the rise. From where he lay hidden, Lorhaiden heard the Leishoranya ride closer. He hitched up on his elbows, peered over the grasstops, and started counting the oncoming enemy, comparing what he could see with what he had sensed earlier. The darkness made his tally uncertain, but reinforced his original estimate of forty-five men.

He lowered his head and lay down again, keeping his thoughts blank. An insect buzzed around his ear, but he ignored it even when bitten. He sought to become such a part of the surrounding ground and grass that no questing mind could detect his presence. He knew where his comrades lay in the darkness to his left and right, but he could not sense or see them.

Heart beating faster now, he carefully parted the dew-dampened grass. The first of the Leishoranya, a tall man riding a tall horse, drew closer. The Leishoran leaned forward in the saddle, poking his speartip into the grass ahead and to each side of his horse, attempting to flush out anything hidden.

Lorhaiden could hear the other Leishoranya now, the muted jingle of harnesses and weapons. Like the man who rode in his direction, they searched the grass with their speartips as they drew nearer through the darkness. *Lords! They're following our tracks like a roadway! They'd have been blind to have missed them!* The grass rustled as the first man came closer. The enemy called softly back and forth to each other, another evidence that they had decided they were alone.

The tall warrior rode only a few paces away: Lorhaiden willed himself to an even greater immobility. Consciously taking short, shallow breaths, he filled his mind with images of grass, the sound of the wind in it, the scent of the plains, and emptiness . . . total emptiness.

Hand trembling on swordhilt, he sensed the Leishoran's speartip pass only a few finger's widths above his head. A thin rivulet of sweat ran down his forehead into his left eye, and another insect hummed around his face. Motionless, he waited for the Leishoran to ride on.

Suddenly, at the very moment he thought the enemy had missed his hidden company, a muffled cry rose from somewhere off to the right. Lorhaiden stiffened: the warrior who had just passed jerked his horse to a stop, wheeled around and called out something sharp in Leishoranji. Though Lorhaiden knew only a smattering of the enemy's language, the meaning of those words was utterly clear.

"Krotànya!"

Lorhaiden shouted to his companions, leapt out of the grass, and shoved his shield in front of the Leishoran's horse. The animal shied violently, throwing its rider off balance. Lorhaiden darted in close, thrust his sword up cleanly between the warrior's ribs—the Leishoran screamed and started to fall. Grabbing the horse's bridle, Lorhaiden shoved the dying man from the saddle and snatched at the pommel. He frantically sought and found the stirrup, then hauled himself astride the panicked horse.

"Krotànya!" he cried again, yanking at the reins and turning his mount around. "For the Light! *Legir! Legir!*"

Silence shattered in a flurry of sound and action as Lorhaiden's men jumped up from their hiding places.

Lorhaiden looked for the spear his enemy had carried, but the grass was too deep and the night too dark. He cursed, wheeled the horse about and rode toward the thickest of the fighting. One of his companions fought wounded against a stronger opponent; Lorhaiden galloped forward and bore down on the startled enemy, giving the Leishoran no time to organize his defense. Lorhaiden's swordstroke nearly beheaded him.

"*Yiiiii-yah!*"

The cry alerted Lorhaiden in time to raise his shield. A Leishoran had ridden in close and stabbed out with his spear—Lorhaiden caught the spearpoint on his shield, pushed it off, rocked in the saddle by the force of the blow. Twisting sideways, he slashed out with his sword at the enemy's arm, missed, and struck again. The Leishoran yelped as Lorhaiden's blade nicked flesh above the wristguard. Kneeing his horse around, Lorhaiden plowed the animal into his opponent's mount, knocking the other horse off its feet. The Leishoran fell under his horse, thrashed a moment, but lay still once the animal had struggled to its feet.

Then, suddenly as it had begun, the battle ended. A horse nickered in the darkness and someone groaned, but all else was still. Lorhaiden glanced about, counting casualties, as Sammàndhir rode to his side.

"Sahmdja. How many dead?"

"Ten, Lord. Seven wounded, but not seriously."

"The enemy?"

"Dead or dying. A few of them fled to the south."

"Hairon?"

"He's all right, Lord. Not a scratch."

Lorhaiden's hands trembled on the reins. *Lords of Light, we were lucky.* He heard another horseman draw near.

"Be you hurt, Lord?" asked Hairon, all but unseen in the dark.

"No. I'm fine." Lorhaiden straightened in the saddle

and sought the minds of his men. *Dismount,* he Sent. *Make sure all of the enemy are dead. Then we'll rest awhile before we ride. And gather our dead. We'll bury them in the hills.*

His men obeyed, many with sighs of relief. Ordering three warriors to stay mounted as lookouts, Lorhaiden swung down from the saddle, his own knees shaking. The stirrups were too short: he fumbled in the dark and lowered them. A warm feeling welled up in his heart: nearly forty Leishoranya dead; two, possibly three, by his own hand. Today alone he had killed nearly—His mind went blank. Numbers were meaningless in the face of Tutuljad's fall. How many of her citizens had died before they could escape? He cringed at the answer, refusing an estimate. *Ah, Kahsir, sword-brother! I'll redeem myself.* The memory of dying Leishoranya filled his mind. *And keep to my Oath. That, too, my Lord.*

He bent, cleaned his sword on the grass, and slid it into its sheath. As his companions prepared to leave, their thoughts spilled over, clear in the darkness: each of them considered himself lucky to be alive. Sammàndhir had supervised the gathering of the dead and the caring for the wounded. Then, he and several other men had rounded up what enemy horses they could find, leaving only six men who needed to ride double. Now, ready to move out, Lorhaiden caught up the reins and mounted.

"Head north," he said. "We should be able to make the hills long before dawn now that we're horsed. But be careful. There could be more war bands close by."

He set off in the lead, finding it hard to adjust to the enemy saddle. The high cantle was bothersome and pushed him forward into an uncomfortable position. He settled in at last and glanced up: the moons had become shadowed faintly by clouds. *Dammit to Darkness! Not rain. Not now. That's the last thing we need. Ah, Lords! At least give us time to reach the hills.*

And Kahsir? Where was he now? How many men rode with him? How many could he or the High-King spare? The faces of other Krotànya commanders filled Lorhaiden's mind. It was spring now throughout the Kingdom of Elyâsai, spring turning to summer; with warmer weather, the battles would come more frequently. He grimaced and looked ahead. Only Elyâsai stood before the enemy, and that fact would embolden them.

Hatred for the enemy rose in his heart. His mind filled with bloody images, scenes of revenge for his slaughtered family: his father, arrowshot; his mother and sisters, burned alive in the great house by Dhumaric, the Leishoran commander, who sat his horse, laughing in the flame-shadowed darkness. Dhumaric had not laughed at the end, on that hilltop a year ago, when he had died under Lorhaiden's sword.

Suddenly, in the midst of his hate, Lorhaiden felt a terrible sense of loss. All those centuries gone by, blurs of darkened years, decades of battles and death—what *might* have been instead. For one brief moment he raged against the path reality had taken. Then, surprised by the tears in his eyes, he looked up at the clouded moons, and rode on through the darkness.

CHAPTER 4

Midday brought no sunshine, only long lines of clouds scudding across the horizon. Kahsir stood by his horse, tested the girth and made sure he had tied his saddlebags securely. He shivered suddenly in the chill wind, looked up and frowned. Rain. Exactly what he did not need if he wanted to reach a position east of Tutuljad by midafternoon. The pause he had allowed his men had taken little time, but a ride through the rain would slow them considerably.

Something had gone wrong with Lorhaiden's defense of the city; though Kahsir was unsure exactly what had happened, a cold feeling coiled at the pit of his stomach. Tutuljad *had* fallen, even sooner than they had feared. He was so certain of the danger of enemy detection, he had ridden tightly shielded, unreachable save for one of the Mind-Born. But now, this close to the city, he left his mind open for contact. He had to know how things stood before he continued much farther.

Horsed, his subcommanders waited, their men alert behind; two scouts had already ridden ahead of his army. Kahsir glanced at the sky once more, shrugged, swung up into the saddle, and turned his horse to the southwest again.

One thousand warriors rode behind—half he had hand-picked from his army. A hard two days' ride lay between his camp and Tutuljad. He had cut that distance in half yesterday by alternating between the mind-road and normal travel, then had taken the mind-road again at dawn. He rubbed his eyes wearily: how much worse off his men must be who were not as used to such rapid travel.

The first heavy drops of rain began to fall, and moments later the downpour began. Behind, all but hidden by the rain, the hundred-commanders called out orders to close ranks. Kahsir glanced upward again, shielding his eyes with an upraised hand. He could not tell how long this storm would last, but it would not be over soon. He sighed, looked down, and settled back in the saddle, prepared for the ride ahead.

Tutuljad: the first of Elyâsai's cities attacked by the enemy; Tutuljad: the first, he feared, to have fallen.

He hid his dark thoughts from the other men who rode behind. What of Lorhaiden? If Tutuljad had fallen already, and Kahsir *knew* it had, it would not have been because of Lorhaiden's inexperience. Oath-ridden as Lorhaiden was, he commanded better than most.

And the three thousand men Lorhaiden led? Small comfort for one who had lost nearly two thousand at last count, and who must have lost more since he had Sent to Tebehrren. Not for the first time, Kahsir questioned the wisdom of going to Lorhaiden's aid, but his oath of sword-brother allowed nothing less. If the enemy army numbered ten thousand, and if they had lost an equal number of men, Kahsir and his thousand would be riding against a force that outnumbered them eight to one. Such an attack would be suicide, and he had no intention of meeting the enemy if he could help it. His first objective to get reinforcements to Lorhaiden must be met—then he could worry about the other tactical problems.

The rain fell harder and it became impossible to see for any distance; Kahsir cursed, slowed his horse, and rode on. The grasslands had already grown sodden, and if the rain continued, low-lying areas would turn into muddy bogs. He shook the rain from his cloak, drew it tight again, then glanced over his shoulder. Behind, hidden by the heavy downpour, his men followed in orderly fashion.

He had left the mind-road hours northeast of Tutuljad, still wanting to arrive unsensed, but now he questioned that choice and longed to Send to Lorhaiden that he brought reinforcements. Though he could cloak his messages far better than most, he was not Mind-Born, to Send unnoticed over such a distance. Secrecy and speed of movement—he had to maintain that if he hoped to surprise his enemy.

Tsingar walked toward the crest of the hill, drawing his cloak closer up around his neck. The tents nearby had fallen silent now, the victory celebration at Tutuljad over. Only a few men stirred at this hour, most on their way to the latrines on the east side of camp.

He reached the hilltop and looked to the north: the fallen city lay before him, hidden now by the mist and rain. Behind him, the army had set up its camp around the crest of a low hill, a place easily defended. Though Mehdaiy had been here only a few days, a greater sense of order prevailed than when he had arrived.

Tsingar smiled slightly. He had distinguished himself in yesterday's battle, bringing honor to his weapons and his Clan; though Lorhaiden had escaped, victory sweetened that disappointment. His people had invaded Elyâsai, last standing of the Krotànya kingdoms, and he could easily guess what this invasion would do to Krotànya morale.

For centuries, millennia, his people had fought the Krotànya, place to place, age to age. Now it seemed the final confrontation Ssenkahdavic longed for had come. Only this time, there would be no escape for the Krotànya.

The trip south from Rodja'âno, the fallen capital of the Kingdom of Tumâs, had been a rough one. Elyâsai stood ringed with defenses, both military and mental, and no quick way existed to travel from north to south. Taking the mind-road across the Kingdom of Elyâsai would have been simplest, but the Krotànya Mind-Born stood in the way of that. So he and his commander Mehdaiy had skirted the borders to that kingdom, going far to the east and back, thousands of leagues out of their way.

He did not like to remember that journey: Mehdaiy demanded speed and instant willingness to go beyond physical limits. No matter that Tsingar did not possess a mind of the same strength as Mehdaiy's. So, he had followed, through jump after jump, moving from one safe base to another. Finally, weary near to dropping, he and Mehdaiy had arrived at the headquarters of the southern army, where Mehdaiy would take over dead Chiyuksai's place.

And then, with admirable swiftness, Mehdaiy had reorganized that army—had taken control with an iron hand, executing several subcommanders who objected to the Queen's choice of him as their new commander. Giving the remaining subcommanders little time to regain their footing, Mehdaiy had set out in a lightning strike to the north, aimed at the border city of Tutuljad.

Tsingar heard footsteps behind, turned and looked up into Mehdaiy's harsh face. *Gods! It's like seeing Dhumaric roused from the dead!*

"Dread Lord," Tsingar said by way of greeting.

"Are you ready to leave?"

"Aye, Dread Lord. Immediately, if you wish."

Mehdaiy nodded and looked off to the fallen city. "You'll be in command of five hundred men," he said. "They're young, Tsingar; don't ride them too hard.

Take the mind-road to the southern edge of the hills. I'll be sending out other companies of the same strength, several to each side of you. We know the Krotànya who escaped scattered in all directions, but I'm sure you'll be following Lorhaiden's trail. You probably won't catch him, but the chase will educate your men."

Tsingar bowed slightly, heavily shielded as always. He had met Mehdaiy only a few times before the audience with the Queen, and then in Dhumaric's presence. With Dhumaric, he usually had known where he stood, how far he could go. But with this one . . . He knew Dhumaric's brother to be, if anything, more dangerous. Friendly one moment, icy the next, his changes in mood proved unsettling. He would have to be very careful with Mehdaiy—very careful indeed.

Grim-faced, pale in the gloomy light, Mehdaiy looked northward. "You seem to have the gift of knowing where that crazy bastard is." The black eyes turned their power away from the city to Tsingar's face. "Use it. Even I can't sense Lorhaiden as truly."

Tsingar stirred at Mehdaiy's admission of failure. "Perhaps it's because I've fought him so long, Dread Lord."

"Perhaps." Mehdaiy looked out at Tutuljad's lifeless bulk again. He shrugged his cloak up around his neck, then glanced back. "I think we've got the Krotànya this time. At last, we can fulfill the task the Gods set upon us. With our victory here, on this continent, we'll have destroyed the greatest enemies that have ever stood before us." Mehdaiy straightened, his pensiveness gone. "I've assigned you a second-in-command. You should feel honored that he rides with you."

Tsingar let the silence stretch out, waiting for Mehdaiy to continue. "Who is it, Master?" he asked at last.

"Aduhar, my sister's great-grandson."

"An honor indeed, Dread Lord," Tsingar murmured,

bowing slightly. Aduhar? He had never met the man, but suspected him a warrior with few peers. Dhumaric and Mehdaiy came from a Clan which had produced many of the best warriors ever to take up weapons.

"Like the rest of your men, he's young," Mehdaiy said. "He fights like the Void's own champion, but—" Again, those inscrutable eyes sought Tsingar's. "He's proud and rightly so, but he's never had a command of any sort before. Don't let him push you around, for the Dark knows he'll try."

Tsingar kept his face expressionless, his mind shielded completely. What was Mehdaiy saying? He shifted uncomfortably. If a warning, regarding what? His own actions, or Aduhar's?

"Teach him, Tsingar," Mehdaiy said. "Teach him well. Don't let him forget *you're* his commanding officer, not the other way around. I want him to return from this southern campaign a seasoned commander, fully qualified to lead in our final attack on the Krotànya. I'm trusting you in this. See that you don't fail me."

"I'll do my best, Dread Lord."

"That will be sufficient. Leave when you're ready."

Tsingar bowed low as Mehdaiy walked off into the heavy mist, then lifted his head and turned toward the city. His stomach had tensed into a thousand writhing balls. *By the Gods! First Chaagut goes after my position as Dhumaric's knife-hand. Then Girdun comes after me to take revenge for Chaagut's death. Now I've got to put up with a spoiled, arrogant young prince.* He straightened; Mehdaiy's words echoed in his head. *If I'm going to command this youngster, I'll do it. But it won't be easy. My life could depend on how I handle this one.*

Rain still fell an hour later, but the worst of the storm had passed. Kahsir stretched his legs in the stirrups and rubbed at the tension in his neck and shoulders. His clothes felt cold, the chainmail and its padding colder: both clung to his body in a sodden mass. Even his boots had barely kept his feet dry. He shifted in the saddle, letting further dampness in, and cursed softly.

Suddenly, another mind touched his, distant at first, then growing stronger with contact.

—Kahs.

He straightened *Grandfather! What—?*

—There's no time, Vlàdor Sent. *You were all but impossible to locate. Tebehrren's helping me cloak this Sending, but we still could be detected. Tutuljad fell— yesterday afternoon.*

—O Lords! Kahsir's heart lurched. *And Lorhaiden?*

—Escaped north to the hills with what was left of his army. They reached them at dawn. Get him those reinforcements, if you can.

—Aye. Wait, Grandfather—don't go yet. Has Ahndrej come back? Is his family all right?

—He's here. Returned this morning. His bother's getting the steading ready to evacuate. Ahndrej says unless the border deteriorates, they probably won't leave for another twenty days. I'm breaking contact. Send to me when you get a chance.

Then Vlàdor's mind-touch was gone, as if it had never existed. Kahsir stared off into the distance and wearily rubbed his eyes. *Dammit! I knew it! Tutuljad's gone! Now the whole southern border will have to restructure defenses. And I'm responsible for that. Lords above! Give me the time!*

Sudden movement came to his left; he started out of his thoughts as Chànnoveth dàn Ostraik, one of his subcommanders, rode to his side.

"Lord." Chànnoveth eased his horse closer. "We should turn south now if we want to approach Tutuljad from the east. The hills are only two hours away."

Kahsir looked off into the easing rain, then back. "I've talked with my grandfather, Chànno. Tutuljad's fallen. Lorhaiden and those who could escaped north to the hills."

Chànnoveth stared.

"Spread the word," Kahsir said. "I want everyone to know. We're changing our course—heading directly to the hills."

"My scouts have returned. Should I send out more than two this time?"

"Two for right now. We'll double that later."

The subcommander nodded, reined his horse around, and cantered toward his five hundred. Kahsir looked forward again and frowned. *If only I'd taken the mind-road to Tutuljad yesterday, perhaps Lorhaiden could have held.* He shook his head. *I can't redo the past. No one can.*

It had nearly stopped raining, and a blowing mist filled the air. Tall grasslands for the most part, the land stretched level save for a few ridges and hollows near the hills. The gloomy weather had leached it of all color and life, but a day of sunlight would change that; now, everything smelled of sodden grass and mud.

Kahsir turned at the sound of muffled hoofbeats to his right. The two men Chànnoveth had chosen as scouts cantered by, saluting as they went, then vanished into the gloom. Kahsir waved back, settled down in his saddle, and drew his cloak tighter against the clinging dampness.

Another half hour. Rain alternated between a virtual downpour and a light drizzle, typical for spring in this area of the plains. Kahsir scanned the horizon, his eyes seldom leaving it. *Where the Dark are those damned scouts? They should have been back to report by now.*

A horse snorted loudly. Kahsir jumped at the sudden noise, snapped his gaze sideways, then looked ahead again to see only empty land and leaden skies. *What the Dark's going on? Why am I so damned nervous?* He tried a subtle probe of the land—nothing. Lifting his hand, he motioned his two subcommanders forward.

"Chànno," Kahsir said, "neither of the scouts you sent out have reported since they left."

Chànnoveth glanced at the other subcommander, Mishta dàn Tekonnen, then looked back. "I told them to contact you every half hour, Lord. You should have received visual signs from them by now."

Kahsir nodded and rubbed the tension from the small of his back. "Something else is wrong. I don't know what, and I can't trace it, but it's getting worse the farther we go." He looked from one man to the other. "Place your five-hundreds on immediate alert and send out two more scouts. And tell them they're to ride in sight of us at all times."

The rain lessened to a mere sprinkle, but thickened clouds turned the afternoon even darker. Kahsir kept his senses open to their fullest, though he did not probe the countryside again. His men came behind: muffled hoofbeats on sodden ground, the muted jingle of harnesses and bits. No other sound disturbed the silence. Each man rode tightly shielded, betraying nothing of his presence.

The grass grew shorter now as the land began to slope up toward a long rise; several small trees grown crooked by the wind stood off to Kahsir's left. He looked for the scouts and saw them both riding half a league ahead. He shifted in the saddle, rubbed the back of his neck, and rode on.

Suddenly, the scouts halted and lifted their spears two-handed over their heads.

Danger . . . possibly immediate.

Kahsir's heart raced: the warriors riding at the front of the army had read the signal, too. There came a faint whisper of swords being unsheathed, and the men's alarm grew noticeable even hidden by their

shields. Kahsir reached for his sword but halted; the
scouts pointed their speartips downward, signing that
armed combat was not necessary yet.

Kicking his horse to a faster pace, followed by
Chànnoveth and Mishta, Kahsir cantered up the low
hill, his heart sinking as he drew close enough to the
scouts to see their expressions. He jerked his horse to
a sliding stop on the wet grass: there, riddled with
enemy arrows, lay the bodies of the first set of scouts
Chànnoveth and Mishta had sent out.

For a brief moment Kahsir sat frozen, then he tore
his gaze away and carefully looked around. A thin
probe of the countryside revealed no enemy.

"Stay mounted!" he ordered his men over his shoulder. "And keep watch!"

Cursing softly, he jumped down from his horse and
walked to the bodies. He sensed some of his men
gathering behind him, but gave his attention to the
dead.

Kneeling before the first of those bodies, he
reached out and briefly touched it. *Damn! Not stiff
yet. How long ago were they killed? The enemy must
have silenced their death-cries, or we would have
Heard.* A cold sweat broke out on his forehead. *Those
bastards could be anywhere!*

"Mishta." He lowered his hand and stood; the subcommander waited at his shoulder. "You've got a real
talent for this. Can you Read these bodies?"

"I'll try, Lord. It shouldn't be hard—they couldn't
have been dead long."

Kahsir moved aside as Mishta came to the first
body. The subcommander stooped, held his hands over
the dead man's forehead, then did the same to the
other. For a moment, Mishta stood between the two
bodies, and then, kneeling beside the first, he
extended his hands again. Fingertips nearly brushing
the skin, he closed his eyes and sought.

Kahsir watched intently, though it appeared nothing

was happening. The expressions on his subcommander's face told otherwise: Mishta was Reading the memories still left in the dead scout's body. Finally, the subcommander let his hands fall, opened his eyes, and looked up at Kahsir.

"This man died last," he said wearily, his gaze still unfocused. "Neither he nor his companion sensed danger after leaving us, and before they knew it, they'd ranged too far ahead. They'd turned around to make their reports to you when they were attacked. The Leishoranya company numbered three hundred, possibly more. The memories concerning that are unfocused."

"Which direction did the enemy take?"

"South, my Lord."

"South? I'd expect them to head north. Those who escaped Tutuljad's fall would . . ."

"Would what, Lord?" prompted Chànnoveth.

Kahsir blinked in the light rain. "There are only two reasons they'd head south: they've found no Krotànya to run down and they've been recalled to Tutuljad; or, they're on their way to join other companies nearby. They must know Lorhaiden and his army took cover in the hills." He looked around, searching for places where the enemy might have set up an ambush. "Mishta. How long ago did these men die?"

"Not over an hour, Lord. Maybe less than that. But I'll bet the enemy's not far away. They probably didn't sense us coming and thought these men survivors from Tutuljad."

"It's also possible they *did* sense us," Chànnoveth said. "If so, they'd have known themselves outnumbered and made a run for it."

Kahsir rubbed his forehead, then straightened his shoulders. "I agree with Mishta," he said at last. "If the enemy sensed us, Chànno, and knew we outnumbered them, they wouldn't have left these bodies behind. What better evidence for us to see?" He

glanced away from his commanders into the rain. "I
don't think they're far away."

Silence fell on the hilltop. Kahsir looked at the bodies
again; he sensed the anger welling up in his men—anger
mingled with sorrow. He gestured helplessly. "We can't
bring them back to life," he said, "but we can avenge
their deaths. See if you can find their horses. We'll take
these bodies with us, and when time allows, we'll give
them the honorable burial they deserve."

He looked up at the grim faces in the rain.

"Scouts to the fore, and stay in sight!" he said.
"Let's go! We've got Leishoranya to hunt."

CHAPTER 5

When Lorhaiden left the great house of the steading he and his men had camped around, it had started raining heavily again. Most of his warriors had bivouacked in the woods close by or in the pasturelands to the south. Several steadings lay in the hills north of Tutuljad, and through blind luck, after an all-night ride, he and his companions had stumbled across one of the largest. They had reached the hills before dawn, but only in the past few hours had the rain stopped long enough for them to bury the dead.

Lorhaiden frowned up at the sky and his shoulders tightened. Hands clenched into fists, he walked through the rain, kicking at the grass. The barn where he had set up headquarters loomed up, a dim shape in the downpour.

He rubbed his eyes with a shaking hand—unlike his companions, he had not been able to sleep. Though the ruler of the steading, Lord Nichàlor, had offered him a room and a dry bed in the great house, he had decided to stay with his men, a choice made to bolster their spirits and, at the same time, limit his anger to those who could understand it. He drew one final

calming breath, then walked across the sodden lawn
that ran down toward the barn.

Sammàndhir stood with Hairon in the wide doorway.
"Lovely weather, isn't it?" said Sammàndhir, moving
aside. "You're drenched."

Lorhaiden paused in the doorway. Warm, musty
smells swept out from inside, bringing with them
memories of days long gone: his father's barn, the
horses, the heaps of fragrant hay. . . . He gave Hairon
his dripping cloak, put on the dry one his shieldman
held out, and then, with Sammàndhir and Hairon coming behind, sought out his corner of the barn.

"What be happening, Lord?" Hairon asked, hanging
Lorhaiden's cloak over a railing. "They got horses
here?"

Lorhaiden sat down in the hay and blinked in weariness. "Not many. These people are vintners. They
only keep a few horses for their own use."

Hairon nodded, sat, and leaned back on one elbow,
stretching his legs out. The wound on his arm had
scabbed over; he scratched at it, looked as if he would
say something, but was silent.

"What now, Lord?" asked Sammàndhir.

"There's a steading close by that breeds horses.
We'll have to try there."

"Huhn." Sammàndhir picked up a stalk of hay and
twirled it idly between his fingertips. "The volunteers
you sent to watch the plains left an hour ago. They'll
report if they see any enemy activity."

Lorhaiden nodded, shifted his weight, and looked
out the barn door: the rain now fell in straight silver
lines beyond. "Have you made a final count of everyone gathered here?"

"Over one thousand, Lord."

Lorhaiden cringed. He could not have expected all
of what remained of his army to find their way to this
steading. More than likely, the rest of the survivors
had found shelter in other areas of the hills. But . . .

one thousand? Out of his original force of over five thousand he had lost—

"Of that number, only half are mounted," Sammàndhir continued, his voice dry in reporting. "But there could be others who haven't been able to find their way here yet."

Lorhaiden glanced away.

"Be the steading's people leaving, Lord?" asked Hairon.

"No." He looked at his shieldman and his second-in-command. "They'll stay." He caught Sammàndhir's skeptical look. "Aye. I was surprised, too. These southern steadings have a reputation for being soft. This one isn't."

Hairon turned over on his side, hay crackling beneath his weight. "I be minded of my own kin, Lord. I know why these folks don't want to leave. It be a part of us Land-Born, this stubbornness. Give up land to the enemy?" He snorted and looked up at the rafters. "Land be like a mother to us. Yet here I be, playing at warrior. A hoe sits better in my hands than a sword."

Sammàndhir grinned and slapped the sole of Hairon's boot. "You're doing a damned fine job to be *playing*." He rubbed his unshaven jaw. "Lord Nichàlor's men could be of great help to us."

"Aye." Lorhaiden pulled at his wet leather jerkin; with luck it would not go stiff beyond comfort. "He's already sent out messengers to the other steadings, warning them of Tutuljad's fall and telling them to watch for any of our army that made it to safety."

"What about Kahsir, Lord?" asked Hairon.

Kahsir. Lorhaiden stiffened and tried to cover his expression with a yawn. "I haven't heard from him yet, but by now the High-King will have told him we made it to the hills."

"Reinforcements?" Sammàndhir asked.

"The High-King told me Kahsir's bringing one thousand men. If I know Kahsir, he'll take no chances on running into the enemy. He'll approach the hills from the east. The High-King said he took the mind-road yesterday, so he should be reasonably close by now."

"This here rain's slowed him down, I'll bet," Hairon said.

Lorhaiden nodded, and leaned back on his elbows; now that he had stopped walking around, his weariness grew overpowering. He yawned again—a true yawn this time—and rubbed his eyes. "I'm going to get some sleep," he said. Drawing his cloak up about his shoulders, he stretched out in the hay. "You two do the same. The Light knows we need it."

"Aye." Sammàndhir stood, waited for Hairon to join him. "Rest easy, Lord. We won't wake you unless there's need."

Lorhaiden nodded, closed his eyes and listened to his companions walk off. Left alone, he opened his eyes again, looked up into the dimness of the rafters above. Tutuljad. Lost. Burned. In the hands of the enemy. *And I'm accountable.* His hands clenched at the hay. *Lords! If I can believe only what I see, just one thousand of my men survived. And now I've got to haul them together, make a fighting force of them again. We've got to throw up our lines north of Tutuljad to keep the enemy from coming farther north. And facing nearly twelve thousand of the enemy, without horses . . . ? By the Light! Am I insane to think I can stand against that many? I'll have to get more reinforcements than Kahsir's bringing if I hope to hold here.*

He shut his eyes but the memory of Tutuljad would not disappear: it hung in his mind, burned there like a brand. He cursed and turned over on his side. *There's got to be more men who survived than just the thousand I know about!* He shifted again, and finally sleep rolled over him in a long dark wave.

Tsingar looked over his shoulder at the five hundred men who followed. *Gods! I've seen more inept idiots before! I must have! Remember. They're young, all of them.* He snorted quietly. Being young gave them no excuse for their behavior. They rode strung out behind him, unable to understand the importance of keeping tight ranks. Though he had harangued them all before leaving Mehdaiy's camp, they still seemed oblivious to the importance of their task.

He cursed and looked forward again. *I'll never catch up to Lorhaiden with these dolts dragging at me!*

"Tsingar."

He cringed at the sound of the cool, half-amused voice. Carefully setting his face to an expression of polite patience, he turned to the man at his left.

Aduhar was everything Tsingar had feared he would be. Beneath an intricately worked helm, the young man's handsome face looked back, one eyebrow lifted slightly in what bordered on disdain. A rain-darkened red cloak—an affectation for one of the high-born— covered Aduhar's tooled leather jerkin, silver-washed chainmail beneath.

"*Tergai?*" Tsingar prompted.

Aduhar's face tightened and his eyes narrowed slightly. The rank of second-in-command, *tergai*, irked the young aristocrat, though he had not complained of it until now. Tsingar considered it part of the young man's lesson. *Teach him,* Mehdaiy had said. *You're his commanding officer, not the other way around.*

"*Tergai?*" Aduhar hissed. "That's *Lord* to you."

Tsingar's stomach tightened, but he kept his eyes locked with Aduhar's. "No." He spaced each word evenly, keeping his voice to an agreeable tone. "Not while I'm in command." Aduhar flushed, his eyes narrowing further. "Your uncle, the Dread Lord"—Tsingar stressed Mehdaiy's rank—"placed you under *my* command. Do you question that, *tergai?*"

Aduhar jerked his eyes away, looked off over the sodden countryside. Tsingar stared at the younger man, willing his attention and, when he got it, nodded to the rear. "Tell those idiots that if they don't close ranks, a Krotànya company half our size could tear us apart. *Go!*"

Aduhar jumped before Tsingar's voice, the crack of authority in it; then, curling his lip, he inclined his head only the barest degree and reined his horse around. Fluid strength lay in every movement. Tsingar closed his eyes and let his breath hiss between his teeth.

Gods! If I have to fight him, I'm dead.

He straightened his shoulders, looked toward the unseen hills, hidden by the rain. He had been riding for an hour now since leaving the mind-road. The land had changed slightly, become less flat; the grass had shortened and he had even encountered a few trees. That damned Lorhaiden could have entered the hills at any point, setting ambushes for anyone who followed.

Something caught Tsingar's eyes, a hint of movement, dim shapes in the gloom. He peered forward, immediately alert. It must be his scouts, returning with a report.

Two men approached at a trot, reined in their horses, and saluted.

"Well?" Tsingar asked, affecting a lazy drawl.

"There's a company of men ahead, Lord," one of the scouts said. "Three hundred."

Tsingar rubbed his chin. It could not be Krotànya. No one but his own people would ride so openly on the grasslands now that Tutuljad had fallen. And yet—

"Are they ours?"

"We didn't probe them," the second scout replied, "but they look like ours. It's hard to see, but I think I recognized one of our company banners."

"Huhn." Tsingar started to send out a probe, then yanked the tendril back. If he faced Krotànya, he would know soon enough. Better to keep them guessing who *he* was. He lifted his hand, beckoned Aduhar forward, and gestured toward where the scouts said the other company rode.

"Send a messenger to those horsemen. I want to know who they are and who leads them."

Aduhar's face was still as stone; his eyes glinted in the dull light, but he nodded briefly and rode off to choose his messenger. Moments later, a warrior disappeared into the rain. Tsingar stared after him: expendable, that one, if it *was* Krotànya approaching. He held up his hand again, signaling for his army to halt, turned and faced the men behind.

"You dung-eating fools!" They stared blankly back, sitting their horses at ease. "We don't know who's out there—it could be a trap." His men hastily searched for their shields and spears. *O Gods! Gods of my ancestors! What a group of half-brained worm-spawned inepts!*

He faced forward again and waited, counting the time he supposed it would take for his messenger to contact the other company and return. Suddenly, he stiffened; the gray shapes of oncoming horsemen drew nearer, eventually taking on form and substance in the rain. His messenger led them forward at a trot.

Tsingar sighed and relaxed. *Damn! Little chance they could have been Krotànya.* The horsemen's leader rode ahead of the others, a rough-looking man whose clothes and weapons spoke of ill-treatment and no time for rest. Reaching Tsingar's side, he jerked his horse to a stop.

"Dvorkun of the Clan of Tillig," the man said, naming himself, his face stiff with caution.

"Where have you come from?" Tsingar assumed the arrogance of commander, omitting name and rank. Let the other man guess at it.

"Northeast," Dvorkun said, gesturing behind. "There's another company north of us—they're about two hundred strong. We haven't seen any Krotànya save two we killed over an hour ago. We're returning to Tutuljad to wait for further orders."

Tsingar stared. "You killed two Krotànya? Northeast of here?"

"Aye . . . Lord," Dvorkun answered, giving in at last to the suspicion that Tsingar outranked him. "Probably escaping from Tutuljad."

Tsingar glanced over Dvorkun's shoulder at the men he could see who sat clustered behind. Rough-clad as their leader, they waited silently, faces slack with weariness. "Only two? That's curious. Were any others close by?"

"Might have been, Lord. We didn't stay to make sure."

"Gods." Tsingar closed his eyes and sighed heavily. He already led five hundred fools; he hardly needed to meet more. "Come with me, Dvorkun," he ordered. "The Dread Lord Mehdaiy has sent me to hunt Lorhaiden."

"Escaped, didn't he?" Dvorkun grinned slightly through his beard. "Now there's a slippery one for a Krotàn."

Slippery? Tsingar sneered inwardly. *You dung-faced idiot! Try facing him yourself. You'll find out how slippery he is.* He straightened in the saddle. "Have your men fall in behind mine. When we meet the other two hundred, I'll have them join us. We'll approach the hills from the east. As for Lorhaiden . . . that crazy bastard's taken refuge in those hills—I'd stake my life on it."

"Lord?"

Lorhaiden grunted and buried his head deeper beneath his cloak.

"Lord." Sammàndhir's voice. "A messenger's here. From the southeastern edge of the hills."

Lorhaiden opened his eyes, pulled the cloak from over his face and blinked up at his second-in-command.

"He's ridden hard, Lord. He must have urgent news."

"I'm coming." Lorhaiden stood, brushed the clinging hay from his clothing. He threw the cloak around his shoulders, yawned, and followed Sammàndhir to the doorway.

The rain still fell, though not as hard as before, and Lorhaiden shivered suddenly in the chill. Drenched to the skin, the messenger waited just inside the barn; his horse stood behind him, steam rising from its flanks as it nibbled at loose strands of hay on the floor.

"Lord." The messenger's voice shook with weariness. "An enemy company five hundred strong rode out of the south. They met another company of about three hundred, joined ranks and rode off again, headed northeast."

Lorhaiden said nothing; his eyes never left the messenger's face. Suddenly, his heart lurched. *"Chuht!* That puts them on a course that would intercept Kahsir." He spun on his heel. "Wake up!" he bellowed into the barn's darkness. Puffy-eyed men rose from the hay and staggered to their feet. "Mount! All who have horses! We're riding out! Hurry!" He turned back to the messenger, his throat tight. "Go to the woods south of here and the pastures beyond. Gather anyone who can get a horse. Have them follow you to the end of this valley. We'll wait for you there."

"Aye, Lord." The messenger saluted, grabbed for his reins, mounted and galloped out of the barn.

For an instant, Lorhaiden stared at the kicked-up hay settling to the wooden floor. His heart lurched again. Shaking his head, he ran to his place and sought after his swords. "How many horses do we have?" he asked Sammàndhir, attaching shortsword and longsword to his weapons belt. "Over two hundred?"

"Aye, Lord." Sammàndhir grabbed up his own weapons. "Those in the woods and pastures have easily twice that."

"Good. Eight hundred Leishoranya—over five hundred of us. If we give us the advantage of surprise, that makes us even, or close enough to it." He glared at several men who stood motionless a few paces away.

"*Fihrkken* idiots!" he snarled. "Mount up! We haven't a moment to lose."

They stared blankly, then ran off to their horses. Lorhaiden snatched for his helm and remembered it gone. Faces taut in the dim light, Hairon and Sammàndhir caught up their own cloaks and helms. Lorhaiden gestured for them to follow, and ran to the end of the barn where their horses were tethered.

He had ordered that none of the horses be unsaddled, only that their bits be removed and the cinches loosened. He found his horse in the confusion, tightened the cinch on the heavy war saddle, fumbling for a moment with the unfamiliar Leishoranya straps and buckles. Pushing the bit between the horse's teeth, he threw the reins over the saddle, sought the stirrup, and swung astride.

"Sahmdja? Hairon?" He reined his horse around. Both men had mounted; Hairon's horse shied, but the stocky farmer stayed seated, fishing for the other stirrup.

"Ready, Lord," Hairon said, his broad face a blur in the dimness.

"Follow me!" Lorhaiden turned his horse toward the barn door, kicked the animal to a gallop and burst out into the rain, the thunder of hooves behind.

"Scouts, Lord."

Tsingar looked up: two warriors rode in his direction through the rain. He glanced sidelong at Aduhar, surprised at the other's civility. His eyes narrowed slightly—what did Aduhar want?

The scouts slowed, then wheeled their horses to ride at Tsingar's side.

"There's a Krotànya army up ahead," one said, wiping the rain from his eyes. "One thousand strong."

Tsingar's eyes flicked to the other scout who grinned wolfishly.

"It's Kahsir, Lord," the second scout said.

Tsingar held his breath for a moment, released it suddenly. "You're sure?"

"Aye. We got close enough to see him."

Damn! Kahsir? So near? By the Gods— "How far away?" he snapped.

"A half hour's ride, Lord," the first scout said.

"Lord." Aduhar's voice shook with eagerness. "I claim my right to lead this battle."

A wave of coldness ran down Tsingar's spine. He jerked his horse to a stop, turned in the saddle, and looked at the young man. "You *what*?"

"It's my right." Aduhar sat very still, his eyes unreadable, his face hewn out of ice. Only his horse moved, fighting the tight reins. "Dhumaric was my uncle."

"You have no rights, *tergai*, save those I grant you. I'm in command here." He felt sweat break out beneath his helm, made his face expressionless. "I urge you to remember that, *tergai*." Behind, the other men sat their horses, silent, listening, faces blank in the rain: he could not lose their respect now. "If you wish," he said, keeping his voice level, "I'll fight you for it . . . *youngster*."

Aduhar flinched, his face sharpened slightly, but he kept silent. Only his eyes burned beneath his fancy helm—burned and seethed with darkness.

Tsingar looked away, feigning disinterest.

"Shall we go after them?" Dvorkun asked, carefully neutral.

Tsingar ignored Dvorkun and turned to the first scout. "What's the land like between here and there?"

"Mostly flat, more hilly to the west."

"Then let's go northwest. If we're lucky, we'll find the high ground first." His five hundred, Dvorkun's three hundred, and the additional two hundred that had joined forces with them, had finally come to attention. "Ride, dammit! Follow me!"

Rain turned to a blowing drizzle, less drenching but still miserable. Lorhaiden held his horse to a canter, over five hundred of his men coming behind. If the messenger had estimated correctly, the Leishoranya had nearly an hour's lead. *Lords! Did he say they were in a hurry or not? Dammit! I can't remember. I've got to assume they were going at a gallop or I'll never make it in time.* He whipped his horse to a faster pace. It was still too close to call.

Bowmen rode in the ranks, but the dampness would hinder them. Lorhaiden frowned. *I wish Vahl was here. If anyone could use a bow in this weather, it's my brother.* He looked behind, then ahead again; he and his men had ridden nearly an hour since leaving the hills. If the enemy had discovered Kahsir early enough, he might be too late.

He cursed again. He could only deal with what he knew, not what he guessed, save in forming strategy. His men rode silent; he had ordered them not to use mind-speech between them and to keep tightly shielded. The most highly trained of all, he subtly reached out his mind, seeking what lay ahead, though the danger of detection grew greater with every passing moment. If he sensed anything, he must sense it quickly.

Suddenly, something cold touched his mind, and he shuddered with revulsion.

He threw up his hand, signaling immediate halt. Slowly, tentatively, he probed again, thinning the contact to a near nothingness. His heart jumped.

Twisting in his saddle, he gestured his commanders forward. "They've found Kahsir," he said. "Somewhere, they must have met another company of two hundred. That gives them a thousand—equal to Kahsir's force. Lharic, take one hundred fifty north. Get as close to the enemy's left flank as possible. Tokkol, you and your one hundred fifty go south and approach to their right. Sahmdja, Hairon—come with me. We'll attack from their rear. Have your bowmen strike first if possible. And for the Light's sake, keep your minds shielded. Don't attack until you've received my signal. Go!"

His subcommanders saluted and returned to their warriors. Lorhaiden rode forward at an easy canter, shielding both himself and his mount as he went.

—Anger . . . a few waves of fear . . . the desire to kill and a sudden urge for speed. The brutal flare of minds that, dying, knew no gentleness in death—

Lorhaiden winced at those thoughts and quickly shut them out. He rode on, the one open part of his mind fixed on the enemy position. The land rose ahead: this and the light rain might hide his company's arrival.

Then caught by a sudden gust of wind, the distant sounds of battle, muffled and indistinct.

He hauled his horse to a sliding stop—Kahsir and his attackers fought over the crest of the rise he faced. His men halted and gathered behind him, tense and ready to fight. Lorhaiden caught up his shield, chewed on his lower lip and glanced up into the cloudy sky. *Wait, idiot! Wait! The rest haven't taken their places yet.*

And then he sensed his other forces in position. He settled his shield closer against his side, lifted his sword over his head.

—*Now, brothers!* he Sent. *Now! Attack!*

Tsingar ducked, kneed his horse into a sidestep: his opponent's sword swept harmlessly past. He whirled around as another warrior rode in his direction. The Krotàn's swordstroke jarred Tsingar's shield against his side; he gasped for air, lashed out with his sword, caught the man from behind, and rode on.

For a moment, he had a chance to look around. His lips drew back in a snarl. *Gods, Gods, Gods! What's gone wrong? There are only one thousand of them, and we took them totally by surprise.*

He had reached the high ground first, and when the Krotànya had ridden into range, he had led his men down the hillside, their charge nearly splitting the hastily formed Krotànya ranks in two. But now— More and more often, the bodies he rode over were those of his people, not Krotànya.

Aduhar fought to his left, power and unbelievable speed in every move. A cold feeling knotted in Tsingar's heart. He had read Aduhar right: if he ever *did* have to fight him, he would lose. He could not escape that conclusion. He would never equal the young man's battle-craft.

Another Krotàn rode out of the rain. Tsingar set his shield again and kicked his horse forward into a gallop. He met his opponent's swordstroke with his own, but his blade slid aside. Turning in the saddle, he saw the warrior coming back. The two weapons met—steel shrieked, but again Tsingar's blade was turned away. He brought his sword around in a savage sweep and missed the Krotàn altogether.

Tsingar snarled and glanced after his foe. The Krotànya had pushed his men back toward the low rise behind. He spat off to one side. *By the Gods! My men are incompetents! It's got to be their youth, their lack of training! We're barely holding our own!*

He sought out another Krotàn, galloped at him and engaged. This warrior was a superb swordsman and Tsingar fought off a barrage of blows with increasing difficulty. *Gods! He's good! Too damned good! He could beat me.*

Then—a blur of dark red: the Krotàn gasped, fell forward, and Tsingar looked into Aduhar's laughing face. The mockery in the cold eyes had the impact of a swordblow.

Suddenly, an angry roar of voices rose over the battlefield as arrows fell out of the rain, striking men who fought to Tsingar's rear. He jerked his horse to a halt, turned in the saddle, and looked up the hillside. More Krotànya galloped into the battle—hundreds of them, recognizable despite the gloom. They came from all sides, from over the concealing rises, materializing out of the rain.

Tsingar froze and quickly looked around. *O Gods! I'm going to die this time. Damn you, Kahsir! Where are you? I'll take you with me if—*

Then, Queen Aeschu's words echoed in his memory: *Don't let revenge cloud your mind. . . .*

Tsingar drew a ragged breath. *No! I'll escape if I can! Later! I'll have other chances later!*

Aduhar! Tsingar looked for Mehdaiy's nephew in the confusion. He could not let Aduhar die, not after Mehdaiy had placed the young man under his protection. *Teach him,* Mehdaiy had said. Tsingar grimaced. *Aye. I'll teach him, Dread Lord. Teach him how to retreat.*

A jolt on his shield, followed by a searing pain: nearly too late, he struck out with his sword at his Krotànya opponent, and felt his blade bite into flesh. As the man fell, Tsingar looked down—a deep gash ran across his thigh, dark blood welling out of it. He swayed in a wave of dizziness, bit his lower lip, and brought the world into focus again.

He reined his horse around, pain running down his leg like fire, and looked for Aduhar again.

Lorhaiden lashed out with his sword on both sides of his horse, his field of vision narrowed to those he killed. He laughed as he fought: somewhere, a small shred of forgotten sanity disapproved. He laughed again, struck out, and another Leishoranya died beneath his steel.

—Kahsir! he Sent. *Sword-brother! We're here! We've come!*

The Krotànya battle cry rang out in the gloom: Lorhaiden yelled it back, and rode deeper into the fight. The enemy milled in confusion, not certain where to turn. *By the Light! We've got them now!*

Then his horse went down, screaming in agony, a spear in its chest. Before the animal hit the ground, Lorhaiden kicked his feet from the stirrups and leapt free of the saddle. Knocked breathless, he struggled up from one knee, but Hairon had ridden to his side, ready to engage any Leishoran who attacked. Lorhaiden glanced around—a wild-eyed riderless horse trotted by. He grabbed at the horse's saddle and reins, and hauled himself astride.

The fighting had grown fiercer, and he had no time to adjust the stirrups. He lifted his sword in salute to Hairon and set off again. His men had taken advantage of the enemy's growing confusion and, backed up by Kahsir's company, began slaying the Leishoranya nearly at will. There was no pity in their hearts—for every foe his comrades killed, they shouted the names of dead cities, murdered kinfolk, and dying dreams.

Lorhaiden stabbed out at a Leishoran, locked swords, and sent the warrior's weapon spinning away. Killing them seemed so easy. He lunged at the warrior, struck cleanly between the Leishoran's ribs, and jerked his sword away.

Tutuljad! Dead city, fallen city! I'll drown your flames with blood!

The Leishoranya fought doomed and knew it, but they seldom retreated. Lorhaiden grinned. *We've got the bastards! I can get fifteen by myself at least!* Then suddenly the Leishoranya turned and galloped off into the light rain through a breach in the Krotànya ranks.

"No!" Lorhaiden shook his sword over his head. "Come back, cowards! Come back!" His voice rose to a howl. "Hairon!" He looked for his shieldman, saw Hairon's pale face close by. "Follow me! We can't let them escape!"

—Lorj!

Lorhaiden stiffened, caught by the warmth of the voice in his mind, and turned. Kahsir rode across the battlefield, his shield battered, a few small cuts his only wounds.

"Lorj!" Kahsir called, aloud this time.

Lorhaiden responded at last: lifting his reins, he

kicked his horse into a canter toward his sword-brother. Reaching Kahsir's side, he clasped the Throne Prince's arm in greeting.

"Ah . . . *baràdor.*" Kahsir grinned. His eyes strayed to Lorhaiden's helmless head, the bloody cloth that bound it. "By all the Lords of Light! I've never been happier to see you!"

Lorhaiden laughed. "And you were coming to give *me* aid!" Warmth slid into his heart at Kahsir's nearness, and he laughed again.

"How many men have we lost?" Kahsir asked.

"I'm not sure, but it can't be many. We took them totally by surprise."

Kahsir's eyes met Lorhaiden's. "And your army, Lorj? How many got away from Tutuljad?"

Lorhaiden swallowed. "One thousand that I know of. There *must* be another thousand and more in the hills somewhere." His shoulders straightened. "The enemy got reinforcements in the night. They had close to twelve thousand men there. I couldn't—"

"Grandfather told me. And now?"

"Now?" Lorhaiden looked over the battlefield from which the enemy fled. Few Leishoranya remained, and those warriors were wounded beyond escaping. Lorhaiden sighed. "Now I try to regroup what's left of my army. We've got to set up our defensive lines to the north of Tutuljad. The enemy may have the city, but if we move quick enough, we can hold the land."

A brief frown touched Kahsir's face. "For awhile."

"For awhile? But we've—"

"Don't you see, Lorj? If the enemy's gained a foothold here in southern Elyâsai, it's going to be damned near impossible to keep them from advancing. We don't have the manpower."

"Then what?"

"Our secondary plan of defense. We'll hold the land as long as possible, but now that the enemy's got a way across the river, I don't know how to keep them from using it. Our main objective will be to make them spend more blood than they like taking it. There aren't any major geographical barriers north of here until the high hills around Dramujh."

"And the escarpment." Lorhaiden nodded. "It's the best we can do, I suppose. But—"

"Do you think you can hold the land here?"

"Aye. But Sahmdja is capable of doing it." His stomach tightened. "Can I expect reinforcements?"

Kahsir nodded. "But not quickly."

"Lords of Light! There are at least ten thousand of the enemy in Tutuljad! If we can't—"

"We don't have the men now, Lorj. Grandfather will send them to you when he's able. Do you want to stay here?"

Lorhaiden met Kahsir's eyes. "I want to see you married, Lord, but if you don't think Sahmdja can take command for a few days, I'll stay."

"Then let's talk to him, you and I." A small smile softened Kahsir's face. "I can't imagine myself being married without my sword-brother at my side."

CHAPTER 6

Bell-song swirled upward on a salty wind that blew up from the sea. Kahsir reined in his horse, sat for a moment in the sunlight, and looked down from the hillside at the city of Hvàlkir. This was one of his favorite views of the capital, and he had chosen to leave the mind-road at this point so he could savor the sight before him. He drew a long, deep breath, his weariness disappearing in the wind and the sound of bells.

Hundreds of bells, thousands, growing louder or softer as the wind picked up and died again. The city stood on the edge of the Bay of Stars, white towers and walls brilliant in the sun. Gulls swooped overhead, their mewling cries interweaving with the bell-song, as they wheeled and dived toward the glittering water.

Kahsir glanced sidelong at Lorhaiden, who had brought his horse to a halt less than a pace away. Lorhaiden's eyes were narrowed in the bright light, but the harsh lines of his face had faded at the sight of the city.

"They're welcoming you home, Lord," Lorhaiden said, gesturing briefly at the city, "and celebrating your coming marriage. The bells haven't rung like this in decades."

Kahsir smiled as he looked at the city. *Aye. I'm home.*
Memory battered at his mind: dead men, wounded men,
darkness left behind in the south. A shattered army that
depended on reinforcements sent by the High-King, and
Sammàndhir's skill to set it right again.

And the enemy invasion of Elyâsai, which could
bring an end to the Krotànya as a people.

His heart swelled as he looked down the hill at
Hvàlkir, the King City, the last of Vyjenor's capitals,
shining in the sunlight as if in defiance of the gathering darkness. That all this beauty, this history, this
pride in life could be destroyed seemed impossible to
believe.

Lorhaiden said something quick and soft to Hairon,
and the two of them laughed. Kahsir smiled again. *Go
ahead—talk about my wedding. You're both glad to be
here and I know it.*

"Lord." Lorhaiden spoke again and Kahsir looked up
from the city. "Company."

Kahsir followed the line of his sword-brother's pointing arm. Riders ascended the hillside: he squinted in
the sunlight and recognized them instantly. His father,
brothers and sister, even his grandfather, and—Eltàrim.
His heart leapt in his chest, and lifting his reins, he
set his horse to a canter down the hill.

She rode slightly ahead of the others, her dark hair
floating behind her. Her face full of expectation, she
smiled in greeting; the lines of her shoulders and back
showed her growing excitement.

In a few more moments, he had reached her side.
"Tahra!" he said, and leaning from his saddle, he
reached out, took Eltàrim's hand in his, and kissed it.

He reluctantly released her hand and turned to his
family, to his grandfather who spoke.

"This is *your* welcome," Vlàdor said, waving toward
the city, and alluding to the ringing bells. His face softened in the sunlight. "Lords, Kahs. It's good to have
you home."

Kahsir reached for Eltàrim's hand again and held it tightly. "If I said I was glad to be here, it would be an understatement."

"Then let's go." Alàric grinned, riding close enough to thump Kahsir's shoulder. And, with an even wider grin: "As if we could keep you away."

Kahsir laughed, glanced at Eltàrim and turned his horse down the hillside. Hand in hand, he rode with her through the tossing grass, beneath a brilliant sun.

Afternoon sunlight beat down on the white steps of the Temple; Kahsir glanced up at the sky and shifted from foot to foot. His finery had grown bothersome: the heavy, embroidered cloak, the formal jerkin, the new boots that squeaked as he walked. He rubbed his forehead just below the slender gold circlet of Throne Prince; it, too, weighed more than he remembered. He squared his shoulders and looked around.

Lorhaiden stood at his side, appearing equally uncomfortable in his formal clothes. But Hairon was the most self-conscious of all—he had probably never been dressed so fine, and his broad face flushed as crimson as his cloak.

Kahsir rubbed his forehead again. Time seemed to have gone wild. He had returned to Hvàlkir only a day ago, but it felt as if more time than that should have passed. Custom decreed that before a couple exchanged vows of marriage, each spend three nights and three days apart from each other. He smiled slightly. His period of waiting was stranger than most men's: two nights and a day riding to battle, and a second day spent fighting it.

Resplendent in his red cloak, Hairon turned to look at the crowds. Kahsir grinned at the farmer and—

—his sight blurred: red, scarlet, the color of blood; fighting in the south. The sounds of bells, of hushed conversation, faded to be replaced by the cries of

dying warriors. From all three borders of the Kingdom
of Elyâsai, blood and death—

He shook his head and closed his eyes. When he
opened them, he stood on the Temple steps again.

"Lord," Lorhaiden said. "Your grandfather's entered
the Temple."

Kahsir nodded, keeping his face expressionless. His
grandfather and sister would be with Eltàrim; kinless, she
had none to stand with her on this, one of the most
important days of her life. His brothers' minds touched
his, full of joy. His father's thoughts were happiest of
all—heirs for the throne of Ràthen, first of Vyjenor's
High-Kings. Kahsir frowned at the old quarrel between
them, and his sight blurred again. Heirs? Heirs to what?
An empire that was empire no more? Dreams that had
been shattered by the hammer of Darkness?

One bell rang, deeper than all the others—his signal
to enter the Temple. His father motioned toward the
doorway, while his brothers, and Vàlkir, Lorhaiden, and
Hairon touched his hands briefly for good luck. For a
brief moment, he stood hesitating at that doorway and
then stepped forward. Eltàrim was waiting. All the
shadows he had Seen vanished before a vision of her
face and her smile.

"Long life and long health!"

Vlàdor's toast rang out over the crowded hall and
the guests raised their cups to return it. Kahsir smiled
at his grandfather, then looked at Eltàrim. *O Lords of
Light! How could I have waited so long?* He stirred
slightly in his chair and shook his head. *She's beautiful—so damned beautiful! I'm an idiot to have put this
off all these years!*

He had granted himself five nights and four days—
all the time he could spend with her. Now that the
enemy had invaded Elyâsai, four days might be too
long. He closed his eyes briefly, shutting all thoughts
of war and dying from his mind.

Awash in laughter, song and merriment, the feasting hall glittered with a golden light from the many hanging lamps and candles that filled it. Kahsir squeezed Eltàrim's hand in his and lifted his cup.

"A toast," he said, looking into her eyes, "for our happiness."

He glanced out at the hall as he lifted his cup. Made of heavy silver, intricately carved, it glittered in the lamplight like—

—swords and spears glinting in the sunlight; death looking out of the sparkling. Darkness coiled at the edges of his vision, shot through the flash of weapons—

"Kahs."

Alàric's voice. He held onto that voice, made it an anchor to the present place and time. Blinking twice, he turned to his youngest brother, and the world settled into normalcy again.

"The feast's nearly done," Alàric said. "Do you want me to signal Grandfather to let you and Eltàrim go?"

Kahsir lowered his cup, set it down by his empty plate and nodded. *Oh, Tahra. I want you so.* His vision blurred again but the moment passed. *Lords of Light! Don't let her see what's happening to me. Not tonight of all times!*

The High-King stood, lifted his hands, and the hall fell silent as all eyes turned toward him. Kahsir tightened his grip on Eltàrim's hand, and felt her longing surge out to meet his own. Standing, he helped her to her feet, and his grandfather turned to face them.

"Long may you live and love," Vlàdor said, his voice pitched to carry over the hall. "Long may you live and love!"

The guests rose to their feet and echoed that toast. Kahsir looked down into Eltàrim's eyes and met her smile with his own.

Cold—terrible cold, numbing cold. And darkness. Terror and despair stalked that darkness; shadows murmured of no hope for dawn. Death waited there, but so did life, each poised on a balance, each of equal weight. Tears came, sorrow before and after. And somewhere in the depths of night more than night, a lone star burned.

The hallway seemed endless, both sides lined by innumerable doors, each door standing as a portal into places and times that might exist. Kahsir walked on; he had been walking forever, hounded by the clustering shadows. He did not know what he sought, only that he would recognize it when he found it.

And finally, eternities later, he stood in front of the last of those doors, which opened of itself before he could touch it.

His heart jumped: he saw himself reflected as if in a mirror. Then, what had been himself became suddenly transformed, and he faced another figure: shadowy, hidden as if by a mist. Yet not hidden enough. Somehow, he knew himself a part of that person, but changed, augmented, taken to the highest of planes. He swallowed heavily, only a breath away from knowing who looked back. Nothing mattered as much as seeing that face, not even what he had glimpsed through the other doorways. He would throw that knowledge away for a single look at—

—then, for the briefest of instants, he saw—truly saw—who stood in that doorway.

Night fell away. Hope was reborn from darkness: hope, and a million stars, each a brightness equal to the sword in that figure's hand. And for an instant, for the briefest of moments, Kahsir understood—understood it all. Then a flood of light swept out from those stars, to fill him, consume him, and carry him exulting into tomorrow.

Kahsir's eyes flew open and he lay for a moment totally disoriented. Slowly, things began to fall into place: the quiet of the palace, the familiar surroundings of his bedchamber, comforting in the dim firelight. Eltàrim still slept at his side, untouched by what he had seen. He rubbed his eyes, looked up at the shadows dancing on the ceiling. All hope for sleep gone, he rose from bed, moving slowly to keep from waking his wife.

"Kahs?"

"Aye?"

He looked at her as she sat up, the coverings gathered around her knees, her long hair falling about her shoulders.

"What happened? Why are you so upset?"

He dropped his shields—she would Read behind them anyway—and walked across the room. Stopping by one of the windows, he pulled the drape aside and stared out into the chill spring night. Her movements quiet in the even quieter room, Eltàrim slipped out of bed and came to his side.

"Your mind's so full of thoughts I can't Read any of them. What happened?"

"I'm not sure, *tahvah*, dearest." He faced her, letting the curtain fall back in place. "I think it was a *lo'fìvàd*."

"A True-Dream?" she echoed. Her eyes filled with curiosity. "Can you remember any of it?"

"Parts." He kissed her forehead, hints of what he had seen at the edge of memory. "Perhaps all."

One of Kahsir's cats rubbed up against his ankles, mewed softly and joined its companions in front of the fireplace. He smiled, led Eltàrim to their bed, and sat down with her on the side closest to the dying fire. The cats' purring sounded loud in the room.

Eltàrim leaned her head on his shoulder. "Was it a dark Dream?"

"It was everything," he replied, looking into the fire. What *had* he seen? Even now it was fading. "Life, death, sorrow, light, joy, darkness—So much more." Words could not tell it; opening his mind, he filled hers with what images remained.

"And those futures you saw," Eltàrim said at last, "can you remember any of them?"

"Not really." He stood, tossed two logs on the embers, then sat down again. "I probably won't recognize what I've seen until I'm so involved in it I won't know if I've foreseen it or not. But I do know this: most of those doors were full of shadows."

"The last one wasn't."

"That's true. It wasn't. But what I saw through it puzzles me the most. I stood there, yet I didn't. It was only part of me."

She ran her fingertips across his shoulder. "Who was it?" she asked quietly. "Do you know?"

"I'm not sure. I think—maybe I do. But I could have been seeing what I wanted to see."

He looked away from the fire into her eyes, his mind now firmly in hers.

"Hjshraiel," she whispered.

"Maybe. Maybe not. I could have put flesh on the hopes of our people."

"And who besides Hjshraiel can be that?"

He smiled and gestured briefly. "But death, sorrow, and darkness will come before."

"We're in that darkness now. There's never been a night without a dawn to follow."

"Ah, *tahvah*." He kissed her forehead. "Go back to sleep now, if you can. I'm sorry I awakened you."

"Since you leave tomorrow," Eltàrim said, "I could hardly see enough of you."

He looked into her eyes, lifted her chin, and sought her lips, leaving the puzzle of his Dream behind.

Kahsir stretched, yawned, and walked down the front steps of the palace into the courtyard where his horse stood tethered, the pack horses grouped to one side. Iowyn waited there, the only one of his family he had seen yet. Dark hair touched by early sunlight, she saw to her own mount and Ahndrej's.

"Kahs." Her eyes met his over the back of her horse. Tall and slim, she walked across the courtyard, her leather riding skirt brushing against her trousered legs. No pampered woman this, his sister, not she. Raised with three brothers, all older, she had trained and hunted with them; she did not wear the slim-bladed sword at her side for show.

"You're up early," he said, taking her elbow in his hand and guiding her into the garden close by.

"Me?" Her smiled widened. "*You're* the one who's newly married. I should be asking why you're up, not the other way around."

He lifted an eyebrow and looked down at her. "I'm not going to start in on that so soon in the morning." He stopped beneath the branches of a *melenor* tree—its white blossoms filled the air with their scent. "Io," he said, and turned her about so she looked directly into his eyes. "Where the Dark did you come up with the idea of going to Vharcwal with Ahndrej?"

Her smile disappeared. "I didn't realize I had to ask *your* permission to go."

He flinched at the ice in her voice. "You don't. But Father—"

"Father knows," she snapped. "Drop the subject. I'm going and you can't keep me from it."

"But—"

"But, nothing! Can't you understand? This is the last time I'll be able to visit Vharcwal." She looked quickly away. "I love it so. . . ."

"I know that." *I might as well give up. She's more stubborn than ever this morning.* He sighed quietly. "Can't *you* understand why I'm concerned for you?"

She lifted her head, fierce pride in her stance. "I'm not a little girl anymore, Kahs. In case you haven't noticed, I've grown up. I can take care of myself."

"I don't doubt that. But even I wouldn't go into Ahndrej's lands now without taking some precautions."

"I'll take them." Her face softened. "This means so

much to Dreja. He wants me to see his estate once more before it's gone forever."

Kahsir sighed again, threw back his head, and stared at the sky.

"Kahs. Do you understand what I'm telling you?"

He looked down at her, at the stubborn set of her shoulders, her hands clenched at her sides. "I understand. But—"

"No buts. I'm going. Ahndrej left his family, his lands, to come to *your* wedding. I can at least show my love for him by going back one last time."

He shook his head and lifted his hands in defeat. "All right. You're going. But if—" He sought her eyes. "At least let me ride with you. I'd feel better if I knew you'd reached his steading safely."

"Lords of Light! The enemy's not *that* close!"

"Listen to me." He reached out and caught at her arm. "The enemy's not that close . . . aye, not *now*. We're managing to hold them back. But Vharcwal is one of Elyâsai's southernmost steadings. A raiding party or a company could—"

"They *could* do anything, Kahs! Dreja and his family are leaving in a few days. Trust me. I'll know when to go. I didn't sleep through all those strategy classes we took while growing up."

"No," he admitted. "You didn't." He let loose her arm. "Let me ride with you. After we've reached Vharcwal, I'll turn east with Lorhaiden and Vàlkir."

She held his gaze and some of the hardness faded from her face. "Only if you promise to leave me there. No other way. Can you *promise* me that?"

He hesitated slightly, then nodded. "I promise." The lines of tension dissolved from her face and body. *Lords! I'm surrounded by some of the most stubborn, hard-headed—*

"You're none too pliable yourself," Iowyn said, "so don't try to make me feel sorry for you."

He snorted. "Between you and Lorhaiden . . ."

She pulled a face and, with a shrug, he smiled.

Tsingar shifted in his chair, licked his dry lips, and looked around the lamp-lit tent. *His* tent. As one of Mehdaiy's commanders, he was entitled to one—another mark of favor of the Great Lords. Memories flooded back: nights spent shivering outside Dhumaric's tent door in the cold—aching bones and muscles from sleeping on the hard ground—exhausted yearnings for dawn. . . .

The tent flap opened; he turned and a dull stab of pain ran through his wounded leg. Mehdaiy stood in the dim lamplight, cloaked in shadow.

"Stay, Tsingar," Mehdaiy said.

Tsingar fell back in his chair as Mehdaiy sat down opposite him. "I've run out of wine, Dread Lord. Shall I send for more?"

Mehdaiy shook his head and extended a wine flask. "I've brought my own. A far better vintage."

Tsingar nodded, reached out for two cups on the table at his side. Buried beneath his shields, he watched his commander pour the wine. *What does he want? Such courtesy isn't normal.*

"You're better by now, I trust?" Mehdaiy asked, leaning back in his chair and crossing one booted foot on the other.

"Aye, Master. My leg's healing, but it's still painful." He drank, unable to see Mehdaiy's face in the shadows. "It's kept me from being much use to you."

Mehdaiy made a gesture of curt dismissal. "Despite the men you lost, you did well. You deserve the days you've rested. And your scouts have served me in your absence."

"Ah?" Tsingar straightened. "They're returned?"

"This afternoon. You were sleeping." Mehdaiy uncrossed his legs, sat forward in the chair, arms across his knees. Though Tsingar could not see Mehdaiy's eyes, he felt their stare. "Kahsir's coming south."

"When?"

"Soon. After that battle in the hills, he went home to be married."

Tsingar laughed. "He won't see much of his wife, then, fighting so far away."

Mehdaiy's stillness sent a wave of ice down Tsingar's spine. *Don't presume on his momentary easiness. Men have died for less.* Mehdaiy relaxed, a subtle shifting in the shadows, and Tsingar let loose his pent-up breath.

"Your scouts caught a Krotànya warrior," Mehdaiy said as if nothing had happened. "They forced his mind and learned some other interesting information." He drank the last of his wine and held out his cup; Tsingar quickly filled it, then his own at Mehdaiy's gesture. "They're *all* coming back," Mehdaiy continued. "The whole damned lot of them: Lorhaiden, Vàlkir. And—" he paused, as if savoring this next piece of information "—Kahsir's sister is riding south with him."

"His *sister*?" Tsingar sat up straighter. "What's *she* doing—"

"She has a lover or betrothed—that's hard to tell— who has a steading not far from the border. We've suspected something of the kind all along, and your scouts proved us right. She often visits him there. I suppose she's coming south to be with him before his people flee."

Tsingar stiffened; something lay hidden behind Mehdaiy's words, something *he* should know. He searched his memory: he had fought the Krotànya for so many centuries he felt he knew most of them personally. Kahsir's sister? He remembered now; she considered herself a warrior—amusing thought—but he actually knew little about her. And now she was coming south. *Damn! If only—*

"Aye," Mehdaiy said. "If only."

Tsingar shrank in his chair, away from the coldness

in Mehdaiy's voice.

"I'll let you handle this, Tsingar. If there's some way you can take this woman prisoner—" Mehdaiy's hands clenched. "Think what we could do with her! *Think* of it!"

"Aye, Master. She'd be lovely bait, wouldn't she, to dangle before Kahsir's nose."

"Keep in contact with your scouts. I want to know where he and his sister are at all times. When they're far enough south to make it worth while, I want you to go after her."

"What of him, Lord?"

"If he can be taken or killed, do it. But I want his sister. Once we've got her, we'll have him."

"And the rest of his family." Tsingar rubbed his nose. "Where's this steading located, Dread Lord?"

"We haven't found out yet, but we will. There are always more Krotànya to catch. One of them is bound to know where this Princess goes when she journeys south."

"Aye, Master. I'll leave when you give me word."

"Good." Mehdaiy leaned back in his chair. "And I want you to take Aduhar with you."

Tsingar winced, covering it with a cough.

"He's still as cocky as ever, but—by the Gods! You stood up to him. Called him *tergai* to his face. No one's ever done that and lived to tell it. He needed the discipline, Tsingar. He'll never lose his arrogance; it's his heritage, and so is his pride. But first he must learn to serve. Those who don't, die."

A heavy mist and gloomy skies hid the late afternoon sun. Kahsir pulled his cloak higher about his neck—at least it had stopped raining. Everywhere he looked, the countryside was obscured by damp grayness. Lorhaiden and Valkir rode at his side; ahead, all laughter and merriment, his sister and the man she loved.

Two hundred warriors rode behind them, bound for

the southern border, men whom he had led from the capital yesterday. Fresh from their ten-day of rest from fighting, they would replace warriors presently in combat. They rode in tight formation, their eagerness and high spirits not yet diminished by war.

But even as they rode, the southern border shrank league by painful league. Two days ago, Sammàndhir had reported that he had managed to regroup Lorhaiden's army, now reduced to half its former size. Good news, for Lorhaiden had feared no more than the thousand he had found in the hills had survived. Later that same day, Sammàndhir had led those men out of the hills to throw up a defensive line north of Tutuljad and to wait for reinforcements. Few natural barriers existed to use against the enemy—only open plains; yet with careful preparation, a skilled commander could turn that to his advantage.

Iowyn laughed lightly and Kahsir looked up from his hands tightly clenched on the reins. Ahndrej said something unheard, and when Iowyn replied, hung on her every word. Kahsir smiled reluctantly: he found it hard to be gloomy around them. Their togetherness only made his longing for Eltàrim harder to bear. *O Lords! If only we could have had a few more days!*

"Not a day fit for travel, is it, Lord?" asked Vàlkir from alongside.

Kahsir turned; the younger man hastily hid his smile.

"We should have waited and hoped this weather would pass." Vàlkir's mischievous smile returned. "Eltàrim wouldn't have minded."

Kahsir grinned. "I wouldn't have, either. But this rain and mist could last for days."

Vàlkir shrugged, leaned forward and looked to Kahsir's left. "Lorj? You're so silent, brother. Brooding again?"

"No," Lorhaiden replied. "Thinking."

Kahsir frowned. Lorhaiden's damned Oath again—

that and his concern over the broken army he had left behind.

The mist thickened to near a rain. Taking the mind-road might bring them out into better weather farther south. Kahsir shook his head; they had done so already today, and a second jump so soon would waste their strength. Despite the weather, their pace had been swift: slightly over a half day's ride separated them from Ahndrej's steading.

"Doesn't it ever dry out around here?" he called forward to Ahndrej.

"Rather this," Ahndrej said, "than snow, ice, and freezing my feet off in the north. I'm one of the Kahràmmir—children of the Sun, lovers of warmth and light."

"No wonder. I haven't seen much of either lately." He glanced up at the sky, judging the time. "Is there somewhere close to camp? It's nearly sunset, and we've ridden far enough today."

Ahndrej looked around. "Aye. Less than an hour's ride ahead. And, if it's any consolation, the weather might be breaking. Maybe tomorrow we'll see the sun."

"Lords! Let's hope so. I don't think I'll ever dry out." Kahsir guided his horse around a large puddle in his path. "An hour, you said? Let's make it sooner." He lifted his hand, motioned to the men who followed, and lightly touching his horse's ribs with his heels, set out at a faster trot.

Ahndrej's choice of a campsite seemed a good one to Kahsir. Surrounded by a stretch of woodlands, the clearing was large enough to give sleeping space to over twenty men. The rest of the company had thrown down their saddlebags in the trees close by; laughing quietly and swapping stories, they finished their evening meal.

Kahsir shifted in his sitting position, easing the stiffness out of his legs and back. He finished the last of his dried meat, wiped his hands on the wet grass, and yawned. Iowyn and Ahndrej had settled down against a large tree, wrapped together in a blanket, whispering and oblivious to the dampness. Vàlkir had already stretched out buried beneath his blankets, but Lorhaiden was nowhere to be seen. *Posting sentries,* Kahsir Read him. *Lords. Let him see to it.*

He shrugged, stood and sought his own blankets. As he lay down beneath a tree, he heard Hairon making a place for Lorhaiden to sleep close by, and the quiet sounds of other men bedding down for the night. Kahsir yawned again, hunting a more comfortable position. Lorhaiden returned and stretched out, a rustle in the darkness. Someone started to snore; heavy breathing came from others falling into deep sleep, trusting in the sentries.

An owl hooted off in the distance, and then was still. Lorhaiden had fallen asleep now—Kahsir sensed his sword-brother's relaxation, the repose of other sleeping minds.

He shifted his weight, blinked and stared up into the dark. The urge to sleep had vanished. Something hovered barely out of reach at the very edges of his mind. The owl hooted again. Kahsir closed his eyes briefly, listening to the silence. He stirred, rubbed his eyes and frowned.

The firelight. The owl. . . . Somewhere, he had seen and heard these things before.

He started: future meeting present—a memory from his Dream.

A wind that was no worldly wind touched the back of his neck. He sat up in his blankets and carefully scanned his surroundings and those who slept close by. Slowly reaching out with his mind, he searched beyond the edge of the woods: the sentries stood there, alert but unconcerned. Nothing was out of the ordinary, yet everything was. The wind that was not a wind came again, and he shivered.

*It's my Dream. We're in it now—living out one of
its possibilities.* He shut his eyes. *Dammit! I can't
remember! What did I see?* Only hints and fragments
of the Dream remained, and, as if in mockery, he
heard himself tell Eltàrim that he would likely not remember what he had seen of a future until he became
locked into it.

He shivered again, pulled his blanket closer, and slid
up into a sitting position against the tree trunk. *One
more time! Try to remember! I've got to try!*

Nothing. Only hints . . . sensations experienced in a
Dream that proved—

"Lord?"

A whisper, a soft step: Kahsir's eyes snapped open.
"Vahl? What are you doing up?"

The younger man knelt, a shadow against the fire.
"Your thoughts woke me. What's the matter?"

It would have been Vàlkir who had awakened; at
times, he showed a level of mental awareness that few
untrained ever achieved. One of the Mind-Born might
have reacted the same way to Kahsir's disturbed
thoughts. He peered at Vàlkir's unseen face and drew
his blanket closer.

"It was a Dream, Vahl."

"A *lo'fivàd*, Lord? You had it tonight?"

"No. The night before we left the capital. I should
have suspected I might. I was Seeing things more
often than usual." He sighed quietly. "I can only
remember one part of it, and that's hazy. But I know
this—we're living out one of its possibilities now."

"Ah."

The hushed response told more than words. Vàlkir
had also dreamt such Dreams, had more than once
become trapped in a memory, a time, a familiar set of
circumstances. Suddenly, Kahsir's mind filled with
sights and sounds—a memory of one of Vàlkir's
Dreams. A vast wall stood wrapped in a sheath of fire

that was not fire but something purer still. And then—
Pain . . . loss . . . anguish. The sense of being left
alone. Ah, Lords! How alone. . . .

Valkir gestured with his right hand, warding off the
memory, unaware that Kahsir had shared it.

"So," Valkir said, and rocked back on his heels to
sit. He gathered his blanket close. "We're living a part
of your Dream. Is it evil, or do you know?"

Kahsir shook his head. "If I could recall more of
the details, I might be able to tell you." He gestured
helplessly. "Not much happens these days that isn't
touched by the Shadow. If we've set out on a dark
future, maybe I can remember enough to avoid it, or
change it somehow."

He flinched inwardly, hearing his own words twice—
once in his Dream, only now remembered, and again
as he spoke them. He shivered anew, chilled by something only he could feel.

The leaves rustled overhead and the owl hooted
once more, only now much farther away. The misting
rain had stopped, though the clearing still smelled sodden. One of the sentries returned to see to the fire
and threw another branch on it; the man glanced
around, nodded a greeting in Kahsir's direction, then
disappeared into the woods.

Silence. Someone murmured in his sleep and then
fell still; Valkir sat waiting patiently. Kahsir glanced
away, leaned his head back on the tree trunk, and
searched his memories. And somewhere, on the very
edge of his awareness, he sensed more than saw the
gathering of shadows.

CHAPTER 7

It was midday before the mist finally lifted and patches of blue sky shone through the clouds. This combination changed everyone's moods; the men who rode behind Kahsir talked and laughed more frequently. He sat straighter and rubbed his eyes, besieged by memories that would not leave.

Vàlkir rode at his side, but Kahsir ignored his scrutiny. He had finally sent his friend to sleep, unable to tell him any more about his Dream. Now, Vàlkir waited for some hint that he had remembered more. Kahsir closed his eyes briefly. Lords! Would that he might!

The sunlight fell warm on his shoulders; the rain had left the land washed clean, and everything seemed to stand out with preternatural clarity. He breathed deeply of the sunlit air, then shivered as the shadow of his Dream passed by—

—leaving him helpless to halt events foreshadowed by that Dream. Every step he took, every sound he heard, everything he saw, he had experienced before.

Where does my Dream leave off, the memories fade, and where does reality begin?

Ahead, Ahndrej rode with Iowyn; now and then, he

pointed to something and he and Iowyn would laugh together. Kahsir looked away and shielded his misgivings so that no one would notice the darkness that preyed on his mind. Valkir had become aware of it, but Lorhaiden, usually so sensitive, seemed untouched. Kahsir frowned: that failure was probably due less to his own talent at shielding than to Lorhaiden's moodiness.

He shifted uneasily in his saddle and scanned the horizon, alert for any hint of danger. Something was wrong—something still hidden. His Dream again, or reality? Or memories of that Dream imbedded in the present?

Another league passed, and another. Ahndrej grew more subdued; Iowyn had fallen quiet too, a mirror of Ahndrej's mood. Kahsir rubbed his eyes, blinked at his double-vision, and rode on.

Valkir's mind touched his; Kahsir looked at the younger man and shook his head. *No answers yet, Vahl. Nothing but the shadows of shadows.* Lorhaiden stared now, and the warriors who rode behind them had fallen silent.

Iowyn looked over her shoulder and Kahsir tried to smile, to assure her nothing was wrong. Closest of all, his sister, bound by blood as well as love. She frowned and looked away, and Kahsir knew his smile had failed.

Damn! Trapped! I'm locked in my Dream with no hope of escaping it. He had foreseen everything, down to his sister's frown: a memory from his Dream. He cursed softly. *Say something. Anything. Keep fixed in the present. It's not as if no one's guessed something's wrong.*

"Dreja," he called. Ahndrej slowed his horse and Kahsir caught up to him. "I never got a chance to talk much with you before my wedding. How's your family doing?"

"They're all right. Upset because they have to leave, but so am I. That steading's been part of our lives for—well, since long before the war. To give it up now, even though we know why we have to go—" He shrugged. "We're not the first to leave our lands."

"Your brother's a fine man. I'm sure he has things well in hand."

Ahndrej's face broke into a smile. "Eldànhi's one of the best! There are times I think *he* should have been born eldest, not me. He has such a way with the land. And wait until you see my newest nephew, Maikha. He's only three. You've never seen him before—he's the very image of his father!"

"Does your family have any alternate plans for leaving Vharcwal?"

Ahndrej's dark face went blank for a moment. "Besides the one we've gone over?"

"Aye. In case they have to leave sooner than you planned."

Ahndrej stared for a moment. "What's wrong?"

"Haven't you sensed anything?"

"I don't—" Ahndrej's eyes narrowed a moment. "You mean the feeling of things being off center?"

Kahsir sighed. *I've got to go slowly . . . pick my way among the strands of my Dream.* "Something's not as it should be. Do you feel the same, or have you sensed my own uneasiness?"

"I'm not sure," Ahndrej said at last. "I'll admit I'm edgy. I don't think it's bled over from you, but I couldn't swear to it." He looked around, eyes glittering in the strong midday sunlight, and gestured. "These are my lands. If anyone should know whether something's wrong, it should be me."

Lords! He's edgy. I can understand that—shielded as I am, I still must be radiating nervousness. Maybe it's only that, and not yet reality. "Have you kept in touch with your family?"

"Aye. I Sent to Eldànhi yesterday. He said Mannishteh dàn Shuvo and his army had passed close to my southernmost pastures. Other than that, he had no news."

Kahsir nodded. "That's fortunate. I'd planned to talk with Mannishteh after we reached Vharcwal."

"If you want, I'll contact Eldànhi—"

"No. Don't bother." An icy feeling swept down Kahsir's spine, gone before he could grasp it. *Dammit! What's that about?* He sought after the feeling, but it had utterly vanished.

Ahndrej frowned. "Do *you* know what's wrong? Your questions—"

Kahsir shook his head. "No. I don't."

Ahndrej stared a moment, obviously unconvinced. "If there's anything I can do—"

"Keep my sister company," Kahsir said lightly, "and leave me to my gloomy thoughts. It's probably nothing." Ahndrej lifted one eyebrow, then trotted forward to Iowyn's side. Kahsir looked at his sister and met her eyes, but she knew no more about what was happening than anyone else. He unclenched his hands from the reins. *Dammit! It was* my *Dream! What the Dark did I see in it? Now's the time when I need those memories the most!*

Vàlkir and Lorhaiden rode to his side, and though neither of them said anything, their heightened state of awareness spoke for them. Kahsir grimaced, touched the hilts of his double swords, and made sure his shield was instantly available. A mad scene of confusion, of attack, filled his mind, and then, like other details of his Dream, it vanished.

He looked around the countryside. Ahndrej raised cattle for the most part, though he also dealt in grains; his lands were hilly and lay broken up into wide pastures where his herds grazed. Even now, Kahsir and the rest rode across one of those pastures, a lush expanse of grass that wound its way between higher land on both sides. To Kahsir, the pasture seemed curiously devoid of life: no cattle grazed here, and only a few birds sang in the trees that clustered the hillsides.

It'll take us two hours to make the great house of

Vharcwal. Maybe I should Send ahead to Ahndrej's brother and tell him how close we are.

No. They would arrive ahead of schedule, and Ahndrej had said something about wanting to surprise his family. Kahsir swatted the ends of his reins at a fly on his horse's neck. Now was hardly the time to panic.

Tsingar looked down from his position halfway up the hill, waiting for his scouts to return. Behind him waited five hundred warriors, the hundred-commanders sitting their horses at Tsingar's side; Aduhar waited among those commanders—silent, withdrawn, his face unreadable. The surrounding countryside had broken up into rolling hills. Tsingar smiled thinly; this far inside the borders of Elyâsai, he welcomed cover of any kind.

The steading of Vharcwal stood just over the horizon. He and his company had waited in Tutuljad camp until someone found out where the steading lay; finally, Mehdaiy's warriors had caught and broken the mind of a Krotàn who knew the steading's location. Armed with that information, Tsingar had found it easy to locate. Distrusting his young warriors, he had scouted Vharcwal himself before dawn and discovered it poorly guarded. Krotànya fools! They lived far enough from the fighting that they thought themselves safe. It would be a simple thing to take the steading, even with only a third of his force.

One of the hundred-commanders said something and pointed off to the left. Tsingar recognized his scouts; looking weary but satisfied, both men whipped their horses up the hillside. Tsingar's heart raced a moment—Kahsir!

"He's coming, Lord." One of the scouts gestured behind. "Several valleys away to the northwest."

"How many ride with him? Still only two hundred?"

"Aye, Lord."

Tsingar sat silent, looking off to the northwest.

"Lord." Aduhar spoke unprompted for the first time since dawn. "By your leave."

The tinge of sarcasm made the words annoying, but not enough to call the young man out. Tsingar looked at Aduhar, kept silent, and waited for him to continue.

"Are you still planning to ambush Kahsir?"

What in the names of all the Gods is the young fool up to now? Tsingar nodded.

"And also attack the steading to keep them from sending him aid?"

Tsingar nodded again. "What do you propose, *tergai?*"

Aduhar's eyes narrowed, but his voice stayed level. "Let me ride ahead. I'll place one hundred fifty men on either side of the valley he'll pass through. Then, I'll attack him when he comes between us. By that time, you and the other two hundred will have had time to destroy the steading."

Tsingar looked off into the valley below. He saw nothing wrong with what Aduhar proposed—it echoed his own plan of attack. Mehdaiy wanted his nephew to learn command, and now might be an excellent time for it; if Aduhar and his men kept themselves heavily shielded, even Kahsir should be taken by surprise. Tsingar's presence this far behind the Krotànya lines was audacious at best, one of the last things the Throne Prince should expect. Mehdaiy had cloaked the company so thoroughly that they had ridden past any detection by the Krotànya Mind-Born.

All right, then. So be it. Aduhar would attack with three hundred warriors and, with that advantage, might keep Kahsir engaged until Tsingar returned from the steading.

He grinned slightly: sending Aduhar up against one of the best warriors alive could solve his most immediate problem. If Aduhar reacted as Tsingar suspected, Kahsir would tear him to bits. Mehdaiy would rage over his nephew's death, but Tsingar would have witnesses that confronting Kahsir was Aduhar's idea.

"Lord?" prompted Aduhar.

"Aye, *tergai*," he said at last, glancing sidelong to make sure he was overheard. "That's a good idea. But don't be overconfident. Lorhaiden's with Kahsir, and you remember what happened the last time we met."

Aduhar nodded slowly; that admission must have cost him much, for as far as he was concerned, none of the Krotànya were worthy of carrying weapons.

Tsingar glanced over his shoulder at his silent warriors. Once more, he led men who were both young and inexperienced. *Maybe I should bring that inexperience to Aduhar's attention. It could make a difference in the way he handles his attack.* He snorted a quiet laugh. *If he can't recognize that by now, he's doomed.*

"It shouldn't take long to destroy the steading. Remember, Aduhar, taking Kahsir's sister is our first goal, but if he himself falls into our hands, don't push him away." Tsingar met Aduhar's cold eyes. "Do what you can. Keep them pinned down. Use your archers, and don't engage the Krotànya unless you have to."

Aduhar's lip curled slightly.

"Listen to me, *tergai*," Tsingar snapped. "In case you've forgotten who you're fighting—"

"I haven't forgotten," Aduhar shot back. "Neither have the warriors. And I've *stressed* the importance of fighting well." A thin, cruel smile, so much like Mehdaiy's, crossed his handsome face. "I'll personally take care of those who don't."

And enjoy doing it, too. "So," Tsingar said, pitching his voice to slight disdain, "don't pay attention to my suggestions. Do it your own way. But if I have to lug your dead body back to your uncle . . . "

Aduhar's face went pale, his eyes glittered dangerously in the sunlight, but he kept silent. "By your leave," he said, matching Tsingar's disdain with his own.

"Go."

Aduhar rode back to the waiting warriors, the set of his shoulders adding to his jauntiness in the saddle. Tsingar snarled silently. *What a fool! He's asking to be defeated. Let him! As long as we get our hands on Kahsir's damned sister, I don't care* what *he does.* Aduhar rode up and down the gathered company, choosing the three hundred men he would lead. *At least the brat's learned something. Not all his three hundred are dolts.*

Done, Aduhar sketched a mocking bow, and set off at the head of his men. Tsingar sighed, and gestured to his remaining two hundred. Turning his horse eastward down the hillside, he set out at a quick pace toward the steading.

Kahsir shifted uneasily in the saddle and looked around as he rode. It had grown far too silent for his liking. The birds had stopped singing, but midday warmth could account for that. He glanced around again, shrugged, and loosened the cloak around his shoulders. As springtime turned to summer in the southlands, the days grew steadily warmer.

Iowyn and Ahndrej rode silent, as did the two hundred who followed them. Lorhaiden and Valkir wordlessly kept their horses at an even pace with his. Kahsir rubbed his chin, his vision blurred with his Dream.

Suddenly he caught the glitter of something on the very edge of his vision, from the dense brush covering the hill ahead and off to his right. He looked quickly in that direction and scanned the hillside: nothing—no repeat of whatever had caused that flash of light. He reached out with his mind, only to suffer the curious sensation of sliding off to the side of his point of concentration. Cold sweat broke out on his hands, and he hastily clamped his shields down.

"Dreja!" he called softly. "Shield yourself! Unless

your brother left sentries who aren't greeting you, there are Leishoranya on the hillside to our right."

Iowyn's indrawn breath hissed in the quietness. The enemy, this far north?

"Sentries?" Ahndrej sounded puzzled. "If Eldànhi had thought that necessary, he would have told me."

"Damn!" Kahsir slowed his horse to a stop, Lorhaiden and Vàlkir reining in their mounts by his side, now fully shielded. He nodded toward the hillside. "I can't tell how many enemy there are—they're hidden in the trees and brush. They probably stationed more men off on that hill to our left."

"Ambush," Vàlkir said.

Kahsir nodded. "I don't think they know I've sensed them. They're waiting for us to get nearer."

"How many, Lord?" asked Lorhaiden.

"I said I don't know," Kahsir snapped. Lorhaiden's eagerness for combat spilled out from behind tight shields. Kahsir probed toward the enemy again, thinning the contact to the utmost. "I'd guess well over one hundred on the hill to the right. They're better shielded on the left-hand hill . . . I can't Read them as well." He looked at Ahndrej. "Can we avoid this valley?"

Ahndrej shook his head, his face pale in the bright sunlight. "Short of turning around and going back the way we came, no. If we did that, we'd have to skirt the hill on our left and then turn south again. Vharcwal lies a bit to the east as we're going."

"Lord!" Lorhaiden's voice was full of tension. "You can't be thinking of going back! We've got two hundred men with us!"

"Dammit, Lorj! We *are* going back. We've got to reach Ahndrej's steading and the protection it gives us. So we've got two hundred. The Leishoranya have nearly that many, and more yet that I can't sense. I can't risk lives on an assumption of the enemy's strength."

"If Kahsir's right," Valkir said, catching at his brother's arm, "you'll soon have your chance to fight. Let's try to avoid battle until we're certain of our ground and of how many we face."

"But, Lord—"

Kahsir glared at Lorhaiden, silencing him in mid-speech. "Rhàjon!" He motioned the commander of the two hundred forward. "We're riding into an ambush. Let's get out of this valley fast as we can."

Rhàjon nodded and cantered back to his warriors.

"Io!" Kahsir looked at his sister, who had moved closer to Ahndrej's side. "If we're trapped, I want you and Dreja to try for the steading. Warn everyone that Leishoranya are in the hills."

"But how did they get here undetected?" she asked, her face gone pale. "And why not Send to Eldànhi?"

"The enemy might not know Vharcwal is linked to us. Move!"

Kahsir turned his horse, lifted his reins, and rode at a canter by the tight ranks of the two hundred who waited behind, angling off to the northeast.

Sudden motion came from the brush at the end of that hill. Mounted Leishoranya warriors over one hundred strong burst out from their cover and whipped their horses down toward the pasture.

Kahsir cursed as Dream and reality fused, became one with the now. Without looking, he knew the enemy hidden on the western hill behind had also begun their charge down to the open field.

"Ride, Dreja, ride!" Kahsir cried. "You and Io! Take ten men with you. Make for Vharcwal, and warn them if you can!"

"But, Kahs—" Iowyn's hand gripped the hilt of her slender sword.

"Get out of here, Io!" he snapped. "Now! While you still have the chance! We'll try to hold them here."

Iowyn glanced at Ahndrej, then back again, her face blank in indecision. Kahsir gestured sharply.

"Dammit, Io! *Go!*"

She nodded and, with Ahndrej and the ten men closest, set her horse to an all-out run to the north.

Tsingar sat his horse on the hilltop of Vharcwal and wiped the sweat from his face. The great house of the steading would not burn properly—the rain that had fallen the day before had soaked its wooden walls and roof—but its defenders had died easily enough once he and his men had broken their initial resistance. He grinned; if only the rest of the Krotànya could be beaten with such relative ease.

He looked around the hilltop. Bodies lay everywhere: men, women and children, in a jagged ring around the great house where they had fallen before his galloping attack. Most had died by arrowshot, but those few who had escaped Tsingar's archers had fallen beneath his men's swords. The Lord of the steading had fought like one possessed; even the women and children had fought. But it made no difference in the end—not a one of the Krotànya had survived.

The smell of smoldering wood swept across the hillside; Tsingar moved upwind of it and looked off to the northwest. By now, Aduhar should have engaged Kahsir and the two hundred who rode with him. Tsingar scratched at his leg, at the all but healed wound. As soon as his men had rested briefly, he would set out to aid Aduhar. *Gods! Smile on me today. Let me not only take the High-King's granddaughter prisoner, but Kahsir as well!*

He denied the latter fantasy: Kahsir's sister was of paramount importance, for with her in hand, Mehdaiy could lure her family into coming after her. He reached out with his mind to where he knew Aduhar fought: aye, the youngster had engaged the enemy, but something about the battle did not feel right. Tsingar intensified his probe, then sat up straighter in the saddle. Aduhar had not used his archers; he had charged down the hillside in a direct attack, giving the Krotànya time to close ranks.

Suddenly, something else touched Tsingar's mind, something odd enough that he focused on it entirely, Aduhar's battle forgotten. His breath caught in his throat. *She* was coming—Kahsir's sister. Riding toward the steading with only her lover and ten men.

He jerked his horse around.

"You!" he called out to one of his two hundred. "Dvorkun!" The subcommander trotted over across the death-strewn hilltop. "Gather the men. I don't care if they're resting. Do it! The Gods have given us a gift. We don't have to chase our quarry—she's coming to us!"

Kahsir glanced away from the oncoming enemy as his two hundred men took up their positions on the valley floor. The sole hope they had of surviving this double charge would be to ride straight at the Leishoranya coming down the eastern hillside—those closest to the path Ahndrej and Iowyn had taken.

"Lorj!" He unsheathed his sword and set his shield in place. Lorhaiden's face was alight with anticipation. "Use the *topàrtis*, spearhead formation. It's our only chance to avoid being surrounded. Don't mind-send to the others—Hairon can spread the word."

Lorhaiden nodded and bellowed out orders to those men who could hear; Hairon cantered off to those who could not. Finished gathering his bowmen, Vàlkir rode to Kahsir's side.

"Are you going to lead us, Lord?" he asked, setting his helm tighter on his head and unstrapping his bow.

Kahsir nodded. "Aye, Vahl." He lowered his voice. "My Dream hasn't been of help yet, but it *might* give me the knowledge I need to prevent a rout."

Vàlkir held his gaze a long moment, then nodded. "Good luck," he said, and rode off to his bowmen.

The enemy riding down the eastern hill had reached

the valley floor now and thundered across it, their cries and shrieks splitting the air. Kahsir held his breath: all his men had assumed their positions, awaiting his command to charge. Exact timing was crucial. If he miscalculated his counterattack by one instant, the Leishoranya coming in from the west would attack them from behind.

"Now!" he cried. "Krotànya! For the Light! *Legir! Legir!*"

Kahsir kicked his horse forward at an all-out gallop, his warriors following in a thunder of hooves. He rode at the very fore, at the tip of the galloping spearhead of men and horses aimed at the Leishoranya.

In the last few moments before battle, Kahsir reached into what he could remember of his Dream, seeking a hint—even the merest suggestion—of where lay the weakest point in the oncoming enemy ranks. A myriad of possible futures flashed through his mind, but only one showed him the way.

The two armies met with a clash of arms. Kahsir swung his sword, caught one of the enemy in the throat, another in the side, and rode on. Carried by the force of the charge through the Leishoranya ranks, he reined his horse around.

Though the Leishoranya carried bows, none had unstrapped them. Kahsir shook his head. *Fools! Who's their leader? Why aren't their archers firing?* Urging his horse into the fighting, he cut down another opponent and signaled his men to hold the milling Leishoranya back. *Now!* he Sent to Vàlkir, and arrows flew.

"Lord!" Lorhaiden's voice. "They're coming, Lord!"

Kahsir glanced around—the rest of the enemy drew closer.

—*Vahl!* Kahsir Sent, transferring the image of the oncoming enemy hundred. *Keep those dung-balls off our backs!*

—*Done, Lord,* came Vàlkir's response. *We'll handle it.*

An enemy warrior armed with a spear charged. Yanking on the reins, Kahsir pulled his mount around, avoiding the spear thrust. The man turned to come back, but suddenly tumbled from his horse, an arrow through his neck.

Another of the enemy rode forward—a young man clad in a red cloak—and Kahsir met the charge. His opponent was good, possibly the best swordsman he had faced in decades, but inexperience made the pattern of the young man's swordstrokes easy to read. Leading the warrior into a series of thrusts and parries, Kahsir suddenly reached out and slashed downward at the Leishoran's unprotected side.

The warrior cried out and fell sideways from his horse. Krotànya arrows hissed overhead and Kahsir glanced up, his red-cloaked opponent forgotten now. He had only enough time before being attacked again to see the front lines of the Leishoranya company fall before those arrows.

After an endless time, he found no one left to fight. Kahsir's swordarm ached as he wiped the sweat from his forehead. For a few moments, he stared at the streak of blood across the back of his hand, then remembered the swordstroke that had grazed his head.

He looked up again and blinked in the sunlight. Their ranks decimated by Vàlkir's bowmen, and all form of command gone, the Leishoranya had ridden off in full retreat, led by the red-cloaked man who had somehow found a horse. Kahsir shook his head. *Lords! That bastard's still alive!*

A cold chill ran down his back. *Iowyn! Where is she?* He glanced up and down the battlefield, his heart thumping in his throat. The dead and wounded, men and animals, lay everywhere, contorted shapes in the pasture, partially hidden by the grass.

"A close fight, Lord." Lorhaiden had reined in at his side, Hairon waiting slightly behind. "They were green," Lorhaiden said in a tone of vast disbelief. He rubbed at a scratch on his cheek. "They must have been, or they wouldn't have broken like that. We're still outnumbered. And why the Dark didn't they use their bows? Our archers saved our necks!"

"True. We were damned lucky today. Where's Vahl?"

"Here, Lord." Valkir rode to Kahsir's side.

"You were with the bowmen," Kahsir said. "Did you see where Io and Dreja went?"

"Aye. Off to the northeast, probably around this hill."

Kahsir sought for his sister's mind but did not find it. Likely she had shielded herself to the utmost—as had Ahndrej and the ten men who rode with them. Still, he should be able . . .

"How many dead?" he asked.

"Nearly eighty," Valkir replied. "The wounded are able to ride."

Kahsir frowned at the number, but the enemy had lost over twice that. "We've got to find Io and Dreja. There might be more Leishoranya in these hills, and the ones we just fought could always come back again. Let's get to Vharcwal fast as we can. We'll come back later to bury the dead."

Tsingar waited among the trees on the crest of the hilltop, holding his horse motionless. His men lay hidden on all sides of the road that led to the steading. He sighed quietly, rubbed his nose, and looked out at the hilltop again.

He counted it a stroke of fortune now that the great house had not burned; the smoke would have alerted anyone riding toward it of what had happened. To further prevent discovery, Tsingar had ordered his men to douse what flames had caught with water drawn from a well that stood close to the house.

He shifted in his saddle. *I wonder how Aduhar's doing in his fight?* He grinned slightly. *The brat's got a lot to learn, and Gods know Kahsir can teach it to him*—if *he lives through the lesson.*

He tensed and stilled his horse: the sound of hoofbeats came from beyond the crest of the hilltop. Twelve riders came into view—eleven men and one woman. They galloped forward, then drew rein so suddenly that several of their horses slid on the grass. For a long moment, they sat stricken by the sight of slaughter before them.

—*Now!* Tsingar Sent, and his hidden archers rose from the brush in the trees, took aim, and fired.

He cursed. Of the eleven arrows shot, only ten found their marks. He snatched his sword from its sheath, gestured at his men who waited behind him, and burst out of his cover toward the man and woman who remained untouched.

His sudden appearance startled them, but the man yanked his sword out and met Tsingar's charge. No warrior, this one, but he fought determinedly enough, and for a moment Tsingar was hard-pressed by the man's furious attack. Yet the Krotàn's clumsiness doomed him—Tsingar slashed out, struck the man's unhelmeted head, and the Krotàn fell heavily from his horse.

He turned and faced the woman—Kahsir's sister. Slitted eyes in a pale face looked back beneath a silver-washed helm. He caught his breath. By all the Gods! She was armed! A slender sword sat in her hand, and she had caught up the shield from behind her saddle. She obviously *did* think herself a warrior. Tsingar waved his men away; he must take her unharmed if he could.

Suddenly she attacked, her quickness taking him off guard. She thrust at him with her swordtip, then slashed at his horse, never letting her blade meet his for too long a time.

Tsingar parried her blows, meeting her sword when he could. *By the Void! She's good! Damned good!*

Where by the Gods did she learn to fight like this?
Another slashing attack; he jerked sideways in the saddle, barely missing her blade. *Damn! I've got to end this quickly or my men will laugh me all the way back to camp!* He bore down upon her, using his superior strength and weight to his advantage, forcing her to meet his sword. If she had been only a little stronger—

He saw his chance, twisted his sword, and sent hers flying off into the grass. She never paused, but grabbed at the dagger that hung at her other hip. He cursed and swung his sword flat-bladed against the side of her head. The blow knocked her helm loose and sent her sliding from her horse. Even then, she struggled upward, her breath coming in loud gasps. He rode at her, slipped his foot from the stirrup, and kicked at her shoulder. She spun around, fell heavily, stirred a moment, and then lay still.

Tsingar sat silent for a moment, his own breath coming hard, then looked up from the woman sprawled in the grass at his horse's feet. A number of his men clustered close by, amazement on their faces.

"That's how a warrior fights, worm-bait," he said. "If any one of you fought as hard—" He left the sentence hanging and glared at his men. "Dvorkun!" The sub-commander rode through the throng, his face still registering disbelief at what he had seen. "Take forty men with you and get her back to Mehdaiy's camp. I'm going to help Aduhar." Dvorkun nodded, dismounted and warily approached the unconscious woman. Tsingar snorted a quiet laugh. *Good. The fool's found some caution.* "And for the Gods' sake, Dvorkun, bind her well." He allowed a thin smile to touch his face. "I don't think you'd like to face her if she breaks free."

Kahsir held his laboring horse to a gallop, riding toward the Hill of Vharcwal. Again, he had sought his

sister's mind, and again he found nothing. *O Lords!
Where is she?* He leaned forward in the saddle, scan-
ning the way ahead. Anxiety—dark hints of his Dream
coiled in his mind. *Dammit! Where is she?*

The hilltop loomed closer, tree-clad, rising out of
the pasturelands about it. He kept his thoughts tightly
shielded, a futile attempt: each man, in one way or
another, had sensed his worry, and they rode with the
same urgency that clawed at his heart.

He cantered up the hill, the way easier now that he
had found the roadway; Lorhaiden and Vàlkir kept at his
side, their hands never far away from their swordhilts.
He glanced over his shoulder: Hairon and the warriors
following looked around with increased alertness.

Kahsir cursed softly. Over the crest of that hill lay
the affirmation or denial of the Dream that had
haunted his sleeping and waking. He took a deep
breath, and rode over the hillcrest.

There, its fire-scarred bulk dominating the hilltop,
lay Ahndrej's great house. Someone cursed softly, and
only instants later did Kahsir recognize the voice as his
own. He shuddered. Dream and reality fused, and the
ghostly wind he had felt before swept by again, filled
now with the chill of death.

CHAPTER 8

"Iowyn!"

Lorhaiden flinched from the agony of Kahsir's cry.
His sword-brother's shout rang across the silent hilltop,
disturbing the carrion birds from their feast—a cloud
of them arose in the quietness, wings snapping angrily.
Before Lorhaiden could stop him, Kahsir leapt down
from his horse, his face gone white, and his sword
appearing with uncanny speed in his hand.

Lorhaiden glanced at Vàlkir and unsheathed his own
sword. Gesturing for his brother to follow, he dismounted, throwing the reins to Hairon who waited
close by. Kahsir had already started off toward the
great house.

"Rhàjon," Lorhaiden called to the commander, as he
and Vàlkir started after Kahsir, "keep the men on
alert!"

"Io!" Again, Kahsir cried, his voice raw with fear.
"Dreja! Io!"

"Lord!" Lorhaiden reached Kahsir's side and grabbed
him by the arm. *O Lords! He won't listen to me. I'm the
one who goes off into rages, not him. Get Vàlkir to talk
him out of it. He'll listen to Vahl!* Lorhaiden glanced at
his brother. "Say something, Vahl! Anything!"

"Think, Lord! Think!" Vàlkir's voice overrode Kahsir's strangled oath. "This could be a death trap."

Kahsir stopped fighting Lorhaiden's grip and drew a deep, shuddering gasp. Lorhaiden nodded to Vàlkir.

"If she's here, Lord, we'll find her," Vàlkir said. He gestured toward the ruined mansion. "We'll go with you. But be careful, Lord."

"Aye," Kahsir said at last. His eyes were as gray as his swordblade, and Lorhaiden flinched from their power. "But if Io . . . "

"We'll find her," Lorhaiden promised. *Please, Lords! Don't make a liar out of me!* "Let's go."

He dropped his hand from Kahsir's arm and set off. Bodies lay everywhere. The first he came across, riddled with enemy arrows, was that of a young man, not even to his majority. Scavenger birds had already been at the body. Lorhaiden looked away, a red haze gathering at the corners of his sight.

Vàlkir knelt by one of the bodies, stood, and turned to Kahsir. "These people died less than two hours ago, Lord."

Lorhaiden drew a ragged breath. Two hours ago? That meant Iowyn and Ahndrej had arrived at the steading soon after the massacre. The enemy must have surprised them, though why they had not seen the smoke of the burning house remained a mystery. Lorhaiden glanced over his shoulder; Rhàjon had spread the men out around the hillside in defensive positions against possible attack. *Good man. The enemy could be out there waiting for us. What better trap than this?*

Kahsir stood silent, lips a grim line of anger and pain. Lorhaiden nodded to Vàlkir, touched Kahsir's shoulder, and walked on.

Dead Leishoranya lay among the bodies, but the fallen Krotànya—men, women and children—far outnumbered their foes. Lorhaiden chewed on his lower lip. *They had no warning. They wouldn't have died this easy otherwise.* From all appearances, the enemy had made a circular attack—fire blackened the two sides of the house he had seen. The enemy had surrounded the mansion and showered it with fire arrows, though he could now see that it had not burned completely. Yesterday's rain could account for that, or—

"Hsst!" Vàlkir halted abruptly. "Did you Hear that?"

Lorhaiden stopped at his brother's side and listened. The carrion birds circled above the hilltop, their harsh cries marring the silence. "What?" he asked. "I didn't Hear anything."

"Listen," Vàlkir said. He pointed off to the right. "There it is again."

"It's Ahndrej." Kahsir spoke at last, certainty filling his voice.

Lorhaiden looked up into Kahsir's eyes and caught the fragment of a memory, something that slipped out from behind tight shields. *Lords! Now I know what's been bothering him. A lo'fivàd! No wonder he's been shielded so tightly. A Dream! And we're all locked into what he's Seen!*

He motioned for his brother to go on and, Kahsir following, went around to the western side of the hilltop. A man who had ridden with Iowyn and Ahndrej lay there, an arrow jutting out from one eye. Lorhaiden clenched his teeth and looked away, the tightness in his chest growing worse.

"Ahndrej!"

Kahsir ran forward and knelt in the grass. Lorhaiden followed, his brother at his shoulder. Ahndrej lay stiffly on the ground, the left side of his face caked with blood.

"Lords of Light! He didn't have a helmet! It's a wonder he's alive!" Kahsir glanced up. "Lorj! Get me water. Hurry!"

Lorhaiden turned around, hunting for the well he had seen at the front of the great house. But Rhàjon had anticipated such a need; the commander came running across the hilltop, water and binding cloth in his hands. Lorhaiden took them, nodded a brief thanks, and knelt at Kahsir's side.

He rocked back on his heels and watched as Kahsir gently cleansed Ahndrej's wound. *Now what? Kahsir's always been the steady one, but this time I've got to steady him!* He shivered uneasily. *I've got to do it! I don't have a choice.*

Kahsir lowered the wet cloth: Ahndrej stirred, mumbled something, moaned, and tried to open his eyes.

"Easy, Ahndrej . . . easy," Kahsir said, holding Ahndrej down in the grass as the other man would have tried to sit up. "Don't try to move yet."

"Io. . . ." Ahndrej's voice was slurred and difficult to follow. "They have her." He opened his eyes and blinked in the strong sunlight. "They were waiting for us—knew we were coming. We've got to follow them! They've taken her—"

"When, Dreja?" Kahsir forced the tenseness from his shoulders and held his voice even. "How long ago? Can you remember?"

"Not all that long." Ahndrej's voice grew stronger as he spoke. "We rode like the Void to get here, to give warning. Instead—My brother . . . his family. They—"

Kahsir winced at the agony he sensed in Ahndrej's mind, the echo of it in Lorhaiden's, those two sharing massacres of family and destruction of a place they loved.

"We'd just arrived," Ahndrej said, his words slow and full of pain, "when they attacked. They shot the men who rode with us. I fought their leader, but he struck me down. He must have thought I was dead, for he left me alone after I fell. Before I lost consciousness, I saw him take Io captive."

Kahsir looked away, out at the corpse-strewn hilltop, his heart thumping loudly in his chest.

"By the Lords of Light! If she's been harmed, I

swear I'll kill them all!" For a brief instant his vision blurred; scattered impressions darted through his mind—ways to take, ways to avoid, memories of the future caught from the past. He glanced at Lorhaiden. "Let's go! I'll show you the way. Rhàjon!" The commander straightened. "Stay here with Ahndrej. Keep him still until he's stronger. And for the Light's sake, be careful. You'll be vulnerable with all your wounded." Kahsir stood, his hands clenched at his sides. "We're going after her."

"But, Lord," Vàlkir said. "It could be a trap. What better way to lure you into danger than for—"

"No, Vahl. It's not a trap. Not this time. Trust me." He looked around at the other men who had ridden closer. "I'll need thirty volunteers," he said, and reached for his sword.

Tsingar rode through the valleys, keeping away from heights. Something was wrong, very wrong, but he could not place it. Afraid of being detected, he probed for Aduhar. Nothing. It was as if Aduhar had never existed. *Gods! If only I could leave that posturing fool here and tell Mehdaiy he was dead.*

No. He had to find Aduhar. Mehdaiy's nephew had bungled things, that was obvious, but *how* was not. Aduhar had not used his archers, had charged headlong down the hillside toward his prey. Still, surprise and numbers should have given him the advantage. Tsingar cursed. Though he had sent Aduhar off hoping the youngster would be killed, that prospect had turned from a wish to a chilling probability. *Mehdaiy will have my hide for this!*

He lifted the reins, clucked between his teeth, and urged his horse across a small stream, his men coming behind. He rubbed his chin. *Where* was *that battle? Not too many hills away.* There—the direction he sought stabilized and he turned that way. *Huhn! Won't surprise me to find all of Aduhar's men slain and the*

*brat dead, too. But I'm free from blame! I warned
Aduhar—warned him more than once.*

He sighed quietly and reined his horse around a
large rock in the pathway. His main objective had been
to capture Kahsir's sister and he had accomplished
that; even now Dvorkun was taking her to Mehdaiy's
camp. He looked quickly around at the hills. If Aduhar
had been defeated, Kahsir might attack Tsingar's men
thinking they held his sister.

Tsingar stirred uncomfortably in his saddle. *Gods
help us if other Krotànya women fight as well! I
wouldn't want to face her on ground of her own
choosing.* He frowned and looked off over the hillsides.
If any of his men had suspected how hard-pressed he
had been in that fight, it would be difficult to lead
them. He rubbed the back of his neck, then scratched
at his healing wound. It was over now; he had accomplished his mission. All he must do now was find
Aduhar and return to Mehdaiy's camp.

Kahsir led the way south down the hillside, his
horse shying several times at bodies in the grass.
There was no turning back now—fully caught up in
the unfolding possibilities of his Dream, the path he
must follow was glaringly clear.

The countryside lay flatter to the south than the
land north of Vharcwal. Kahsir kicked his horse into a
canter: the open terrain would make the going quicker,
but the enemy would have the same advantage.

*Io! Lords above! When I find you, those bastards
will wish they'd never touched you!* He tried to keep
his mind calm, his thoughts fixed on his goal. *Why the
Dark did they go after her and not me?* A chill ran
down his spine and he shivered though the air felt
warm. At times, the enemy would take a Krotàn of
high rank prisoner, then lure that captive's kin into
unthinking retaliation—vengeance usually resulting in
death. He shook his head: he *had* ridden off after his

sister but, unlike other distraught kin, he had a Dream to lead him.

Exhausted from battle and the ride to Vharcwal afterward, his horse stumbled slightly. Kahsir eased to a trot and glanced over his shoulder; the men who followed had slowed their pace as well.

The slight touch of Lorhaiden's mind brushed his own. He shook his head sharply, motioned for his sword-brother to ride closer.

"No mind-speech, Lorj," he said over the sound of hooves. "We can't risk it."

"Aye." Lorhaiden's face was expressionless in the afternoon sunlight. "Are you sure of your path, Lord?"

Kahsir nodded. "They've got over an hour's lead on us. If we're lucky, they'll think no one followed."

"How many are there?"

"I'm not sure. From the looks of their tracks, at least the same number as us."

"We'll catch them, Lord," Lorhaiden said. "They'll have to stop sometime. And *we* have more to lose."

Kahsir shrugged, looked up at the sun, judging the time: they had several hours of riding left in the day. He had to hold the pace to a canter or a trot with frequent periods of walking, or the horses would give out long before he and his companions caught up to the Leishoranya. He cursed softly. *Damn! If only I knew how many are in that war band. If the enemy severely outnumber us—*

He looked forward to the southern horizon though the few hills ahead prevented any view of great distance. More trees grew this far south of the steading than he had seen to the north; he avoided those small groves, wary of ambush. Glancing at the sun again, he slowed his horse to a walk, and let the animal catch its breath and cool down.

It's taking us too fihrkken *long! But they'd sense our coming if we took the mind-road and be gone before we could follow. O Lords! Keep Io safe!* He shifted in the saddle and started keeping count of his horse's hoofbeats: twenty-seven, twenty-eight, twenty-nine. *We'll never catch them!* Thirty-one, thirty-two. He looked at the sun again, trying to keep Iowyn's plight out of his mind. *Concentrate on the pathway ahead, or we'll be lost.* It was hopeless. As if she stood before him, her face was there, wordlessly pleading, asking understanding for her fear.

He leaned forward, felt his horse's neck; sweat had dried on the animal's coat and the skin was cooler to his touch. He set off at a slow canter again, his companions matching his pace. His sister's name rang out in his mind in time with the hoofbeats: Io—Io—Io. He looked at the sun again, and this time it had fallen closer to the horizon.

He rubbed his eyes, flexed the tension from his shoulders and reached inward again, linking even closer to his Dream, his remembrance of it. The pathway was still clear, mentally and physically—tracks in the grass showed where horses had passed not all that long ago. It might have been any group of horsemen riding in between steadings, but the scent of Leishoranya was plain.

The sun lay setting and shadows spread from the west across the plains. The path taken by the Leishoranya had not varied: straight as the land would allow, it led off to the southeast. Kahsir looked over his shoulder: his men followed in grim silence, expressions showing the strain of the journey. Valkir and Lorhaiden rode beside him; their faces were blank, though their eyes glittered in the fading sunlight. Both had withdrawn behind their shields, but he felt the warmth of their concern. Hairon came doggedly just behind Lorhaiden, his features slack with exhaustion.

Kahsir sighed, slipped his feet from the stirrups, stretched his legs, then fished for the stirrups again. Then suddenly—a brief onslaught of visual impressions.

Forty. Only forty Leishoranya. And Iowyn. For one brief, dizzying moment he saw their position, their intended goal. He threw up his hand to signal a halt and reined his horse to a stop.

"There!" Kahsir pointed off to his left, to a low line of hills, western slopes bloodied by the setting sun. "That's where the enemy will make camp for the night."

His men shifted in their saddles and stared, puzzled how he could know such a thing without making a mind-search.

"What odds?" Lorhaiden asked.

"Close to even, baràdor. Six more than us. And we have thirty bowmen—thirty-one, counting Vahl."

"Our horses be near spent, Lord," Hairon said. "Much more and they be useless."

"Aye." Kahsir leaned forward and rubbed his horse's neck. His hand came away damp with foam. "Now's the time to rest. We can't do anything until dark. Dismount."

A nearly audible sigh of relief passed through his men as they stiffly slid down from their saddles. Kahsir dismounted, legs trembling slightly. The horses simply stood there, heads lowered, their quick breathing loud in the sudden silence.

"We'll rest here awhile," Kahsir said. "Keep your minds shielded but open. And watch carefully. I don't sense anyone out here but us, but we can't afford to be attacked. Try to sleep a little. I don't want to move on until dusk."

Several of the men nodded and led their horses a short way off. Finding a place to stretch out, they lay down in the grass, reins wrapped tightly around their hands. Hairon stood attentively nearby but at Lorhaiden's gesture walked off, slightly unsteady on his feet, to join the other men.

"Do you have a plan, Lord?" Valkir asked, leaning one arm on his saddle.

"Aye." Kahsir looked from Valkir to Lorhaiden, then off again at the hills to the southeast. "The enemy will be camping for the night. If we leave at dusk, and hold our pace, we should be there by full dark. Then, we'll attack."

Lorhaiden's brow furrowed. "But, Lord, are you *sure* they'll stop for the night? What's to keep them from taking the mind-road? If they do that, we'll never catch them. They're too far away to track."

"Even if I *wasn't* sure, I don't think they'd risk it. They haven't jumped anywhere yet. They're tired, they're riding blind in country they don't know, and they can't be sure they won't be observed, or mind-road it into the midst of one of our patrols. No. They'll stop, if for nothing more than to rest before they try taking the mind-road." Kahsir's throat tightened. "Iowyn's no weakling. Dragging her through a jump wouldn't be the easiest thing they ever tried."

He met Lorhaiden's eyes and his sword-brother nodded. Rubbing his horse's nose, Kahsir led the animal away from where the other members of his band lay. With a low sigh, he sank down in the grass, reins looped around his wrist, and sat silent, gazing off over the plains. Crickets sang loud now in the grass; a puff of a breeze stirred his hair on his shoulders. He removed his helm and rubbed at the chafe mark on his forehead.

Grass rustled behind: he turned and looked up at Lorhaiden and Valkir.

"I'll keep watch, Lord," Lorhaiden said. "I managed to sleep a bit in the saddle."

Kahsir nodded and lay back in the grass, Valkir stretching out at his side.

"Only an hour, Lorj," he said. "Wake us then."

Kahsir stood in the darkness, listening to the silence. Shadows in the night, his men had gathered close around him and waited quietly for orders. He glanced at them, then cocked his ear toward the hillside again.

"Listen to me," he whispered. "The enemy's camped on top of the hill. Vahl, take fifteen men and go around to the east. The rest of us will swing around to the west. For the Lords' sakes, keep yourselves tightly shielded. One small lapse could cost us all our lives." He paused, letting that warning sink in. "Spread out so we can cover as much of the hill as we can. Timing's critical—remember that." He looked up at the hillside once more. "They'll have posted pickets. Take them first, but for the Light's sake, do it quietly. Forty men are up there. If two are standing guard, that leaves thirty-eight more for our archers."

Someone grunted quietly, a wordless complaint.

"I know. We've only got thirty-one bowmen." He shifted his weight from foot to foot. "That means you'll have to be good with your shots, doesn't it? Questions?" No one replied. "All right," he said. "Let's go. But don't attack until you get my signal."

Shadows moved within shadows as Vàlkir and his chosen fifteen moved off into the night. The moons had not risen yet; there was only the starlight above. Kahsir gestured broadly to his seventeen, unsheathed his sword, turned and crept up the hillside. A low wind rustled through the grass and the small trees he and his men passed; its slight noise would help cover their approach.

Halfway up the hillside, he sank to his belly and crawled. The last little distance seemed agony. He lay close to the earth near the hillcrest, taking slow, shallow breaths. For an unendurably long moment he held motionless, hidden by the grass and trees. Then, hand trembling on his swordhilt, he cautiously lifted his head.

It was as he had suspected: the enemy had placed two pickets by their camp. From where he lay, he could see them easily; they walked about the far perimeter of the camp, weapons glinting in the firelight. The other Leishoranya sat or lay around the fire. And there, arms and feet tied securely, her dark hair partially hiding her face, sat Iowyn.

Kahsir hissed in anger—though bound and helpless, Iowyn was guarded by two men, one sitting on either side of her. He glanced around the hilltop and frowned. Either the Leishoranya thought themselves alone in these lands, or they were inexperienced. The tight control of other enemy camps he had seen was totally lacking here.

His heart lurched. *Or have I misread my Dream? Are there more of them, somewhere off in the night? This looks too simple. Too unorganized.*

He watched the pickets again. Suddenly, a shadow leapt out of the darkness, clamped a hand over one picket's mouth. A quick flash of firelight glittered on a knifeblade drawn across the Leishoran's throat. In less than a heartbeat, it was over. Kahsir looked at the other picket. *If he felt his comrade's mind in its death-cry, we're done!* But Vàlkir's man had been careful. The other Leishoran merely scratched the back of his neck and walked on.

A low rustle, nearly unheard over the wind in the trees, came from Kahsir's left: one of his men crept closer to where the other picket would pass. Kahsir held his breath, waiting. The picket paused and stared off into the darkness, suddenly alert. Kahsir cursed silently. *Lords of Light, don't—*

His man struck and the second picket died, throat neatly slit as that of the first.

Kahsir jerked his eyes to the campsite, and his mouth went dry as he saw the Leishoranya grouped around the fire alert and reaching for weapons.

—Now! he Sent. *Attack!*

He heard the snap of bowstrings. At the same instant, he leapt to his feet, shield up, and sprinted across the hilltop toward the fire, Lorhaiden at his left side in the place of shieldman.

Close to twenty of the enemy fell dead or dying, yet

the two men who stood on either side of Iowyn had
not been touched. Bowstrings snapped again, and more
enemy fell. One of the two Leishoranya guarding
Iowyn lurched heavily backward, clawing at the arrow
buried in his chest, but the other rolled to the ground,
avoiding the arrows.

Suddenly, time stopped.

Kahsir felt as if he ran through loose sand, his legs
made of lead. The lines of probability and What Was
met: Dream and reality joined, fused into the now.

And in that instant, he knew he would never reach
his sister's side in time.

Lorhaiden ran toward the startled Leishoranya, his
sword lifted and shield close to his side. Kahsir ran
beside him toward the fire where Iowyn sat. Lorhaiden
clenched his teeth. *You fihrkken bastards! Dammit!
Don't run away! Turn and face me!*

Bearded face contorted with anger, the Leishoran at
Iowyn's side scrambled to his knees and snatched at
her. Firelight glittered on the knifeblade as he brought
it up in a disemboweling stroke.

Kahsir screamed a Word.

A brilliant explosion of light, pure and clean, lit the
hilltop. Lorhaiden threw his swordhand up before his
face and, squinting, looked again.

The bearded warrior knelt screaming in agony—his
knife had melted, fused to his hand, searing through
flesh to bone. The other Leishoranya lay in contorted
shapes around the fire, those who still lived blinded by
the light. Kahsir's men stood on the perimeters, eyes
narrowed against the brilliance.

Then the light was gone—shut off—vanished as if it
had never been. Too late, Lorhaiden jumped for his
sword-brother's side. Face frozen in a mask of concentration, Kahsir fell forward, sword jarred loose from his
hand.

"Vahl!" Lorhaiden yelled and looked for his brother.

His heart jumped: Vàlkir had fallen to his knees, blood covering his shoulder. Lorhaiden tore his eyes away and searched the fire-lit hilltop for his own shieldman. "Hairon!" The stocky farmer turned, face unreadable in the near darkness. "Help Iowyn! Hurry!"

Lorhaiden knelt by Kahsir, slipped the shield from his arm, and gently turned him over in the grass. Seldom did any Krotàn call up the enormous power that Kahsir had used. Only a few ever had, and they were either Mind-Born or had the star-blood in their veins. And, so far as he knew, no one had ever used such power to kill, even in self-defense.

Until now.

"Kahs!" Unsteady on her feet, Iowyn walked across the campsite to kneel at Kahsir's side. Her face pale in the firelight, her eyes darted up to Lorhaiden. "Lords of Light! Did you see what he *did*? Will he . . . ?"

"He'll live, Lady." He glanced down at Kahsir. "He needs rest now, more than anything we could give him."

"And Dreja?" she asked, reaching up to rub the side of her face, the ugly bruise that lay across her cheek visible even in the semi-darkness.

"Wounded, but not badly."

Hairon and Vàlkir sank to their knees beside them. Lorhaiden looked at his brother: Vàlkir's face was drawn in pain, and though he held a hand tightly over his shoulder, blood seeped through his fingers.

"Ahndrej will be all right, Lady," Vàlkir said, his voice trembling. "And Kahsir needs what Lorj says— rest."

Iowyn nodded, closed her eyes and covered her face with her hands. Lorhaiden caught Hairon's attention and nodded toward the fire. Murmuring something soft, Hairon stood, lifted Iowyn to her feet, and led her to the fire.

Lorhaiden glared at his brother. "Go lie down, Vahl! Now! And get someone to bind that shoulder." Kahsir's face was relaxed, his breathing even now, deep and rhythmic. He loosened Kahsir's collar and gently removed the crowned helm. Valkir's presence still intruded. "Get out of here. Take care of yourself. Go, Vahl."

Valkir left. Lorhaiden rocked back on his heels and took a deep breath. There was little he could do—little any of them could do but wait. He rubbed at his cheek and found crusted blood beneath his fingertips. *Now what? Kahsir's going to be unconscious for quite awhile. There's no escaping the backlash of the power he used.*

A scuffling came from the brush close by: Kahsir's men were dragging the dead Leishoranya away from the campsite. A chill ran down Lorhaiden's spine. *Lords! Kahsir killed all those we didn't. All of them. And only using his mind!*

He blinked several times in the firelight and rubbed his eyes with a shaking hand. He had to get Kahsir close to the fire lest he take a chill. And then? What remained of the two hundred who had ridden south from the capital had probably stayed camped around Vharcwal. Close as they were to the border, he would have to risk a Sending to them. He could not afford for his men and Rhàjon's to be separated for long.

Kahsir stirred slightly. Lorhaiden reached down, slipped his arms under Kahsir's arms, and lifted his sword-brother from the grass. Slowly staggering to his feet, he tottered a bit at first, then walked the unconscious Throne Prince toward the fire. *Take care of Kahsir first. Tomorrow you'll figure out what to do. Tomorrow.*

CHAPTER 9

The carrion birds should have been warning enough. Tsingar blinked and looked down into the valley again: the dead lay everywhere—all men who had ridden out with Aduhar to ambush Kahsir and Lorhaiden. Tsingar cursed and slammed his fist down on his knee. His men radiated their discomfort, shifted in their saddles, and murmured quietly among themselves.

By the Void! How many dead are there? He counted for a moment, his eyes traveling slowly over the field. *Nearly two hundred. And no Krotànya bodies. None! They must have suffered casualties, too. Gods! That means there were enough of them alive after the battle to take their dead away to bury.*

He rubbed his eyes. Of his original two hundred, one hundred forty-seven men had survived the attack on the steading; he had sent forty of them off to Mehdaiy's camp with Kahsir's sister. Aduhar had ridden out with three hundred and had lost over half that number in the valley. He frowned. *Gods of my ancestors! I don't know how many Krotànya were killed. I could run into a force the size of my own. And these fools with me are next to useless.*

First things first. Where would Aduhar and the rest

of his men have gone? South, most likely, toward Mehdaiy's camp. If they had enough sense to remember its location. And himself? He was in trouble—deadly trouble. He could hear the laughter of his fellow officers. *Tsingar,* they would say. *He's good at losing men.*

If only I could turn my back on the whole thing and leave Aduhar food for the birds and worms.

"To the rear," he ordered. "And be careful. We've got to find our survivors and the Dread Lord's nephew." He gestured south, over the ridge of hills. "Ride, idiots!" he snarled. "And if you don't keep those ranks closed, I'll throw you to the first Krotànya we meet."

Kahsir opened his eyes, flat on his back, and looked up into a morning-bright sky. A pair of hawks wheeled slowly, riding the air currents in search of prey. For a moment, he was totally disoriented; he tried to remember what had happened, but his mind was blank. Then, with startling clarity, it all came flooding back.

Iowyn! He sought her mind and found it, along with those of the other men close by. She was safe, unharmed. Warmth filled his heart, relief following quickly afterward. He sensed no turbulence in his surroundings: wherever he lay was well protected.

Again, the memories came. He had rescued his sister, aye, rescued her from certain death; but it was the *how* of that rescue that loomed darkly, terrifying in its implications.

He squeezed his eyes shut, trying to black out those memories, the feelings they brought with them. He found that impossible. Everything he had done seemed as vivid as if it had happened moments before: the knife stabbing up toward Iowyn, and the something that had snapped in his mind at the sight. Unthinking, he had sought his power and it had come, so naturally it scarcely needed guiding. And before he could see whether he had acted in time, he had fallen into blackness, his sister's name shrieking in his mind.

His face went hot and he clenched his teeth; still the memories would not go. *O Lords! I've broken the Law. And everyone on that hilltop saw it.*

He flinched away from what he had done, but could not deny the elation he had felt seeing the enemy fall blasted by his power. The feeling haunted him. And suddenly as he lay there in the sunshine, he remembered a still, far-off part of him that had whispered: *You're wrong! You're wrong!*

He clenched his teeth again. *Dammit! I'm innocent. Innocent! I didn't know what I was doing. Surely that can't be held against me.*

He drew a deep breath, still keeping his eyes tightly closed. *I threw it away . . . all of it. All the things I've been taught—everything I believe. I'm no better than the Leishoranya. I'm a . . . mind-killer!*

Lords of Light! What else could I have done? I didn't know! How could I know I could do that? All I wanted to do was save Iowyn.

And everyone had seen it. Even if he buried his own memories, he could not change what the others had seen. His House was gifted with power, like the other Star-Born Houses, but this—

I've got to tell Grandfather. Get a message to him somehow. He'll know what to do.

But will he? How can I depend on that? He's never done what I've done. No one has. What can he tell me save the obvious? I'm no better than the enemy I fight against.

Suddenly, all the teachings of the Mind-Born swept through his mind, reinforcing his guilt.

I can't escape it. Only Hjshraiel can fight the enemy that way. Mental powers are only for defense.

The thought sent ice through his heart. Hjshraiel. The Dream. Could it be . . . ?

No! He shook his head in denial. *Not me!*
Hjshraiel.

He trembled before a descending wave of utter despair. With all his new-found power, he stilled his mind and pushed the memory of what he had done to one side, knowing he could never banish it. *Now what do I do? What do I say? Io, Lorhaiden, Vàlkir—the other men. They saw. What can I say to them?*

He opened his eyes again and grimaced, his mouth full of a sour taste, his mind sluggish. Someone had propped his head up, probably on his saddle; he could see a little of where he lay. He tried to sit up straighter and was staggered by the effort it took—he was so damnably weak.

"Kahs." Iowyn spoke at his side. "Lorhaiden! Vàlkir! Kahsir's awake!"

Lorhaiden knelt by Kahsir's side and looked carefully into his sword-brother's eyes. No power shone in them save what he always saw there . . . no indication of what went on inside Kahsir's head. Lorhaiden's mind lay open, ready to receive anything, but Kahsir was shielded as never before. A new power resided in that shielding; Lorhaiden could feel its strength.

He glanced sidelong at Iowyn, but she was looking at Kahsir as if any moment he might disappear. Vàlkir knelt alongside; Lorhaiden touched his brother's mind softly and found nothing but jumbled thoughts, all overlaid with pain, and emotions so mixed that none were clear.

And Kahsir? Lorhaiden looked at his sword-brother. *How can he be so calm? If I'd done what he did—* He rubbed the cut on his cheek and glanced up at the sky. *Lords of Light! All that power housed in one man! What I wouldn't give to have just a part of it!*

"Lord," he said, smiling. "You're better?"

"Aye. I'm better." Kahsir's voice sounded rough. He stirred and winced from the movement of limbs long unused. "For the love of Light, get me something to drink. I'm so dry I can't even spit."

With Iowyn's help, Lorhaiden reached out and eased Kahsir into a sitting position. He held Kahsir upright as Iowyn put another blanket between her brother's back and the saddle. Kahsir blinked in the bright light, seeming dazed by it.

Hairon knelt and extended a waterskin. "There be fresh water here, Lord. Got it myself awhile back."

"Ah!" Kahsir took the waterskin and drank.

Lorhaiden watched Kahsir's hands tremble and glanced over at Iowyn. "No more," he said. "You'll make yourself sick."

"By the stars!" Kahsir lowered the waterskin. "I've never tasted better."

Lorhaiden met Kahsir's gaze and held it an instant as Hairon took the waterskin; once more, he could not guess what Kahsir was thinking.

"I'm so damned weak." Kahsir lifted one hand to show how it shook. "Weak as a newborn." He laughed, but Lorhaiden heard the hollowness behind the laughter.

"Weak?" Lorhaiden said. "It would be a wonder if you weren't."

Kahsir's eyes jerked up. Lorhaiden started—it seemed his sword-brother stared right into the depths of his heart. The instant passed, and Lorhaiden could breathe again.

"How long have I been unconscious?" Kahsir asked, neither his voice nor face indicating anything unusual.

"Two nights and one day," Valkir said.

Kahsir looked at Valkir, at his shoulder. "How bad is it, Vahl?"

"Bad enough. I can't use a sword or bow. But I should be healed in a few days, at least enough so that I can be of some use."

Lorhaiden straightened and rubbed the small of his back. *He's hiding himself in small talk. Why is he so silent? Does he think we've forgotten what happened?*

He studied his sword-brother, searching for some hint of what Kahsir was thinking. "Are you hungry?"

"Hungry?" Kahsir echoed. "I'm famished!"

"I'll get you something, Kahs," said Iowyn.

Lorhaiden met her eyes for a brief instant, and she shook her head slightly, warning him not to speak.

"Stay right where you are, Kahs," Iowyn said, when Kahsir started to sit up straighter. She looked at Lorhaiden. "Don't let him move. He'll try."

Kahsir watched his sister stand and walk away, then shut his eyes. The sun felt warm on his face and a slight wind blew across the plains. *They're not saying anything—any of them! They know what I've done, but they're not saying a thing!*

Hjshraiel.

He shook his head in denial and looked at Lorhaiden. "Where are we?" he asked, striving to keep his voice neutral.

"Close to the enemy campsite. We're hidden well enough, but closer to the border than I'd like. You weren't in any condition to be moved."

"Huhn."

A sudden touch of that now-familiar ghostly wind brushed his mind. His Dream! He reached out for it, felt it fade before his search, and frowned. If only he could see into his Dream again, perhaps it could provide the answers he sought. He ran a hand through the grass at his side, feeling some of his strength returning. Lorhaiden still knelt there, waiting patiently.

"Have you heard from Rhàjon and the men we left at Vharcwal?"

"They're here," Lorhaiden said. "They buried the dead and followed us."

Suddenly, too much memory: the dead, the carrion birds. . . . He sensed Iowyn returning and buried all hints of his inner turmoil. Though her face was calm, the shields she had thrown up stood between them.

"Here, Kahs," she said, extending a steaming portion of prairie hen on a travel plate. "And don't bolt it down."

He sat up straighter, took the plate, his hunger doubled in an instant. "*Aii'ya!*" He dropped the meat and shook his hand. "It's scalding! This is torture, Io! It's too hot to eat!"

"Patience, Kahs. It won't take long to cool." She stood and withdrew even farther behind her shields. "I'll be back."

Fanning his meal with one hand, he watched her walk off down the hillside.

"Ahndrej?" he asked, lifting an eyebrow, head cocked at Lorhaiden.

Lorhaiden rocked back on his heels and sat. "Aye. Ahndrej. I'm worried about him, Lord. He's taking his family's deaths hard. He's hardly slept at all, and he's slipping deeper and deeper into himself." He spread his hands. "And Iowyn—she sits up with him when he's unable to sleep."

Kahsir glanced down at his food and tried to pick it up again; this time it had tolerably cooled. "Each man suffers in his own way, Lorj," he said, taking a tentative bite. He swallowed and looked at his sword-brother. "Ahndrej's taken another path than you would have—in the same circumstances."

"Ah, I know." A curious half-smile touched Lorhaiden's face. "I'm crazy—my Oath's warped me. But I can see as well as the next man. I'm still worried about him." With a hint of defiance, Lorhaiden looked at his brother, at Hairon, then back. "Don't you see? He's not *doing* anything about it. He's deathly afraid of sleep. If that persists, if he fears what he might see in his dreams, he'll become useless to himself and anyone else." He shrugged. "Acceptance isn't easy. I know that more than most. But he's got to face the deaths of his family and pass beyond."

Kahsir took another bite, chewed silently, his eyes

locked with Lorhaiden's. He wiped his mouth and
reached for the waterskin. "What do you want me to
do, Lorj? What can any of us do?" He drank, replaced
the stopper, and set the skin down at his side. "I can't
talk to him about it. It's a personal thing—something
he'll have to deal with himself. And Lords know *you*
can't talk to him. The two of you are opposites in tem-
perament and personality. You've chosen your own way
of dealing with your grief and your anger. Let him
choose his." He picked up his meat and tore off another mouthful. "If anyone can help him, it's Iowyn."

Lorhaiden shrugged again. "That's true. But the time
will come when he may need a mental shaking."

Kahsir nodded. All that Lorhaiden had said was
true, but the fact remained—only Ahndrej could heal
himself, and first he must realize he needed healing.

And what of me? My own healing?

"Did Rhàjon and the other men find anyone alive at
Vharcwal?" he asked, setting aside his plate.

Vàlkir shook his head. "No, Lord. They're dead. All
of them."

"They were caught totally by surprise," Lorhaiden
offered. "If only they'd been more alert, they—"

"Leave it, Lorj," Kahsir said. He leaned against the
saddle and looked off across the plains. "I'm bothered
by the whole thing. There are too many unanswered
questions. Vharcwal isn't any more isolated than other
steadings hereabouts. Where were these people during
the raid?" He looked at his three companions, seeking
but not expecting answers. "And since Eldànhi knew
we were coming south with Ahndrej, why didn't he
call to us for help?"

"The quickness of the attack," Vàlkir suggested, rubbing at the bridge of his nose. "They probably didn't
have a chance to do more than fight for their lives."

"That still doesn't tell us why no call for help was
Sent," Lorhaiden said. "You can fight and Send at the
same time."

Though Lorhaiden's voice was level, Kahsir heard the tension in it. *What's he hiding that he wants to say? Why are they all afraid of me?* He shivered slightly in the warm sunlight. *Or is it that they're afraid of what I can do?*

"Might be that Sending been blocked," Hairon said. "Them bastards can do it, too."

Kahsir nodded. Leishoranya or Krotànya—the talent for blocking was the same: his men had hidden the enemy pickets' death-cries in their ambush of the campsite. "It's possible." He stirred against the saddle. "Mannishteh dàn Shuvo and his army are stationed close by. If we can find him, maybe he can tell us what's been happening around here." He looked at Lorhaiden, aware of his sword-brother's unease. *I've got to talk to someone—see how things stand. We're all shielded so tightly.* "Lorj, tell Rhàjon to send out a few scouts. As soon as I can ride, we're getting out of here. Having this many of us so close to the border makes me nervous."

"Aye, Lord." Lorhaiden rose to go.

"Vahl." Kahsir turned to Lorhaiden's brother. "I want you to rest that shoulder. And Lorhaiden—tell Io I'd like to talk with her. Alone."

Lorhaiden looked for Iowyn when he reached the campsite farther down the hillside and found her with Ahndrej. The two of them sat close together, their conversation an inaudible murmur. Lorhaiden frowned; Ahndrej's behavior had grown more disturbing, more skewed from what was normal for him. If something did not change soon, Ahndrej could be permanently scarred.

He walked around to stand behind Ahndrej and gestured slightly to Iowyn. She saw the gesture, nodded, and lightly touching Ahndrej's cheek, rose and came to Lorhaiden's side.

"Kahsir wants to see you," he said, motioning with

his eyes to a place away from the rest, where they could talk unheard. She followed rapidly enough, though her reluctance was obvious.

"Has he said anything?" Iowyn asked, glancing up the hillside to where Kahsir sat.

Lorhaiden shook his head. "Nothing. He's so shielded I can't Read the slightest thought. Maybe you—"

She snorted. "Don't count on it. If he doesn't want to talk about it, there's no power on earth that can drag it out of him."

He shivered suddenly and shifted from foot to foot. "You don't think he's going to let it die, do you?"

Her brow furrowed in thought. "I don't think so. He's too responsible. He knows what he's done." She looked into his eyes, the directness of her gaze unnerving. "And we're going to have to swear ourselves to silence, Lorhaiden—each of us who saw him use that power. You understand that, don't you?"

He nodded slowly. "Aye."

"Good. I'll go talk to him. What I want you to do is get oaths of silence from everyone who was there when he rescued me."

"That won't be difficult." He matched her level gaze with his own. "No one's breathed a word of it."

"Nothing of what he's done must get out. We've been taught all our lives that we can't use our minds to kill—" She shook her head slightly. "That's a terrible burden to bear, Lorhaiden—terrible."

"Then why the Dark doesn't he talk? We saw what he did and he knows it. If he can't even talk about it with his sister . . . He's *got* to let it out. Keeping such a thing—hiding it—will only make it worse."

"That's a fine thing for you to say," she snapped. "You with your Oath."

Lorhaiden blinked. "My Oath doesn't have anything to do with this. We're talking about your brother, not me."

She looked away, her face still set in lines of anger.

"Forget your differences with me," he said. "It's Kahsir who's in trouble now. Go to him, Iowyn. Let him talk it out if he wants to. He's not saying anything to me."

She sighed so softly he nearly missed it. An expression of utter weariness passed over her face, making her look decades older. She looked up, her eyes narrowed slightly. "All right. I'll go. But don't expect much."

Left alone, Kahsir reached around and shifted the blankets between his back and the saddle. His heart still beat raggedly with the effort it had taken to remain outwardly calm.

His Dream had gone, and he had no idea if it would ever return. He sought for it again and found only the barest hint of its presence. *Grandfather! Lords! If only I could talk with him!* Impossible. He was not strong enough yet to make a Sending across such distance, and what he had done was certainly nothing to explain in a Sending, tightly shielded though it might be.

And Lorhaiden? His sword-brother was obviously bewildered by what had happened. And yet— *O Lords! If Lorhaiden could do what I did, what would he become?*

For that matter, what will I become?

Iowyn's footsteps disturbed the grass.

"Kahs? You wanted to see me?"

"Aye." He motioned for her to sit at his side. "First things first." He sought her eyes. "When we rescued you, did you see exactly what happened?"

She was silent for a few moments. "If you're referring to what *you* did—aye, I saw it all."

He rubbed his forehead with a hand that still trembled slightly. "For what I did, for the method I used in freeing you—"

"Kahs." She caught his hand in her own and held it. "You did what you thought best."

"But I broke the Law," he said, his face heating. "I went against everything we've been taught."

"I'm glad you did, for if you hadn't, I wouldn't be alive." The pupils of her eyes dilated. "There's no way I could have avoided that knife."

"But—"

"As far as the rest of us are concerned, nothing out of the ordinary happened that night. Lorhaiden, Valkir, Hairon, myself, those who rode with you—we're binding ourselves to secrecy."

His heart lurched. "Do you realize what you're doing—all of you? You're making yourselves party to my actions."

"You can't bear it by yourself." Her gaze dropped and he sensed a hint of terror. "And you'd be in deadly danger if word of it ever got out."

He stared for a moment, then nodded. If the Leishoranya knew he had used such power—that one of the Krotànya who had been taught from infancy never to strike out with the minds save to use them in defense had *killed* . . . The enemy would never believe he would not use those powers again. *Lords! They'd hunt me down to the earth's far corners. I'd be too great a danger to them to let me live.*

"But for those men who didn't see it—how have you explained my being unconscious for so long?"

"No trouble there," she said, and released his hand. "Everyone assumed the Leishoranya had struck you down."

He held her eyes for a long moment, then looked away. *I've solved nothing save get oaths of silence. Not one single answer as to what I should do. Somehow, I'm going to have to tell Grandfather without Sending to him.* He looked back at his sister. "For what you and the rest have done—"

"Forget about that, Kahs. I can't tell you what to do, but I can at least assure you of our silence."

"All right. I'll accept that with thanks. Now, tell me about Dreja, Io. All of it."

She drew her knees up to her chin, wrapped her arms around them, and looked off over the grasslands. "There's not much to tell," she said at last. She turned her head and he winced at the pain he saw on her face. "As long as he doesn't sleep, he's all right." Her voice faltered but she went on. "I don't know what to do for him. What can *anyone* do?"

"He'll have to make peace with his own torments. We can't do that for him." He willed her to meet his eyes and kept his own gaze level. "And as for you—"

"Don't say it, Kahs." Her voice was thin, brittle to his ears. "I'm not going home. Not now. Of all times, not now. Dreja needs me."

He sighed. "If nothing else, take him home with you. Maybe one of the Mind-Born can help him. Besides, Grandfather needs you, too."

Her face hardened and she moved as if to stand. "One more word on the subject and I'm going back down the hillside. I swear it."

"You stubborn, self-willed—"

"It must run in the family," she said wryly. "And don't name-call. It won't do you any good."

"Have it your way," he said at last. "But if you persist in staying here in the south, then at least you can help me."

"How?" Curiosity lit her face. "Ask. If I can, I'll do it."

"Go north to Dramujh. Many of the refugees fleeing from the south pass by that city. Also, supply trains come there from the capital. Your talents for organization and your knowledge of warfare could be invaluable to me and the governor. To say nothing of your simply *being* there."

Her eyes became wary again. "And Dreja?"

"Take him with you, though I think he should come with me and join my army. Sometimes action and combat can help where nothing else can." He lifted a hand, holding her to silence. "If he chooses to go with you, that's his decision, too." He remembered Lorhaiden's words. "But he has to do *something*, Io—something besides drive himself crazy from lack of sleep."

She sat motionless for a long moment, the wind stirring her hair on her shoulders. "All right," she said, her voice very quiet. "I'll go to Dramujh, and whatever Ahndrej decides, I'll abide by it." Her back straightened. "But I'm *not* going home. And if Dreja *does* go with you, and if anything happens to him, I'll find him, wherever you and your army may be."

Tsingar reined in his horse, stretched the stiffness from his neck and shoulders. After two days of riding, he had been up and down every hillside in the region. The wounded rode with his men, along with those who had fought Kahsir and escaped unharmed. *Perhaps this will teach them. Damned idiots! Warfare isn't learned overnight.*

"Lord!" the man riding next to him said.

One of his outriders was returning. The man cantered to Tsingar's side and gestured behind.

"We've found the Dread Lord's nephew."

Tsingar's heart jumped. "Dead?"

"No, Lord." The scout turned his horse so that it stood next to Tsingar's. "But close to it."

"How far?"

"Over that rise, Lord."

Tsingar motioned the scout forward. He kicked his horse to a trot, his men following. *Close to death? Huhn. The Gods couldn't be that kind to me.*

Aduhar had taken a bad wound, one which must be hurting him terribly. A long gash ran down his right side, not deep enough to injure any vital organs, but severe enough to have cost a lot of blood. The other scout Tsingar had sent out was sitting by the young man, busy binding his side.

"Aduhar." Tsingar dismounted and knelt by him. Aduhar's eyes flickered open, darker than usual against his pallid face. "Can you hear me?"

Aduhar licked his lips and struggled to sit up. Tsingar gestured and the scout held him down. "Aye. I hear you," Aduhar said, his voice surprisingly clear.

"Can you ride?"

"If someone gets me on a horse, I'll make it."

"Do you want something for the pain?"

The old mocking tone crept into Aduhar's voice. "Pain is for lesser men," he said, closing his eyes. "Surely *you* know that . . . Lord."

Tsingar's jaw tightened. "Suffer then," he snapped. "I should leave you here to die, for all the good you've done us." He stood and clenched his fists. "Why the Void didn't you use your archers against Kahsir? What were you using for brains, boy? Horse dung?"

Aduhar's eyes flew open, glittering coldly in his pallid face.

"I was fighting two of the best Krotànya commanders alive! *You* haven't done all that well against them, either."

Tsingar spat off into the grass. "At least I have the good sense not to get in deeper than my head. Do you realize how many men you lost because of your idiocy? Nearly two hundred, if not more. How am I going to explain your foolishness to Mehdaiy?"

"Listen to me, low-born," Aduhar said, pain and rage making his voice tremble. "If you so much as mention that *I* had anything to do with this defeat, I'll have your head! I swear to you by all the Gods—I'll have your head!"

Tsingar looked off across the hillside, feigning unconcern. His heart hammered loudly in his chest. "You'll have to come take it, boy, and from the looks of you it's going to be some time before you're strong enough to try." Someone snickered behind; Tsingar whirled around, stared at those who had ridden close

enough to hear. "You!" He pointed at one of the men,
the one he sensed had laughed. "Get off that horse."
He gestured at two more warriors. "You and you. Help
me get this young fool mounted." He turned back to
Aduhar, visually inspecting his bindings. The scout had
torn Aduhar's red cloak to stanch the bleeding. Tsingar
smiled coldly. *What a shame. The poor lad's returning
in less than glorified condition.*

Suddenly he shuddered before an icy wave of fear.
*And me? When I get back to Mehdaiy's camp? Gods!
What will happen to me?*

CHAPTER 10

Kahsir looked up toward the hill of Vharcwal, then over at Ahndrej who rode at his side. Iowyn held her horse's gait to match Ahndrej's, riding close enough so Kahsir could easily see her face, her expression of weariness. He sighed and looked forward again, his mouth thinning into a frown. Ahndrej was still silent, sleepless save when total exhaustion left him no alternative. And then the nightmares followed. Ahndrej had awakened several hours before dawn, had sat silent in the darkness, shaking with fear at what he had seen.

And now Ahndrej was returning home for the last time, to stand by his brother's grave, and the graves of his brother's wife and their children. Weakened by his wounds, he had lacked the strength of body and mind to watch the burials. And by the time Rhàjon had led what remained of Kahsir's men south to join Lorhaiden and the volunteers who had rescued Iowyn, Ahndrej had still been unable to face the physical evidence of his family's massacre. So, haltingly, absent his usual self-control, Ahndrej had begged Kahsir to return to Vharcwal before riding on to his army.

Though it meant a loss of time, Kahsir had given in

to this request, sensing this last journey more than necessary for Ahndrej's peace of mind.

And his own mental peace? Kahsir frowned again. He had all but lost his Dream, though he had sought it more than once since awakening on the hillside. But, as if in recompense, his power had been augmented, along with his ability to shield his thoughts. Iowyn, Lorhaiden and all those who had seen what he had done that night had so far kept their silence. He was certain that none outside this group knew what had happened.

I'm a mind-killer.

He flinched at his own accusation and attempted to concentrate on other things—anything other than what he had done.

It was impossible. Now that he had used his mind to strike out against another—to kill—he would find it easier the next time. In the night, he had agonized over that knowledge; he posed a deadly threat not only to himself, but to all those around him. The temptation to break the Law—he knew himself too well to fear for that. But to *bend* the Law . . . ?

I could be Ssenkahdavic's equal . . . save entire armies from destruction. Cause events to happen that—

NO!

He glanced sidelong at Ahndrej and Iowyn, and knew they had Heard his mental shout, as had Lorhaiden and Vàlkir who rode to his left. Kahsir looked straight forward and shielded his mind with all his new-found power.

His two scouts waited at the edge of the hill of Vharcwal, hands raised to indicate safety. He relaxed some at that, looked at Ahndrej, then to Iowyn, assessing their reactions. Iowyn's face was pale, all softness vanished from it; Ahndrej rode stiff in the saddle, eyes glittering in the morning sunlight, his knuckles white on the reins.

Rhàjon had directed that the steading folk be buried

separately from the family of dàn Herahlu. Ahndrej's brother, his brother's wife and children, Rhàjon had buried off to one side of the ruined house, giving them a place of their own to lie. As Kahsir and the other men dismounted, Iowyn caught his eyes and shook her head. He nodded: he and his companions would stay behind, leaving Ahndrej and Iowyn alone.

A bird sang off to Kahsir's right, hidden by the trees—another answered, then another. The wind blew up from the fields around the hill of Vharcwal, fresh with the scents of morning. Kahsir stood by his horse's head, rubbed the velvet chin, and looked up at the piercing blueness of the sky; the world went on, the sun rose and set, the birds still sang. Yet his life, his sister's, and the lives of the men who had ridden with him in her rescue had been changed forever.

Why not use the power I have? I could change *things, by just reaching down inside myself for the strength I have.* . . .

Kahsir squeezed his eyes shut, turned and leaned his forehead against his horse's cheek. For a brief moment the possibilities of what he could do shone blindingly clear. His horse moved away and he jerked back to what was. And suddenly, as if suspended above the hill, he saw the thirty volunteers who had ridden with him to rescue Iowyn gathered close by, felt their uneasiness, their fear of him and what he had done.

He blinked several times and gazed over the fields below. A gust of wind blew the acrid smells of charred wood from the ruined house. He met Lorhaiden's curious eyes and looked away.

Iowyn stood quietly at Ahndrej's side, close enough to touch if he wanted. She looked at him as he stood there, silent, his face harsh in the morning sunlight. For a long moment, she heard nothing but the wind through the trees, the call of birds, and the snorting of the horses tethered behind her. Then she heard the low sound of Ahndrej's weeping, of his agony. Tears ran down his face now—the first tears he had wept since the massacre. She closed her eyes: if anything could help him, giving in to his grief would let the healing begin.

Ahndrej stirred; she glanced sidelong at him, saw him dry-eyed. But instead of the expression of comparative peace she expected, there was only a hard, angular mask of the man she loved.

"Dreja. . . ."

He shook his head sharply, forbidding speech, and she kept silent. *Dreja. How can I help you if you won't let me?*

"Iowyn." He turned away from the graves. "I'm going with Kahsir to his army. He offered to let me fight with him."

"But your fields . . . your cattle. Who will—"

"Kahsir assured me he'd find someone to take care of those details for me."

She sighed quietly. "I wish you'd come with me."

"And what the Dark would I do in Dramujh? Sit around and be useless?"

She flinched before his thinly veiled sarcasm. "No one's said you're useless. In fact, I'd welcome any help you could give me. The refugees—"

"No." With utter flatness. "I'm going with Kahsir." Ahndrej motioned behind at the graves. "There's vengeance to take, and even you can't rob me of it."

"Vengeance? Now you're starting to talk like Lorhaiden. Come with me, *tahvah*, dearest . . . let me help you get a better hold on—"

"I won't say it again, dammit! I'm going with Kahsir. You can go to Dramujh, but don't expect *me* to come with you."

"I asked you to come, even before Kahsir offered you the chance to fight." She reached out for his hands, but he stepped away. "What's happened to you? By the Lords! What's going on in your mind?"

Ahndrej laughed, a harsh croak. "Look around you. You see those graves, you see what's left of my house? How can you *dare* ask what's happened!" He turned away. "Go to your brother, Iowyn. Go seek *his* comfort. I don't have any to give."

Tears started in her eyes. "Dreja, don't! Don't let yourself go like this. It's not like you. . . ."

"Go, Iowyn," he said, still keeping his back turned. "I'll send you off to your duties with good wishes. Have the courtesy to send me to mine with the same."

Lorhaiden sat on the edge of the hilltop, idly watching the plains to the east. He picked away the last of the scab on his cheek, ran a hand across his chin, then stiffened. There—distant, unrecognizable—a company of riders came toward the hill of Vharcwal. Lorhaiden's heart thumped loudly as he counted the oncoming horsemen: there were only around one hundred, less than Kahsir's men gathered on the hilltop. He touched Valkir's shoulder and pointed, and sensed his brother's attention focus on the approaching riders.

"They're Krotànya, Lorj," Valkir said, shading his eyes against the sun.

"Who the Dark . . . ?" He sensed Kahsir come up behind. "Horsemen, Lord," he said, gesturing. "Krotànya."

Kahsir stared for a long moment at the riders, then nodded. "Perhaps it's Mannishteh," he said, though his tone of voice indicated he thought otherwise. "We'll wait for them here. Let the warriors know we're getting company. And send several men out to meet those riders. I don't want any more surprises."

Lorhaiden dipped his head in acknowledgement and walked to where Rhàjon and the rest of the men waited by their horses. Some of the warriors had also seen the riders coming: they fingered their swordhilts uneasily, whispering to their comrades.

"Rhàjon," Lorhaiden said, "those horsemen are

Krotànya. Take ten men with you and ride out to greet them. Tell them what's happened here at Vharcwal if they don't already know."

Rhàjon saluted and motioned to a group of men standing closest. They mounted and set off at a trot down the hillside.

Lorhaiden looked to where Kahsir stood, still staring off at the approaching riders, and started up the hillside. Suddenly, he dreaded Kahsir's company, an unexpected and frightening reaction. He sensed something going on deep within Kahsir, hidden from even those he loved best. *It must be what he's done. He's agonizing over it. Even shielded tightly as he is, I can feel it.*

He shook his head. *Lords! To have all that power and be forbidden to use it! If I had only half what I sense within Kahsir, I'd—* Images flashed in his mind: his Oath, his vowed destruction of every Leishoran he faced. . . . With power like Kahsir's, all he would need do would be to *think* the enemy dead. He saw them fall before him—hundreds of them, armies of them. . . . He drew a deep breath, denying himself the completion of his vision. *By the Light! I'm not sure what I'd do. Perhaps it's better that I don't know.*

Accompanied by Rhàjon and his ten men, the company of horsemen rode over the top of the hill of Vharcwal; for a long moment, they sat silent, struck by what lay before them. Kahsir gestured to Vàlkir and Lorhaiden, and walked across the hilltop to greet the newcomers.

They were led by a tall, red-haired warrior. Kahsir had seen the man before, but never fought with him. Motioning their men to join the other warriors who waited on the opposite side of the hilltop, Rhàjon and the stranger dismounted.

"Lord," Rhàjon said, nodding toward the redhead. "Chàrion dàn Cwyvonna, one of Mannishteh's subcommanders."

"Chàrion," Kahsir said, grasping the man's arm in greeting. He weighed the other briefly, liking what he saw. "Where's Mannishteh? I'd hoped to speak with him."

Chàrion looked around the hilltop, still seeming shocked by what lay about him, then shook his head slightly, as if in denial. "Mannishteh's four days east of here, Lord. Rhàjon told us what happened. But now that I've seen it . . ." He paused, looked around again. "Where's Ahndrej?"

Kahsir pointed off across the hilltop. "With my sister. He wanted to see his family's graves one last time." He caught Rhàjon's eyes and silently bade him leave. "Where were you when Vharcwal was attacked, Chàrion?"

"Two days east of here. The Leishoranya had attacked another steading and we were fortunate enough to be close by."

"Did you hear any calls for help from that steading?"

"None, Lord. I know . . . that's unusual. We were close enough a child could have Sent to us."

Kahsir nodded slowly. Things were beginning to fall in place. "The same happened here. We must have been only hours away when the enemy attacked Vharcwal, yet we received no calls for aid."

"Mind-blocking?" Chàrion asked, gray eyes slitted in the sunlight.

"Likely. And if what I suspect is true, these steadings weren't the only ones attacked that day. It looks like the enemy coordinated these raids to keep us off balance. These were quick strikes, a back and forth across the border, not intended for prolonged combat."

"What of the Mind-Born?" asked Chàrion. "Surely *they* must have been aware something was going on."

"I don't know. Maybe so many enemy companies crossed the border at once it confused them." He shifted his weight, kept his mind heavily shielded. "What else has happened around here lately? We've been involved in situations where no Sendings could have reached us."

Chàrion rubbed his forehead, removed his helm, and ran a hand through his unruly hair. "I can't speak for more than the area we patrol. We're spread pitifully thin, Lord. Grigorda lost an army, or nearly all of it, to the east of here."

"Damn!" Kahsir's heart constricted. "When was that?"

"Three days ago. If you were out of touch, you couldn't have heard about it. Now we have to ride four days' length of border instead of the usual two. Mannishteh's broken half his army into small companies like mine, keeping us in constant motion. There aren't enough of us to cover all that distance if we stay together."

Kahsir glanced sidelong at Lorhaiden and Vàlkir. "You've heard nothing else? How do the other armies fare?"

Chàrion shrugged. "The Leishoranya are starting to put terrible pressure on us, Lord. We're in need of reinforcements, but news from the capital tells us there aren't any."

"Not now. But Grandfather will be sending men south soon."

"I hope it's *very* soon, Lord, or we could be overrun." Chàrion glanced toward Ahndrej's and Iowyn's unseen position. "Rhàjon told me Leishoranya ambushed your sister and Ahndrej, and that you'd rescued her after defeating another enemy force of near three hundred. Did many escape?"

"I'd guess over two hundred, if you count those who attacked this steading." Kahsir looked away. "We killed the forty men who had taken Iowyn captive. I don't know where the rest of them are."

"They shouldn't be a factor in our defense," Lorhaiden said hastily. "They probably returned to their camp after being beaten so badly."

Kahsir threw his sword-brother a look of thanks. *Lords! If I have to explain what happened that night, I'm doomed. I never was good at lying.*

Why should I lie? If I use the power, I could halt this invasion here in the south!

"Lord?"

Kahsir heard puzzlement in the subcommander's voice. "I'm all right, Chàrion," he said, forcing steadiness into his voice. "We're all bone tired. We've been on the run for several days."

Chàrion seemed satisfied with the explanation. "Are you going back to your army, Lord?"

"Aye. Lorhaiden and Vàlkir to theirs, too. I'll probably set up my headquarters in Dramujh, but spend an equal time in the field. From what you've told me, the sooner we return to our commands, the better."

Iowyn turned from Ahndrej, her tears making it hard to see, and blundered off across the hilltop toward a group of trees. *What's happened to him? What's changed him so? He can't bring his family back to life—no one can do that.* She struggled to get hold of her emotions. *The war's hurt all of us in one way or another. We're all different. But he's turning into another Lorhaiden.*

The thought chilled: it could not happen . . . she must not *let* it happen.

She peered out from the trees, wiped the tears from her cheeks; Ahndrej still faced his family's graves, his shoulders and back stiff with suppressed emotion. She looked the other way, to where her brother waited. A stranger stood there, red hair flaming in the sunlight. Lorhaiden and Vàlkir waited close by, and she breathed a little easier at that—it would be agonizing for Kahsir if he had to talk about what happened during the past few days without someone to turn those questions away.

More composed now, she stepped out from under the trees.

Kahsir turned his head as she walked to his side, eyes flickering slightly as he saw her alone. She nodded to him, trying to assure him that she was all right.

—*Talk alone?* she Sent on the deep level used by siblings when they wanted total privacy.

"My sister Iowyn," Kahsir said to the stranger. "Io, this is Chàrion, one of Mannishteh's subcommanders."

"Lady," Chàrion said, bowing. "I'm sorry about what happened here. I wish we'd been closer. Is Ahndrej around? I'd like to offer my sympathy to him."

"He's still at the graves," she said, holding her voice under firm control.

Chàrion took the hint. "Then I'll talk to him later."

"If you'll excuse me a moment," Kahsir said, "I want to have a few moments alone with my sister."

Iowyn nodded in response to Chàrion's bow and walked to the other side of the hilltop with her brother. When they were far enough away so that no one could hear, he turned to her.

"What happened, Io? What did Ahndrej say to make you so upset?"

She started at his words, sure she had shielded herself sufficiently so not even he would notice her state of mind. "I don't know what happened. Dreja's changed. . . . He's so different from the man I knew a few days ago."

"Losing his family could account for that," he said quietly.

"You know what I'm talking about. You've seen what's happened to him. He's acting like . . . like Lorhaiden! When he stood by those graves, he cried; I thought—" She blinked her tears away and glanced off across the hill. "When I asked him to come with me to Dramujh, he all but shoved me away. He said he's going with you."

His mind reached out and touched hers, soft with understanding.

"Ah, let him go," he said. "You can't expect him to

be rational right now. At least he's made a decision to do *something*. And as for his turning into another Lorhaiden . . . where did you come up with *that* idea?"

"His own words." She looked back at him, held her gaze level. "He's after revenge. That's why he wants to ride with you—not to lose himself in the fighting."

He frowned slightly. "That may be, and if so, he's not the first. When the enemy killed Grandmother . . . remember? Only when I realized I couldn't bring her back, no matter how many Leishoranya I killed, did I give up thoughts of vengeance. Ahndrej will come out of it."

"Lorhaiden didn't."

"Lorhaiden had an Oath to hold him. I can't see Ahndrej taking one. It's simply not in his nature."

"It's not his nature to brood like this, either."

"I'll keep an eye on him," Kahsir promised. "He'll be fighting with me, and I'll make certain he's never far away. Besides, I'm sure he'll Send to you when it's safe."

The next few words were agony. "Be careful. He doesn't have any idea what happened when you rescued me. If he knows . . ." She shook her head. "In his state of mind, it's hard to tell *what* he'd do."

"I'll be careful," he said, and she sensed the tightness of his control, his sudden need for a change of subject. "I was thinking of sending forty of my own men with you to Dramujh, but now that Chàrion's here, I'd like to send him along. There's something about the man I like. I trust him."

"But isn't he fighting with Mannishteh?"

"Aye. But I don't think Mannishteh will mind if I take one of his subcommanders and forty men from him. I'll send word with the other sixty of what I've done."

"If Chàrion agrees, I'd be happy to have him. I'll need all the help I can get if the situation at Dramujh

is anything like I think it is." Thoughts of Ahndrej
intruded again. "And, Kahs, please keep watch over
Dreja. I'm frightened for him."

He smiled in reassurance. "Don't worry, Io. I'll
watch him." Then a curious expression crossed his
face; he closed his eyes briefly and she felt the brush
of something powerful across her mind. "Would you
send Vahl to me?" he asked, looking away. "I need to
talk with him."

What's he hiding? What's happening to him? Suddenly, all the events of the past few days began to pile
up, one on another, leaving more confusion in their
wake.

"And give my apologies to Chàrion," he murmured.
The brief flash of agony in his eyes was even more
unnerving. "Tell him I'm discussing strategy. He'll
understand."

After Iowyn had gone off to find Vàlkir, Kahsir
began to pace up and down by the edge of the hill.

*Why deny it? As surely as I can kill, I can heal.
Ahndrej needs that healing. . . .*

He shook the thought aside and turned all his
strength to finding his Dream. *Dammit to Darkness!
Why can't I find the* fìhrkken *thing when I need it?*

"Lord?"

It was Vàlkir. Kahsir turned, looked at the younger
man, and tried to weigh his state of mind.

"Your shoulder, Vahl?"

Vàlkir lifted one eyebrow, not diverted by the question, and Kahsir smiled inwardly. With someone this
sensitive, he would always have to be on guard.

"Better," Vàlkir answered. That penetrating look
returned to his eyes. "Why?"

"I'm sending you back to the capital. As far as anyone knows, it's to speed your recovery."

"But, Lord . . . I'm healing quickly. I don't see
why—"

"Vahl." Kahsir took Valkir's elbow and led him off to one side. "I don't need to tell you what's bothering me. You've sensed more than you let on. What I did when I rescued Iowyn . . . hasn't been without consequences. I desperately need to get word of it to Grandfather. I can't trust such news to a Sending, no matter how well I cloak it."

A Sending? I'm worried about a Sending? I've got enough power to Send across the world without the Mind-Born knowing about it.

Valkir stood silent, carefully watching.

"Ordering you home for rest is the only way I can get Grandfather news of what's happened," Kahsir said tightly.

"My oath of silence—"

"Negated. I want you to tell him *everything*—the whole bloody mess! He'll know what to do. And bury your knowledge of it deeper than you've ever buried anything before. I could be in tremendous danger if knowledge of what I did leaked out."

Valkir held his gaze steady. "The Leishoranya."

"Aye. Leave soon, today if you can. I'll help you take the mind-road if you need the added strength." He drew a long breath. "I'm sorry for placing you in such a situation, but I can't send anyone else."

"What should I say to the other men? And Lorhaiden—he'll sense a lie. I can't—"

"Tell them I'm sending you to Hvalkir for rest. You won't be lying. After you've told Grandfather what I've done, I want you to stay in the capital until you feel stronger."

Valkir kept silent for a long moment. "Aye," he said finally, "I'll go, Lord."

Immediately, some of the weight left Kahsir's heart. *Grandfather can help me. He'll tell me what to do.*

And if not? He looked away, and shivered though the sunlight felt warm.

CHAPTER 11

Vàlkir rode out of the mind-road into a clinging blanket of fog that had settled over the courtyard of Vlàdor's palace. He glanced behind as the gateway vanished; though he had had Kahsir's help in taking the mind-road, he still felt tired, and his shoulder hurt more than he had thought it would.

He dismounted, flipped the reins over his horse's head, and led the animal toward the front stairs. Someone loomed up in the fog: one of the palace retainers.

Vàlkir drew his cloak tighter about his shoulders. "Is the High-King here?"

"Aye, Lord."

He handed the reins to the retainer and trotted up the steps to the front porch, past the houseguards who saluted him and opened the doors.

No one waited inside. Vàlkir sent out a quick probe: the High-King was in his study, the rest of the family elsewhere. Shielding his mind, Vàlkir hurried up the stairs and down the hall to Vlàdor's study.

With a quick glance behind him, Vàlkir knocked softly on one of the closed double doors, opened it, and entered the study. Vlàdor had stepped around his

161

desk and now stood in the center of the room, his expression one of profound concern.

"My Lord," Vàlkir said, shutting the door. "Please . . . it's urgent. No one must know I've been here."

Vlàdor nodded and gestured Vàlkir into the room. "I thought you were with Kahsir."

Vàlkir swallowed heavily. "That's why I'm here. Have you heard from him?"

"Not since before you were supposed to reach Vharcwal, and long enough ago to know there's been trouble." The High-King's eyes strayed to Vàlkir's bandaged shoulder. "How the Dark did you get that?"

"It's all part of my story. Will we be left alone?"

"Aye." Vlàdor's forehead furrowed in puzzlement. "But I'll seal the door if you wish."

"Please, Lord. You'll understand why."

He felt the High-King's mind reach out and set a seal on the door; now no one could enter without Vlàdor's permission.

"All right, Vahl. Out with it."

Vàlkir swallowed again. "Vharcwal's gone. The enemy destroyed it and murdered all its people. Another company of Leishoranya ambushed us on our way there, and Kahsir sent Iowyn and Ahndrej ahead to warn the steading."

Vlàdor's hands tightened into fists, but he held his gaze steady, even when Vàlkir told the rest of the tale . . . of how Iowyn had fallen captive.

"Iowyn's all right," Vàlkir said quickly, "and so is Kahsir. But . . ." He carefully picked his way forward again, telling of Kahsir's True-Dream, of the ride to rescue Iowyn after the enemy ambush. All the while, the High-King stood unmoving, his face and eyes still.

"You told me she's all right," Vlàdor said when Vàlkir paused again, "so Kahs must have succeeded. But there's more, isn't there, Vahl? Kahs obviously trusted you with a message he dared not Send. Now trust me. You haven't lived under this roof all these centuries to fear what I'll say."

"I'm sorry. I've been through so much in the last few days, I can't keep things straight." Again, he briefly told of the chase after Iowyn's captors and the assault on the Leishoranya camp. But when he reached Kahsir's part in Iowyn's rescue, Valkir's voice broke. "Kahsir. Lord . . . He killed the Leishoran who was going to knife Iowyn . . . killed him with a thought—him, and all the other enemy warriors who were still alive."

The stillness that followed seemed deafening. Valkir looked down at his feet, exhausted.

"Vahl." Vlàdor's voice trembled only slightly. "Look at me."

Valkir lifted his head and met the High-King's eyes. Even in the lamplight and candlelight, he could see the bleakness in them.

"Did Kahs know what he was doing?"

Each of Vlàdor's words was evenly spaced, precise, and taut with control.

"No. I'd stake my life on that. No one could have reached her in time. He acted out of instinct." Valkir gestured and his words came out in a rush. "He asked me to come to you, to tell you what he's done. He needs your help, Lord; he needs it badly. I'm sensitive enough to know how he's suffering, though he's shielded strongly. He's always been the most level-headed of us all. To do what he did . . ."

"Aye." Vlàdor's voice was laden with a weariness Valkir had never heard in him. "I can imagine what he's going through. How many others saw what happened?"

"Only those of us who had followed him to that hill-top. Iowyn and Lorhaiden got us all to give our oaths of silence, though Kahsir released me from mine to talk to you." He stirred uneasily. "Not that any of us would tell anyone. The secret's safe."

"You didn't meet anyone on your way upstairs, did you?"

"No, Lord."

Vlàdor rubbed his eyes, and motioned to the chairs in front of the desk.

"You know what kind of power the Star-Born Houses carry," he said, sitting down. "It's our heritage and, in a way, our curse. What exactly did Kahs ask you to do?"

Valkir eased himself down into the other chair. "To tell you what happened. Beyond that, nothing. I think he felt certain you could help him."

Vlàdor sat up straighter. "And that's exactly what I *can't* do," he murmured. "We're trapped in this . . . all of us. We can't let anyone know."

"Even the Mind-Born?" Valkir asked, his heart tightening. "Surely *they* could help him if you can't."

"Least of all the Mind-Born. That's not to say I don't trust them . . . I do. But can't you see? Even *they* must not know. If I told Tebehrren, how many others of his kind would learn of it? No, that's doing him a disservice. He'd keep his silence. And that would put *him* in a moral predicament." Vlàdor's eyes locked with Valkir's. "And think of this: what a tool Kahsir could become if someone was tempted to use him."

"The Mind-Born?" Valkir started in shock. "Do you think any of them would—"

"No. I don't. But I can't tell you the future. If one of the Mind-Born ever defected—was ever, by some mischance, taken over by the enemy . . ."

Valkir shivered suddenly.

"Aye, Vahl. So here we sit, the two of us, unable to do a damned thing. No one must ever know what happened, not even Eltàrim, unless Kahs tells her himself. His position as Throne Prince could be jeopardized by what he's done. There's no help for it: he'll have to deal with it alone." Pain crossed the High-King's face. "If only you knew how much I wish I *could* do something. But I'm at a loss. I have no knowledge, no precedent, to draw on. How would I judge him? How would the Mind-Born judge him? As far as I know, nothing like this has ever happened before."

"But, Lord . . ." Valkir bit his lower lip, kept other words he knew useless from spilling out. "What can I tell him? He's trusting you."

"Tell him I love him," Vlàdor said. "That's all I can give him right now."

Kahsir sat apart from the other men and watched the sun set over the fields that stretched out from the hill of Vharcwal. They would misinterpret his silence and moodiness, but at this stage he hardly cared. His men and Chàrion's lay camped down the hillside, away from the devastation of Ahndrej's steading. Lorhaiden and Iowyn had kept people away from where he sat, explaining that he was still weak from the wounds he had taken.

He frowned and stretched his legs out. Valkir must have reached the capital and spoken to Vlàdor by now; he had left Vharcwal slightly after midday. Why had Vlàdor not answered?

He could not expect his grandfather to deal openly with the subject, but there were ways Vlàdor could express what he wanted to say without saying it. Yet nothing had come from him . . . not even a hint of a Sending.

And did I really expect anything else? Grandfather can't help me. Only I can do that. And by denying what I've become—

Kahsir frowned deeply. *What I've become. . . . What have I become? I now know how to do evil with my mind. Does that mean—* He denied the next thought with all his strength, yet it came. *I could become another Ssenkahdavic.*

"No," he whispered. "No. I'll kill myself first."

The sound of his own voice drew him back to reality. He stood and began to pace up and down through the trees that stood at the western edge of the hilltop. And suddenly—

—Kahs. Vlàdor's Sending was clear and strong.

*Vàlkir's spoken to me. Tell Iowyn I'm glad she's safe. I
agree with you . . . send Chàrion to Dramujh with
her. He sounds like he's the kind of captain she needs.
Give Ahndrej my deepest sympathy for Vharcwal. And
keep an eye on him. From what Vahl tells me, he'll
bear watching. Send to me when you reach your army.*

—*Grandfather!* He tried to keep the panic from his
Sending. *Has Vahl told you everything?*

—*Aye. All of it. Now break contact. I can only keep
this Sending shielded so long.*

Kahsir's breath caught in his throat. That meant his
grandfather had not trusted any of the Mind-Born to
help him. —*But . . . what am I to do?*

—*Send to me later. And be careful. I love you.*

Vlàdor's Sending was gone, leaving a void in Kahsir's
mind. For a moment he stood motionless, disbelief
weakening his knees. He looked around, found a place
to sit, and slowly lowered himself to the ground.

I was right. He's not going to help me. He can't—

Kahsir stared blankly over the fields, his mouth
gone dry. Vlàdor had not sent Vàlkir back; instead he
had made a routine Sending, avoiding any mention of
the problem. No other conclusion could be drawn: his
grandfather expected him to find the answer himself.

He buried his face in his hands, drew a long breath to
calm his heart, and considered what he must do now. The
war would go on, whatever happened in his mind. He
must send Iowyn north to Dramujh along with Chàrion,
who had agreed to go. Then he must turn east to his own
army, taking with him an Ahndrej who was a stranger.

In blind desperation he reached out for his Dream
again. But it, like his hope for help, was gone.

Iowyn looked out the window of her chamber in the
governor's house at the rain falling on the rooftops below. The city was a dreary sketch in shades of gray
and shadowed beiges; only the red tile roofs of the
buildings lent any color at all. She frowned, keenly

aware that the rain was not responsible for her gloomy mood.

Kahsir had returned to the front two days ago, leaving her with a mental picture clearer than any map of how the defense of the southern border stood. Tutuljad, now headquarters for the enemy army, lay four days' ride directly to the southeast of Vharcwal. Dramujh stood to the northwest of Vharcwal, over fifteen days' distance from the ruined steading.

Her brother commanded all the armies strung across the shrinking southern border, each of those armies patrolling an area never farther from one another than a two day journey. Lorhaiden led the regrouped army north of Tutuljad, Mannishteh the army to his west, south of Vharcwal, while Vàlkir commanded the army that stood east of Lorhaiden's. Kahsir's army, led in his absence by Pohlàntyr, stood to Vàlkir's east.

Beyond, father east and west, lay other armies, each as evenly spaced as possible along the border. Reinforcements had swelled each of those armies to near five thousand men, yet the enemy had more. Since Grigorda's death and the loss of nearly all his men, Kahsir, Lorhaiden, Vàlkir, and Mannishteh had spread their armies thinner than they would have liked, trying to fill the empty space left behind after that loss.

And now she stood co-governor of the city of Dramujh, guardian of the hills that led to the high plains to its north. It was a key of highest military importance: if Dramujh stood long enough, supplies and reinforcements could be filtered south with relative ease. She harbored no illusions regarding the war to the south. Sheer manpower was the enemy's greatest ally. There had always been so many more Leishoranya than Krotànya. . . .

That summed up the military positions held by the enemy and the Krotànya. The refugee situation was harder to grasp all at once. Up and down the southern borders, people fled their cities, their towns, their steadings. Some folk left behind everything they owned in their flight, the enemy coming too close behind them, while others came to Dramujh with wagons and pack horses loaded to capacity. But all of them—nobles, farmers, merchants—fled north, away from the invading Leishoranya. And Iowyn found it harder and harder to look at their faces, the hopelessness and the fear.

And increasingly difficult to order what menfolk had come north with the refugees south again, only this time as hastily trained warriors. Every man who was strong enough, who could bear a weapon, she culled from the refugees. Kahsir had given her the authority to do so, as had her grandfather; Tahrkan dàn Adelgai, governor of Dramujh, gladly relinquished his command in this area, free now to deal only with the problems of the citizens of the city itself. And though the refugees recognized the authority vested in her and knew the reasons for her actions, they loved her less for it.

So she held Dramujh, sending supply trains to the armies fighting to the south and dispatching reinforcements when they reached her; an equally important part played by the city was that of being headquarters for the scouts she sent out through the countryside. Those scouts might prove invaluable, letting her know if any of the enemy had slipped behind either the lines held by the Krotànya armies, or the Mind-Born scattered across the countryside.

The day darkened perceptibly, throwing the room into deeper shadow. *Lords! I can't stand it any longer! I've got to get out!* Iowyn walked quickly to the door, opened it, stepped into the hall. Voices drifted up from the entry hall; she hurried down the stairs, eager for company and any news her scouts might bring her.

A small group of warriors had gathered below, close to the front door; she looked at them, seeking faces she knew, and recognized several of the men who had ridden north with her from Vharcwal. A tall woman stood by the arched doorway of the common room, bow and quiverful of arrows over her shoulder. Her dark blond hair, pulled behind her back into a braid, dripped water from its tip.

"Jhadàvis," Iowyn said.

The woman turned, candlelight and lamplight glittering on the chainmail she wore beneath her long leather riding dress. She had only just come in out of the rain; her leathers were blackened by the water.

"Any news?" Iowyn asked.

"None, Lady," Jhadàvis said. Her face was lined with weariness and dark circles showed beneath her eyes.

"The scouts I sent out? Have they returned?"

Jhadàvis shook her head. "Not yet." She took her bow and quiver from her back and, setting them up against the wall, walked ahead of Iowyn across the common room to the large fireplace where other men and a few women had gathered.

"They're overdue, Jhada."

"Only by a few hours, Lady. The rain's slowed them."

Iowyn frowned, held her hands out to the fire. The old stone house was cool, even close as the season was to summer. The dampness ate at everyone and she longed for a day or two of sunlight.

"Lady?"

She turned, saw one of the men she had ridden with to Dramujh.

"Report from the gate, Lady. Your scouts are coming."

Iowyn closed her eyes with relief. Now, perhaps, she would find out what was happening to the south. The refugees were always full of news, but that was tangled and suspect; she trusted more to her own methods of gathering information.

"Thank you, Domhar. Send them to me the moment they arrive." The man turned to go. "And bring me some wine, will you?"

The man bowed again and left the room.

"To the Dark with this rain," Jhadàvis said. "Be days

'fore I get my bowstrings dried out."

Iowyn nodded, stepped up to the fireplace. "I don't think any of us will dry out. No wonder the grass around here stays lush all the way into summer. After all these centuries, I'm still amazed the rain doesn't drown it first." She looked at Jhadàvis. "You'd best get out of those leathers, Jhada. You'll catch your death of cold."

"Aye, Lady. I'll go. Call if you need me."

Jhadàvis bowed, went and retrieved her bow and quiver. Iowyn watched her; she considered it a stroke of luck to have met Jhadàvis. Virtually kinless, Jhadàvis fought alongside the men . . . had their respect, too; not a bad companion for a woman co-governing a city, even if that woman happened to be the High-King's granddaughter.

Iowyn moved closer to the fire. *Lords of Light! What do they expect us women to do? Stay huddled around the hearths, praying for victory?* Even Maiwyn, her almost sister-in-law, who had never been warrior-trained, who had been brought up in a noble house, was learning to fight. Alàric's doing, most of that, but Maiwyn had never objected. Eltàrim, as well as working with the resistance fighters, could hold her own with the bow and slender sword most fighting women carried. Iowyn shook her head. *One of these days there will be more of us, and we'll be accepted for what we are.* She looked up at the warriors who stood in the entry hall and measured their bulk against hers. One on one, in close combat, she knew she could not hold her own for long. But from a distance, with bow or sling . . .

The door opened and a darkly clad man entered, removed his helm, and stood blinking in the lamplight. Someone pointed to the common room and the fireplace; he turned and walked toward it.

"Lady," he said, bowing.

"Where are your companions?"

"I sent them to rest, Lady. I can give you the news you want. I've talked with folk who've seen Kahsir and Ahndrej. They're both in good health. Ahndrej is near healed; he'll probably fight soon. So far, Kahsir's held him from it." He ran a hand through his wet hair, shaking the rain from his fingertips. "Also, more refugees are coming. Rumor has it that this group is larger than the last."

Iowyn groaned inwardly. *Where are we going to put them? The people resting in the city will have to move on. Damn! I dread telling them that, but there's not enough room for them all.*

"Thank you," she said. "As soon as you can, find other men who would ride south for me. I want to be kept apprised of what's going on with my brother. Tell the governor we're expecting more people. And I want to know what's going on with the other refugee bands headed our way. How many more are coming, and how soon." And when he nodded, waiting further orders: "Go rest now. My thanks to your companions, too."

The man bowed and left the room. Iowyn looked into the fire. *Lords! Get me out of this city, this dampness, and especially this house!* But she could not go, not without breaking her promise to Kahsir. *Dammit! I wish I'd never agreed to come to Dramujh!* She knew she was needed here—her very presence in the city had given back a spark of hope to the people who still lived in it.

She looked up at the firelight dancing on the beamed ceiling and sighed, wishing for sunlight and escape.

Ahndrej sat crouched on the rocky bank in the gathering darkness, his sword across his knees. The sun had disappeared behind the hills to his back and the valley below lay wrapped in shadows. He wanted to stretch his legs, to get up and walk, but sat motionless. He lifted his head and sniffed: it had rained only yesterday and the evening wind was full of the sweet smell of open grasslands.

The other men lay hidden, scattered about on the valley walls; Kahsir knelt only a few paces away, just slightly higher up the steep incline. Ahndrej absently checked the cutting edge of his sword, then jerked his hand away. This was to be his first battle; he had fought the Leishoran who had captured Iowyn at Vharcwal, but that was different than a battle.

He shuddered and closed his eyes, but could not shut away the memories. *Eldànhi, brother! To die like that . . . !* He shook his head and blinked in the twilight. *Just give me a chance at one of the scum! Just one.*

One hundred Krotànya sat hidden in the rocks and brush of the valley, and if he turned, Ahndrej could have pointed to several of his invisible companions. Kahsir had taken to raiding these days, never giving the enemy one large, consolidated target. Ahndrej shifted slightly on his heels. *Lords! I'm afraid.* He wiped the sweat from his hands on his knee and gripped his sword tighter.

"Hsst!"

The whisper jerked Ahndrej's attention to the valley below. Hidden by both the rocks and gathering darkness, one of Kahsir's men crept up the bank. Ahndrej's heart beat faster: the Leishoranya were coming. He tightened his mental shields and forced himself into total stillness.

The first two enemy scouts entered the valley, around a league from where Ahndrej sat: they rode a few paces apart, looking up and down the rocky, shrub-covered walls. Ahndrej sensed their minds probing and held his shields tight. The scouts paused for a moment, rode close and conferred together, then motioned for the warriors behind them to follow.

The enemy tactic was not usual these days; they

moved hidden in valleys and kept to dark places, still tentative about riding across the border into the King- dom of Elyâsai. Ahndrej squinted in the twilight: more than one hundred rode in this company, but surprise had become one of Kahsir's greatest weapons.

Utter concentration wrapped the hidden Krotànya. As the enemy moved forward, the sound of hooves on an occasional exposed rock seemed loud to Ahndrej's ears. He licked his lips with a tongue gone suddenly dry, and forced himself to watch the advancing Leishoranya. A curious feeling welled up in his heart, shoving his fear aside.

The last of the Leishoranya entered the valley. Ahndrej tensed and closed his eyes briefly: the faces of his brother Eldànhi, of Eldànhi's wife Zhadànna, and their four children swam in his memory. He trembled and tightened his hand on his sword.

—*Now! At them, brothers!*

Kahsir's Sending echoed in Ahndrej's mind. He leapt to his feet, set his shield in place and ran down the steep bank, his world narrowed into a space only wide enough to contain his enemy. He heard the rest of Kahsir's men bursting from their cover, close to the valley floor.

One of the Leishoranya fell, then another and another, struck by Krotànya arrows. The light had grown treacherous, but some of Kahsir's bowmen had tried their luck to give them better odds.

Ahndrej lengthened his stride and ran on, feeling an odd sense of detachment, euphoric in its power. A Leishoran on a gray horse had reined in ahead, frozen in momentary surprise. Ahndrej covered the short dis- tance in a few bounds, all sense of personal safety forgotten now. The days upon days of training came back: he thrust upward and drove his sword into the Leishoran's unprotected right side.

"Eldànhi!" he cried. "Eldànhi! dàn Herahlu!"

Other shouts rang out, but he barely heard them.

The Leishoran tumbled to the ground; Ahndrej stepped out of the way of the panicked horse and whirled around. Another of the enemy rode in his direction through the fading light.

Ahndrej set himself, called upon all his native horsemanship. He dropped his shield, ducked beneath the Leishoran's swordstroke, and clawed his way up behind the man as the warrior rode past. The saddle was in the way, but Ahndrej threw his free arm around the Leishoran's neck, slit the man's throat, then shoved him from the saddle.

The Leishoran's foot caught in the stirrup: the horse bolted and Ahndrej fell sideways, rolled free, to come up on his feet. He saw another riderless horse, ran toward it, grabbed at the saddle, and hauled himself astride. The horse began to buck and twist, and the stirrups banged into his ankles. He caught at the reins, missed, snatched again, then jerked them back, bringing the horse to a sudden stop.

He laughed in exhilaration and sought the stirrups, but found them too long for his use. There—another Leishoran! He lifted his sword, yelled his brother's name, and charged straight for the warrior. "Death!" he cried. "Death to you all! Eldànhi! Eldànhi!"

He sword rang out against his opponent's, shrieked as it slid away. As he jerked his horse around, the animal faltered but regained its balance. The Leishoran was slower in turning: Ahndrej caught him in the back with a clumsy swordstroke. The man yelled something that ended in a howl of pain, and tumbled from the saddle.

Suddenly, the fighting ended. Silence fell on the valley, broken only by the moans of the wounded and dying. What little light left faded quickly, but Ahndrej saw Kahsir standing in the valley's center, leaning on his sword. Few Krotànya had died in the ambush, while Kahsir's men had killed most of the enemy. Even now, some of the Krotànya went slowly from body to body, delivering the mercy stroke where needed.

"Dreja."

He turned at the sound of Kahsir's voice and, sliding down from the nervous horse, looked around for his shield. It lay a few paces off and he walked over to pick it up. Kahsir stopped at his side.

"You didn't do badly, Dreja. Are you all right?"

"Aye." He stretched his arms and shifted his weight. "I was lucky."

"Lucky, indeed." Kahsir turned as one of his men came to his side.

"Do we rest, Lord, or move on?" the warrior asked.

"We move, Dovic'hàn. Spread the word. I want us out of here as soon as possible."

The man saluted and walked off. Ahndrej closed his eyes, only now feeling tired. *Ah, Eldànhi. Rest well, brother. Three of the enemy fell for you tonight and I'll never be the same again. Rest well . . . sleep safe. Trouble my dreams no longer.*

"Dreja?"

Kahsir had spoken again. Ahndrej opened his eyes, looked up.

"You *are* all right, aren't you?" Kahsir asked.

"I'm fine." A sudden rush of excitement followed his exhaustion—visions of enemy warriors falling beneath his sword. Lords of Light! It would be good to see them die. He laughed, his voice gone rough from shouting. "Are we going to fight again soon?"

The look of shock that crossed Kahsir's face was puzzling. Ahndrej gestured toward the enemy bodies.

"I'll kill more of them next time," he said. "By my brother's grave, I promise you that!"

CHAPTER 12

Tsingar cursed softly, set on edge by the increased activity in Mehdaiy's camp. The commotion did not even die after sunset; more and more men had gathered beneath Mehdaiy's banners in preparation for the full-scale invasion of Elyâsai.

Aimless now that he had fallen into virtual disgrace, Tsingar walked through the darkened camp. He cursed again and tightened his shields. For the thousandth time, he wondered why he had saved Aduhar's life. Little good it had done. From the moment he had brought Aduhar back to camp, the young man had done nothing but lie to his uncle about Tsingar's part in what had happened and protest his own innocence of any wrongdoing. Tsingar's acquaintances would have discounted much of what Aduhar had said, yet Mehdaiy had believed those lies.

Or had he?

Tsingar was not sure. He simply knew that he had been kept in camp, held from riding out with the companies that harried the Krotànya countryside. He spat off into the darkness between two tents. To make matters worse, he did not like the camp's new position: father west than Mehdaiy's first camp, it lay close to

the same wide, slow-moving river that bordered
Tutuljad to the south. But where the land around
Tutuljad rose to meet the hills to the north, this country lay flat and marshy, and the dampness proliferated
insects. After dark on some evenings it seemed impossible to breathe without inhaling clouds of them.

He had told Mehdaiy the true story of what had
happened. Expressionless, Mehdaiy had listened to
Tsingar's recounting of the battle with Kahsir and
Lorhaiden, then turned to hear Aduhar's tale. The two
stories were wildly divergent. And the outcome?
Mehdaiy had stripped Tsingar of his command, and
put him in charge of the scouts that went out into the
countryside beyond.

Tsingar stopped, blinking at the sight of his own
tent, unsure how he had come to it. He remembered
nothing of his walk through the camp, save the feeling
he had been watched and laughed at. He bit back an
angry curse. If cursing made any difference, Aduhar
would have been dead long ago.

Wishful thinking, that. Tsingar entered his tent,
snatched the wineskin from the center pole, unstopped
it, and drank. *Gods! What I wouldn't give to see that
insolent pup get what he's due.* Visions of what he
could do to the youngling prince flashed before his
eyes. If he could spring a trap—

No. That was *one* thing he dared not do. He
thought of Chaagut. Doubtless Ssenkahdavic had told
Mehdaiy how Tsingar had rid himself of Chaagut's bid
for power. He shook his head, sat down in the one of
the chairs, and kicked angrily at a travel box close by.
No accident, then. There must be other ways he could
get back at Aduhar.

A fight broke out in front of his tent. He stopped
the wineskin, slammed it down in the other chair,
stood and went to the tent door.

Two warriors had faced off in the wide aisle
between the tents, their boot-knives glittering in the

torchlight. A circle of curious onlookers had gathered around the combatants; voices rose, calling bets back and forth. Tsingar cursed quietly, stepped out of his tent, and walked over to the growing circle that surrounded the two warriors.

"You dung-heads!" he bellowed. "Get out of here."

Most of the onlookers turned at his voice; some jeered, making rude gestures, but other warriors began to wander off. Tsingar elbowed his way through the crowd. The two men had begun to fight—they circled one another, knife blades stabbing out in feints as each tested the other's reflexes and tried to find any weakness he could exploit.

"Curse you for worm-bait!" Tsingar yelled. "If you idiots want to fight, do it somewhere else! Now get out of here!" He kicked at one of the men, brought him down in a cursing heap. The other whirled around. "Put up that knife, scum," Tsingar said. "Take your squabble elsewhere!"

The tripped man had struggled to his feet and stood undecided to Tsingar's right. Tsingar whirled on him, put his hand to swordhilt and the warrior's eyes fell; he hefted his knife thoughtfully in his hand, then shrugged and walked away. The other man yelled obscenities after him, but fell silent as Tsingar half drew his sword.

"You," Tsingar barked. "Get out of my sight! If I see you again, you'll regret it."

The man left, followed by at least half the crowd. They murmured among themselves as they went, and several looked back, their faces puzzled. Tsingar turned on those who remained. "What are you? Men or dogs? Get out of here!"

Without seeing if they complied, he spun on his heel, slammed his blade home, and stalked back to his tent. Once inside, his knees began shaking; he fell down in his chair, and reached for the wineskin.

Gods! What's come over me? We're all bored, those

of us held in camp. A little fight like that might have made the evening a bit more interesting.

He drank again, dimly aware he had been drinking more than he should. He shrugged and stopped the wineskin. It did not matter now. His scouts did all his work. *Let me drink . . . that's all I'm good for.*

Where were Kahsir and Lorhaiden? Retreating slowly north with the rest of their men, most likely. Tsingar's hand clenched around the neck of the wineskin. If he could only get out of camp, ride free again. Between his scouts and his own strange ability to sense where Kahsir or Lorhaiden were, he could find them quickly. He wondered what Mehdaiy would think if—

If, if, if. He glared at the tent wall. There had to be a way back into Mehdaiy's good graces. He looked up at the lamp-shadowed ceiling. At least Mehdaiy had not taken his tent away. That said something.

Unbidden, the face of Kahsir's sister loomed up in Tsingar's mind. When he had brought Aduhar back into camp, he had expected to find her in Mehdaiy's hands. But Dvorkun and the forty men he had chosen to take her to Mehdaiy were missing. Another chance lost to impress the Dread Lord. When Mehdaiy had asked about it, all he could say was he had taken Iowyn prisoner and sent her south under guard. Beyond that, it was anyone's guess as to what had happened.

Someone scratched on the tent door. Tsingar looked up from his crossed legs, set the wineskin down on a small table, and rose.

"Enter."

It was one of his scouts. The man saluted and stood silent, waiting to be addressed again.

"Speak," Tsingar said. "What have you found?"

"Not much, Lord." The scout scratched his neck, mouth curled up in a grimace. "The Krotànya are in slow retreat. They—"

"I know . . . they retreat, they retreat! But damned

slowly, and they also attack." He glared at the scout. "Granted, they attack in squads and companies from out of the dark, but they attack. I want to know *where* those companies are. We can't do much if we're constantly hounded by an enemy we can't see." He closed his eyes, feeling dizzy. *Cut back on the wine, Tsingar,* an inner voice whispered. *You still have to think.* He gestured at the tent door. "Go. When the other scouts return, send them to me."

"Lord," the man said, and was gone.

Tsingar stood motionless in the center of the tent, swaying on his feet. He looked at the wineskin on the table next to his chair, then with deliberate slowness turned and walked to his pallet. *Good for nothing, am I?* He sank down on his knees and rolled over onto his back. The flickering shadows on the tent ceiling set his stomach churning; he closed his eyes, but that only made things worse. *Good for nothing?* He laughed, startled at the bark he heard in his own ears. *And who, besides me, will be the first to learn where Kahsir or Lorhaiden are? By the Gods . . . I'm not useless yet.*

Kahsir closed his eyes briefly, reopened them and concentrated on keeping straight in the saddle, on anything but his weariness. Two ten-days of fighting since he had led the valley ambush had taken its toll. The five-day-old sword cut across his arm had begun to heal now and itched intolerably. He scratched at it, forced his hand away, and glanced over his shoulder.

His men followed, what he had left of them. Time and again, they had fought against enemy forces that outnumbered them at least three to one. All things considered, he was fortunate to have escaped even greater losses.

His hands clenched on the reins and his chest tightened. *Dammit! How the Dark can I be expected to hold the enemy back outnumbered as I am?* He knew all too well that the High-King had few men to send south as reinforcements, and was sending all he could. Not taking into consideration the warriors his grandfather had sent him since Tutuljad fell, Kahsir judged he only had around three thousand men left of the original five thousand he had started with in early spring. And now, since they rode in companies spread out across the countryside, raiding the Leishoranya when and where they could, he found it harder to keep an accurate count of who had died and who still lived.

This doesn't have to be! I could avoid all these deaths if I would—

He refused to follow his thoughts to a conclusion.

Ahndrej rode to his right, silent and withdrawn. Kahsir had thought Ahndrej would have come back to himself after he had fought and killed. Not so. He glanced sidelong at Ahndrej and cursed this war and what it did to those who fought it. Ahndrej had lost his innocence, but an even greater loss was his grip on sanity. Not for the first time Kahsir felt Lorhaiden rode at his side.

He saw one of his scouts returning: the horseman rode low on the hillsides, avoiding the setting sun to his back. Kahsir straightened in the saddle, wincing slightly. *Lords! Grant he's found somewhere we can stop.* The wounded needed it badly and all of them were starved for rest.

The scout reined in his horse, turned it about so he rode at Kahsir's side. "Lord," he said, gesturing to the northwest. "I've found us a spot to camp for the evening."

"Defensible?"

"Aye, Lord."

"How far?"

"Half an hour."

Kahsir sighed, nodded at the man to ride off again. As the scout cantered away, Kahsir hitched around in the saddle and signed to his men that a campsite was near—relief passed through the minds close by. He turned around and increased his horse's gait to a slow canter, his men following at a similar pace.

The land had broken up into low hills again, dotted with wind-twisted trees. Kahsir looked for the scout, saw him not all that far ahead, and altered his men's course. He glanced once more at Ahndrej, but Iowyn's lover still kept hidden behind his shields.

The scouts had found an excellent campsite: trees clustered about the hilltop and a stream ran close to the south. Kahsir's horse tried to drink as it crossed the stream, but he jerked its head up; there would be time for that later when the animal was not so hot and winded. Now all Kahsir wanted was to get out of the saddle and sit down on something that did not move.

He dismounted stiffly, handed his reins to one of the scouts. There was a chorus of sighs and groans from the men close by as they slid down from their saddles, and low talk among some who were less tired than the others.

"Place sentries around this hill—five of them, at least," Kahsir instructed the scout. He sighed, stretched the stiffness from his shoulders and back, his arm itching again. "Ahndrej?"

"Aye, Lord?" Ahndrej stepped closer, holding his horse's reins loosely in one hand.

"Get some sleep. You need it as badly as the rest of us."

"Less. My people are Kahràmmir, born and bred to horseback. I'm used to all this riding. I'll be one of the five to stand watch, if you'll let me."

Kahsir gestured Ahndrej away with a weary hand. *Lords above! Does he never tire? He's killed more than any of us and still keeps looking for more.*

"Water, Lord?"

He turned, took the still dripping waterbag from the scout who stood at his side and drank, feeling some of his energy return. Wiping his mouth, he passed the waterbag back.

"How are the wounded?"

"Better than yesterday, Lord, but Taràs has taken a turn for the worse."

"I'll be there in a little while, sooner if he calls for me. Make sure he and the other wounded are fed first."

"Aye, Lord."

Kahsir made his way to the shelter of a small tree. He had spent far too long a time in the field, away from his headquarters in Dramujh, but until recently he had not felt he could leave his men. Now that they had found a campsite where they could rest for several days, he thought he might be able to take the mindroad to the provincial capital, if even for a day.

He glanced up and saw Ahndrej standing not all that far away. He frowned. A potential problem, leaving Ahndrej by himself; besides, he had promised Iowyn he would not let her lover be alone.

"Dreja," he called. The figure at the edge of the hill turned, and Kahsir gestured. "Only a moment of your time."

Ahndrej walked to the small tree and hunkered down at Kahsir's side.

"I'm going to Dramujh tomorrow for a day or two. Why don't you come with me?"

"I'd rather not," Ahndrej said, looking away.

Kahsir lifted an eyebrow. "Why?"

Ahndrej drew a deep breath and slowly let it out. "I'd rather not. I have my reasons." He looked back. "If you order me to, I will."

"Iowyn would like you to come see her."

"Give her my apologies, then. I feel I'm needed more here."

Kahsir stared, and smothered the angry words he felt like saying. *Damn! What the Dark is still eating at him? And who can I leave to keep him in line?* He rubbed his eyes and shrugged. "Whatever you want. I think you're being damnably stubborn about things."

Ahndrej did not reply, merely sat looking across the countryside.

"Go," Kahsir said, waving a hand at the place Ahndrej had set up as his vantage point. "I'll let you know when I leave if you have any message for her."

"No need." Ahndrej stood. "Tell her I wish her luck with the city."

"Huhn." Kahsir closed his eyes as Ahndrej walked off. His second-in-command, Tyndhyar, had a level head on his shoulders; he of all the men in the company seemed a logical choice to keep watch on Ahndrej. Shaking his head, Kahsir stood, sought Tyndhyar's mind, and walked across the hilltop to speak with him.

When Kahsir left the mind-road in front of the governor's mansion, he was assaulted by the noise of the city itself. Though the home sat at the highest point in the city, the sounds from the streets below rose to him as he handed the reins of his horse to one of the soldiers who stood at the foot of the steps. After so long in the wild, Kahsir found the invisible pressure of the mass of people in Dramujh unsettling.

"Kahs!"

He looked up; his sister came down the stairs, a smile on her face. But her eyes strayed over the courtyard, looking to see if anyone had accompanied him.

"You seem well," he said, embracing her and kissing her forehead. "Where can we talk?"

She glanced around the courtyard one last time, some of the happiness fading from her eyes. "The common room is fairly empty . . . or do you want privacy?"

"What I need is a soft bed, something to eat and drink, and a quiet place to talk . . . not necessarily in that order."

"You *do* look exhausted," she agreed, leading the

way into the mansion. Instead of turning into the common room, she gestured him into a small side room across the entry hall. A retainer hovered at her elbow. "Wine, bread, and cheese," Iowyn said. "I'll join my brother."

"Aye, Lady. My Lord." The retainer bowed and set off toward the kitchens.

"Lords of Light!" Kahsir sank down into a comfortable chair, stretched his feet out, and closed his eyes. He heard his sister close the door and sit down in the chair next to him. "This is better than any saddle I know of."

She laughed quietly, but then kept silent, waiting for him to speak.

"How are things going?" he asked, and sensed the slight hesitation before she replied.

"About as well as might be expected. A supply train was ambushed around twenty leagues north of here by an enemy suicide squad. We managed to kill all of them, but not before they'd ruined the wagons."

He opened his eyes and sat straighter in the chair. "Damn! Has this been happening with regularity?"

"No. But we're going to have to step up our vigilance. Maybe have a Mind-Born ride with any supply train from now on."

"What I want to know is how a suicide squad got past the Mind-Born in the first place. That's one of their jobs, guarding the frontiers."

She shrugged, an expression of frustration touching her face. "This isn't the first time it's happened, and it won't be the last."

"I'll talk to Grandfather about it, unless you've already done so."

"I have. But if you talk to him, too, maybe he'll move a little quicker."

A soft knock sounded at the door. The retainer let himself in, laid the bread, cheese, and wine out on the table between the two chairs, and let himself out again.

Kahsir poured Iowyn a glass of wine, then one for himself. "The city's packed with people, isn't it?"

Her laugh was slightly brittle. "Packed is hardly the word. Lords, Kahs! I don't think I've ever seen more refugees."

"Where are they all coming from?"

She gestured. "Several towns and steadings to the southeast—Dhidorova, Padalaiki are the largest of the towns. The steadings—"

"Are you having trouble persuading them to keep heading north?" he interrupted.

"Most go willingly."

"Most? What about the rest?"

"We've had trouble with some of them," she admitted, "but nothing we couldn't handle."

"Thank the Light you're here. Before you arrived, the place was a nightmare."

"I can imagine. Tahrkan certainly wasn't upset at having me take charge of the refugee problem. Or, for that matter, the military one." She cut a slice of bread from the loaf, spread some cheese on it, and handed it across the table. "But I'm not winning any friends among the refugees, taking their menfolk from them. I've heard myself described as the Ice Princess who has no heart."

Kahsir frowned. "Do they honestly think you're doing it for your amusement?"

"No. But to a woman who has only one son left alive, who sees him taken off to be taught warrior skills, I'm far from understanding." She took a drink of wine. "How long can you stay?"

"A day . . . not more. I left my men in a secluded campsite, but I don't feel right about being off in comfort while they suffer."

She said nothing, busy with her own bread and cheese, but he noticed the hurt that touched her face.

"How's Dreja?" she asked, her voice tightly controlled. "Is he still—?"

"Aye." He debated telling her of Ahndrej's refusal to return to Dramujh, and thought better of it. He chose his next words with care. "I thought he'd come out of it, Io. I really did. But he's still after Leishoranya with Lorhaiden's intensity." He sensed the flare of her concern and had a vision of her leaping onto her horse and riding south in an instant. "He's all right," he assured her hastily. "And at this stage, he's about the only one of us who is."

"Is it still as bad, Kahs?"

"Aye." He Sent her his memories of the past few days' fighting and what had happened afterward, layering that Sending with information about what he knew of the other armies on the southern front. "If we aren't sent some reinforcements— Dammit, Io! We can't hold them back much longer. We're being torn to bits!"

"Have you heard from Lorhaiden or Vàlkir?"

He nodded. "They're facing the same odds. I'm going to have to talk with Grandfather. I might even have to return to the capital. I know he's sending as many men as he can when he has them, but it's just not enough." He watched her stand, wineglass in hand, and walk to the window overlooking the courtyard. *And the solution to our problems here in the south is as plain as day, isn't it? All I have to do is to let myself go, use my power to—* He banished the thoughts with an inner grimace.

"I wish Ahndrej had come along with you," Iowyn said softly. "Or that I could ride south to be with him."

"I know." He let his mind touch hers, trying to share his concern, love, and understanding. "But it's vital that you stay here. Without you, the whole place could fall apart. The refugees would *never* make it north."

She did not reply, only stood silent, looking into the

courtyard for a face he knew she would not find.

Tsingar blinked in the morning sunlight as he stuck his head out of the tent. He rubbed his eyes with the heels of his hands and ducked back inside. His mouth was dry and he wanted another drink, but after the last episode with the wineskin, he had tried to avoid anything that tasted like alcohol.

Standing motionless for a moment in the center of his tent, he yawned and dressed. He was gathering his weapons when he heard the tent flap pulled aside. His heart lurched—he turned, knife in hand. Mehdaiy.

Gods! What does he want?

Mehdaiy stood halfway into the tent, the slant of the early morning's sunlight making his face look harsh and foreboding. Tsingar hastily sheathed the knife in his boot.

"Dread Lord?"

"Two more of your scouts came in. They're badly wounded."

Tsingar's heart caught. "Where are they, Master?"

"By my tent. Come."

Tsingar quickly attached his weapons to his belt and followed Mehdaiy outside. Mehdaiy kept silent, his attitude a warning that he did not want to be disturbed. Tsingar walked slightly behind his commander, still befogged by sleep. *Wounded? Where the Void have those scum-sucking idiots gotten to that they've been wounded?*

Neither of the two men waiting by Mehdaiy's tent was so injured he could not sit. One had taken a long, deep sword cut to his thigh, while the other's left arm hung useless, likely broken beneath his shield. Mehdaiy stepped aside so that Tsingar could squat before the scouts.

"Irguhn . . . Dhavash." Tsingar hissed their names, looking from one to the other. Clear-eyed, they looked back, pain sharpening their features. "What did you find?"

"Krotànya, Lord," said Dhavash, the shorter of the two. He cradled his useless arm in his right hand. "Lots of Krotànya."

"Where?"

"About thirty leagues north of here," Irguhn said. "We followed a band of refugees, Lord. They rode with their minds wide open—they were heading toward the provincial capital, about six days' ride to the north. We managed to capture one of the sluggards. I guess we were careless. Several Krotànya warriors discovered us, and we barely escaped with our lives."

Tsingar rocked back on his heels. "What did you learn from this fellow you'd captured?"

"Woman," Dhavash said. "It was a woman, Lord. It seems Kahsir's sister is in this provincial capital. Among other things, she's coordinating the refugees' retreat."

Tsingar stiffened, sat down cross-legged, feeling Mehdaiy's stare. *O Gods! What have these fools done?* "She's there? I would have thought she'd have been sent home." He glared at the two scouts. "Why did you go after a woman? I'd think a man, possibly a warrior, would have had better information."

Neither scout said anything; they both shifted their weight uncomfortably.

"Answer me!" he snapped, reaching out and grabbing hold of Dhavash's broken arm. He twisted it savagely. "Why?"

Dhavash screamed in agony, his face gone sickly white. Tsingar pushed him away, hard enough that he fell onto his broken limb. He turned to Irguhn.

"Well?" Tsingar snarled. "Looking for a little fun, eh?"

"She was armed, Lord . . . a warrior. She would have known—" He cringed before Tsingar's raised fist and swallowed heavily. "I . . . we were tired, Lord, and thought we wouldn't have to fight all that hard to subdue her."

Tsingar groaned inwardly. "You were tired—" He took the scout by his collar. "You fools! I supposed you didn't keep watch while interrogating this woman, did you?"

Irguhn winced in pain, but kept silent.

Mehdaiy's presence loomed close behind. Tsingar swallowed heavily. "And where's Kahsir? Lorhaiden? Did you find out *anything* concerning them?"

Irguhn shook his head. "No, Lord. Nothing."

Tsingar shoved the scout away and the man fell over onto his side, grabbing for his blood-crusted leg.

"These men are useless to me, Master," Tsingar said, standing and looking at Mehdaiy's closed face. "I won't tolerate careless scouts. Do I have your leave to execute them?"

Both scouts cried out suddenly in the following silence. Tsingar gestured them silent.

"Of course, Tsingar." Mehdaiy's smile was lazy, half-amused.

"Lord," Dhavash whimpered. He had worked his way up to a sitting position again; Irguhn sat beside him, his pale face slick with sweat. "We got away, didn't we? We brought you the information about Kahsir's sister you wanted!"

"Aye. And think how much *more* you might have learned if you hadn't been so damned tired, or kept such poor watch." Tsingar spat at the scouts' feet. "Idiots! Dung-brained fools!" His mind was whirling, turning over what the scouts had said. "Dread Lord," he said to Mehdaiy. "May I have a word with you . . . in private?"

Mehdaiy nodded. Tsingar motioned to several men who stood close by, drawn by the screams.

"Guard these idiots," he said. "If they're gone when I return, you'll die for it."

He spun on his heel and followed Mehdaiy around

to the front of the tent. Just as Mehdaiy reached out for the door flap, a strong, gold-braceleted hand pulled it back, and Aduhar stood in the entrance.

Tsingar stiffened. Aduhar's slitted eyes grew colder yet, and a slow, disdainful smile spread over his face.

"Rather nicely done," he drawled, hitching his new red cloak over his shoulders, "though I would have preferred a bit more torture." His smile turned into a sneer. "How's it feel to be sober, Tsingar?"

"Aduhar." Mehdaiy's voice was emotionless but clipped. "Get out!"

Aduhar blinked slightly and stood hesitating in the doorway.

"Out!" Mehdaiy hissed. "Now!"

Aduhar ducked his head and, throwing a hateful look in Tsingar's direction, quickly left the tent. Tsingar struggled to keep his face composed, and followed Mehdaiy inside.

"Well, Tsingar?" Mehdaiy sat down. "What do you want to talk about?"

Tsingar wet his lips with a too-dry tongue. *Gods! A drink!* "I've been thinking, Dread Lord. We might have another chance to get at Kahsir's sister."

Mehdaiy lifted one eyebrow. "Oh?"

"If I can find out more about this provincial capital, how many men guard it, what the comings and goings of the refugees are, I might be able to take her prisoner again."

For a long moment Mehdaiy sat silent, his eyes hooded. "And?"

"There's another thing that could aid us, Dread Lord. Her lover is fighting with Kahsir."

Mehdaiy nodded slowly. "It's a good idea, but it wants further planning. How are you going to take her? By ambush? What if she never leaves the city? Surely it must be defended. If so, by how many warriors?" He leaned back in his chair, lazily running a fingertip across one knee. "The city's far within

Krotànya-held lands. What about the Krotànya Mind-Born? You wouldn't be able to depend on any help from us once you got that far north. Have you considered these things?"

"I think so, Dread Lord," Tsingar said. "I'll—"

Suddenly, Mehdaiy's mind moved against his, broke down all but his innermost shields, and went rummaging through his memories, his plans regarding Kahsir's sister. He held his breath and waited trembling until Mehdaiy had satisfied his curiosity. As Mehdaiy's mind faded from his, Tsingar staggered on his feet, drained and shaken.

"I'm not going to ride off today, Master," he said, struggling to regain his composure. "I want to send out more scouts, get more information. I'll need answers to all your questions before I leave."

Mehdaiy nodded absently, withdrawn now, coldly remote. Tsingar glanced around the tent and saw a waterbag hanging on the center pole. Mehdaiy sighed and gestured.

"Drink, Tsingar. It's water."

Tsingar lifted the waterbag from its post.

"I'm sending Aduhar with you again," Mehdaiy said.

Tsingar paused in unstopping the waterbag. His heart lurched and he knew his face held a look of such shock that he could not hide it. Honesty alone was his only choice of action.

"Dread Lord? After what he's said about me? After all he's—"

"Sit, Tsingar." Mehdaiy motioned curtly to a chair, waited until Tsingar sat in it. "Go on . . . drink!"

Tsingar drank quickly, his hands shaking so that the water dribbled down his chin. He restopped the waterbag, set it down beside his chair, and looked up at Mehdaiy.

"I warned you about my nephew," Mehdaiy said. "He's not one to be taken lightly. And he's never met anyone who's crossed him as many times as you. As for what he's said . . ." Mehdaiy dismissed those poisonous words with a flip of his hand. "I believe what I want to believe, not what others tell me. Even my nephew. Yet I know what you told me was truer than anything Aduhar said."

"Then why punish me like this? I'm yours to command, Dread Lord, but I can't serve you by being held here in camp."

"You said several things to Aduhar I could not excuse. No one—not even Aduhar's commander—has the right to abuse him the way you did."

Tsingar choked back other words he longed to say. *Don't push things,* he cautioned himself. *Let it be. You'll get your chance later.* He straightened his shoulders.

"Do I have my command again?"

Mehdaiy stared at him. "Of course. Go, Tsingar. You've two scouts to execute."

"Aye, Master." Tsingar rose and hung the waterbag on the pole.

"And keep me advised."

Tsingar bowed and stepped out of the tent, his knees quivering with relief.

CHAPTER 13

People seldom came to this unfrequented end of the governor's house. Nevertheless, Iowyn looked down the hallway to make sure it was empty, then hitched herself up sideways on the wide sill of the recessed window.

As she opened the window, pushing it outward, a warm breeze stirred her hair. The tile roofs of the buildings gleamed in the sunlight; their wide overhangs, built to shade the space below them, threw the walkways and porches into deep shadow. Dramujh sat atop the highest hill in the area, and the governor's house held the summit of the town. Wide streets wound their way from the house toward the wall, and a few children played a noisy game somewhere off beyond her view.

She stretched one trousered leg out on the window-sill, brought her other knee up to her chin, and wrapped her arms around it. Flowers filled the garden below now; they seemed to have bloomed all at once after the last few days of rain. She made a face. Lords forbid she see rain for the next ten-day or so.

Distant voices drifted up from the courtyard on the other side of the house, and she frowned: the argument between two refugee leaders was still going on.

Lords! If it gets any worse, I'll have to go settle it.

The number of refugees caused the major problem; she had never imagined so many people could be headed in one direction. They came north in a steady stream now—villages, steadings, and the few towns that lay south emptied of their inhabitants. *By the Light! Where do they think they're going? Surely not to Hvàlkir, to the capital. There's not enough room for them and all those more to follow.*

A blur of memory—other refugee flights, other times and places. She rubbed her eyes, trying to keep those memories buried, but it did no good. Centuries piled one on the other: decades, years of war, of death. One event seemed to blur with another, but if she concentrated, she would remember each time and place as if she had come from there only yesterday.

But yesterday—decades and centuries past—there had been somewhere to retreat. Now there was only the sea, death and . . .

She clenched her hands into fists and felt her shoulders tense as she looked down into the garden. It would do no good to lose her temper now. She had bordered on the verge of it when she had fled the courtyard and the argument, and until she was calmer, she dared not go back.

Kahsir   was   in   slow   retreat   before   the Leishoranya—he, Vàlkir, Lorhaiden, and the rest of the commanders on the southern border. With too few warriors at their backs, time and again they threw themselves against the enemy in a futile attempt to halt the invasion. Amazingly enough, they had been successful to some degree: the Leishoranya had bought every league they had taken with enormous loss of life. But this desperate defense could only last so long. She had Sent to her grandfather, begging for more men, but received the same answer as Kahsir: Vlàdor simply had no more to send at this time. The recuperating wounded he *could* send south still needed rest, and the newly recruited required more training.

So Kahsir had ordered a war on the land: everything the enemy could possibly use was destroyed. Villages and steadings were burned, foodstuffs ruined or taken with escaping refugees, livestock driven north or butchered and left to rot. What few roads existed were torn apart to make it as hard as possible for the enemy to drive their wagons across the countryside. It was imperative that the Leishoranya be kept from establishing their supply lines.

And every able-bodied man who came with the refugees Iowyn ordered into the care of Chàrion, who then armed them and sent them off to various captains who tried to teach them what they could of warfare before sending them off to defend the countryside. Much to her relief, all but a few seemed eager to take up arms and had proven able students.

A bird sang out from one of the trees that grew close by the garden wall; another answered from somewhere farther off to the left. Iowyn rubbed her forehead, blinked a few times, and leaned against the wall.

And Ahndrej. Lords above! What had happened to him? Where was the man she used to know, whom she loved so well?

She blinked back sudden tears. If only she could go to him, talk to him, hold him in her arms and tell him he was not alone. She sighed, brought her other knee up to her chin, and rested her head on her crossed arms. She had promised Kahsir she would stay in Dramujh unless Ahndrej was wounded. Damn! Did that promise cover lingering damage to the mind? And the fact that he had not Sent to her for over—

Footsteps came from the hallway; she stiffened, curled her legs up, and drew her long riding skirt down over her trousers, then relaxed. It was Jhadàvis.

"Lady?" The footsteps came closer. "Be you alone, Lady?"

She sighed. "Hsst!" she whispered, leaning out from the windowsill and gesturing. "Down here, Jhada."

The tall woman smiled her slow smile in greeting, and walked toward the window, her long strides easy and relaxed.

"I been hunting you, Lady. That argument downstairs be getting worse."

Iowyn moved over on the sill, gestured Jhadàvis to join her. "Won't they listen to anyone else?"

"No, Lady." Jhadàvis hitched herself up, back toward the window, and sat there swinging her heels against the wall. "You'll be needing to end it sooner or later. Them folks! The last lot of refugees must've taken this for home the way they be fighting leaving."

"Huhn." Iowyn glanced sideways at Jhadàvis, remembering again how very young she was. Only forty—seven years past the age of majority, and still in some ways quite innocent. "What's the problem, Jhada?"

"Lords only know. Now me, I think they be so tired of running that any place that smells of security looks like a good spot to stop."

"*Aii'ya!* Eventually *everyone* will have to leave, including us." A strange look flashed behind Jhadàvis' eyes and Iowyn winced. *Damn! And if the enemy's making their final push as Kahs is afraid they are, that day's not far off, either. I wonder if Jhada's contemplated this herself?*

"I suppose it crossed their minds once or twice." Jhadàvis shrugged. "You know how it be, Lady. Them folks want to ignore what they don't want to think about."

Iowyn smiled thinly. *As do we all.*

The voices in the courtyard had grown louder and she sighed; she could no longer avoid it. "Damn! I'll have to talk to them. Better now than when they've come to blows." She slid down from the windowsill. "Come with me, Jhada. And for the Light's sake, look formidable. We may have to face them down."

Jhadàvis joined her as she walked down the hallway. "Do you want me to bring my bow?"

Iowyn glanced sidelong, saw Jhadàvis' mocking expression, and laughed. "It's a good idea, but I don't think they'd appreciate it."

The argument had grown fiercer since she had left. Dhàvi, one of the warriors she had ridden with from Vharcwal, stood at the head of the stairs by the front door of the house. Two men who had the look of village leaders about them faced him, gesturing at each other, and arguing in loud voices, neither listening to a word the other said. Iowyn briefly brushed Dhàvi's mind and he turned to her, vastly relieved.

Iowyn reached out and touched the minds of the two arguing men. —Dammit! Stop! she snapped mentally. They both halted in mid-sentence and faced her.

"Haven't you settled this yet?" she asked, pitching her voice to convey boredom. "Children would carry on so. I don't see what the problem is. One group of you has to go."

"But, Lady," the shorter man said, bearded and dressed in his best. "My people are exhausted!"

"And his aren't?" Iowyn gestured at the other man. "His people arrived here three days behind yours. It's obvious which group needs to leave first."

"But, Lady," the first man said. "My wounded—"

"Dammit! What of his?" She clenched her fists at her sides and struggled to keep from shouting. "There's only so much room within these walls. If you," she said to the first man, "and your people wish to camp outside them, you're more than welcome. His people have the right to come in." The bearded man started to say something, but she interrupted. "I give you until tomorrow to have your people out of Dramujh. That's an order."

It was so silent now in the courtyard she could hear the birds off in the trees.

"Lady," the bearded man said. He bowed stiffly and stalked off down the stairs.

Iowyn turned to the other man who waited silently. "Tell your people," she said, keeping her voice level, "they'll be able to come into the city tomorrow."

"My thanks, Lady," he said, and left.

She sat down on the stairs. "Dhàvi," she said to the man behind her. "I want that order to stick. See that it does. Inform the governor of my decision. If you have any trouble, get back to me or Chàrion."

"Aye, Lady." She heard amusement in his voice. "Thank you."

She nodded absently and he walked off. Jhadàvis sat down on the steps in a creak of leather clothing.

"Fools," she said, her voice full of youthful disdain. "Be there anything else for me to do, Lady?"

Iowyn shook her head. "No. Not now. I'm waiting for my scouts to return."

Kahsir had left three days ago, and since then she had not received a Sending from him. During the entire time he had spent in Dramujh, he had never once mentioned what he had done while rescuing her, or how he was dealing with it. He had made only one allusion to the incident, telling her that he had asked Vlàdor for more than reinforcements. From this, she judged her grandfather had offered no help handling either problem. She shook her head; how Kahsir managed to keep on, bearing the burden of what he had done, remained a mystery.

Somewhere a dog started barking; the birds continued to sing, undisturbed by the dog or impending doom. Iowyn ran a hand through her hair, shook it loose on her shoulders, and stretched her legs out on the stairs.

"I suppose," she said, thinking of Jhadàvis' offer to help, "you could ride with me, Jhada. I want to take a look at the refugee camps outside the walls." She rose and waited for her companion. "If nothing else, it will get me out of this damnable place before I lose my mind."

*   *   *

Tsingar sat hidden in the brush, waiting for the sun to set, his men concealed on the hillsides all around. No one would have found it an easy job keeping two hundred of them hidden, much less quiet, during the day, but at least this time Mehdaiy had given him experienced warriors.

The provincial capital of Dramujh lay over an hour's ride to the northeast. Tsingar had chosen his hiding place with care, wary of the hapless refugees that trekked toward the city. The camp lay in the hills, far from the city fields, a place Tsingar sensed safe from discovery; he trusted it was also hidden from anyone who might hunt or herd his beasts to pasture. Still, he had taken extra precautions to keep the horses farther to the south, had forbidden any cooking fires, and was scrupulous about the maintenance of the latrines. Smells from a large group of men and animals could carry for extraordinary distances.

And, above all, he had ordered instant death for anyone caught stealing as much as one chicken from the farms around the city. Nothing would alert the peasantry to his company's presence as quickly as such a theft.

He heard Aduhar, somewhere off to his right, hidden by the brush. He snorted. *At least I don't have to look at him.* The young man had kept silent for the most part since leaving Mehdaiy's campsite, content to surround himself with other young warriors, all of whom seemed eager to curry his favor. *Damn! I wonder what Mehdaiy said to Aduhar before we left. He's been uncommonly civil.*

Tsingar glanced at the sky, judging the time by the sunlight. Soon dusk would fall and he could risk another look at the city himself; this time, he would go closer and verify the information his scouts had reported. He frowned. The country around the city itself was hilly, narrow valleys full of trees and brush.

As for Dramujh, it—like most Krotànya cities—was surrounded by a high wall. This could make it hard to tell exactly how many warriors were stationed in and around it. He had never once believed it unguarded, though it lay far from the southern border. The Krotànya might be many things, but they were far from stupid.

He scratched at a bug bite, reached for his waterbag, and drank. The inactivity had begun to drive his men crazy; discipline had turned into a serious problem. He leaned back on the hillside, propped up on his elbows, sighed quietly and closed his eyes.

The crackling of brush came at his side: he jumped, grabbed for his sword and scrambled to his feet. One of his scouts stood there, shoulders slumped, face lined with weariness. Tsingar let loose his pent-up breath, curtly gestured the man to sit, then, hunkering down on his heels, he extended his waterbag to the scout.

"What did you see?" he asked.

"Kahsir's sister," the scout said, lowering the waterbag. "She rode out from the city again this afternoon. I supposed she was inspecting the refugees."

"Guarded as before?"

The scout nodded. "By five men, maybe four. I think a woman rode with her. I wasn't close enough to tell for sure."

"Did she ride far?"

"Not today, Lord. She visited a large group of refugees who've gathered by the south wall."

"A large group. How many, exactly?"

The scout tugged at his mustache. "Around a thousand, Lord."

"Mostly women and children?"

"Aye, Lord."

Tsingar scratched his chin, looked off into the trees. Kahsir's sister took few chances, far from the border though she was. She seldom rode out accompanied by a smaller escort.

He closed his eyes and considered various ways to take her alive. The information he had collected before he had come north indicated that the city served as garrison for Krotànya troops. In addition, a number of the Krotànya Mind-Born dwelt in Dramujh. So much for a quick jump inside the city walls. This left the seemingly regular rides; and if she did not go far from the city itself, any attack he made could prove disastrous.

Tsingar glanced at the scout. "Could you see how many men guard the city?"

"No, Lord."

"Damn. Make an estimate from what you've seen."

The scout shrugged. "That's impossible to tell, Lord. Several times I've watched around five hundred warriors practicing arms outside the city walls."

"Are they always the same men?"

"I don't know, Lord."

Tsingar sighed. "What insignia do they wear? Does it vary?"

"No insignia. But I don't think they're all locals. Some of them have got a practiced edge—a discipline."

Imperial troops, then, at least five hundred of them. Those numbers corresponded with what Tsingar's scouts had told him, but there *had* to be more warriors: aside from serving as a garrison, Dramujh was a provincial capital. And, Tsingar's scouts had seen various companies of men riding off to the south; from the looks of some of those warriors, they were refugees newly trained to fight. Tsingar chewed on the inside of his lower lip.

"How much smoke did you see over the city?"

"A fair amount, Lord. More than I'd think five hundred men *and* the city's inhabitants could make."

Tsingar nodded. He estimated the city at one time had held thirty thousand people. Now that the fighting drew closer, some of the citizens of Dramujh had likely left their homes, heading north along with the refugees.

He shifted his weight. At the very least, five hundred imperial troops; refugees numbering several thousand, if he counted those inside the city; a home guard he estimated could be as large as one thousand. If someone had put him in charge of that city, what would *he* do? Either Kahsir's sister had many more men within those walls, or she was trying by those exercises to give the impression of greater numbers than she possessed. He shook his head. *Quit jumping to conclusions. We've kept our minds tightly shielded: as far as she knows, we're not here.*

"Go rest," he said to the scout. "And send me my captains."

The scout returned the waterbag, saluted, and walked off into the brush. Tsingar stoppered the bag, set it at his feet, and thought over the situation again.

Not knowing the strength of Dramujh, he dared not attack the city itself, even if he had ten times the men he had now. It seemed he had but one choice—a swift strike against Kahsir's sister and her guard when they rode far enough away from the city to make it feasible.

He contemplated that. A few more days in hiding might establish a pattern he could use. So far, she had left the city every day, save when it rained, sometimes for nothing more than a wild ride around the walls. Would she continue to take those rides? And what kind of cover lay close to the city? He cursed; he had a fairly good idea but he had forgotten to ask the scout. Likely brush and trees. The countryside this far north seemed much the same.

He heard the movement of men approaching off to his left: his two hundred-commanders. Someone walked behind them.

Aduhar.

"Lord?" Khartu, the taller of the hundred-commanders hunkered down; Chevig, the other commander, sat down beside him. "You wanted to see us?"

Tsingar nodded, looking at Aduhar. Mehdaiy's

nephew returned the look with one totally unreadable, then gathered his red cloak closer and sat slightly off to one side, his entire attitude reeking of disdain.

"So far Kahsir's sister has ridden out from Dramujh every day," Tsingar said. "I doubt we'll be able to tell how many warriors stand in the city's defense, so if we're going to take her, it will have to be from ambush."

The two hundred-commanders exchanged a glance and nodded. Aduhar looked up at the darkening sky, his expression politely bored.

"I suppose," Aduhar said, still staring off into nothing, "you've decided on the place we'll attack her from."

Tsingar stiffened. "Not yet. All my scouts aren't back, and I don't know the land well enough. But from what I've seen and what I've been told, there should be ample cover for an ambush."

Aduhar looked down, met Tsingar's gaze, his eyes shadowed in the fading light. "I claim command of that attack," he said, his voice very soft.

Tsingar's breath caught in his throat; he sensed his hundred-commanders watching, waiting for him to reply.

"No, *tergai*," he said, keeping his voice soft and level as Aduhar's. "I gave you a command before. This time, we'll do it my way."

Aduhar sat motionless for a long moment, coiled, ready to spring. The menace in him was so intense, Tsingar shifted his weight slightly forward, ready to defend himself.

"You can't deny me this time, Tsingar. Not again. My uncle sent me with you to learn to command. By the Dark! How am I going to do that if I'm never given the chance?"

"You had your chance, *tergai*," Tsingar said, hands clenched in the sparse grass at his sides. He fought down the urge to yell, to say things he knew Aduhar would repeat to Mehdaiy, things that could put him in disgrace once again.

A swift, cold smile crossed Aduhar's face. "I'll fight you for it."

For a long moment Tsingar sat frozen, unable to reply. If he fought Aduhar, he would lose; he knew that, without deprecating his own skill. Aduhar was too good, too fast. Yet, if he did not fight, what would his commanders think?

He swallowed, hoped his nervousness went unnoticed in the twilight. "No." Suddenly, he jumped forward and grabbed Aduhar by a fold of his red cloak. "You listen to me, *tergai*. Your uncle spoke to me in private before we left. He told me you were to learn to serve, *tergai*. Serve! Do you know the meaning of the word?" He felt the sweat bead his forehead. "Tell me," he whispered, letting loose of Aduhar's cloak and shoving the young man away, "tell me, *tergai*, what's the punishment for disobedience to a commanding officer?"

Aduhar gathered his cloak up on his shoulder, his gaze still fixed on Tsingar's face. For a few moments, the tension was palpable. Then Aduhar dropped his eyes. "Death," he said, his voice very soft.

"Remember that," Tsingar snapped, sitting down, "the next time you think to challenge my orders."

The two hundred-commanders shifted uneasily. Tsingar looked at them; both were heavily shielded, and he could not guess what they were thinking.

"Lord," said Chevig. "Someone's coming."

A man walked up the hillside—Etenjai, another scout.

"Well?" Tsingar asked.

"Lord," Etenjai said, sitting down at Tsingar's side. "Mandahun and I just returned from the city."

"Where is he?"

"Hurt, Lord." The scout went on in a rush. "We got close to the city, Lord . . . very close. We waited there nearly all day and then started back. We stumbled across two Krotànya—scouts, I'd guess. We killed one and caught the other. We were going to break his mind, try to find out more about the city, but he got away."

Tsingar felt all his plans dissolve. "He got away. You good for nothing dung-head! How could you let him escape? He'll ride to the city and—"

"He won't go far, Lord," Etenjai said, shrinking before Tsingar's anger. "Not knifed in his back and his side."

Knifed twice. By the Gods! Was that enough? Tsingar shook his head, fighting off his rage. What was done was done. "How far away from the city were you when you found these Krotànya?"

"Over an hour's ride, Lord."

Tsingar took a deep breath. It would be amazing if the man could last half that time. He looked at Etenjai's shadowed face, wishing the light were better so he could see the man's eyes.

"Rest," he said. "As soon as you and the other scouts are able, return to the city. Stay several days if need be. I want to know if there's any pattern to the rides Kahsir's sister makes and, more importantly, whether or not that Krotànya scout made it back to the city alive." He looked off into the twilight. "Once we've established those things, we'll go after her."

Iowyn raced down the stairs, her boot heels loud on the stone, her heart beating raggedly as she neared the entry hall. A group of men had gathered by the opened doorway; faces blurred as she ran past them. She heard her name called—a hand grabbed at her sleeve.

"Lady Iowyn!"

Iowyn glanced sidelong and gestured for Jhadàvis to follow. The gathered men parted as she thrust her way among them, then ran down into the courtyard. The twilight air felt cool now that the sun had set.

She saw the horse first, then the man. *Lords of Light! It's one of my scouts!* Two warriors held the man upright between them, and from the limpness of his body, she thought him dead.

"No, Lady," one of the warriors said. "He's still alive. Barely. Is there a healer close by?"

"Jhada! There's a Mind-Born among the refugees. Go—"

But Jhadàvis had gone off at a run, heading toward the houses where the new band of refugees had taken up quarters. Iowyn stared at the unconscious man's face and recognized him in the torchlight. She licked her lips and looked up to the warriors who held him.

"It's Rehkor," she said. "Get him into the common room. Quickly."

She trotted up the stairs, scattering onlookers who clogged the doorway. They parted, drawing back into the entry hall, curious heads craning in the lamplight to see who had been brought wounded into this house.

Iowyn led the way into the empty common room, and stood undecided for a moment in its center.

"Get a blanket," she said to a man near the doorway. He ran off before she could add water and binding cloth to her wants. She drew a ragged breath. *What the Void's happened to Rehkor? Surely the enemy can't be this close to us yet!*

The two warriors carried Rehkor over to a corner of the common room and stretched him out on the floor. One made a pillow out of Rehkor's cloak, wadded and thrust under his head. The other looked up at Iowyn.

"Knifed," he said. "Twice."

Iowyn came closer: the long deep cut in Rehkor's side still oozed dark blood. She wondered that he was alive. He must have taken the other wound in the back. Footsteps thudded down the stairway. She looked up, saw the man she had sent off enter the room, blanket, binding cloth and a water jar in his hands.

Curious onlookers had gathered in the doorway to the common room, many spilling over into the room itself. Iowyn's head began to pound with the beginnings of a headache, and her chest tightened. "Leave us!" She gestured toward the courtyard. "He doesn't need an audience!"

They muttered among themselves, but most of them went quickly enough. The few who remained stood a good distance away, friends of the injured scout. Jhadàvis came into the entry hall, followed by a short, dark-skinned woman dressed in white. Iowyn felt the Mind-Born's power wash into the room.

"Lady." The woman walked to Iowyn's side, glanced down at Rehkor, then bowed. "I'm Ahthysa. May I serve you?"

"Him better," Iowyn said. "You're a healer?"

"Aye, Lady. Sometimes." The white-clad woman knelt by the scout.

Iowyn stepped around her to get a better view. "Talvir!" She motioned the man with the water jar forward. "Help the Lady Ahthysa."

"No." The Mind-Born looked up, her face hard to read. "There's nothing you can give him now, Lady, save burial."

Iowyn closed her eyes and swayed slightly on her feet. How . . . ? She found her voice with difficulty. "Can you Read him, Ahthysa?"

The Mind-Born nodded. "I'll try, Lady. I'm not trained for that, but I'll try." Her face seemed even darker in the lamplight. "Is there anything in particular—?"

"Who, Ahthysa," Iowyn said. "I want to know who did it. How long ago. The circumstances surrounding it. Everything you can pick up from him."

"Aye, Lady."

Iowyn heard someone drag a chair up behind her.

"Sit," Jhadàvis said.

Still not taking her eyes off the Mind-Born or the body, Iowyn sat down. She gnawed at her upper lip in frustration, then fought her mind under control: the Mind-Born hardly needed that distraction.

For a long time nothing seemed to happen, then the Mind-Born rocked back on her heels, rubbed her eyes, and looked across the room. Iowyn stood and gestured to her chair.

"My thanks, Lady," Ahthysa said, sitting down. Jhadàvis shoved another chair over.

Iowyn took it. "Were you able to Read him?"

"Aye." Ahthysa's voice was weary. "It was the enemy, Lady . . . two of them."

Iowyn stared, hearing the hiss of indrawn breaths around her.

"Rehkor and his companion were attacked from ambush," Ahthysa said. "The Leishoranya killed the other warrior and then tried to take Rehkor alive. Even though they knifed him, he escaped. Now, his memories become confused."

"Wine, Jhada, if you can find some," Iowyn said, holding the Mind-Born's gaze. "Slowly, Ahthysa. Try to remember everything."

The Mind-Born shook her head. "Remembering isn't the hard part, Lady. It's sorting this man's memories. There's a lot of overlapping information; part was his— the rest I think he sensed from the Leishoranya." Jhadàvis returned, extended a glass of wine to the Mind-Born. "From what I can tell," Ahthysa said, taking a quick swallow, "there's an enemy company hidden close to us here."

Iowyn's heart lurched, then beat steadily again. "How many?"

"Well over a hundred . . . likely two." She met Iowyn's eyes. "I'll share, Lady."

Iowyn nodded, opened her mind, and was suddenly filled with all the information Ahthysa had Read from Rehkor's body. For an agonizing moment she felt paralyzed, unable to think. What the Void was the enemy doing so far within Elyâsai's borders? Suddenly her throat tightened.

"Ahthysa," she said, "I know you're weary from your

Reading, but I have one more thing to ask. I need to contact my brother. If the enemy's as close as I'm afraid they are, then any Sending I make could be sensed. Could you aid me—help cloak my Sending?"

The Mind-Born nodded, took another swallow of wine. "That I can do with little trouble." She glanced down at Rehkor's body. "Now, Lady? Or later?"

Iowyn looked over her shoulder—Rehkor's friends and the two warriors who had carried him in from the courtyard waited silently. She rose and motioned them forward.

"I'm sorry," she said, her voice rough. She glanced at Jhadàvis, gesturing toward the doorway with her eyes, and then looked at the men. "I'll be there when you bury him."

They nodded; faces composed but touched with loss, the two warriors picked up the body between them. Jhadàvis led the way from the common room; Iowyn could hear her order the bystanders out of the way.

And now her Sending. A sudden cold thought: she knew it imperative to have one of the Mind-Born help shield the Sending with the enemy this close to Dramujh, yet all her memories of Kahsir were there and vulnerable. She stood silent for a long moment, fully shielded, and sought to bury those memories—to hide them far down in the dark recesses of her mind where Ahthysa could find them only if she knew they were there.

She looked at the doorway, saw it and the common room empty. Trusting she had hidden those memories sufficiently, she sat down again. "Now, Ahthysa, help with my Sending. The sooner I make it, the better."

Ahthysa nodded and settled back in her chair, holding her glass between her hands.

Iowyn sensed the Mind-Born's readiness and sought her own power. She closed her eyes, felt the touch of Ahthysa's mind on the surface of her own, the added strength that came from it. Fully hidden now, she reached for her brother.

—*Kahs!*

His surprise was genuine. *What's wrong, Io?*

—*Leishoranya. A company of them close to Dra-mujh. Likely to the south. Probably close to two hundred.*

For a long moment he did not reply. *You stay right where you are,* he Sent. *Don't dare go out like you've been doing in the past.*

—*I hadn't planned to. I think they're after me again.*

—*You're probably right. You still have the thousand men with you in Dramujh?*

—*Aye. If necessary, I could raise another five thousand from the home guard and citizenry.*

—*Are you certain of the enemy's number?*

—*Fairly. I've been aided by a Mind-Born, the Lady Ahthysa. She's the one who's helping cloak this message. The enemy killed one of my scouts and knifed the other. Somehow he made it to the city alive. He died shortly after he got here. What we know we got from him. Sensing the need for quickness, she filled her brother's mind with memories of events that had happened before and after.*

—*Can you give me this company's exact location?*

—*No. Try my memories again. What Ahthysa Read from Rehkor's body should be there.*

For a brief moment, Iowyn felt Kahsir's mind fully in her own, present with a new strength and power she had never sensed before.

—*I've got the location, or as close as your memories can provide.* He paused. *I'll bet the enemy sent a strike force north to get at you again if they can. Stay right where you are. Keep most of your warriors hidden—the enemy must be forced to guess at your strength. Your men still aren't wearing any insignia, are they?*

—*None.*

—*Excellent. That should confuse any enemy watchers.*

And under no circumstances leave the city. I'm coming north.

—*No, Kahs! You mustn't. That's exactly what they want you to do. Don't worry about me. I can handle things here. I simply wanted to let you know what's happened.*

There was a long pause: she felt the touch of something cold on Kahsir's mind.

—*I'm coming, Io.* The tone of his Sending forbade any argument. *Tomorrow. Sooner if I can.*

And suddenly, he was gone.

CHAPTER 14

Kahsir broke contact with his sister, opened his eyes and stared up at the tent ceiling. For a long moment he sat there, then he cursed softly, rose, threw his cloak about his shoulders, and left his tent.

It was cooler outside than he expected, even though the tent flap had been pulled aside. He waited a moment for his eyes to adjust to the dark, and then walked off toward the trees at the edge of camp. Someone called a friendly greeting as he passed; he lifted his hand, waved in the general direction of the voice, and kept walking.

Hints of his Dream were back—or at least part of it. The instant before he had promised he would go to Dramujh to help Iowyn, he had felt a brush of that Dream on his mind. And now it was gone again, leaving behind only hints of its presence.

Had he done the right thing? He paused, leaned his shoulder against a tree and stared off into the dark. Iowyn could undoubtedly take care of herself. Lords knew she had enough men; the enemy company, far from any reinforcements, could not begin to equal her manpower. All she had to do was stay in the city. He grimaced, familiar as he was with his sister's vacillating moods.

Yet he had Seen himself—Heard himself—telling Iowyn he would come . . . all through one of the doorways in his Dream.

Now he was committed, had said he was riding north to help her. He looked up at the sky, at the stars that shone in undiminished glory before the moons rose. What of his own men? If the enemy company Iowyn said lay hidden around Dramujh was near two hundred strong, he would need to take three hundred warriors with him. Now was no time for heroics and valiant stands. He needed a sure victory, an edge on the enemy. Three hundred men. Immediate departure. He had only six hundred warriors in camp with him at this time, and he could not afford to withdraw more from other key positions.

He cursed again and felt his shoulders tighten. Lords! Suddenly, everything had gone complicated beyond what he could have guessed. His men were exhausted. Only in the past day had this six hundred gathered from their various areas of patrol. Now, they rested, enjoying a brief respite before the enemy attacked again. He could hardly march them out at dawn, expect them to take the mind-road, and then be fit to fight afterward.

What had possessed him to tell Iowyn he could help her? He had been begging reinforcements from his grandfather for days now. But in the moment he had told her he would come to Dramujh, he could have done nothing else. *I'm trapped again, trapped in my Dream. Only this time it's gone. It's not there to guide me.*

He sighed. What was done was done—he could hardly back out at this stage. She was probably counting on him more than she would ever admit. He had no choice: he must gather what warriors he could and ride north with the help he had promised.

A gust of wind blew through the trees, rustling the new spring leaves above. He gathered his cloak about his shoulders, turned and walked into camp. Most of the men had gone to sleep now, stretched out under their blankets. He looked across the campsite, at the banked fires that burned in the darkness. Sentry change had taken place within the last half hour, so the men who stood watch would be alert and rested.

Pohlàntyr: he would have to tell his second-in-command what had happened. Then, he would need to ask for volunteers to ride north. Tomorrow morning . . he would do it then, after his men had rested. He snorted a laugh. *Trying to avoid what you've gotten yourself into?* he chided himself. *Do it, and quit stalling.*

A Sending to Pohlàntyr on the edge of his mind, he walked into his tent and drew up short.

"Lorj! What the Dark are *you* doing here?"

Lorhaiden turned toward the tent door, grinned and leaned back in his chair. "Drinking your wine," he said, gesturing to the cup sitting on the map table before him.

As Lorhaiden stood, Kahsir crossed the tent to his side in a few steps, and gripped his sword-brother's arm in greeting.

"Obviously you're drinking my wine," he said, motioning Lorhaiden to sit. He drew up another chair and sat down opposite. "But *why* are you here?"

"I've been in the capital. I finally got reinforcements—five hundred men. I thought I'd stop to see you before I went back to my own army."

Kahsir lifted one eyebrow. "And how did you manage to get reinforcements when the rest of us are crying for them?"

"I suppose—" Lorhaiden flushed slightly. "I was in another battle where I lost a lot of men."

"Where are they?"

"The five hundred?" Lorhaiden gestured vaguely. "Off to the west, several hills away. Hidden for the most part. You've got more of your warriors together than I've seen in awhile. Are you tired of raiding?"

"No." Kahsir reached for the wineskin that hung on the center pole and poured a cup of wine. "Periodic war council, that's all." He returned the wineskin to its place and leaned back in his chair. "Is Vahl all right?"

"Aye." Lorhaiden crossed one leg on his knee. "How's Iowyn doing with the refugees?"

Suddenly the problem returned—all of it. Kahsir took a long drink, then set his cup on the table.

"She's in trouble," he said. "I just had a Sending from her tonight. There's a Leishoranya company about two hundred strong somewhere around Dramujh. She thinks the enemy's after her, to use her against me."

Lorhaiden uncrossed his legs, leaned forward, arms across his knees. He reached for his wine. "Likely," he granted. His shadowed eyes glinted. "What are you going to do? Send her aid?"

"Aye." Kahsir stood, began to pace the length of the tent, his indecision returning. He looked at Lorhaiden. "Is Sammàndhir still commanding your army while you're gone?"

"No. Tahbril dàn Hravha."

"What happened to Sammàndhir? He's not—?"

"No. He's in the capital. He needed the rest."

"Huhn. This Tahbril . . . I've never heard of him."

"He's one of my hundred-commanders," Lorhaiden said, his face sharpening with curiosity. "Why?"

"Lorj—" Kahsir paused, then spoke quickly so Lorhaiden could not interrupt. "I want you to stay here . . . with my army. Only for a few days. You can go on to your own command when I return."

"When you *what*?"

"I've got to help Iowyn. I told her I would come."

"Why not send Pohlàntyr—"

"I'm leaving him here. He's been in command before. Lords know he's damn near seen as much of it as I have lately. But I'd feel better if you stayed with him. You could send half your warriors on west and keep the rest of them here. I'm going to be taking three hundred men with me when—"

"I'm going with you."

Kahsir sighed softly. "You've just arrived. And right now I need you here."

"You don't," Lorhaiden said, standing. "You just told me Pohlàntyr could take command."

Kahsir glared. "Dammit, Lorj. I'm not going to fight you about it. And don't try your shieldman arguments on me, either. You're a commander now, and we're running short of them. You're staying, and that's an order."

He caught his breath, realizing his voice had risen. Lorhaiden stared a moment, then sat down in his chair.

"Aye, Lord. But—"

"No more. Can't you see? I need your men here in place of those I'll be taking with me. If the enemy attacks while I'm gone . . ."

Lorhaiden nodded. "I can *see* that. But wouldn't it make more sense if I took my warriors, men fresh from—"

"No."

Lorhaiden's brow furrowed. "No?"

"No, you're not going. I'm more familiar with this area of the country than you are."

Lorhaiden reached for his cup and finished his wine. "Your argument's full of holes, but I'll stay if you like. When are you leaving?"

"I don't know. As soon as possible."

"Tonight?"

"I'd like to, but my men are too exhausted. Tomorrow afternoon, most likely. We'll have to take the mind-road and we're going to need help for that. Do you know the Mind-Born Stefendhi?"

"The healer? Aye."

"Good. Find him for me. We'll need his help in shielding. Tell him I want to leave as soon as possible." Kahsir began pacing the length of his tent again.

"And I'm going to need volunteers—three hundred men. Try to find archers, Lorj. I want to take as many bowmen with me as I can."

Lorhaiden stood. "At least take a hundred of my own men," he said, "or more. They're rested and yours are not." He stepped to the tent door. "I don't know any of the particulars about this thing, but from what I can sense, it's not going to be quick or easy."

Kahsir nodded reluctantly. "No, it's not," he agreed. He rubbed the bridge of his nose. "All right, Lorj. I'll take one hundred fifty of your men, the rest from my own." He met Lorhaiden's eyes. "And do your best while I'm away. I'll be depending on you."

Lorhaiden stood silent for a moment, nodded, and left the tent.

A fitful wind rustled the trees and brush. It smelled of rain again, and Tsingar frowned up at the evening sky. *Not now, Gods, not now. I'm sick to death of rain.* He leaned back on the hillside and stretched his legs out. An argument erupted close by in the dark and he hoped it would resolve itself. He was far too comfortable to get up and stop it.

I wonder where Aduhar is? Ever since I threatened him, he's avoided me. Probably out hunting allies. He spent all afternoon with the younger warriors. Tsingar shrugged. Not having to constantly endure Aduhar's barely civil presence was a pleasure; keeping an eye on him, a necessity. Aduhar was dangerous, more dangerous than Tsingar had calculated at first—not very subtle yet, but that would come with time. He was so young, so full of unbridled passions; if he could manage to stay alive, Gods protect anyone who got in his way when he was older.

Tsingar looked in the direction of the city where Iowyn stayed. *Damn! I wish I knew more about the city, how many warriors are in it. Those idiot scouts never have been able to give me a solid answer.* The city's strength was surely over the five hundred men everyone reported seeing; Dramujh lay in country the Krotànya would think very much their own. It was still a long ride to the fighting on the borders.

The brush rustled and Tsingar sat up straighter, waiting. The argument had broken off, either by mutual consent or because the men involved wanted to hear what was going on.

"Lord?"

Tsingar relaxed, recognizing Bhanikai, the last of his scouts to return from the city. Bhanikai sat down on the hillside and made himself comfortable.

"I just got here," he said in a low voice. "Kahsir's sister rode out again today, guarded as before. I still can't tell how many guard the city. I see warriors on the walls and in the fields close by, but never enough to make an accurate count."

"What's your estimate?"

Bhanikai paused before answering. "Speculation, Lord. I think there may be well over five hundred in the city. I'm sure I've seen enough different men to make up a greater number than we reckoned at first."

"There's no sign they know they're being watched?"

"Not that I can sense, Lord."

Something pulled at the edge of Tsingar's mind—an uneasiness he could not ignore. He looked toward the scout, but the other man was only a darker shadow in the shadowy night. "Mandahun and Etenjai killed a Krotàn late this afternoon. His companion escaped, but not before they knifed him twice. Now I'm beginning to think he might have made it back to Dramujh alive." The quarrel began again, only this time the voices had grown louder. "That's all, Bhanikai," Tsingar said. "Get some rest. And tell those two idiots in the brush over there that if they're so damned eager to fight, I'll truss them and drop them down in front of the city."

"Aye, Lord."

Tsingar leaned back on the hillside, listened to the scout move off through the night. The two voices kept arguing; another, Bhanikai's, overrode them. Silence fell; the brush rustled again and then was still.

Damn, it's quiet! Too quiet. And those dung-headed fools I lead—I'll go mad keeping them hidden and away from each other's throats! A twig snapped off in the darkness and Tsingar jumped. *Gods, I'm on edge. I suppose fighting with Aduhar hasn't helped that.* Tsingar shifted position and swatted at something buzzing around his ear.

If he was correct in assuming that at the most one thousand men guarded the city, perhaps he stood a chance of taking it, *if* he had reinforcements. A lightning strike against a city totally unprepared to defend itself had worked before. If he could approach Dramujh in the darkest part of night after the moons had set . . . if the Krotànya had left the gates open. . . . If, if. He spat off into the brush. He could not attack on the weight of ifs. And yet—

He sat up straighter. He knew it a danger to make a Sending so deep in Krotànya territory, but he was better than most at masking his thoughts. He scratched at the insect bite. It seemed worth the chance.

"Hsst!" He whispered into the darkness. "Chevig! Come here!"

The brush rustled as the hundred-commander walked up the hillside.

"I'm going to contact Mehdaiy," Tsingar said. "Help me cloak the Sending."

"Is that wise, Lord?"

"You question me?"

"No, Lord," Chevig said, sitting down.

Tsingar closed his eyes, concentrated on Mehdaiy's location, and felt Chevig's mind touch his own. Chevig had a real talent for this, and Tsingar needed the support if he hoped to slip this Sending past the Krotànya Mind-Born. Drawing a deep breath, he reached out with his mind and found Mehdaiy awake, seated in his tent.

—*Dread Lord,* he Sent.

—*Tsingar? What the Void are you doing?*

—*A possible problem, Lord. I need advice.*

—*Quickly, then. You're cloaked, but not well enough.*

—*We've watched the city, Master. As far as I can tell, none of the Krotànya have noticed us. But late this afternoon two of my men ran across Krotànya scouts returning to Dramujh. They killed one, but the other escaped. I spoke with one of the men when he returned to camp. He swore he and his companion had mortally wounded the Krotàn who got away.*

Mehdaiy was a long time answering. *So? And for this news you risk a Sending?*

—*There's more, Dread Lord.* Tsingar swallowed and kept an iron grip on his mind. *I'm beginning to think the Krotàn didn't die, that he lived long enough to make it to the city. If so, Kahsir's sister must know we're out here. I haven't been able to get a firm count on how many warriors are in the city, but I'd guess it at not much more than a thousand. I think the only way I can get at Iowyn is to attack the city by night.*

—*Attack the city?* Mehdaiy echoed. *Idiotic! Even if I did send you reinforcements, how can you conceive of attacking the city when you don't know how many men defend it? You say you think they might have one thousand? What about all the refugees? The citizens of the city who still live there? And what of Krotànya troops who might be close to the city? Do you think they wouldn't notice? Use your brain! If Iowyn's as good as you say she is, she's not stupid. Don't complicate matters. Wait. Watch the city. You'll get a chance at her.*

—*But, Master.* Tsingar gathered his thoughts, tried to keep the urgency from them. *If we stay hidden much longer, I can't answer for what might happen to my men. They're already fighting among themselves.*

Mehdaiy's amusement stung like fire. *Are you a commander or a nursemaid? Tell those fools to obey you—obey you, or die.*

—*Aye, Master.*

—*Don't try this again, Tsingar, unless your need is truly urgent. I've shielded you as much as I can. If the Krotànya Mind-Born noticed your Sending, only the Gods can help you now.*

Mehdaiy broke contact with startling suddenness. Once more, Tsingar sat on the hill, Chevig at his side, the fitful wind rattling the leaves around him.

"Lord?" asked Chevig. "The Sending—?"

"Well done," Tsingar said, allowing none of his dismay to color his voice. *Idiot, am I?* Mehdaiy's accusation hurt. *We'll see how much of an idiot I am. I'll make this plan succeed in spite of my lack of men.* Tsingar rubbed the back of his neck, swatted at another insect, and stared off into the dark. "Talk to the scouts. Tell them I want the watch on Dramujh doubled. The land around it, the places of cover where we might hide—I want to know that, too. We'll get our hands on Iowyn only by surprise and stealth." He smiled in anticipation, some of his confidence returning. "When the time comes, I want us to be ready. Now, go!"

Kahsir rocked back on his heels and looked down at his saddlebags, at all the things he planned to take. His hands clenched on his knees. Damn! Somehow, two hundred Leishoranya had managed to ride undetected deep into Krotànya lands. Though the enemy company had penetrated far enough behind Krotànya defensive lines to make receiving reinforcements difficult, they had come with too few men to be planning an actual assault on the city. Lords only knew how long they might have been hiding in the hills.

He rubbed his eyes. Two hundred enemy. Why the

Dark had the Mind-Born not detected such a serious breach in defenses? The moment he asked himself the question, Kahsir had the answer: a diversion somewhere—something that had momentarily drawn the Mind-Borns' attention from the borders they guarded. The Mind-Born would have to be told what happened, yet he dared not make a Sending. *They'll sense what I've done, sure as rain. Maybe Grandfather can relay the information. He should know what's happened anyway. Huhn. He didn't help me when I asked him before. Why start now? I'll tell Iowyn to let the Mind-Born know, so—*

Someone scratched on the tent door. Kahsir turned, looked over his shoulder, and saw Ahndrej.

"Come in, Dreja," he said, returning his attention to his saddlebags. "I thought you were standing sentry tonight."

"I was. I found another to watch in my place."

He glanced up as Ahndrej entered the tent. "Why? You volunteered to—"

"You've spoken with Iowyn," Ahndrej interrupted, standing just behind Kahsir's left shoulder, "haven't you?"

Kahsir hitched around, balanced on one knee, and looked up into Ahndrej's expressionless face. "Aye," he said, keeping his voice level. "I have."

"She's in danger, isn't she?"

Dammit, Lorj! If you told Dreja what's happening, I'll—

"Lorhaiden said nothing to me. I haven't spoken with him."

Shields locked in place, Kahsir looked at Ahndrej, seeking something of the man he had known. Ahndrej stared back, dark face inscrutable, all harsh planes and shadows in the lamplight.

"Dreja—"

"She's in danger," Ahndrej repeated, his eyes glittering in the lamplight.

Kahsir sighed. "Not now."

"Aye, not now." Ahndrej's voice was flat, leached of emotion. "But she *could* be . . . and soon. I can sense that."

"Not if she uses her head. She's not unprotected in the city."

"Still, her chances of meeting danger have increased, haven't they? Enough so that she let you know she faced trouble? I know you and I know your sister. I don't have to read your thoughts to know you're going north."

Kahsir glanced away. *O Lords! Here it comes.* He stood and looked down at Ahndrej. "Aye, Dreja. You're right. I'm going north."

"And I'm coming with you."

"You are *not*! I'll have all the men I need, and you'll be of far more help to me here."

Ahndrej shifted his weight. His jaw tightened and he gestured sharply. "You've got plenty of other men who—"

"Enough!" Kahsir motioned to one of the chairs. "Sit. It's time you and I had a talk." Ahndrej stiffened and set his jaw. "Sit, dammit!" Ahndrej's resolve crumbled, and he did as he was told, sat and looked off at some unseeable point on the tent wall. Kahsir took the other chair. "I don't know what's going on in your mind anymore, Dreja. It's been closed—sealed against anyone for days upon days now." He tried to meet Ahndrej's eyes. "What the Dark's happened to you? What's changed you so?"

Ahndrej's head jerked around. "*You* should know that—you of all people."

"Vharcwal." Kahsir kept his voice level. "Aye. But the path you've chosen for yourself isn't the best . . . for you or for those around you."

"You say that, while your shieldman—"

"Leave Lorhaiden out of this! We're talking about you, not him. Even when he was young, Lorj had a bent for vengeance. You did not. It's not in your nature to—"

"Who's to say what my nature is," Ahndrej said. "Things change, Lord; people change, too. The path I choose to walk is my business and no one else's."

Lord, is it now? Kahsir bit back angry words he would later regret saying. "So. You've chosen your path." He leaned forward in his chair. "Consider Lorhaiden, since you brought him into this. He's chosen his path, too . . . oathed himself to it. Has that made it any easier for those around him to understand? Extremes in anything are dangerous; before Vharcwal, you would have agreed with that." He sought Ahndrej's eyes again, and this time made contact. "Don't lose yourself, Dreja. Don't bury yourself beneath a load of vengeance." He drew a deep breath. "Have you ever thought about Iowyn?"

Ahndrej looked away. "If she loves me," he murmured, "she'll accept it. Just as *you* have learned to accept Lorhaiden's ways."

"Dammit, Dreja! You can't bring your family back! They're dead . . . gone! Nothing you do can change that. You can kill Leishoranya from now until the Last Day, and your brother, his wife, their children . . . they'll all be just as dead."

Ahndrej's hands clenched and his shoulders tightened; he looked up. "You're damned cruel."

"Me? What about *you*—the way you've treated my sister! Why the Dark did you turn on her, Ahndrej? All she wanted was to comfort you. And since you left her—you haven't Sent to her once, have you?"

Ahndrej was silent.

"Answer me. I'm at least owed that much."

"There are some things between your sister and me that aren't meant to be aired in front of other people. Even you."

"Then you'd better be a little quicker about solving your problems. And as for your family . . . your family's buried. Out of your reach. You can't bring them back. Ever."

"Speak to me when *you've* lost," Ahndrej said, his voice raw with bitterness, "when those you loved and cared for have been murdered. Then I'll listen."

"You fool!" Kahsir snapped. "You idiotic, blind fool! Speak to you when *I've* lost? Lords of Light, Dreja! Where have you been all these years? What's happened to your memory? I've lost . . . Lords know how I've lost. My mother, my grandmother—at the hands of the enemy. Do they count for nothing?" He stared off into the shadows in the tent. "We found enough of my grandmother's body to bury after the Leishoranya were through with it. And I watched my mother die . . . *watched!* Powerless to do anything at all." He tried to hide those memories again, shut them off from his conscious mind. "Not a one of us hasn't lost in this war. Don't think yourself so *fihrkken* unique!"

Ahndrej kept silent, staring once more at his feet. He shifted his weight, looked up. "So you fight for the living, then?"

"Aye. For the living, for those unborn. But I can't bring the dead back. None of us can do that."

"Then I'll fight for those still alive. For Iowyn." Ahndrej sat up straighter, his shoulders squared. "You can't keep me from riding with you."

Kahsir closed his eyes, rubbed them with the heels of his hands. "I can," he said, "and I will. I turned down Lorhaiden's offer to accompany me, and he's my shieldman. You don't have an oath to bind you to my side."

"No," Ahndrej said, his face still and remote. "I don't. But I have Iowyn."

Kahsir sighed. "I want you *here*, Dreja. I need your skill in border fighting. Lords know you're good at it. You're one of the best I have. It's *because* of Iowyn that I forbid you to come with me. Since she's involved—since she could be in danger—you won't be thinking clearly."

Ahndrej smiled thinly. "And you?" he asked. "What will her danger do to you? Make you think more *logically*?" He snorted a laugh. "Try another argument. That one won't work."

Kahsir cursed softly. He stood, walked to his saddle-bags and knelt. "I suppose not," he said, resuming his packing. "Come along then, Dreja. I can't seem to keep you from it."

CHAPTER 15

The midday sun shone warm on his shoulders as Kahsir brought his horse from the mind-road to a hilltop just northeast of Dramujh. His company followed; Stefendhi had brought them all to this point, cloaked and, so far as Kahsir could tell, unnoticed by the enemy.

Turning in the saddle, he watched the last of his men appear on the wide hilltop. Stefendhi sat mounted somewhat to one side, his young face taut with concentration as he watched the gateway; when the last of Kahsir's men had left the gate, it dissolved behind them into a million fragments of starlight. Kahsir edged his horse away from the other men and studied the hills nearby, then the city of Dramujh which held the highest of those hills.

The city lay quiet now at midday; the tile roofs of its buildings caught and held the sun in an eye-watering glare. Distant figures manned the city walls, speartips glittering in the light. To the left ran the only road that led to Dramujh from the southeast. Kahsir frowned, his eyes following the course it took between the hills. None too safe, that road; an ambush could be launched from any of the nearby hillsides.

He turned to the hilltop where his men were waiting, gestured broadly to either side of the hill, and the warriors drifted away into the undergrowth. He dismounted, stretched the tension from his shoulders, and removed his helm to run a hand through his hair. A slight wind blew out of the south, pleasant in the midday warmth.

"Tirril!"

One of the hundred-commanders stood nearby, loosening the cinch on his saddle; as Kahsir called his name, he glanced up. "Aye, Lord?"

"Get all the men in hiding. I want them to rest . . . *each* of them. This was no easy riding. Only those who volunteered to stand sentry should be on their feet."

"Aye, Lord."

Kahsir reset his helm and reached for the reins; leading his horse across the hilltop to a grove of small trees, he loosened the girth and tethered the animal to a sapling. Rubbing his horse's chin, he took his waterskin down from the saddle and drank.

I'll have to Send to Iowyn and tell her we've arrived. He rubbed his eyes. Later. He needed to rest now. Any Sending he made at this point would be ragged and easily sensed.

Would it? Tired as I am, I could still—

He silenced the inner voice, clamping down on his mind with ruthless strength. Pouring a handful of water, he offered it to his horse, let it drink, then poured another. After his horse was finished, he restopped the waterbag, hung it on his saddle and sat down beneath one of the trees.

Now that he was here, what next? Iowyn thought the enemy had hidden themselves to the south of the city and, looking at the fold of one hill leading to another, he agreed. Likely to the southwest. They had to be aware of the traffic that went down the road and had doubtless picked a campsite far away from it.

Damn! If I hadn't been so eager to help Iowyn, I

might have had more time to think this through. My Dream's trapped me into taking action again, like it did before I rescued her. Only this time I can't see a clear pathway to take.

And where was that Dream now? Still hidden, save for hints, as it had been since Iowyn's rescue. He cursed softly. In the cold light of reason, he would have found it easier to simply send her reinforcements.

But he had promised, given his word, and he could not back out at this stage. Somehow, *something* would come out of what he had done . . . something important enough to lie in his Dream.

Suddenly, his heart lurched and he sat up straighter and looked around. His men had concealed themselves in the brush and trees on the hilltop and down its sides. From where he sat, he could see no one. But something jarred his sense of rightness. Ahndrej. Where was Ahndrej?

He cursed, rose, and walked out from the small grove and scanned the hilltop. A few horses stood visible, tethered to small trees. He opened his mind, searching among his hidden men.

"Tirril!"

The hundred-commander's head appeared from behind a tree. His eyes were sleepy and his face slack with weariness. "Aye, Lord?"

"Have you seen Ahndrej?"

Tirril stood, shook his head, and came to Kahsir's side. "No, Lord. Not since leaving. He was riding right behind you, wasn't he?"

"Aye. But I can't sense him anywhere. Was he one of those who offered to stand sentry? That would be like him."

"No, Lord. I don't believe so."

"Find him for me, Tirril. It's important. I want to talk with him."

"Aye, Lord."

The hundred-commander walked off across the

hilltop, stopping now and then at places where other
men had stretched out to rest. Kahsir rubbed the back
of his neck. Where the Dark was Ahndrej? He began
to pace, then went off on his own search.

He returned to the hilltop at last, having found
nothing; no one he had talked to had seen Ahndrej.
Pebbles rattled behind him: Kahsir turned as Tirril
came to his side, threading a way between several
large boulders.

"Well?"

"Gone, Lord. Not a trace."

"Ah, *chuht*!" Kahsir looked off toward the city.
"Where's Stefendhi?"

"Asleep, Lord. He was most exhausted of us all, I
think."

"Small wonder. My thanks, Tirril. Go back to sleep."

The hundred-commander blinked in the strong sunlight, bowed slightly, and returned to his place in the
brush. Kahsir walked down to the other end of the
grove; Stefendhi's horse stood tethered to a tree, and
the young Mind-Born lay stretched out beneath the
bushes. The instant Kahsir stepped closer, Stefendhi's
eyes opened.

"Lord?" he said, moving from sleep to alertness in
an instant. "What's wrong?"

Kahsir hunkered down on his heels, held a branch
of the bush away from his face. "I'm not sure. Make a
search for me—a heavily cloaked search. I can't find
Ahndrej."

Stefendhi hitched up on his elbows. "He was with
us when we left the mind-road. Are you sure he's not
off somewhere sleeping?"

"I couldn't find him. Tirril looked, too. No one's
seen him since we arrived."

"I'll search, then."

Kahsir moved back fractionally, giving the Mind-
Born more room. Stefendhi sat up, rubbed his eyes,

then closed them. Even close as he knelt to the Mind-Born, Kahsir could sense only a hint of power, so skilled was Stefendhi's search. Time seemed to drag. A fly buzzed around Kahsir's ears; he brushed it away with his free hand. Finally, Stefendhi opened his eyes.

"He's not here, Lord," he said, his gaze still slightly unfocused. "I could find everyone else. But not Ahndrej."

"You're *sure* he was with us when we left the mind-road?"

Stefendhi nodded. "Absolutely. I kept track of each man who rode with us and each who came to this hill-top."

"*Aii'ya!*" Kahsir drew a deep breath. "My thanks, Stefendhi."

"Wait, Lord . . . I'll try again. He *was* here."

Kahsir shook his head. "No, Stefendhi. Rest. I'll call you if I need you."

"But—"

"Rest, Stefendhi."

The Mind-Born nodded and stretched out again. Kahsir stood, let the branch swing back, and turned away. For a moment, he stood undecided. *O Lords! Where is that* fihrkken *idiot? He left the mind-road with the rest of us on this hilltop. I know it!* He walked out into the sunlight, paused and stared down the hillside. His shoulders tensed. *Lords of Light! The fool's gone off! That's the only answer. He's gone to Iowyn!*

Or—with a scowl—*after the enemy.*

He began to pace, hands locked behind his back. *No. That's Lorhaiden's way. Ahndrej hasn't turned that crazy! Yet. O Lords! Keep him from that! I can't take two of them!*

He scowled again. *Here I am, hidden with my men on a brushy hilltop, the enemy off in their camp somewhere to the southwest, and Ahndrej disappears! Damn him! I should have guessed this would happen. Nothing the idiot*

*does anymore is predictable! And I can't make a search
for him without giving away my position.*

And why not? he asked himself. *With my powers I
could—*

He refused the temptation and returned to his place
in the trees. There was little he could do about it—little
anyone could do, given the present circumstances.
Ahndrej was on his own.

Late afternoon sunlight slanted down through the
trees, and though he sat in the shade Tsingar felt
warm. His fingers drummed a nervous rhythm on his
knee and he jerked his hand away. It was quiet on the
hillside; most of his men were either asleep or farther
down the slope in the clearing where the cooks had
set up mess.

Tsingar cursed softly. Kahsir's sister had not ridden
out from the city all day; the scouts who had returned
to camp agreed on that. In fact, there had been little
activity in the city at all. Such a departure from habit-
ual actions told much. Though knifed, the Krotànya
scout must have lived long enough to return to Dramujh and report of the ambush. Tsingar could only
guess at what else.

"Scouts, Lord."

Tsingar straightened; Khartu, one of his hundred-
commanders, pushed through the undergrowth and sat
down at his side.

"They've got a Krotàn with them," Khartu said.

"Ah?"

"Bound and unconscious, Lord."

Tsingar listened to the rustling coming closer, drew his
boot-dagger, and buried it point down close at hand.

The brush parted and two of his scouts struggled to
his side. Behind them, they dragged the unconscious
body of a Krotànya warrior, hands and feet securely
bound. A small tree caught at one of the captive's
empty scabbards. The shorter of the two scouts cursed,

jerked the scabbard away, and helped his companion lay the warrior at Tsingar's feet.

Tsingar leaned forward, looked at the Krotàn, and stiffened with a jolt of familiarity.

"Where did you find this one?" he asked.

"Trying to sneak around to the north gate, Lord," the first scout said. His arm oozed blood from a long, shallow sword cut. "He's the Void's own fighter. It took Duhvul and me both to bring him down, and then only because I hit him from behind."

"Turn him over, Ghitoka. I want to look at his face."

Ghitoka roughly shoved the unconscious man over onto his back. It was one of the short ones—the dark-skinned Krotànya. Tsingar stared at the slack face and scratched at a healing bug bite. He had seen this man before . . . somewhere.

The underbrush snapped and cracked. Tsingar looked up from the bound warrior; Aduhar stood there, boot-knife unsheathed in his hand.

"Shall we play with him a bit?" Aduhar asked, smiling coldly. His eyes met Tsingar's. "We haven't had any amusement around here for days. Perhaps a few small cuts on the face to wake him . . . make him tell us what he knows."

"Sit down, Aduhar," Tsingar said in a flat voice. "We'll get the information we want. I think I've seen him before."

"Remember that while I work at him." Aduhar grinned and sat down by the Krotàn's head—a quick flick of his knife opened a short cut over the Krotàn's left eye. The man turned his head away and groaned. "For that matter, why not kill him? He probably doesn't know anything new."

Tsingar leaned over, caught Aduhar's knife-hand in his own, and jerked it away. "I said, leave him alone. Can't you hear?"

Aduhar struggled briefly, then shrugged. "Going soft in your old age, Tsingar?"

Tsingar dropped Aduhar's knife-hand, glared at the young man for a long moment, then looked down at the Krotàn's face. Suddenly, memory took him to that steading he and his men had burned. That was it. Could this man have been—

"At least let me wake him up for you," Aduhar offered, driving his fist into the unconscious man's abdomen, then twisting his hand savagely. The Krotàn whimpered, jerked with pain; he gasped loudly and his eyes fluttered open.

"Aduhar!" Tsingar snapped. "Get out of here. Now!"

Aduhar's eyes narrowed; he set his jaw and flexed his shoulders, but at last stood and stalked off through the brush, muttering as he went. Tsingar stared after him for a moment, then looked down into the dark face. This man had ridden with Kahsir's sister—he was sure of it. Could this be her lover?

Recognition and just a hint of fear crossed the Krotàn's face, instantly replaced by cold hatred. He struggled in his bounds, cursed in his own tongue, then glared at Tsingar, blinking away the blood that ran into the corner of his eye.

Tsingar reached for his boot-knife, lifted it in one hand, and made a show of testing its sharpness. Let the fool think *he* had cut him, not Aduhar. He searched his mind for what few words of the Krotànya language he knew.

"Iowyn," he said. "She . . . you . . ." He made a rude gesture with his hands.

The Krotàn leapt against the ropes that held him fast; Ghitoka and Duhvul both held him down on the hillside. Tsingar smiled. What a stroke of luck! This man was Iowyn's lover. Now Tsingar had a lure the Princess would be unable to resist.

The Krotàn yelled something, his words interspersed with strangled gasps. Tsingar tried to catch what he said, but it all came too fast. He heard the words for brother, for death. Suddenly, things started to make sense. The steading. It had been this man's steading, not his brother's. Tsingar closed his eyes, quit listening to the words, and tried to sense what was in the Krotàn's mind. He found that difficult, for few rational thoughts escaped.

The yelling finally got on Tsingar's nerves. He reached out, left-handed, and slapped the man into silence. For a long moment, he held the Krotàn's hate-filled stare, then looked away.

"What's he talking about, Lord?" asked Khartu.

"Something about a steading, about his brother being killed." Tsingar smiled. "I think I did that. It was when Aduhar and I rode north to go after Kahsir's sister. We killed the family who lived in the steading Kahsir and his sister were riding to. I think it was this man's steading, that the people we killed were his family." He rubbed his chin. "I *knew* I'd seen him before, but I thought I'd killed him."

"Who is he, Lord?"

"Her lover," Tsingar said. He glanced down at the Krotàn, who was struggling again. The man glared back, said something quick in an icy voice, then fell silent as Tsingar lifted his fist. Tsingar looked at Khartu. "I think we've finally got her. You know how these Krotànya are. The women are fiercely loyal to their men. I'll bet if she knows we've got her lover, she'll react."

"How can we let her know, Lord," asked Duhvul, "short of dragging him out before the city itself?"

"There are ways," Tsingar said, wiping the knife blade on his pants leg and sheathing the weapon in his boot. He looked down at the Krotàn, and nudged him in the chest with his toe. "You . . . Iowyn," he said, lifting an eyebrow. "You . . . she . . . " He made the rude gestures again.

The prisoner cried out in rage, his words running together, and Tsingar made the gestures more graphic. Blind with anger now, the Krotàn tore at his bindings, cursed and spat. Tsingar quickly touched the Krotàn's crotch with a boot toe. "Good, heh, Krotàn? She good?"

The Krotàn howled in anger now, and suddenly, Tsingar sensed what he had been waiting for: a Sending . . . a Sending of great power, aimed at the city. The Krotàn Sent again and Tsingar briefly caught part of it. He had hoped for this: the Krotàn had called to Iowyn, told her he was a prisoner, and begged her not to leave the city for any reason. Tsingar let the man Send a third time, then kicked him in the chin.

"Enough!" he snarled. The Krotàn fell silent, licked at the blood seeping from the corner of his mouth; only his eyes moved, and Tsingar flinched inwardly from the hatred in them. He looked up at Khartu and the two scouts. "So. You see how easily he obliges us? If Iowyn didn't Hear that Sending, she's Deaf!"

"What do we do with him now?" asked Khartu.

"Keep him bound. Tightly. You saw how he fought. The last thing I want is for this one to escape." He looked at the two scouts. "Duhvul . . . Ghitoka. Tie him to a tree—a stout tree. Make sure he's not harmed."

Duhvul nodded at Ghitoka, and the two of them took the prisoner by the armpits and ankles and dragged him off. The Krotàn twisted in their grasp, trying to squirm his way free, and then began cursing again; Ghitoka's voice overrode the angry words and the captive fell silent. Tsingar smiled and leaned back on the hillside.

"And now, Lord?" Khartu asked.

"Now we wait," Tsingar said, and glanced at his companion. "Iowyn will react to her lover's Sending. She'll probably guess we're luring her into a trap, so we'll need him to goad her into action." He grinned and lifted his hand, slowly clenching it into a fist. "We've got her, Khartu. I think we've got her at last!"

*   *   *

The garden darkened and trembled before Iowyn's eyes, birdsong only a memory. She shivered in the warm sunlight, saw only gathering shadows, and swayed on her feet.

"Lady! My Lady Iowyn! What be happening?"

A voice . . . someone had called her name. Iowyn blinked, shook her head, and the garden reappeared—calm, sun-filled and quiet. She gasped and sat down on a stone bench beneath one of the trees.

"My Lady . . . be you all right?"

She turned her head: Jhadàvis knelt at her side.

"Dreja . . ." Unable to go on, Iowyn licked her lips with a dry tongue, and tried again. "It's Ahndrej. . . . Didn't you Hear the Sending, Jhada?"

"What Sending, Lady? I Heard nothing." Jhadàvis sat down on the bench. "Are you sure you be all right?"

Iowyn drew a deep, sobbing breath and stared up into the branches. "It's Ahndrej. The Leishoranya have got him."

Jhadàvis frowned. "Where be he, Lady? And how did they take him—be Kahsir come north to help us?"

Iowyn stared at her hands clenched tightly on her knees. "I'm not sure where Dreja is, Jhada—somewhere off to the southwest. I don't know how the Leishoranya caught him, but if he's here, then Kahsir's somewhere close by."

"Stay here, Lady," Jhadàvis said. "I'll be back."

Iowyn nodded, closed her eyes, then shuddered briefly. Not only had Ahndrej fallen prisoner to the enemy, but his Sending indicated the Leishoran who held him was the same one who had slaughtered his family. She rubbed her eyes, and stared off at the garden wall.

"Lady."

Jhadàvis stood at her side, a glass of wine in her extended hand. Iowyn took the offered cup, drank, and held it tightly.

"Be you better now?" Jhadàvis asked.

Iowyn nodded slowly; panic would not help Ahndrej. "Go find the Lady Ahthysa. I don't care what she's doing. Bring her to me."

"Lady," Jhadàvis said and left.

Iowyn looked down into her cup and finished the last of the wine. Her heart began to beat raggedly; she drew a long breath to calm it, then set the cup down on the bench at her side, rose and began to pace.

How the Leishoranya had caught Ahndrej no longer mattered. She felt certain they would use him as bait to draw her out. Disturbed as Ahndrej had become, he would not have made the trip north without Kahsir. And where *was* Kahsir? Why had he not made a Sending if he camped close by? She frowned and blinked away sudden tears.

Footsteps grated on the stone stairs. She turned as Lady Ahthysa and Jhadàvis came down into the garden.

"My Lady Iowyn," the Mind-Born said. "How may I help you?"

Iowyn's voice shook as she spoke. "I need to make a Sending," she said, certain she had all memories of what Kahsir had done in his rescue deeply buried. "I think Kahsir's somewhere around the city, possibly in the hills to the north. Find him if you can. I need to talk to him, and it's of utmost importance that the enemy senses none of this."

"I'll do my best, Lady."

The Mind-Born closed her eyes, silent in the late afternoon sunlight. She looked much like some statue there in the garden, the bright flowers behind her, her white robes brilliant in the light. Iowyn waited quietly, not even daring to move. Finally, Ahthysa opened her eyes.

"I've found him, Lady," she said. "He's in the hills northeast of the city, as you suspected. He and his army arrived around midday. Nearly all of his men are asleep, wearied from the mind-road."

Iowyn nodded. "Thank you. Now, the Sending." She

picked up her glass, handed it to Jhadàvis, then motioned to the bench. "Sit, Ahthysa."

The Mind-Born complied and Iowyn joined her. Closing her eyes, she sensed Ahthysa's patient waiting; then Ahthysa's mind joined hers, guiding her thoughts to where Kahsir lay hidden.

—*Kahs! Are you awake?*

His mind filled hers, immediate, clear and strong. *Aye, Io. You're cloaked well. Is it the Lady Ahthysa again?*

She Sent affirmation, then hesitated. *Ahndrej*—

—*Have you heard from him? He was with us when we came to this hilltop, but now he's gone.*

She fought to keep her mind steady. *He's been taken prisoner by the Leishoranya company that lies to the south.*

—*I was afraid of that,* Kahsir returned bitterly. *He was probably trying to get into the city to see you.*

—*How could you let him go off like that? How?*

—*Dammit, Io!* His mind cracked whip-sharp across hers. *Don't you start, too. I didn't let him do anything! He had gone before anyone knew it. As for him being here—I tried to keep him from coming. I guessed he might do something stupid like this.* He paused and she sensed his uneasiness. *They'll use him to draw you out of the city. You know that, don't you?*

—*Aye. But I want to come to you. I've got to find him.*

—*Come to me? I'm in the opposite direction from him. Get a hold on yourself, Io! Think!*

She flinched slightly. *Then I'll go out on my own to*—

—*Have you lost your mind? You're not going anywhere! You understand me? You're staying right there.*

—*Kahs. . . .*

—*Don't, Io. Don't fight me. My temper's not the best right now as far as Ahndrej is concerned.*

Her throat tightened. *You can't keep me here. If I*

want to leave, I'll—

—Io!

She recoiled before his anger.

—You listen to me, and listen well. The last thing I need is you set against me, too. Ahndrej has caused me enough grief as it is. If you're so damned bent on helping him, listen to what I say.

—All right. I'll listen.

—Let the Leishoranya think you've fallen for their bait. Not now, mind you. I don't want you to stir from the city for at least another day.

—But they'll do something terrible to him if I don't—

—That's his problem.

She shrank before the coldness in Kahsir's Sending.

—When you hear from me next, he continued, *gather a small company of men, around fifty or so. I don't want you taking more. Fifty will be a bait the enemy can't resist. Take the road and ride south as if you're going to hunt for Ahndrej. By then I'll have my company hidden in the hills near the road.*

—How many men did you bring with you?

—Three hundred. We've got a Mind-Born with us and arrived undetected. The Leishoranya will only see you and your fifty warriors. I want to force the enemy's hand . . . make him do what he hadn't planned. And I'll need your help in this.

—I'll do whatever I can.

—Good. I want you to alert the thousand troops you have in the city that they might have to move out at any time. Keep your Mind-Born ready to make and receive Sendings.

—Done, Kahs. Anything else?

—No. Until you leave, stay hidden. Don't even show yourself on the walls. Let's make the Leishoranya guess what we're going to do next.

CHAPTER 16

Tsingar looked down at the dried meat he held in his hands and grimaced. He could do little about the food he and his men had shared since they had taken up hiding. Even though he had revealed his presence to Kahsir's sister through her lover's Sending, he still refused to allow his men to build small cooking fires. They grumbled and cursed, but he knew better. He and his company might be hidden, and shielded from all but a concerted effort of many of the Mind-Born, but it would not take many Krotànya to destroy them. He ran a risk of being discovered every day he lingered here, this far behind the front lines.

Finished eating, he rubbed his hands on the grass and looked off through the sunlit bushes. The Krotàn had cursed half the night, never seeming to run out of breath, and it had been a relief when he had fallen asleep at last. In an odd way, Tsingar admired the man: anyone who could sustain such a maddened rage this long was worthy of some respect.

He rose, pushed his way from the bushes and walked down the hillside to where the captive sat bound to a tree. Moving silently, he stopped just beyond the Krotàn's view and watched. Dried blood still caked the Krotàn's chin and forehead, but he was silent now, glowering at the two men Tsingar had chosen as his guards. Tsingar stepped forward and, at the sound of rustling undergrowth, the captive glanced up.

"Have you fed him yet?" Tsingar asked the guards.

"Aye, Lord," one said.

The other man grinned slightly. "Don't get close to him, Lord. He'll bite your hand off. We had to make him eat from the ground like a dog."

Tsingar sat down in such a position so he could watch the Krotàn. "I'm thirsty. Do you have water?"

"Aye, Lord." The first guard found his waterskin and extended it. He jerked a thumb at the captive. "Damn fool's been cursing us all morning long."

Tsingar drank and returned the waterskin. "Did you pick up any of his thoughts?"

"A few," the second guard said. "Nothing important."

The Krotàn continued to glare at Tsingar through narrowed eyes. Tsingar tried to touch the man's mind, but met a shielding strong as he had ever encountered. Doubtless hatred strengthened it. He rubbed his chin and considered forcing the captive's mind, but gave up the idea. If he planned to hurt the Krotàn, drive him into another Sending, he wanted the man's mind unharmed—it would radiate pain far more effectively.

Still, a little baiting can't hurt. Aduhar was right—hiding's a terrible bore.

"Krotàn," he said, cursing his limitations with the man's language. The captive stiffened, set his jaw and stared coldly back. "We take Iowyn," Tsingar said, watching the Krotàn's reactions closely. "She come for you. Then I—" he pointed at himself "—I . . . she . . ." He gestured rudely.

The Krotàn spat at Tsingar so suddenly he barely had time to avoid being hit. One of the guards slapped the captive across the face, hard enough to jerk the man's head to one side. Tsingar laughed.

"When I do," he said, "find Iowyn good . . . then give him." He pointed to the guard who had slapped the Krotàn's face. "Then him," he said, gesturing at the other guard. "She much good . . . no?"

The captive began to rage again; his words tumbled one over the other, making it impossible to guess what he said, but his emotions flared clearly enough. Tsingar let the Krotàn go on, trying to get sense of what the man was thinking. Hatred loomed uppermost in the Krotàn's mind. Once more, Tsingar caught memories of the burning steading, of kin slain, of a loss that burned like fire. And—deep within the Krotàn—revenge. Tsingar sensed plenty of that: a longing to kill him and the other men in his company.

Tsingar raised his fist, leaned forward, and the prisoner fell silent. "Krotànya," he sneered. "Cowards. Many times cowards. Little men. No good warriors. Iowyn be ours. Krotànya die."

The captive cursed, caught between anger and cold rage. Tsingar stared off into the brush. Pretending disinterest, he sought along the edges of the Krotàn's mind, hoping for a crack in the tightly held shields. Then suddenly one word . . . one name . . . stood out from the twisting thoughts: *Kahsir!*

Tsingar's heart beat hard—once, twice—then settled into its normal rhythm. Kahsir? Could it be? He glanced at the Krotàn; his hand stole to his boot-dagger and he slipped it free from its sheath. The captive saw the motion, and stopped his cursing in mid-breath. Tsingar nodded to the guards; they drew their own weapons and moved closer.

"Kahsir?" Tsingar said, holding the daggerpoint under the captive's chin. "Where Kahsir? Here? Kahsir close?"

The captive's dark face paled, as if he only now realized what he had done. He swallowed heavily but remained silent, eyes never wavering from Tsingar's face.

"So, Krotàn," Tsingar asked again. "Where Kahsir?"

The man remained stubbornly silent.

"Shall we cut at him a little, Lord?" asked the second guard. "We'll make him talk."

"No," Tsingar said, still keeping his eyes locked with the Krotàn's. "Not yet. I think I've found out what I need to know." He pricked the captive's neck with his daggerpoint: a small bead of blood welled up. "Krotàn," he said. "You coward. All Krotànya cowards. Kahsir coward. Soon you, Kahsir, all Krotànya dead." He laughed coldly, drew his dagger back and sheathed it in his boot. "Keep him quiet," he said to the guards, "but don't hurt him too much."

"Aye, Lord."

Tsingar stood and pushed his way through the brush. Kahsir. Somewhere close by. He felt sure of it. The Krotàn's refusal to talk, even to curse and deny, underscored Tsingar's suppositions. If one thought like a Krotàn, it made sense. It would be reasonable to believe Kahsir would not ignore his sister's peril if he had learned that Tsingar stalked her.

Damned Krotànya! They're never logical.

Tsingar stopped for a moment and rubbed the scar on his forehead. If Kahsir had come to Dramujh, then perhaps he could go after him as well. If he had more men. He had no accurate sense of how many men Kahsir led, but the captive had thought in terms of hundreds. Likely two hundred—maybe more. The fighting along the southern border had grown fierce enough that the Krotànya could not afford to withdraw any great number of men from their positions.

Tsingar looked around for his second-in-command, Chevig, and saw him standing nearby.

"Come with me," Tsingar said, motioning toward his own place on the hillside. "I'm going to make another Sending."

Chevig followed readily enough. "To Mehdaiy again, Lord?"

"Aye." Tsingar sat down and waited for the hundred-commander to join him. "Hide me well."

As Chevig closed his eyes, Tsingar focused his thoughts, reached out and touched Mehdaiy's mind.

—*Tsingar! What are you doing Sending to me again?*

—*Necessity, Dread Lord. Kahsir's here.*

—*Kahsir? Are you sure?*

—*I'd wager much on it, Master. We caught a Krotàn yesterday . . . Iowyn's lover. I managed to crack his shields. He evidently came north with Kahsir.*

—*How many men does Kahsir lead?*

Tsingar sensed his commander's excitement. *Between two and three hundred, Master. If you could send me more men, I think I might be able to take him, too.*

—*Perhaps,* Mehdaiy Sent, caution replacing his eagerness. *Perhaps. What about the men in the city? If there are a thousand of them, they could tear you to bits.*

—*Aye, Lord. It's a risk I'll take. If you could send me enough men to guard my back against any attack from Dramujh, I could crush Kahsir.* He hesitated. *Given enough men.*

—*Can you trust this information? Are you certain this Krotàn is her lover?*

—*Aye, Lord. He was at the steading when I first caught her. In fact, I thought I'd killed him.*

Mehdaiy fell silent for a moment. *Our primary objective's always been to take Kahsir prisoner. If we do that, she's of little account.*

—*Aye, Master,* Tsingar replied. He had baited the captive with lewd remarks about Kahsir's sister, but everything he had said held some degree of truth. Memories came of her at the steading, of the way she had fought him. He would not mind bedding that one . . . not one bit.

—*Tsingar?* Mehdaiy's impatience cracked through the Sending.

—Apologies, Dread Lord. He hastily buried his thoughts deep behind his shields. *I was thinking of how to get at Kahsir.*

—You've got your scouts, Mehdaiy snapped. *Use them. And use that Krotàn you've caught. See if you can lure Kahsir's sister out of the city.*

—Aye, Lord.

—Good. We've got men to spare. I'll send you seven hundred . . . three hundred for you, and an additional four hundred to guard your back. They'll be coming by the mind-road tonight.

—I'll be watching for them, Master.

—And Tsingar— Mehdaiy's Sending was cold *—forget the Krotàn bitch. I don't think you'd enjoy her company.*

Guiding his horse around a large stone in the pathway, Kahsir looked up at the sky and saw a circling hawk, but no other evidence of life. His men followed quietly, only the snorting of their horses and the muted thud of hooves betraying their presence. He had led his company south, keeping the city to his right, and had now turned them west. Shading his eyes with an upraised hand, he looked ahead to the unseen road, knowing where it ran by the revealing fold of the hills.

At the top of the next hill Kahsir drew rein, his men drawing up behind him. The road lay below, flat, its pavement dusty looking in the sunlight, but empty.

"Stefendhi."

The Mind-Born worked his way forward through the clustered warriors, and reined in his horse at Kahsir's side. Kahsir gestured at the road.

"Search for me, Stefendhi. Is anyone using this road? I don't want us seen, even by our own people."

Stefendhi closed his eyes briefly, then reopened them. "No, Lord. It's empty now."

"Good." Kahsir hitched around in his saddle and

looked at his men: those he could see sat silent, awaiting his orders. "Tirril, Rhàjon, Havahr." He called out
his hundred-commanders' names and they rode forward. He pointed across the road. "Tirril, Rhàjon—take
half the men to the west side of the road. Havahr and
I will stay here with the rest. Hide and don't spread
out too much. No mind-speech. If there's any commu-
nicating to be done, let Stefendhi handle it. And don't
be stingy with your sentries; you'll have the
Leishoranya at your backs."

The commanders nodded and rode off to gather
their warriors. Havahr sat quietly next to Kahsir, idly
chewing on a long stalk of grass.

"Havahr, deploy our men along the edge of the
road. I don't want us too close to it, but we're going
to need a clear way off these hillsides. Does everyone
have enough food and water?"

"Aye, Lord. For at least a three days' wait."

"Good. Go."

Havahr nodded and reined his horse around. Stefendhi alone remained, looking down the road toward
the city, his blond hair shining in the sunlight.

"Lord," Stefendhi said. "Your sister wants to talk
with you."

"Ah? Why didn't she—?" Kahsir caught the words
back; Iowyn had probably judged it too dangerous to
Send anything herself. Using the Lady Ahthysa, who
could link with another Mind-Born close by, would
give her the secrecy she sought. Though he knew his
sister had hidden her knowledge of his misuse of
power, he trusted more to his new-found mental
strength to hold the secret tight. He looked at Stefendhi. "Link me to her."

He felt the sudden touch of Stefendhi's mind on the
edges of his own, and then Iowyn was there, her
Sending clear but heavily cloaked.

—*Kahs! They've hurt Dreja again.*

He cringed at the agony in her Sending and tried to

keep his return calm. *We knew they would. Could you tell how badly?*

—*He's in a lot of pain. I can't stand it, Kahs! I've got to do something! I can't just sit here*—

—*If you want to see him alive again, you'll have to. I'm setting my men up on either side of the road now. We're about a half hour's ride south of the city. As far as I can tell, the enemy didn't sense us.*

—*But what about Dreja?*

—*There's not a damned thing we can do for him now. You know that.*

—*Kahs*—

—*We're playing a dangerous game here. The next move is the enemy's. Here's what I want you to do. This afternoon, take more warriors with you, and Jhadàvis if you wish, and ride out to visit the refugees. Aren't some of them still camped at the south wall?*

—*Aye.*

—*So. When you ride out, keep looking off to the south. Let anyone watching know you're thinking of Ahndrej, and that you want to go after him. Have an argument with someone over it. Be overly broad in your gestures. I want the enemy to know you're chafing to be off.*

She laughed bitterly. *I won't have to pretend about that.*

—*I know.* He tried to soften his touch on her mind. *Now, listen to me. Once you've staged your argument, return to the city—reluctantly. Let a few thoughts of setting out on your own slip past your shields. We want those enemy scouts to tell their commander you're falling for the bait. The Leishoranya will likely move in closer toward the city, waiting for you to take the road south.*

—*But Dreja . . . they'll*—

He hesitated. *I know. But they won't kill him. Not yet. Trust me in this. If there's any way we can get him away from them, we'll find it.* He shifted in his saddle and rubbed his chin. *Now comes the important part. I won't be able to keep my presence a secret for long. Leave the city again tomorrow. Take your fifty men along with you. Make it apparent you're riding out in haste and secrecy. I'll be waiting by the road as you pass by. Come just far enough south so the Leishoranya will think you're in their trap. When you see them, turn and ride for the city. We'll be waiting for you to pass. Do you understand?*

—*Aye. But what if the Leishoranya don't come? What if they suspect and stay away?*

—*You'll sense that. If it happens, try again the next day. But after all the trouble they've taken with Ahndrej, I can't imagine them not being there. Is there anything else?*

She was silent a long moment. *Aye. Why don't we take the thousand men we have here in the city, join them with your three hundred, and destroy the enemy? We could easily crush them.*

—*It wouldn't work. They'd sense our numbers and be off before we could confront them. And a ten-day or so later they'd be back again, and we'd have to go through this whole thing once more. If they got past the Mind-Born once, they can get past them again. Besides, I can't be sure there aren't more Leishoranya companies than this one in the hills. If there are, we'd be leaving the city undefended save for the home guard, and whatever support they could get from the citizens of Dramujh and the refugees.*

—*It was a thought.*

—*Aye, and not a bad one. But circumstances make it a poor choice at best. Any more questions?*

—*No.*

—*Good. This will have to be the last time we Send to each other. It's going to be too dangerous. Even the Mind-Born can cloak our thoughts only so long.*

—*I understand. I'll try to do my best.*

—*Remember to keep the city on alert. Tell the*

*governor what you're doing, so that he can respond
instantly if need be. And be careful. Lords know I
don't want to lose you again. Now break contact. With
any luck, I'll see you tomorrow. Let's hope the enemy's
grown predictable.*

—*Good hunting, Kahs,* she Sent.

He broke contact, looked across the roadway, and
hoped his plans held together.

Tsingar stared at the two scouts who stood silent before him.

"You're sure?" he asked.

"Aye, Lord." Etenjai looked at the other scout, a
thin, bearded man, who nodded emphatically.

"It's true," the second scout said. "We got close
enough to the city to hear her arguing with her men.
We couldn't understand a thing she said, but her
thoughts say she knows where her lover is."

Tsingar looked sidelong at Khartu and Chevig, who
stood at his side. "Then why did she go back to the
city?"

"Caution, Lord," Etenjai suggested.

"Maybe the men overruled her," said Mandahun.

Tsingar snorted. "Iowyn's a Princess, fool. She rules
them, not the other way around. Where's Ghitoka?"

Mandahun and Etenjai shrugged and silently shook
their heads. Tsingar turned to his hundred-commanders.

"Have you seen him?"

"No, Lord," Chevig said.

"Damn! He was supposed to have been the first one
back." Tsingar worried at his scar, then forced his hand
away. "I don't like this. Something's wrong."

"What, Lord?" asked Khartu.

"If I knew that, I wouldn't be worrying about it!"

Khartu glanced at Chevig. "Does this mean we're
not going after Kahsir's sister as we'd planned?"

"Not yet," Tsingar said. "Until I know what's gone
wrong, I don't want to risk it. We're too far from help,

and we don't know where Kahsir is. No one's been able to find him."

"*If* he's here at all," Chevig said. "The prisoner could have been lying."

"No. I didn't sense a lie." He straightened. "Let me think about it."

Khartu stirred uneasily. "She might take the mind-road in here and try to lift him out."

Tsingar shook his head. "She's not stupid. She'll come, and she'll come in quietly, not with a troop, and not so we can sense her."

"I agree with you, Lord," Chevig said. "And I don't think she'll take to the hills . . . not right off. She'll probably follow that road south, then turn toward us. But consider this, Lord—if we aren't in position tonight, we could miss our chance at her."

"I said let me think about it," Tsingar snapped. "Let *her* make the move. Now go away. And when Ghitoka returns, I want to see him immediately."

"Aye, Lord," Khartu said.

Tsingar watched them go, his mind racing. Gods! What had gone wrong? What had happened to Ghitoka? All the other scouts had returned, Etenjai and Mandahun the last to report in. Tsingar rubbed at his scar again and glanced up at the fading daylight. He had sent Ghitoka to watch the city's northeastern walls and had expected him back by midafternoon. A sudden chill ran down Tsingar's spine. What if Kahsir was hiding northeast of the city and had captured Ghitoka? All plans would be useless, the ambush foreknown.

"Gods!" Tsingar shook his head. There was nothing he could do now save wait. The reinforcements Mehdaiy had promised had not arrived yet, and he could not risk having the Krotànya come at him from the city. Damn! He had come close to telling Chevig and Khartu about the reinforcements, but had concealed the information. Some small voice deep in his mind had urged utter caution, even with his subordinates. He sighed heavily and walked down the hillside to get his dinner.

A number of men had already gathered in the clearing around the store of food. Tsingar longed for something besides dried meat, but in a few days, he and his men would be out of here, and once again he could have something hot and cooked. His mouth watered at the thought. Gods, he was hungry.

Suddenly, he felt the prick of something sharp at the nape of his neck.

"If you value your worthless life, Tsingar, don't move."

Aduhar's voice. Tsingar's breath caught in his throat; holding himself very still, he straightened. The tip of the swordblade on his neck never moved.

"What are you doing, boy?" he hissed, starting to turn. The pressure of the swordblade increased. He halted the movement and stood sweating in the twilight.

"Now," Aduhar said softly. "Turn around. Slowly . . . very slowly."

Tsingar drew a deep breath and turned. Aduhar kept his sword steady.

"*Aduhar!* What the Void are you doing?"

"What I should have done long ago. Taking over your command. You've grown soft, Tsingar . . . soft and hesitant. My uncle sent me with you to learn command. All I've learned from you is how to wait."

Tsingar narrowed his eyes. "You certainly didn't have to learn how to lose men. You already knew that." He glanced sidelong at his hundred-commanders: they stood silent, faces expressionless in the dimming light. Only Chevig shifted slightly on his feet, but Tsingar could not Read what passed in his mind. The other men in the clearing were motionless, halted in whatever they had been doing.

Tsingar cleared his throat. "I'll forget this ever happened, Aduhar, if—"

"You'll forget nothing, low-born," Aduhar said, the sword still and steady in his hand. His eyes flicked up toward a position behind Tsingar's shoulder. "Bosahr . . . Waigan. Bind him."

Rough hands grabbed Tsingar's arms, pulled them behind his back. Not a one of the other men seemed ready to come to his aid.

Gods! How could this have happened?

Brief memories returned of Aduhar talking with various warriors at different times, all younger men. Tsingar shut his eyes, cursing himself for having been so blind.

One of the men pulled the ropes too tight and Tsingar winced, but struggling would only make it worse. He clenched his teeth, tried to forget the swordpoint at his throat, and looked into Aduhar's eyes.

"Do you have any idea what you've done, boy?" he asked scornfully. "You've condemned yourself to death—you and all your lot. When your uncle finds out what you've done—"

"He'll ask why I didn't do it sooner." Aduhar's cold smile recalled Dhumaric . . . and Mehdaiy. "And he'll question his own wisdom in asking for you to serve him. You're no commander—you're just a spy-master who's fooled people into thinking he had the talent."

That stung. Tsingar drew himself fully erect, and forced ice into his voice. "I suppose that includes Ssenkahdavic?" he asked, each word clipped and precise, pitched so everyone close by could hear.

Aduhar's eyes wavered for a moment's time; his voice was less sure when he spoke. "It was my uncle who asked for your services, not the Dark Lord." He looked to the men who stood out of Tsingar's sight. Another cold smile crossed his face. "And since you've become so solicitous of the Krotàn's welfare, we'll tie you to a neighboring tree. Cowards should keep each other company."

Aduhar's cohorts tightened their grip on Tsingar's

arms. He thought of kicking out at them, but the swordpoint at his throat changed his mind. He flinched and closed his eyes in shame as one of Aduhar's men took his two swords and boot-knife from their sheaths. No one would harm them: such an act would bring a curse too terrible to contemplate. But a man without his weapons—

"Aduhar," he said. "I'm giving you one last chance to turn back from this."

Aduhar laughed in his face. "You fool! When I return to camp with Kahsir *and* his sister, my uncle will forget everything, save that you were a failure. Bosahr . . . Waigan . . . take him away. And tie his feet to the tree. He'd better be exactly where you left him when I come back. Chevig . . . Khartu. Gather the warriors. We're riding out."

One of the men had begun to bind Tsingar's feet, leaving only enough slack in the rope to walk. His heart sank. He tried reason one last time.

"Aduhar, do you even know where you're going? Do you know where Kahsir is? Think, boy. You could be riding into a trap."

Aduhar lowered his sword. "I know where I'm going. Each time the scouts reported to you, I talked to them afterward. You've told me what you were planning. It's not a bad idea, Tsingar. In fact, there's a certain merit in it. It amazes me that a spy-master could think of it." He turned to the two hundred-commanders. "Choose ten warriors to stay here at camp. Keep the Krotàn and our former commander under constant guard. The rest of us will ride out within the half-hour."

Chevig and Khartu nodded briefly, turned and walked off into the brush. Aduhar's supporters glanced at each other, and Tsingar felt their longing to be gone from this place, to be active again. Aduhar sheathed his sword.

"Don't try to escape, Tsingar," he said sweetly.

"You'll die the moment you do." An amused expression crossed his face, leaving his eyes untouched. "You won't have to wait long. We'll come back for you tomorrow. In the meantime, you and the Krotàn can become better friends. I'm sure the two of you have much to discuss."

Aduhar gestured. The two men holding Tsingar's bonds jerked him around; he nearly lost his balance, and fought to stay on his feet to leave the clearing with some dignity. His captors, both young warriors, laughed and started off to where Tsingar had ordered the Krotàn bound, dragging on the ropes as they walked. Behind, voice sharp with authority, Aduhar gave out his orders.

Tsingar closed his eyes, stumbled, and opened them again. A bitter taste filled his mouth—he longed to spit, but swallowed instead. He had no idea if he would be given water or not, certain he would not be fed; but he had gone hungry and thirsty before. Though the two young men had stopped laughing, he sensed their amusement. He repeated their names, memorized their faces; when he got free, he would take special delight in seeing how long he could keep them alive before he killed them.

The Krotàn glanced up as the two men shoved Tsingar up against a tree. Tsingar shuddered briefly. Gods! Would he have to stand all that time? No . . . Aduhar's men shoved him down to a sitting position, but one in which his feet were out of reach of his hands. He pulled at the ropes and found them tighter.

The two men checked the knots they had tied, then returned to the clearing without so much as one backward look. Tsingar glared off after them, swallowed convulsively and shifted his weight, trying to find a more comfortable position.

The Krotàn laughed. Tsingar jerked his head around and stared at the man. From all outward appearances, the Krotàn appeared untouched save for the cut above his eye and his swollen jaw; most of his abuse had been mental. The Krotàn looked directly at Tsingar and laughed again. Then he said something quick in his own language and stared off into the trees, smiling like some idiot.

Tsingar bowed his head, shut the Krotàn from his mind. Of all the punishments Aduhar could have ordered, enduring the Krotàn's laughter hurt the most.

CHAPTER 17

Iowyn entered the small, brightly lamp-lit room and
took her chair at the end of the table. Jhadàvis had
already taken her place, and Chàrion came through the
door only moments later. The tall, red-haired warrior
carried a map case under one arm; he shoved the case
across the table as he sat down.

"Maps, Lady. In case you need them."

Iowyn nodded and looked carefully at her two companions. The room was illumined well enough that she
could see the lines of tension on their faces.

And her own face? She struggled to keep it calm. If
either of them knew just how nervous she felt, how
very much she wished tomorrow was over—

She remembered the argument she and Ahndrej
had had in the capital before Kahsir's wedding, of how
she had told him she did not know if she could command *and* be in love at the same time. Now, those
words came back to haunt her.

Iowyn felt steadied by Chàrion's presence. Kahsir
had not misread this warrior when he had ordered him
north. Time and again, Iowyn had benefitted from his
skill, the ease with which he assumed co-command
over the warriors who defended Dramujh.

And now, that experience was exactly what she needed.

I've commanded before, but never in battle. Lords! I hope he understands!

"The men I've chosen to ride with you tomorrow are ready, Lady," he said. "Are you still leaving in the early afternoon?"

"I'd like to. I don't want the Leishoranya to think I've lost my resolve. Are all the scouts in?"

"Aye. They got brief impressions the enemy might have left their camp."

Iowyn's heart jumped. "Then they've taken our bait."

Chàrion nodded. "Let's hope so. As for our plans—I want to change them a bit. I'm coming with you tomorrow."

"But—"

"Your brother entrusted you to my care, Lady. I can't watch over you if I stay behind."

"Then you'll be leaving Nehaiden in command?"

"Aye. It shouldn't cause a problem."

She nodded. Nehaiden dàn Lhossef had commanded the thousand troops that manned Dramujh before she had arrived. "Have you briefed him?"

"Fully. And the governor, too."

Iowyn squared her shoulders, reached for the map case and unscrewed the end. "All right. We still don't know where the enemy camp is. We can only assume it's to the southwest. If they *have* fallen for our ruse, they'll attack us on the road somewhere—" her finger moved down the dark line on the map that represented the Dramujh Road "—likely from its western side."

Jhadàvis leaned forward in her chair. "*That* bothers me. Can we be sure where?"

"No. But Kahsir will be waiting for us. We won't be attacked without his knowing it."

"Too damned dangerous for my liking, Lady."

Iowyn looked at Jhadàvis, at the stubborn set of her

friend's jaw. "What choice do we have, Jhada? If I don't go through with this, and if the enemy gets enough reinforcements, they *could* come at the city. It's *me* they want, not Dreja."

"Still—"

"We argued this out earlier, Jhada. I'm going." She straightened in her chair. "When you and Chàrion go over our plans with the men tomorrow, don't tell them Kahsir will be out there."

"Lady," Chàrion said, "I understand this is for security reasons, but the men might freeze when they see how outnumbered they are."

Iowyn forced a smile. "Not if *you* chose them. I trust your judgment more than that."

Jhadàvis made a small noise of complaint; Iowyn turned to her.

"And Jhada—make sure most of the warriors who ride with us are archers. You'll be in charge of them. They're to carry all the extra arrows they can."

"Aye, Lady. But I don't like seeing you put yourself in such danger."

"Don't argue. It's too late to turn back."

"Any further orders, Lady?" Chàrion asked.

"No. Kahsir's men are in position on either side of the road. It's our turn now. Tomorrow will prove *our* test."

"I'm for bed, then. I've told everyone who's coming with us to sleep well tonight. Until morning, Lady." He stood, bowed to her, nodded to Jhadàvis, and left the room.

"Do you think it will work?"

"I trust Kahs. He knows what he's doing." Iowyn glanced at Jhadàvis. "It's late, Jhada. Get some rest."

Jhadàvis shook her head slightly, shoved her chair back, and rose. "Sleep well, Lady."

For a long while Iowyn sat staring at the map before her. Both Jhadàvis and Chàrion had misgivings about tomorrow's ride. So did she, in spite of her trust in Kahsir. So many things could go wrong. The enemy might not be where Kahsir expected them. And— worse yet—something might happen to Kahsir, or to his men.

She sighed softly and rolled up the map. And Ahndrej? The enemy had tortured him again today— she had *felt* his pain clearly. Now that the Leishoranya thought they had her in their trap, what good was Ahndrej to them? They could kill him and be done with it.

"Lords of Light!" Her hushed voice was overloud in the room. She slid the map into its case, screwed the end on, and stood. "Kahs," she whispered. "This had better damned well go right."

Tsingar's thirst seemed worse than his hunger. His guards had given him nothing to eat or drink since last night. Even worse, he had been forced to relieve himself in full sight of the other men and the Krotàn. He clenched his teeth and shifted position, the ropes cutting in that small movement.

The Krotàn had not spoken yet this morning. Tsingar glanced at him, found him staring, though that was nothing unusual: he had stared all last night and most of the morning, and the hatred in his eyes had never lessened.

Raucous laughter came from beyond the brush and trees; the men Aduhar had left on guard were fully drunk by now. They had guzzled wine all last evening, and had started drinking again even though the day was young. Tsingar tried to spit, but found his mouth too dry. Animals. Some of them were nearly too drunk to stand. Take away any form of command and they deteriorated into everything a warrior should not be.

A slight noise: Tsingar looked at the prisoner. The man had changed positions again, shifting his arms and legs, trying to keep circulation in his limbs. Tsingar met the hate-filled eyes, made himself look without glancing away. Then the man spoke, only this time in the Speech, though the Krotànya were notoriously stubborn in their refusal to speak anything but their own tongue.

"Dark-One. You kill brother. Kill family. Burn home-place. One day soon, I kill you. Slow, Dark-One. Slow. You suffer much. I swear it. You suffer."

Tsingar turned his head away.

The laughter from the drunken warriors grew louder; someone threw up, and Tsingar twisted his mouth in disgust. *Why be so surprised? If Aduhar had half a brain, he'd have left someone in command who knew what he was doing. Drunken idiots!*

A rustling came from his right. Tsingar's heart lurched as he looked at the prisoner: somehow the Krotàn had managed to weaken his bonds.

"Guards!" Tsingar bellowed. "Guards! The prisoner's escaping!"

"Oh, shut up!" one of them roared. "All you want is a drink!"

"You idiots!" Tsingar cried. "He's escaping!"

Someone said something that Tsingar could not hear, and the rest laughed uproariously. Brush rattled and one of the warriors pulled back a few branches and looked down at Tsingar, then over at the Krotàn who was sitting still now, arms behind him. The warrior swayed on his feet, wiped his mouth with the back of one hand, and belched.

"Thought so," he said, his speech slightly slurred. "That bastard's going nowhere. He's tied tight as you."

"Damn you, can't you—"

"Shut your mouth!" the warrior shouted. He swayed again, nearly lost his balance, and caught himself on a tree. "Suffer! Think of us . . . all that good wine—"

"Check his ropes, dung-head! At least check his ropes! He's nearly freed himself!"

The warrior belched again, waved an unsteady hand in Tsingar's direction, and lurched off through the brush. Shaking with rage, Tsingar glared after him.

The Krotàn laughed.

"Fools," the Krotàn said, struggling once more with his bindings. "You all fools." He lunged forward, grunting sharply in pain, and snapped his arms around in front of him. He had rubbed the rope against the tree trunk last night until it had come near to breaking. Blood ran down the Krotàn's wrists, but no pain showed on his face.

The captive rubbed his wrists, flexed his hands, then fumbled at the knots on the ropes binding his feet.

"Guards!" Tsingar cried. *O Gods! If the Krotàn escapes, I'll have to face Mehdaiy for it!* "Guards! Get up here!"

"Choke on it!" one of them yelled.

Tsingar glanced at the Krotàn. The man had his feet free now; he rubbed his legs and ankles, stretching them out in front of him, then staggered to his feet. Tottering a moment, he grabbed the tree he had been tied to.

"Want kill you now," the Krotàn said, his voice thin with pain. "I go. You live. I promise . . . I kill you one day."

"Guards!" Tsingar yelled, but this time no one answered. He glared up at the Krotàn and, gathering what strength he had, concentrated and lashed out at the man's shields. The Krotàn staggered against the tree, seemingly unprepared for such an attack. Tsingar tried again, but this time felt his blow turned.

"Dung-eater!" the Krotàn hissed. He let go of the tree, staggered to Tsingar's side, and drew back his fist.

Tsingar lashed out again, but the Krotàn's shields were too strong. He cringed, expecting the captive to hit him, but instead the Krotàn spat in his face. Tsingar jerked his head back and grunted in pain as it hit the tree trunk. The Krotàn turned, stood swaying a moment, then walked unsteadily off into the brush.

Tsingar blinked the spittle from his eyes and tore at his own ropes, but could not loosen them. He yelled obscenities. The laughter from the drunken warriors grew louder.

The Leishoranya had moved closer during the night; Kahsir sensed them out there, south of his own position. Despite his augmented powers, he had not probed for their exact location—they had come far too close to his company and doubtless would be alert for any such search.

Kahsir looked across the empty road, the early afternoon sunlight warm on his face. North, toward the city, he could see rapidly building storm clouds on the horizon. He looked down at the road, rubbed the tense muscles in his neck, and started pacing.

Iowyn meant to leave the city sometime in the afternoon; now all he and his men could do was hold their positions until she passed. It was a damned chancy thing. If his Dream had not compelled him, he would have cursed his rashness. He glanced down at the stone road again, but it stretched empty as before.

Here I am, waiting for Lords know what . . . brought here by the touch of a Dream that won't come back. He reached down into his mind—slowly, tentatively—but found nothing.

Boot heels clicked on stone; Stefendhi stopped at his side.

"She's coming, Lord," the young Mind-Born said. "She's left the city."

Kahsir's stomach tightened. "Good. It's about the same time she rode out yesterday. Can you sense the enemy at all?"

"Not easily, Lord, though some of the shields they've thrown up are ragged. Young and inexperienced, likely."

"All the better for us," Kahsir said. "I'll call for you when it's time for us to move."

The Mind-Born ducked his head in a slight bow and returned to his place in the trees. Kahsir gestured at Havahr; the hundred-commander rose from the rock he had been sitting on.

"Lord?"

"Iowyn's left the city. Have someone signal Tirril and Rhàjon. I want us ready to move out on a moment's notice."

"How long before she passes us?" asked Havahr.

Kahsir glanced at the city. "It could be awhile yet. We're a half hour's ride away." He looked at Havahr. "Go over the plans with your men again. We're to parallel her as she rides south down the road. It's not going to be easy on horseback, but from what the scouts say, the trees are thick enough to hide us without posing much of a problem."

"Aye, Lord."

Havahr trotted off, motioning to warriors who had began to gather. Kahsir looked at the hillside behind him, until he saw a brief flash of sunlight reflected from the mirror Havahr carried. The light flashed once more, and then stopped. Kahsir glanced across the road: the answering signal was equally brief.

He walked over to his tethered horse; the animal turned its head, a grass stem hanging from its mouth. Kahsir moved the saddle higher on the horse's withers and began tightening the cinch, thinking of Iowyn. He could visualize her progress down the road, though he had not tried to make direct contact with her. That delicate business he left to Stefendhi.

Kahsir glanced up at the sun to gauge the time. Iowyn was no idiot: she knew exactly what she had to do, and he trusted her to accomplish it. He began pacing again: up and down in front of his horse, over to the edge of the trees, then back again. His men had gathered in the trees close by. Once more, he reviewed his plans, going over and over them until he knew he could act without thinking. Act without thinking—he laughed silently. If anything, he thought too much.

"Lord." Stefendhi, a few paces away, pointed down toward the road. "She's coming."

Kahsir grabbed for his reins, led his horse out from the undergrowth, and mounted. Men appeared all along the hillside, most of them already in the saddle; the rest leapt astride their horses at his signal. He turned, sensing Stefendhi at his side.

"Shall I alert Tirril and Rhàjon now, Lord?"

Kahsir nodded. The Mind-Born's face froze for a moment in intense concentration as he made a Sending so cloaked Kahsir could not have detected it unless he knew what to expect.

Stefendhi gestured, indicating the two hundred-commanders had received his Sending. Kahsir set his horse moving down the steep hillside. He sensed his sister draw closer. His horse snorted, shook its head, and continued on. Behind, the rest of the men had spread out over the hillside, all slowly working their way down to a position halfway between the hilltops and the road.

Kahsir could hear distant hoofbeats now. He drew rein and sat in the shade of a tree, his eyes fixed on the roadway; finally, Iowyn and her company rounded the curve. Beside Iowyn rode a tall woman he easily recognized as Jhadàvis. Behind them came fifty men, all in tight formation. And Chàrion.

Kahsir shifted in the saddle; Iowyn must know he was close—they were linked strongly, even for siblings. He scanned the weapons she and her company carried, and sighed quietly in relief. Thank the Lords she had thought to bring bowmen with her.

He held himself motionless and watched. As the last of Iowyn's men rode past his hidden position, he motioned to Stefendhi and those warriors he could see. He began following his sister, leaning hillward as his mount negotiated the steep slope. Stefendhi's mind momentarily brushed his own: the Mind-Born had signaled those on the other side of the road to start their way south.

Kahsir's hands started to sweat; he let the reins drop over his horse's neck and wiped his palms on his thighs. This was Iowyn's first field campaign and *he* was nervous. He remembered his own first time at commanding in battle and wondered what she was thinking.

She'll do all right. She's followed by hand-picked men: Chàrion's riding just behind her. Still—

He shook his head, lifted his reins again, and concentrated on keeping his horse to the easiest path possible. He was committed now; they were all committed—Iowyn, her men, his own, the enemy—to the dictates of a Dream that had vanished, leaving only questions behind.

Iowyn sensed Kahsir's presence up on the hillside somewhere, but only because they were kin-bound; without making a search, she knew he rode off to her left. She could barely sense him or the warriors about him. He was damned skilled to keep three hundred men so well hidden on the brushy hillsides. If she had not been so strongly tied to him, she might have ridden on, never knowing there was anyone close.

The roadway she and her squad followed ran straight for the most part south of Dramujh, broken only by a few wide curves and gentle rises in the land. Iowyn looked from one side of the road to the other, at the tree-clad hills, her muscles set to respond instantly to the foreseen attack.

She rubbed the sweat from her forehead; her mouth had gone suddenly dry. The waterskin hanging from her saddle by her right knee was inviting, but she knew better than to drink with action imminent. She frowned and, to ignore her tension, concentrated on nothing but the steady sound of hoofbeats behind.

Her concentration dissolved. Something had happened to Ahndrej again during the morning and, though she had not known what, severe pain had torn through him for a moment. The enemy must have tortured him again, doing Lords only know what to body and mind. Only her promise to her brother had prevented her leaving the city early. She chewed on her lip and looked at Jhadàvis: the tall woman rode expressionless, bow across her saddle, a quiverful of arrows at her knee.

"Lady."

Chàrion trotted his horse forward so he rode to Iowyn's left in the position of shieldman. Gray eyes narrowed in the sunlight, he glanced now and again to the hillsides on either hand.

"We're over a half hour's ride from the city," he said. "The enemy could come down those hillsides any moment now."

She held Chàrion's eyes briefly, then turned to Jhadàvis.

"We be ready, Lady," Jhadàvis said, a brief smile of encouragement crossing her face. "If anyone ever rode more aware into an ambush, I'd like to know who."

Iowyn grinned stiffly at her two companions. "Remember . . . at my signal, turn and ride like wrath to the city. But only at my signal. I don't want to break too soon."

"That's damned dangerous, Lady," Chàrion said. "Better to run at the first opportunity."

"Aye. It would be smarter, that's sure. But we have to lure the enemy to Kahs. Though we're a small enough company to be an attractive target, if we leave too much distance between us and the enemy, they might sense a trap."

"Then guard your back," Chàrion said. "They'll surely have bowmen among them."

Iowyn laughed, startled at the harshness of her own voice. "Of us all, I'm the least likely target. They want me alive so they can get at Kahs."

Chàrion nodded slowly, still looking unconvinced. "If they can't get you alive, Lady, they'll try for you dead. Be careful."

"Always." She tried to smile. "Pass the word, Chàrion. Everyone on battle alert."

He nodded briefly and reined back to ride with the squadron.

Iowyn rubbed the back of her neck and drew a deep breath. *As much as I hate that damned city, I'd give a lot to be there now. Lords of Light! I wish that none of this had ever happened!* She straightened her shoulders and stared forward at the road. Things could not be changed; she could not turn back now from this, the most dangerous maneuver she had ever undertaken.

Sudden movement ahead brought Iowyn to instant alert: Leishoranya charged down the hillside to her right. Chàrion barked orders in a clear voice, and Iowyn sensed her men preparing to run. She glanced around; an odd sort of detachment swept through her mind, leaving her thoughts cool and strangely clear. Whoever led the enemy was a fool. He had not stationed men across the road, and rather than wait until she and her company had drawn even to his position, he had charged down the hillsides too soon.

Damn! What was going on to the rear? Could the whole thing be a trap? She twisted in the saddle, glanced behind, and sent out a quick probe. No. The Leishoranya were all in front of her.

She watched the enemy warriors coming closer to the road and methodically counted her heartbeats. *Lords! There must be two hundred of them!* At the count of four she would give the order to turn for the city. Sunlight glittered on uplifted swords and off enemy helms as the Leishoranya hit the flat ground next to the road.

"Run!" She jerked her horse around, kicked the animal in the sides, and galloped in retreat. Jhadàvis already had her bow in hand, arrow nocked. Chàrion drew aside, letting Iowyn by; as she rode past the red-haired warrior, she glimpsed bowmen falling into position.

Kahsir! What if something had happened to him?

She ruthlessly shoved those thoughts away and concentrated on keeping low over her horse's neck, presenting as small a target as possible to any enemy archer who might have drawn close enough to shoot.

Chàrion rode close to her left side. He pointed to the rear and shouted, half of what he said carried away by the wind.

"They're close, Lady!" he cried. "Too close. Faster!"

She bit down on her lip and kicked her horse into an all-out run. Jhadàvis was no longer to her right: she had fallen back with the bowmen. Iowyn blanked her mind of all thoughts save those of her hidden brother, and the nagging fear that she had waited too long to run.

CHAPTER 18

Kahsir strained his ears but still could hear nothing. The light dimmed as the sun disappeared behind a cloud; he glanced to the north and saw the storm drawing nearer. His horse fought the bit and he loosened the reins, aware he had been holding them too tightly. Where was Iowyn? He listened again, but only heard the wind rustling in the brush and trees and the snort of someone's horse close by.

Suddenly—riders, coming down the road at great speed. He slowly settled his arm into his shield; muffled sounds came to his left and right from the other warriors who were arming themselves. He drew his sword, pushed his helm down tighter on his head, and waited.

He glanced sidelong. "Stefendhi."

The Mind-Born reached out, linking minds with the company.

"Archers to the ready," Kahsir said, never taking his eyes from the road. A subtle brush across his consciousness was all he sensed of Stefendhi relaying his orders to the bowmen. He moved closer to the road, taking care to remain fully hidden.

There . . . Iowyn . . . riding like the wind from

the Void came at her back. She darted a glance
behind her, leaning low over her horse's neck. Kahsir
licked his lips and tightened the grip on his sword;
the enemy must be closer than she had planned. Her
men followed close behind, bowmen bringing up the
rear.

Then he saw the Leishoranya behind them. *Lords!
How did they get that* fihrkken *close to her?* The
enemy leader came clearly into view—a man riding a
black horse, red cloak snapping behind him in the
wind. Kahsir started in recognition: he had fought that
man before . . . he *knew* it.

His sister galloped past his position, her men spilling over from the roadway onto the broad grassy banks
beside. The road was only wide enough to let eight
horsemen ride abreast, but that would hinder the
enemy as well. The Leishoranya came on: Kahsir
forced himself to wait until they drew even with his
hidden company.

"Archers!" he called to Stefendhi. "Now!"

Stefendhi's silent command brushed his mind, then
arrows hissed from the woods.

The first ranks of the enemy crumpled; many of the
pursuing warriors wavered in their saddles, and a few
fell from their horses, ridden over by their comrade
from behind. Another volley of arrows descended on
the Leishoranya.

"At them!" Kahsir cried, Sending to those who could
not hear. "*Legir!* For the Light! *Legir! Legir!*"

The enemy thundered past, their speed difficult to
check. Kahsir lifted his reins, kicked his horse out
from cover, and into a charge down the hillside. He
sensed his men alongside and across the roadway. The
enemy warriors had managed to stop and were trying
to regroup on the road and the grassy margin.

Kahsir's horse reached level ground and found its
footing in the grass. He rode toward the enemy, his
shield tight against his side. The first Leishoran he met

had no time to turn and fight—Kahsir's swordstroke cut him down before he could move.

And then he was in the thick of it. All rational thought vanished. He struck out, only dimly seeing the enemy he wounded or killed. The sounds of battle grew deafening: horses screamed, steel rang against steel, and men cursed and yelled at each other.

He looked for his sister but could not see her. A Leishoran rode in his direction, pale face twisted by hate; Kahsir set himself, met the enemy's charge, and engaged him. The Leishoran's horse turned suddenly, throwing its rider off balance, and Kahsir slashed out with his sword. Not waiting to see if he had badly wounded the warrior, he jerked his mount around and sought another opponent.

Iowyn had given him an accurate estimation of the enemy's strength: close to two hundred Leishoranya rode in this company, which meant he and his own men did not have the advantage of numbers he would have wanted. Again, he looked for his sister, but caught only a brief glimpse of Chàrion.

And of Rhàjon, fighting nearby. "Rhàj!" he called. "Take as many men as you can and try to make it through the flank to Iowyn. She only has fifty men— the enemy might break through her ranks."

He had enough time to see Rhàjon turn before he was set upon by another opponent. His world narrowed now—only he and the Leishoran existed. Kahsir cursed as the warrior's sword nicked his forearm; he freed his right foot from the stirrup and kicked out at the Leishoran's knee. The man grunted, lurched in the saddle, and Kahsir stabbed his sword up and under the uplifted shield. The Leishoran fell out of the saddle, and for a panicked moment Kahsir thought his weapon had caught between the man's ribs. He managed to hang onto the swordhilt and jerked the weapon free.

He glanced around again. These Leishoranya proved

far better fighters than he had guessed at first; after their initial confusion and losses to Krotànya arrows, they had regrouped and now fought with deadly grimness. But they were outnumbered, faced by Kahsir's men from before and Iowyn's behind.

Of a sudden he saw the red-cloaked man again. The young warrior turned his horse, his eyes met Kahsir's, and a wild look of anticipation crossed his beautiful face.

Steel rang against steel as Kahsir met the Leishoran's charging swordstroke. The man's movements were nearly too fast to follow, but Kahsir trusted his own skill and, even more, his experience. The Leishoran was young, and Kahsir remembered fighting him before.

Kahsir winced as the Leishoran's sword opened another cut on his forearm. *Lords! He's too damned good for me to be clumsy! I've got to get centered!* His mind settled, strove for inner balance, the widening of perspective linked with a tighter focus. The Leishoran's shield raised slightly: Kahsir lunged, but his swordstroke merely nicked the warrior's side.

Suddenly, Kahsir's horse tripped over a body—he had an instant to see the Leishoran aim a slashing blow at him, one he knew he could not avoid. He ducked low over his horse's neck, and his opponent's blade struck his helmet.

The world dissolved in pain and for an instant he could not see. He shook his head violently from side to side, trying to clear his vision. Warned by the Leishoran's cry, he instinctively twisted and lifted his shield: the force of his enemy's blow rocked him in his saddle. His vision cleared. He brought his sword up, met the Leishoran's blade with his own, bound and bound again, trying to get inside.

Suddenly, he fell from the saddle. Another Leishoran had ridden up from behind him and rammed into his horse, nearly knocking the animal

onto its side. Kahsir tried to roll as he hit the ground;
stunned, he shook his head, then staggered to his feet.
The man in the red cloak yelled something and turned
his horse to come at Kahsir, his sword lifted for a killing stroke.

Kahsir jumped aside. His opponent's sword grazed
his helmet, and he fell again. Scrambling dizzily to his
feet, he glanced behind—saw the Leishoran turning his
horse for another charge, and loosened the shield from
his arm.

At the last possible moment, Kahsir dodged sideways and shoved his shield between the horse's back
legs—the animal squealed in startled pain and tumbled
down in a heap. The Leishoran lay trapped, struggling
to claw his way free; his horse finally lurched to its
feet and limped away. Kahsir snatched for his shield,
took the grips, and whirled on his downed opponent.

The man scrambled to his feet, stood weaving
slightly, but still ready to fight. Kahsir had never met
the Leishoran afoot: the man was tall, broad-shouldered and well-muscled. But Kahsir was taller yet,
weighed more, and had the longer reach. He grinned
as his opponent recognized these facts; then he lifted
his sword and cut at the Leishoran. Blades rang.
Lords! He's so damned quick! Kahsir brought his
longer reach into play—a downward slash opened a
deep cut on the side of the young man's face. The
Leishoran yelped in pain, his eyes took on a panicked
expression, but he stood his ground, his sword meeting
Kahsir's at every turn.

Kahsir felt the sweat dripping down his sides.
*Damn! I've got to end it quickly! I could be cut down
from behind.* He saw an opening in his enemy's guard,
slashed at the man's right leg, and felt his sword bite
deep. The Leishoran cried out and lurched sideways:
Kahsir lunged, knocked him off his feet, and cut
downward, slashing through chainmail and leathers to
open a deep wound in the warrior's side.

The man screamed briefly, a high, shrill sound, then his face twisted in anguish and went slack. Kahsir jerked his blade away.

"Lord! Behind you!"

Havahr's voice. Kahsir rolled aside just in time to avoid being speared by a passing Leishoran. He rose to his knees, and brought his sword and shield up to guard. The enemy warrior turned his horse, but one of Kahsir's men was quicker and cut the Leishoran down.

"My Lord Kahsir!" Havahr cried again.

Kahsir stood, located his hundred-commander, and ran toward him, where Havahr held his captured horse steady by its bridle. Kahsir grabbed the saddle, and vaulted onto the animal's back.

"Lords of Light!" Havahr said, his face pale. "I thought you were finished!"

"You should have been here earlier," Kahsir panted, taking up the reins and feeling after the other stirrup. He looked around—his own losses were nearly the same as the enemy's. He might have victory today, but not without more hard fighting. "I think I just killed their leader," he said, glancing at Havahr. "Let's hope they take it hard."

Tsingar started awake. He had dozed off, exhausted after trying to work free of his ropes. Someone had touched his shoulder; he could see nothing but trees, and his visitor had shielded himself to the point that Tsingar could not Read him. The clearing was quiet, the guards likely sleeping off all they had drunk during the day.

"Lord."

Tsingar stiffened, recognizing Ghitoka's voice coming from directly behind him.

"What in the Gods' names is going on here, Lord?"

"Ghitoka!" Tsingar's voice cracked in relief. "Cut me free, man! Now! Do it!"

Tsingar's wrists throbbed with pain as Ghitoka

started cutting the ropes that bound them. The ropes pulled against his raw skin—Tsingar gasped and kept his teeth clenched until Ghitoka had finished. His arms fell to his sides, numb from being held so long in the same position.

"My feet, Ghitoka," he said, flinching with pain as he rubbed his wrists.

The scout crept around to Tsingar's legs—only then could he see that Ghitoka moved with a decided limp.

"What happened to you?" he asked, briefly closing his eyes and leaning his head back against the tree trunk.

"I fell, Lord." The scout bent over his work, long black hair hiding his face. "It was stupid of me and I paid for it. I twisted my ankle, damned near broke it." He glanced up from Tsingar's feet. "What happened to you? Where are—?"

"Quietly!" Tsingar hissed. "Aduhar surprised me from behind, usurped my command, and rode off with all the men to go after Kahsir's sister."

"And those drunkards asleep around the fire?" Ghitoka asked, finally severing the ropes around Tsingar's ankles.

"Aduhar ordered them to stay behind, to guard me and the campsite." Tsingar's mouth felt like someone had poured dust in it. "For the Dark's sake, do you have any water?"

Ghitoka nodded and unfastened his waterskin from his belt. Tsingar reached for it, unstopped it and drank. He lowered the skin, looked at Ghitoka; that Ghitoka had obeyed his orders gave evidence of the scout's loyalty.

"Are all those dung-heads asleep?" he asked, pointing toward the clearing. The muscles in his arm rebelled, and his hand wavered.

"Aye, Lord." Ghitoka's face twisted in disgust. "Smells like the inside of a wine barrel down there."

"Good. Help me up."

Ghitoka rose unsteadily to his feet, favoring his left ankle, and grasped Tsingar's arms. Tsingar winced in pain again, and for a moment thought he would fall. He reached out for the tree trunk, steadied himself, taking his weight from Ghitoka.

Then froze at a sudden noise. Horsemen . . . many of them. His hand darted to his side, but his weapons were gone. He glanced sidelong—Ghitoka seemed equally surprised.

Ancestors! Tsingar swallowed heavily. *I can't run, not in my condition! If Aduhar's come back to camp, I'm dead!*

"Tsingar!"

Though the voice sounded familiar, it was not Aduhar's.

"Up here!" Tsingar cried.

Brush rattled noisily, and a man pushed his way through the bushes. For an instant, surprise washed all other expressions from the warrior's face. Tsingar let his breath hiss through his teeth in relief as he recognized D'Yeto, another of Mehdaiy's commanders.

"What's going on?" D'Yeto demanded.

"Did you come from Mehdaiy?" Tsingar asked.

"Aye." D'Yeto gestured down the hill. "With three hundred men. What happened to you?"

"Do me a favor. Those drunkards in the clearing— have your men tie them up and bring them to their senses."

D'Yeto called orders over his shoulder, then turned as men came charging through the brush. "All right . . . tell me what's happened."

Tsingar told him. As he spoke, D'Yeto's face paled slightly.

"And the lover escaped? Gods! What's Mehdaiy going to make of this?"

"He'll have no damn choice in the matter. The Law says Aduhar dies, along with every man who helped him." Tsingar's wrists and ankles still throbbed, and he rubbed them, trying to get his circulation moving again. "I told the fool that, but he wouldn't listen."

D'Yeto shook his head. "Even the Great Lords know how to obey. He's not exempt from that, despite his lineage." He glanced at Tsingar's raw wrists, at the ropes that still clung to his feet. "Are you able to walk?"

"I think so." Tsingar took one experimental step, wavered, then steadied. "We have to get out of here. If I know Aduhar, he's got his men in trouble. Again. The idiot never *could* learn to wait."

D'Yeto shrugged, held the branches away so that Tsingar could walk down to where the commander's men were cleaning up. Ghitoka followed, limping heavily.

The mutineers sat herded together around what was left of their feast. Some were too drunk to sit upright and lay on their sides, faces turned to the grass. The place reeked of spilled wine and vomit. Tsingar spat in disgust. Warriors filled the floor of the ravine—horses snorted and stamped in the sudden silence that fell as he and D'Yeto came out into the clearing.

Tsingar faced those men, keeping all expression from his face, hiding his stiffness and pain beneath the veneer of a high ranking officer. But he noticed a few warriors glance at his empty scabbards, and his face heated.

"Ghitoka. Aduhar took my weapons and hid them someplace. Find them for me."

The scout nodded and limped away.

"Why are you so late, D'Yeto?" Tsingar asked, glancing sidelong at his companion.

"Damned Krotànya slowed us up. We were only able to leave this afternoon."

"Did Mehdaiy send the other four hundred to stand between us and the city?"

D'Yeto nodded. "They're in place, back along the road, about two leagues beyond the point you gave as your intended position to attack Kahsir's sister."

"You took the mind-road?"

"Aye, and we're tired, too. Those cursed Krotànya Mind-Born have tightened their watch. We had to shield ourselves like never before."

Tsingar rubbed at his scar. "There's no hope for it. We'll have to ride out immediately if we're going to get our hands on Kahsir's sister, much less Kahsir himself."

"Huhn." D'Yeto's eyes strayed to Tsingar's empty scabbards. "Are you sure Aduhar left your weapons here?"

Tsingar shifted uncomfortably. "They're around here somewhere. Even Aduhar wouldn't have dared do anything to them."

"He dared take your command," D'Yeto pointed out.

Tsingar chilled and glanced around the campsite.

D'Yeto's eyes narrowed. "Where's Aduhar going to stage his attack?"

"The same spot I had picked. I know where it is, so we can take the mind-road."

"Gods, Tsingar! We can't make it."

Tsingar frowned, then nodded reluctantly—D'Yeto was only telling the truth. But he sensed a need for haste. The late afternoon sky had started to cloud over, and the air held promise of storm. *Gods, Gods, Gods! Don't let it rain! Not yet!* Closing his eyes, he concentrated on where he had planned to ambush Iowyn. If he, D'Yeto, and the three hundred men rode swiftly, they could reach that part of the Dramujh Road in just over a half hour.

"All right. We won't take the mind-road. But we're going to have to ride hard."

"That we can do."

"Lord," Ghitoka called. "Your weapons . . . they're all here."

Tsingar's knees shook as he walked to Ghitoka's side. Heart in his throat, he knelt before his weapons, fearing the worst, but they appeared unharmed. *Gods!*

Ancestors! Krotànya blood to you for this gift! Gently, he kissed each of the blades; running his fingertips down them, he sheathed the swords, slipped the boot-dagger into its place, and stood, whole again.

"D'Yeto." Tsingar turned D'Yeto aside and stood shoulder to shoulder with him. "There's too much bad blood between Aduhar and me. I want your oath on this: if the Krotànya got to him first, I'm going to let him die. Don't give me that look. He deserves it. Mehdaiy will kill him anyway when he gets hold of him. I want the pleasure of knowing the last thing Aduhar sees in this lifetime will be me, restored to my command."

D'Yeto stirred uneasily. "I can't give you my oath on that, and you know it. I'm bound to bring Aduhar back to his uncle." A thin smile crossed his face. "But if he's hurt badly enough, I could be conveniently absent."

Tsingar laughed. "Good. We understand each other then." He straightened. "We've got to leave here as soon as we can. And as for those drunkards—those dung-heads who think they're warriors—let's kill them now. I can't spare the men to guard them and I'll be damned if they ride with us. I wish we had more time—I'd like to make it last awhile."

"Aye." D'Yeto grinned, eyes glittering in the fading light. "The first cuts are yours, Tsingar."

Tsingar's hand fondled his swordhilt. "Get your men ready. We'll leave right after."

Ahndrej sat beneath a tree, surrounded on all sides by thick undergrowth, his head swimming, his wrists and ankles bands of fire. His captors had kicked his ribs and stomach—it hurt to simply breathe. He licked his lips with a dry tongue and swallowed, then closed his eyes, trying to reconstruct the landscape in his mind. So near the hills, there had to be a stream close by.

Then into the vision of the land swam Iowyn's face—pale and anxious. He concentrated on the image. Anxious . . . aye, and afraid.

His face went hot with shame; he was a fool, he was more than a fool. *Lords! How could I have been so stupid? I've put everyone I love in danger—Iowyn, Kahs—all of them. Because of me, they could die! I've been more help to the enemy than hindrance.* His eyes filled with tears and he brushed them away. *Kahs was right, dammit! I could have doomed us all.*

Iowyn was in danger at this moment, possibly fighting for her life. He knew this without making a probe. And here he sat, racked by pain, weakened from lack of food or water, his knees aching from the fall he had taken moments before.

A bird called out from a tree not far away. The sky had darkened, and he smelled distant rain. Lords! Weakened as he was, if he was caught in rain chill and had to wait it out in the brush through the night, he could easily die. He ground his teeth, his hands clenching into fists on his knees.

What he could *not* do was wait much longer. He had to reach help somewhere. He stood, swayed slightly, and pushed his way out from the undergrowth. The bird resumed singing in the fading light.

He saw the loose stone an instant too late—his foot slipped over it, and he lost his balance. Flailing at the trees nearby, he tried to break his fall, but rolled halfway down the hillside before he came to rest. He closed his eyes tightly, blackness washing the edges of his sight. His ribs were afire with pain now, and his right leg throbbed in agony. *Fool! Idiot! I deserve to die out here!*

He clawed his way up the tree trunk he had rolled into and sat there, panting in the silence. Then he heard it: the distant rush of water over stone. He swallowed convulsively and tried to stand; he swayed, dangerously close to falling, but kept to his feet. For a long moment he stood there, hanging onto the tree, then, summoning what strength he had left, limped down the hillside, slipping now and then as he went.

A small stream ran at the bottom of a steep valley; Ahndrej fell to his knees on the low bank, grunted in pain, and plunged his face into the icy water.

He was getting nowhere, so weakened and hurt. His thrashing about in the thickets could help no one. He knew of only one thing left to do, and he flinched from the thought.

He frowned then, denying himself a choice, for he had none. A distant rumble of thunder sounded to the north, and he glanced up at the sky. Weather-wise, he knew it would not rain for some time yet, but it made little difference. He closed his eyes, banished all thought from his mind, and concentrated. If the enemy hunted him close by, this concentration alone would instantly betray his position: he lacked the strength to maintain his shields. He shrugged the thought away, and fixed his mind firmly on his goal.

He felt it long before he opened his eyes: the gateway shimmered before him, poorly wrought, wavering at the edges, but as firm as he could make it. Head swimming in exhaustion, he struggled to his feet and lurched toward the glowing doorway. One more step . . . one more, and he would be there. *Got to concentrate! Got to see to the other side!*

He plunged headlong through the gate, and saw nothing but blackness as he fell.

Hidden by the thick woods, Tsingar reined in his horse and looked down on the battle. D'Yeto said something; Tsingar motioned for silence. The gloom made it hard to tell exactly what had happened but, from his first glimpse of the fighting, Tsingar knew Aduhar had bungled things again.

The Krotànya outnumbered Aduhar's men, not by a

great margin but by enough to give them victory. The roadway and grassy slopes beside it were littered with bodies.

Tsingar squinted in the stormy darkness, not stopping to count how many on each side had fallen. He could see Kahsir clearly: the Krotànya Throne Prince was taller than the other men who fought around him. And there—fighting alongside her brother—Iowyn. Those two he recognized, but he could not find Aduhar.

"D'Yeto." The commander nudged his horse closer and Tsingar pointed at the battle. "If we can slip around behind, we'll be able to trap them."

D'Yeto's eyes narrowed as he assessed the situation. "Aye. We could do that. But we'll lose time."

"Time." Tsingar spat. "We have a choice. Lose time or lose Kahsir and his sister. If we attack from this side, we'll only drive them head-on to the city."

"You're right," D'Yeto admitted. "Damn! If we're going to do it, we'd better move!" A brief rumble of thunder. "This storm's not going to hold off much longer."

Tsingar nodded. "Pass the word." He pointed off to his left, at a low ridge of hills that paralleled the road. "Once we reach the road, turn and charge straight at the Krotànya. They won't have anywhere to go."

"Aye."

Tsingar listened as D'Yeto relayed the orders to the hundred-commanders who waited a few paces away, then glanced at the road. Gods! Where was Aduhar? He rubbed his eyes wearily, cursing his stiffness and sore muscles. D'Yeto called in a soft voice; Tsingar reined his horse around and rode to his co-commander's side.

The other men had started moving north now, still high on the hill, behind a screen of woods. Tsingar urged his horse to a faster gait, hearing D'Yeto come along behind. The Krotànya had pushed Aduhar's men southward on the road, away from the city, and would hardly expect attack from the rear. With what was left from the two hundred men Aduhar had, and D'Yeto's three hundred, Tsingar would outnumber the Krotànya nearly four to one.

Tsingar looked at the road, saw it curve toward the west. He caught D'Yeto's attention, gestured sharply, and motioned farther on.

"Let's go down around that bend. We'll be hidden from sight and we can get our speed up in a charge."

D'Yeto grinned and called out his orders to the hundred-commanders. As Tsingar thought of coming battle, his exhaustion vanished. He reached for his shield, pulled it onto his left arm, wincing slightly at the pain in his wrist. Several of the men had already started down the hillside; Tsingar unsheathed his sword, kissed its blade, and trotted after them. Thunder rolled over the hills, but still there was no rain.

He reached the level ground by the road. The men who had gone ahead waited patiently, weapons gleaming dully in the dim light. Tsingar turned as D'Yeto came to his side, and watched the rest of the three hundred warriors ride down out of the brush onto the road.

"We'll have to charge in tight ranks," D'Yeto said, eyeing the width of the roadway and the grassy slopes beside it. "That could pose a problem."

Tsingar nodded. "Aye, but the Krotànya will face the same. Neither of us will have much maneuverability." Thunder rolled again, closer this time. "If this storm gets noisier, and if they stay busy with Aduhar, they won't hear us coming." Tsingar hitched around in the saddle and looked at the men who waited behind. "Keep your ranks tight!" he called, raising his voice so it would carry to the last of them. "Stay on the road if at all possible. Hit the Krotànya hard as you can. Remember, if you meet Kahsir or his sister, I don't want them killed. Take them prisoner if possible. Ride at my command."

He turned around as lightning flickered over the hillsides and the road. Lifting his sword above his head, hilt in one hand and the blade balanced on the other, he threw back his head.

"Ancestors! Guide our hands!" he cried. "Gods of Darkness, lead us to victory!"

CHAPTER 19

"Kahs!"

Kahsir dropped his opponent and turned toward his sister's voice. Her face was drawn with weariness, pale in the gloomy light; a thin trickle of blood traced the angle of her jaw. She gestured sharply.

"Behind you!" she cried. "Look behind!"

He whirled his horse around and his heart lurched in his chest. Leishoranya! He could see them now, coming at a gallop from the north, dim shapes through the storm-light.

By the Light! I've been outflanked!

"Lord!" Chàrion's voice carried across the battle. "They're going to hit us and hit us hard!"

For an agonizing eternity, Kahsir's mind went blank; he glanced frantically around, seeking an escape route.

Then, coming from out of nowhere, his Dream filled his mind. He Saw a route he might take, a way to possible safety . . . Saw that and a blur of other things, forgotten even before he remembered them.

He looked again, tried to link what he had Seen in his Dream with what he knew about the region and what his maps had told him. A narrow, canyon-like toward it.

"Chàrion! Get everyone up that valley! Now! Disengage where you can!"

"Lord!"

Kahsir turned toward the new voice: it came from one of Iowyn's men who fought close by.

"Lord!" the man shouted. "That valley's—"

A Leishoran cut him down from behind and he died. Kahsir cursed; Chàrion wheeled his horse around and engaged the Leishoran, finally downing him with a hacking swordstroke.

"Now, Chàrion!" Kahsir cried. "Get up that valley! We'll escape across the hilltops!" He sought Tirril, Havahr, and Rhàjon, found them within shouting distance. "Tirril!" The hundred-commander turned his head. "Come with me! Bring as many men as you can! We've got to hold them on that road!"

"No, Kahs!" Iowyn nudged her horse closer. "You can't go up against them. You'll be slaughtered!"

He glared at her. "Don't argue with me, Io! Someone has to command up that valley, and you're it. Now, follow Chàrion!"

He reined his horse around. His men's thoughts boiled in his mind: they had sensed the enemy's charge even as they fought. Chàrion bellowed out Kahsir's orders over the noise, speaking in battle code lest the enemy understand; Iowyn's higher voice was nearly lost in the commotion. Tirril rode to Kahsir's side, signaling he was ready. Kahsir nodded, brought his hand down in the order to charge, and set his horse to a gallop.

He looked over his shoulder and saw that he was followed by at least seventy men. The rest were gradually easing their way toward the narrow valley, holding the Leishoranya off with growing difficulty. Kahsir turned forward again, braced his shield against his side, and rode headlong at the approaching enemy.

The width of the roadway was his only advantage.

The Leishoranya behind the front ranks of the charging warriors would be blocked off from fighting at first. He picked one of the enemy at random and guided his horse straight at the man.

The two horses collided and Kahsir was nearly thrown from the saddle. He lashed out with his sword, felt the blade bite flesh, and whirled to face another warrior. Krotànya battle cries rang out in his ears, but were soon lost in the thunder and the cheers of the attacking Leishoranya. He slashed to the side again, not even seeing which enemy he hit. *Lords! There are too many of them for us to handle! Too many!*

The first heavy drops of rain began to fall. Kahsir cursed, brought his sword down, and met a parry. He turned and reengaged, finally able to stab up under the Leishoran's shield into the man's side.

The enemy slowly forced them back, driving them toward the fighting to the rear. Tirril's voice rang out, calling desperate coded orders. The rain started pelting down. Kahsir blinked it from his eyes; his horse slipped on the wet road and caught itself in a desperate scramble. He glanced quickly over his shoulder; the fighting to his rear had intensified. The Krotànya who faced Red-Cloak's men were fewer now, but they still held, waiting until Kahsir and his men could have a clear run at the valley.

He looked at the Leishoranya—at the beautiful faces, outlined by occasional flashes of lightning. He brought his sword up, deflected a new opponent's blow, then with a quick hook of the guards, sent the Leishoran's blade spinning off into the gloom. Leaning forward, he cut sideways at the man's side before the warrior could react.

Now! Instinct clamored. They had been holding their own before the enemy, but they could not last; he ran the risk of becoming surrounded if he did not move. He looked for Tirril, saw him fighting not more than a few paces away.

"Tirril!" he bellowed over the battle's noise. "Run for it!"

Tirril shook his head. "Only after you go, Lord! I'll follow!"

Kahsir opened his mouth to object, then turned his horse and cantered off down the road. Behind him, he heard a roar of excitement from the enemy and risked a look—Tirril and the others had disengaged and were following him at a gallop.

The valley cut off into the hills beside the road, its mouth barely wide enough for five men to ride up it abreast. Kahsir jerked on the reins and brought his horse to a sliding stop on the grassy margin. The rain had eased somewhat, but visibility was still chancy. The valley vanished to his left in the murky light, its grade probably steeper than it looked.

"Come on!" he shouted to his warriors, waving to the valley and to the few holding from the opposite direction. "Archers! Shoot if you can! Give us protection!"

He was asking a lot from the archers and knew it. Even though they had treated their bowstrings to retard dampness, accuracy in this kind of weather was next to impossible. Still, it was better than nothing, and he and his men needed all the cover they could get.

A tall woman loomed up at his side, her hair plastered against her cheeks. She gripped a bow in one hand and held an arrow nocked with the other, guiding her horse by knee pressure alone.

"Lord!" she cried. "Go! I got bowmen with me. We'll keep those motherless dogs off your backs! Go!"

He hesitated, recognizing Jhadàvis. "Not until the last man's in this valley."

She frowned, then gestured to the archers who followed her. They spread out across the opening of

the valley and began firing at any Leishoran who came
too close. Kahsir's heart beat raggedly in his chest; the
last of his men galloped ahead of the enemy toward
the valley.

Kahsir backed his horse up as more men scrambled
past him from the road. His heart in his throat, he
waved them on—the Leishoranya had regrouped and
were riding closer. Men shouted to each other as they
urged their horses up the rocky grade. Jhadàvis and
her bowmen still fired at the gathering enemy below.
*Damn! That woman's got ice for blood. If I don't order
her to leave, she'll stay here and die.*

"Jhadàvis!" He rode closer to her and shouted her
name again over another rumble of thunder.

She turned, eyes narrowed against the rain.

"Get out of here! Now!" He signaled to the other
bowmen, Sending to those who could not hear him.
"Fall back a bit! Move!"

Jhadàvis reined her horse around and started up the
valley, firing behind at the enemy as she went. Her horse
slipped to its knees on the rain-slickened stones, then
jerked to its feet—her shot flew high and wild. Kahsir
Sent his order to withdraw again: men jostled against
each other as they forced their mounts farther up the
valley. An enemy arrow hissed past Kahsir's head and
bounced off the rocky walls. He kicked his horse into a
trot and scrambled up the valley behind the archers.

"Lord!"

Jhadàvis waited for him, waving her men past.

"If some of us don't stay behind, the enemy'll come
after us!"

He nodded. "Stay, then. We'll make a stand after
we've regrouped."

"We be soaked, Lord. We'll divide up—half of us
will restring our bows, then relieve the others." Her
eyes were dark smudges in the gloom. "And when we
run out of arrows—what then?"

His hands clenched into fists on the reins. "Then,"

he said, "I suppose we'll have to fight our way free."

Tsingar sat beneath the shelter his men had hastily erected by the road and stared at the weary bowman who stood before him. D'Yeto had brought the man into the shelter, and now sat silently at Tsingar's side. The rain drummed on the blankets stretched across lashed spears, but Tsingar was soaked through.

And what the man had told him—it took all Tsingar's effort to keep his face calm and his voice level.

"So you've found Aduhar," he said, looking at the man who stood silent in the dusk.

The warrior nodded, his face difficult to read in the gloom.

"Where is he?"

"Dead, Lord," the man said.

Tsingar spared a sidelong glance at D'Yeto. "Are you sure?"

"See for yourself, Lord."

The dead were everywhere. Tsingar looked at them as he passed with D'Yeto at his side, unnerved to find over half the slain were D'Yeto's men or Aduhar's. Gone were the days when the Krotànya could be run down like vermin and slain out of hand.

The archer who led the way halted, outlined momentarily against the gloom by a flash of lightning, his shoulders slumped with weariness. He pointed toward a tangle of bodies.

"There, Lord. Aduhar lies there."

"Go," Tsingar said.

The warrior saluted and left. Tsingar walked slowly to those bodies, looked down, and saw Aduhar.

The young man lay under several dead. Tsingar shoved at the bodies with his foot, pushing and rolling them aside.

"Gods, Tsingar," D'Yeto said, gesturing at Aduhar's ruined face and bloody side. "Who the Dark could have done *that*? I never saw anyone move as fast as Aduhar."

"I know."

D'Yeto shrugged. "It's over now. And if we're going to storm that valley, we've got to rest."

Tsingar stared at Aduhar's body, somehow empty and burned out inside now that the object of his hatred was gone.

"Tsingar?" D'Yeto prompted.

He turned. "Remember what we discussed. Aduhar fell in battle. I don't want Mehdaiy thinking *I* killed him."

D'Yeto nodded. "I'll still have to tell him about Aduhar's mutiny. We've got to deal with the rest of his cohorts."

Tsingar started toward the shelter. "If we can find them. The Krotànya probably killed them, too. Well over half Aduhar's men are dead."

D'Yeto snorted something. "As for taking that valley, how the Void do you propose we do that?"

"I'm not sure yet. We'll have to do something soon, or the Krotànya will escape to the city. And think about this: if our battle here went unnoticed by the Krotànya Mind-Born, we're damned lucky. We could end up with Krotànya companies crawling all over the hillsides looking for us."

"Aye." D'Yeto grimaced. "You realize it's possible that Kahsir and his men have already escaped."

Tsingar stopped by the shelter, utterly exhausted. "No. I've probed the valley. They're still in it. They're just as tired as we are, and you don't see too many of *us* walking around."

"Maybe not. But Kahsir knows we've got the manpower to surround the valley. He might do something desperate." D'Yeto looked off into the darkening evening. Thunder still rumbled overhead, but the worst of the storm seemed over. "My suggestion is to take the hills on either side of that valley."

Tsingar ducked inside the shelter, shook the worst of

the rain from his cloak, and sat down as D'Yeto joined him. "That won't solve much. They're probably gathered at the end of that valley, and by the time we fight our way to it, they'll have had the chance to escape over its other side. I've sent a few squads to set up watch. The Krotànya won't be able to escape without us knowing."

"We hold the road, Tsingar," D'Yeto persisted. "Send out more men and surround the valley. We've got the numbers to do it."

Though darkness hid D'Yeto's face and expression, Tsingar heard the exasperation in his voice. And something about that particular valley stuck in Tsingar's mind. His men had scouted the area thoroughly, reporting suitable points for staging an ambush. *Damn! What did they tell me about that valley? I can't remember.*

He rubbed his eyes. "Get our maps. We'll need to look at them before we do anything. And what we need right now is sleep."

D'Yeto sighed heavily. "I know. But dammit, Tsingar, if we lose them . . ."

Tsingar shifted his cloak higher around his neck. "My men have scouted this territory. After we've looked at the maps, we'll know more about what lies around that valley, and the valley itself. And as for losing Kahsir and his sister . . . The Krotànya are wounded. We have them bottled up for now. But the war won't turn on it. Mehdaiy knows this. Queen Aeschu knows this. We've got to keep things in perspective. *If* we can take Kahsir—*if* we can take his sister—well, then we've succeeded in one small part of our invasion. But we can't lose our company doing it. Let's look at the maps, man, and get some sleep. The Krotànya aren't made of any sterner stuff than we are."

"But—"

Tsingar glared in D'Yeto's direction. "I've fought Kahsir so many times I've lost count of them. Dhumaric and I faced him on battlefield after battlefield. Kahsir always slipped out of our grasp like he had the Gods' own luck. If he escapes again, it won't be fresh news."

D'Yeto shrugged, a rustle in the darkness. "I'm still going to send out more warriors to join the squads around that valley. If the Krotànya try to escape, at least we'll have enough men to hold them until we can get there."

"Do what you want to." Tsingar was so tired now he had trouble thinking. "The maps, D'Yeto. The maps."

D'Yeto slipped out from the shelter.

The rain had started again: it beat down on the sodden cloaks above Tsingar's head. A steady drip of water fell onto his face—he moved slightly to one side and found a drier position. If Kahsir, his sister, and the other Krotànya managed to escape from their valley, they would have found some source of energy no one else had tapped. He considered the four hundred men who stood between his position beside the road and the city. He could order them back, thereby increasing his odds— No. Trust the Krotànya to get a Sending off to the city, and Gods only knew how many men Iowyn could call to her aid.

Tsingar shrugged, wrapped his cloak tight, then curled up on his side and went to sleep.

A flash of lightning lit up the narrow valley and the steep wall that rose near vertically at its end. Kahsir glared at that dead end, then at the valley walls on either side.

Trapped.

He sought a way into his Dream again, yet it was nowhere to be found. *Dammit! I can't believe it led me so wrong!* Yet his Dream had never guaranteed anything. It had merely served as a look into alternate futures—the way things *might* be if certain choices were made and not others.

He cursed softly. He could *feel* the Dream there, sense it hovering just beyond his reach. Its very absence mocked him, rendered the choices he had already made inconsequential.

"Lord."

Kahsir started. Chàrion stood close by, having arrived unheard and unnoticed.

"I've checked the valley thoroughly, Lord," Chàrion said. "There's no way out except the way we came." Thunder rumbled loudly, drowning out the rest of his words. He tried again. "If we leave the horses, I suppose we could—"

"Rest, Chàrion," Kahsir said. "Go rest now."

"But what the Dark are we going to do about—?"

"Rest, dammit!" He faced Chàrion full on. "None of us can think straight weary as we are."

Chàrion bowed his head. "Aye, Lord."

Kahsir turned and stared at the valley's dead end, listening to Chàrion walk away. Once he knew the commander gone, he let his shoulders slump, and sank down to sit on a large rock. Another rumble of thunder rolled down the valley, and the rain still fell, though not as heavily as before.

Lords of Light! How am I going to get us out of this one? He refused to look at the end of the valley and clenched his fists on his knees. After an endless while, the fury left and he could think clearly again.

He sensed Iowyn long before he heard her footsteps, and knew Chàrion had spoken with her.

"Kahs?"

He motioned to the rock at his side, still looking off into the gathering gloom. Iowyn sat down, pulled her knees up to her chin, crossed her arms on them, and stared at him.

"So," he said, gesturing to the end of the valley, "I've really got us into a fine mess now."

"You had no way of knowing this was a dead end," she said, her voice very quiet. "Don't blame yourself."

"If I'd only had the sense to thoroughly scout this area. . . ." He looked away and then, as she started to say something, glanced back. "And don't ask me what we're going to do. I don't know . . . I simply don't know." He rubbed at the tensed muscles at the back of his neck. "Chàrion suggested, or *tried* to suggest, leaving the horses and climbing out of this valley."

"That's not a bad idea."

"Huhn. Chancy at best."

"Why? The enemy's as tired as we are."

"Aye. But they're hardly stupid. They'll have posted squads of lookouts on the hillsides."

She was silent for a long time. "We could take the mind-road."

He snorted a laugh. "As exhausted and hurt as we are? We'd get about as far as their lines."

She shrugged in the gloom. A low rumble of thunder followed a distant flash of lightning, and she flinched. He looked at her shadowed features; she had never been one to be frightened of storms.

"Io," he said. "What's the matter?"

"I think Dreja's dead."

Fresh energy charged him. "Are you sure?"

"I can't sense him," she said, her voice gone to a whisper. "Anywhere."

"Perhaps you're mistaken. There can be other reasons."

She shook her head, a slight motion in the shadows. "O Lords! If all this had never been!"

"I'm responsible. If I'd listened to myself, paid attention to what my mind told me, I'd have never let Ahndrej ride north."

She made a small noise of protest. "He would have followed you anyway, whether you willed it or not. And now—now he's . . ."

"I don't think he's dead, though I can't tell you why." He put an arm around her trembling shoulders.

"In war, you don't make assumptions until you've counted all the bodies."

She nodded. For a long moment she was silent, then she straightened. "And tomorrow, Kahs? What happens tomorrow?"

"I've told you I don't know. If I did, I'd be doing something about it. One thing's certain: we're going to have to fight again."

"I still think we ought to try the mind-road," Iowyn said, her voice steady now. "The city's not that far away."

"No. We couldn't make it."

"We could get close."

"Do you know for certain there aren't other enemy companies in the hills around Dramujh?"

She set her jaw. "No. But we'd have a better chance in the open countryside than bottled up here."

"We're so damned tired, Io, we'd just stumble into the enemy's hands."

"It seems to me you're only thinking about ways we *can't* escape."

He drew a long, deep breath—keeping silent for a long moment because he feared what he might say. "Don't you imagine the enemy's thought of every suggestion you've made? They're waiting for us to try. Sendings and the mind-road can be blocked. Remember what happened at Vharcwal."

"But we have Stefendhi with us. Surely he could get a message through to the city asking for help."

"I imagine he could. But you already left orders for Nehaiden to send out a company at dawn of over three hundred if we didn't make it back to Dramujh by nightfall, or he didn't hear from us. The enemy doesn't know that."

She straightened. "If the Leishoranya have another company between us and . . ." She turned her head toward him. "Lords, Kahs! That's even more reason to Send to the city. Nehaiden—"

"All right, Io. Let's say Stefendhi *does* get a message to Dramujh, warning of possible ambush. Say that Nehaiden doubles the number of men he sends to help us. Where would he send them? To join us here? The valley won't hold half that many men."

"Dammit, Kahs! He could send them to attack the Leishoranya who've got us trapped here."

"Possibly. But we don't know what the enemy's got out there in the hills. Having now sent six hundred of his thousand out on a rescue mission, Nehaiden would be left with one company, the home guard, and a town full of noncombatants."

"They'll fight well enough."

"I'm not disputing that. Think, Io! If the enemy's decided to make an effort to take Dramujh, *and* force a corridor north from their lines, they could command companies totalling in the thousands. We could lose the damn town!"

"We could Send further off . . . ask for enough men to turn things in our favor."

"Where?" he snapped, dropping his arm from her shoulder. "If you know of someplace that's over-full of warriors, tell me."

After a moment's silence, she gestured helplessly. "Do you honestly think the enemy would attack the city?"

He shrugged. "The enemy commander could have decided this was an excellent time to do just that. They've already sent a strike force here to go after you. Whoever's in charge of the Leishoranya we're facing has likely sent him reports of what they've found here. Why *not* attack the city?"

"Aye," she said at last. "Why not? What you say makes sense. But there's got to be some way we can—"

He turned toward her, making an effort to keep his voice calm. "Look at our alternatives. We've already acknowledged that we can't take the mind-road. We both know we can't stay here: the enemy will storm this valley sure as the sun will rise tomorrow. We don't know how many enemy troops are operating around Dramujh, so we can't leave the city under-defended. If you have a solution, I'll jump at it."

Again, thunder rumbled down the valley. He rubbed his eyes and waited for her answer, but sensed she had none.

She stood. "I wish Grandfather were here," she said, turning away. She cursed as she lost her footing on the slippery rocks. "He'd know what to do."

He stared blankly after her as she walked off into the darkness. "Io!" he called, his throat tight. "Dammit! Come back here!"

But she was gone. Kahsir rubbed his eyes again. *Even if Vlàdor were here, I doubt he'd see a clear way out.* The thought was strengthening. He would sleep for a few hours; then, perhaps, with a clearer mind, he could think of a way to escape this trap.

CHAPTER 20

"Tsingar!"

Tsingar jerked out of sleep, blinked his eyes open and stared up into D'Yeto's face. The commander was kneeling close by in the dim light. Behind stood a man carrying a lit traveling lamp and a map case.

"We've got them, Tsingar!" D'Yeto said, his voice full of excitement. "We've *got* them!"

Tsingar shook his head and sat up. "Why did you let me sleep so long? It's nearly dawn."

D'Yeto motioned the man behind him forward. "Didn't you hear me, Tsingar? The Krotànya are trapped! We've got them now!"

"What?" Sleepiness vanished in an instant. "Trapped how?"

"The valley they scrambled into—look!" D'Yeto opened the map case, took the rolled paper out, and spread it across the soggy blanket he knelt on. He pointed. "Your scouts did a thorough job. This valley— it's a dead end, Tsingar. The only way the Krotànya can get out is to run straight into our army."

Tsingar stared; his mind started working again. He rubbed his eyes. "Don't you suppose they know that?" he asked, handing the map to D'Yeto and standing.

The storm had spent itself during the night, and the pre-dawn air was cool. He gathered his cloak closer, left the shelter, and glanced sidelong as D'Yeto joined him. "I can't imagine Kahsir doesn't know he's trapped."

"There's not much he can do about it. I've had that valley watched all night. Not a one of the Krotànya has tried to leave."

"Even by the mind-road?"

D'Yeto shook his head. "I anticipated that, too. I figured they were too tired to try until they'd rested. Even so, I stationed Bundyai and his men around the valley. They're trained for this; they'll keep the Krotànya from breaking out."

Tsingar looked around the roadway where his company had camped with D'Yeto's. Most of the warriors were up and moving around, trying to ease the stiffness from their bodies. "Let me see that map again."

D'Yeto handed it over. For a long moment, Tsingar studied it.

"So. The Krotànya are trapped. That doesn't help us much. We still have to storm that valley, and from what I can tell, it's narrow enough that we can't mount a good charge."

"We outnumber them, Tsingar, probably three to one. Given those odds, we can wear them down."

"Maybe. We could always recall the four hundred men you sent closer to the city. Then we'd—"

"No." D'Yeto lifted a hand. "There's a Krotànya company of three hundred men on its way south from Dramujh. They just left. We're going to need those four hundred to keep the Krotànya off our backs."

Tsingar winced. *Gods! How long can we keep two engagements hidden from the Krotànya Mind-Born? We're going to have to make this as quick as possible and then get the Void out of here.* "Are you sure there's only three hundred of them?"

"That's what the scout said."

"He'd damned well better be right!" Tsingar walked slowly back and forth in front of the shelter, rolling and unrolling the map in his hands. "Is there any way we can get at Kahsir from the sides of the valley?"

"No. It's too steep. And there's just enough cover to keep our archers from having clear shots."

"Damn! I guess we don't have a choice. We'll *have* to storm it. But I don't like the idea of spending all those men."

D'Yeto stared. "After all this time—after all the chasing around and lying in wait—you're concerned over the loss of men?"

"Gods! Do you think I care whether these scum live or die? But consider this: Queen Aeschu herself told Mehdaiy and me that *if* the chance presented itself, we were to take Kahsir prisoner."

"This seems to me to be that chance."

Tsingar handed the map to the man who still held the case. He glanced up toward the narrow valley and shrugged. "If we knew precisely how many Krotànya patrol these hills, I'd agree."

"Then all the better to move *now!*" D'Yeto said. "Let's use our superiority of numbers while we still have them."

"If this were anywhere else, I couldn't find fault with your argument. Follow my thinking on this, D'Yeto, and tell me if I'm wrong. You say we've got men to spare; that's true, but we'll lose most of them. We're deep in Krotànya-held lands, and you can't tell me the battle yesterday and the one we're planning will go unnoticed. Once we've caught Kahsir and his sister—if they survive—we've still got to make it back to Mehdaiy. I don't relish the idea of doing that without a lot of men behind me."

Gradually, the look of incredulity faded from D'Yeto's face. "I see what you mean. But I'd rather face Mehdaiy having made the attempt than not." He dropped his eyes momentarily. "From what Mehdaiy told me, he assumes you've got a good chance to go after both Kahsir and his sister. If he hadn't believed this true, I don't think he would have sent me and my men north to aid you."

Tsingar let the veiled comment pass, then glanced up at the sky. "Let's wait until the sun's higher. Light's good enough here, but it won't be in that valley. We've a lot of Krotànya to kill, and if we can see what we're doing, it will make the job easier." He rubbed his stubbled chin, then looked at D'Yeto. "It's a shame Aduhar's dead. He would have been one of the first I'd have sent up that valley."

The Leishoranya roared out cheers as another wave of them charged the shieldwall that stretched across the valley. From where Iowyn stood, their numbers seemed endless. She put another rock in her sling, whirled it about her head, and let fly.

"My Lady Iowyn!"

She glanced over her shoulder. Chàrion waited several paces away and gestured up the valley.

"Your brother wants to see you, Lady," he called.

Iowyn nodded and lowered her sling. Chàrion called her name again; she waved to let him know she had heard. Turning from battle, bent low to avoid arrows, she followed the red-headed warrior.

Kahsir stood waiting for her, his sword bloodied to its hilt, and a strip of cloth around his swordarm near his shoulder. She caught sight of his face and her heard lurched: he had not looked so grim for decades—so grim and so dangerous. She remembered what she had said to him the night before, and now wanted more than anything to unsay those harsh words.

"Io," he said. "Are you all right?"

She nodded, her arm and shoulder aching from unaccustomed use of the sling.

He glanced down the valley. "I wish the same could be

said for the rest of us. Chàrion, get more bowmen down there. And remind Jhadàvis they're not to fire unless their shots are sure. We're running short of arrows."

"Aye, Lord."

Chàrion trotted off, hunting for Jhadàvis. Iowyn watched him go, her heart in her throat. *Lords of Light! Keep Jhada safe!* Her shield dragged at her arm so she set it at her feet, glancing up at her brother as she straightened.

"How much longer can we hold them off?"

He shrugged, his face still unreadable. "Awhile," he said. His voice had gone rough from shouting. "They have to rest, too. The only thing that's saved us so far is the narrowness of this valley. They can't send any more men against us than we can meet. But they've got the advantage of numbers; they're killing us off one by one."

She nodded and looked down to the entrance of the valley, to the enemy that clogged it, rank upon rank deep. She peered into the confusion, hunting for Jhadàvis.

"Have you sensed Ahndrej yet?"

Her heart jumped with a pang of loss. "No."

"I'm sorry. Not knowing is sometimes harder than knowing the worst. If it's of any consolation, I still don't think he's dead."

"That's all I can hope for," she murmured, glancing away. *I've got to think of other things. Anything but Dreja!* "How many wounded do we have?"

Kahsir glanced over his shoulder. Behind, ministered to by Stefendhi and several others, lay a number of men, most severely wounded. "At last count, twenty-five this morning. Nearly the same number killed."

She grimaced. Counting the men Kahsir had brought north and the fifty she had taken from the city, three hundred and fifty Krotànya had been alive at the start of this battle: now, only around one hundred could fight.

"We can't hold much longer if they keep this up.

Several hours, at most. Soon, they'll have worn us down to the point they can walk right over us." She looked up at her brother, choosing her words with care. "Have you considered what to do when we finally break?"

He held her eyes for a long time, then nodded slowly. "Chàrion's spreading the word. When that moment comes, each of us is to take the mind-road."

"It's blocked. I tried for it as an experiment. The Leishoranya must have heavy help up there."

"You haven't heard the rest. I want the wounded out of here first, then those of us who are weariest. If the rest of us are able to join minds, we might be able to break that block."

"*Aiii*, Kahs! Tired as we are? Do you honestly think—?"

"Also," he said, his eyes straying down to the edge of the valley, "I'll give them something to take their minds from blocking us. I'll be in the front ranks, begging them to come at me."

Her heart froze. "No! You mustn't! Not you! Of us all, not you!"

"Think, Io. Who are they after here? Me, that's who. They went after you to use as a lure to get me. If I dangle myself before them, do you honestly think they'd turn down the chance to come after me?"

"But, Kahs—"

"No buts. That's the way it's going to be. I've already told Stefendhi he's to help the men who've been hurt. Chàrion's telling those of us who are too exhausted to fight anymore that they're to escape, too. The rest of us— We'll stand . . . somehow we'll stand. Then, at the last moment, we'll take the mind-road, too."

"But where?"

He waved a hand. "Everywhere. Anywhere. Back to the city . . . to the hills around us. Wherever anyone can go. Those of us with greater power can travel farthest. We'll have to get reinforcements somewhere. Once we're out of this valley, Dramujh could be in danger. *Might be* in danger even as we speak."

"The men Nehaiden sent from the city?" Her heart sank. "Have they—?"

"I don't know. Stefendhi managed to crack the mind-block for a moment. He said the Leishoranya have another company north of us, about two leagues away. They've met and engaged Nehaiden's men."

"O Lords! Then we could be—" She reached out and caught at his arm. "Promise me this . . . give me your oath on it. Don't make me go until you're ready to escape. Please."

He met her gaze and held it. "All right. You have my word."

She closed her eyes to hide the tears that stung them. Again came the roar of Leishoranya cheers, lifted in anticipation of victory; Chàrion's deep voice calling more men forward was nearly lost in the noise. Iowyn bent, lifted her shield, then slipped it onto her arm.

"We'll make it, Kahs," she said. "We've got to believe that we can!"

From where he stood, Tsingar could tell the Krotànya were close to breaking—they had already stood far longer than he would have guessed. He and D'Yeto had thrown their warriors into that narrow valley with reckless abandon, and they had obeyed—obeyed and died. He glanced at the fighting, frowned, and started pacing again. His men's bodies lay piled up around the edge of the valley, sometimes two and three deep. *Gods! The Krotànya can't last much longer!*

"Tsingar!"

Face flushed and grim in the morning sunlight, D'Yeto walked in his direction.

"We'll have to go at them with all we've got!"

D'Yeto said, glancing over his shoulder. "We've lost too many men."

And who was it told me we had them to spare? "How many exactly?"

"Gods . . . over two hundred. They're piled up in front of that valley like kindling."

Tsingar looked from D'Yeto to the battle, then back. "I agree. We're losing the advantage of numbers we once had. We'll have to—" He drew up short. "No . . . wait! If we do this right, we needn't lose all that many more men."

"What are you proposing?"

"We'll get the Krotànya where they can be hurt the worst," Tsingar said. "Recall those men who are maintaining the mind-block. And gather the strongest minds you can find!"

"But . . ."

"Do it!" Tsingar threw back his head and laughed. "Ah, Gods . . . Gods and my Ancestors! Why didn't I think of this sooner?"

"What, dammit? What are you talking about?"

"The Krotànya," Tsingar said softly. "They won't even be able to fight us. Their idiot laws forbid it. We'll go after their minds, D'Yeto! We'll go after their minds!"

Another wave of pain seared through Kahsir's head, burning in its passage like fire. With all his newly acquired strength, he tightened his shields and threw protection over his mind. The pain receded, subsiding to an annoying ache. Other warriors were fighting off this unseen attack, though a few had succumbed and knelt holding their heads in their hands, weapons fallen useless at their sides.

Kahsir turned to the Mind-Born at his side. "Stefendhi! Do something! Anything!"

"I'm trying." Stefendhi's face had gone pale with effort. "They're strong . . . and there are many of them." He licked his lips. "I'm weary, Lord. I can only last so long."

Kahsir nodded and looked down at the mouth of the valley, his head still throbbing. He wiped the sweat from his brow with a shaking hand.

Lords of Light! We're going to die here—every one of us!

Why? Why should we die? I know what I can do. I did it once before when I saved Iowyn.

He remembered the flow of power, focused and channeled against his enemies.

Hjshraiel!

He froze inside. The concept that had haunted his waking and sleeping. Every legend about this mysterious figure said that he would not know his own identity at first . . . that—

No! He shook his head, denying the temptation. *No! If I'm Hjshraiel, I'd know it!*

Would I? Would I really?

He swallowed heavily. He *was* gifted with fearsome mental powers, and he had already misused them once. What was one more time? If he already stood damned in the sight of his people, then at least let it be for saving lives, for preventing a defeat that could open the way for the enemy's full scale invasion of Elyâsai.

Besides, no one knows what I did. And those who do have sworn themselves to silence. I can exact the same oath here.

He looked toward the enemy again, his decision made even before he knew he had made it.

"Chàrion!" he yelled across the noise, his shields established now and his mind free of pain. "The Leishoranya . . . they're massing for a charge!"

Chàrion stood farther down toward the battle. He swung around and gestured over his shoulder. "Men, Lord!" he called. "I need more men!"

Kahsir threw his arms wide. "Where the Dark do I

get them from? My saddlebags? Stand, Chàrion . . .
stand! If only for awhile!"

Without looking back, he spun around and ran up
the valley floor to where he had tethered his horse
alongside the other mounts. Snatching up the reins, he
sought the stirrups and swung up into his saddle.

*Iowyn and the rest must live! They've got to have a
chance! And I can give it to them.*

He reined his horse around and set his shield firmly
on his left arm. As he passed the wounded, they glanced
up, eyes glazed with physical and mental pain. He
brought his horse to a halt and turned in the saddle.

"Mount!" he cried to the men who stood near the
horses. "Mount and ride with me! Spread the word—
the rest of us must try to escape!"

"Kahs!"

His sister's voice cut through the noise. He grimaced, looked steadfastly forward, and rode on.

"Kahs! Where are you—?" Her voice rose in a
scream; he sensed someone holding her, preventing
her from following. "Kahs! Don't! For the love of
Light, Kahs! *Don't do it!*"

His men rode behind him: hoofbeats rattled on
exposed rock. He methodically checked his boot knife,
his shortsword. His sister's cries were only a noise
now; he shoved them from his consciousness. Eyes
held to the seething mass of fighting men at the opening to the valley, he rode on.

"Chàrion!" he yelled ahead. "Back us up, Chàrion!
Then all of you—escape as best you can!"

Chàrion turned; his face went whiter yet, but he
nodded and called out to Jhadàvis for archery support.

Kahsir looked forward again. Everything had disappeared now save the end of that valley and the waiting
Leishoranya. He croaked a laugh. This would give
them something to think about—a sally into their
midst. In the moment he rode out from the valley, he
would have all their attention, tearing it away from his

companions who remained behind. And then he would use his power—blast all the Leishoranya to nothingness. He envisioned it, *saw* it happen, schooled his mind to what he would ask it to do.

The valley floor grew flatter. Most of the enemy fought afoot now; horses would take up too much room in their assault. This was the one advantage he and the men who rode with him had, and he intended to make it count. He urged his horse to a quicker trot and lifted his sword, sensing the warriors behind him preparing for this last desperate charge into the enemy.

Forgive me, Grandfather. And if I die, understand why I had to do this. His family's faces swam in his mind's eye, supplanted by that of his wife. His heart tore wide with agony. *Eltàrim! My heart . . . my life! We'll meet and love again, beyond these stars we know!*

The way was clear now; Chàrion and the men who fought at the entrance to the valley began moving aside. Kahsir brought the flat of his sword down on his horse's rump, kicking the animal into a canter.

"For the Light!" he cried, lifting his sword over his head. *"Legir!* For the Light! *Legir! Legir!"*

"Tsingar!"

D'Yeto's voice carried over the sounds of battle, tinged with such urgency that Tsingar spun around on his heel. His fellow commander was fighting a nervous horse close to the mouth of the narrow valley and gesturing madly.

"Tsingar!" D'Yeto called again. "Hurry!"

Tsingar acted without thinking, spurred by something beyond D'Yeto's frantic gestures and excited tone of voice. He grabbed for his reins, hauled himself astride his horse, and cantered toward the battle. The fighting had grown fiercer around the entrance to the valley; he peered ahead, trying to see into the seething mass of men.

"It's Kahsir!" D'Yeto cried, pointing up the valley.

"Gods, Tsingar! He's coming out! The fool's leading a charge straight into us!"

Tsingar's heart lurched and he jerked his horse to a stop at D'Yeto's side. "You're joking! Surely not. . . ."

"Look for yourself, then." D'Yeto waved at the valley. "He's got men with him—about thirty-five . . . forty, I'd guess. I can't tell. There are too many people milling around here."

Tsingar urged his horse closer to the fighting and stared over the men who fought on foot. It was true. He had no trouble picking out Kahsir's tall figure: he *was* leading a charge out from that valley, just as D'Yeto had said.

"What's he trying to do?" Tsingar asked. "Get himself killed?"

D'Yeto shrugged. "The Dark only knows. Gods! He's hit our front rank! He must have rested men with him—they're cutting ours down like they were children."

Tsingar glanced wildly about, looking at the warriors who stood back from the battle, unable to get closer to the valley. He shook his head: though they were not fighting, they were exhausted. "We need fresh men. If I'm going to have a chance at Kahsir, now's the time. Fresh men, D'Yeto. Where are they?"

"Everyone's been fighting up here." D'Yeto wiped the sweat from his face. "We've been taking turns. We don't have anyone who's fresh save the men who are keeping up the mental attack."

"Then let's use them. We don't have much time to lose."

"But—"

"Do it!" Tsingar snapped. "Kahsir's death is more important than the other Krotànya!"

D'Yeto paused, then turned his horse, stood high in the stirrups, and gestured broadly, calling those men from their posts.

Tsingar looked up into the valley. *Kahsir. The battle*

must have driven him mad! He's trying to— O Gods!

"D'Yeto!" he called. "Hurry! Kahsir's not seeking death: he's trying to escape!"

D'Yeto nodded, gestured sharply at several more men who rode forward. Tsingar recognized them as the warriors who had been attacking the Krotànya minds. They were the most physically rested of all his men, and with them he had a chance of stopping Kahsir's desperate charge. He reached behind his saddle, grabbed up his shield and set it on his left arm.

"Are you ready, D'Yeto?" he called.

D'Yeto nodded again. Nearly fifty fresh men had gathered behind him, armed for immediate combat. "Lead us, Tsingar. It's your honor."

Tsingar unsheathed his sword, set his helm tighter on his head, and trotted his horse to D'Yeto's side. He glanced at the warriors clustered behind them.

"Follow me," he called out. "Take Kahsir alive if you can."

He turned toward the valley and kicked his horse into a fast trot; men gave way and moved aside, jumping out of the path of the oncoming horses. D'Yeto rode to Tsingar's left and slightly behind: the rest of the warriors followed closely. Tsingar drew a deep breath, trying to achieve a sense of calm . . . of fighting detachment.

Gods! O Gods! Let this be the day that brings an end to Kahsir's battle-luck!

Kahsir fought with cold, dispassionate swordstrokes, waiting for the right moment to come. He glanced at the enemy, saw their confusion, and sensed they had called fresh men to meet his unexpected charge.

O Lords! I've got to use my power soon, before more of my warriors die!

He shook his head. *Not yet. It's too soon. The Leishoranya are gathering. I'll want the largest target I can get.*

Hjshraiel!

No! he answered himself, then smiled bitterly. *It doesn't make any difference who I am. No difference in the end at all.*

The Krotànya who rode with Kahsir fought like madmen, and Tsingar was hard pressed by the opponents he met. He kept his eyes fixed on Kahsir's tall figure, aiming himself toward it.

Suddenly, a hard blow hit his shield—he swayed sideways in the saddle, regained his balance, and lashed out at the Kròtan who had attacked. His blade struck the warrior solidly; the man screamed, fell backward out of his saddle, and disappeared from sight.

The impetus of Kahsir's charge was gone now. Tsingar glanced around. His men had slain or wounded nearly a quarter of the Krotànya in their first charge and were now holding them. His heart strained with excitement; Kahsir was close—closer now than Tsingar had been to him in decades. He laughed wildly, slashed out with his sword, and cut down another Krotànya warrior who was already wounded.

"Kahsir!" he cried, his voice pitched to a near scream.

The Krotànya Throne Prince turned in his saddle, and for a brief moment his eyes met Tsingar's.

"Die, Kahsir!" Tsingar yelled in the Krotànya speech. "You die! For Dhumaric! Come, coward! Face me!"

Tsingar's men seemed to share his excitement. Screaming their battle cries, they threw themselves at the Krotànya who clustered around Kahsir. The fighting grew more intense. The noise of combat, of yelling men and neighing horses made it hard to think. Yet it would be over soon. Tsingar's warriors were forcing the Krotànya back now and it was only a matter of time before—

Then even over the battle's noise, Tsingar heard the

distant sound of horns.

"Lord! Do you hear it?"

Chàrion's voice disturbed Kahsir's concentration, drew his mind away from his coming task. He turned his head: Chàrion rode close by, fighting at his left hand in the position of shieldman. The commander wiped at the blood that trickled down into his right eye and yelled again.

"Horns, Lord! Listen!"

Then Kahsir heard. His heart leapt and he nearly laughed aloud. Horns . . . those were Krotànya horns! From all sides came the sound of their blowing. Suddenly all his plans, his weariness, and despair disappeared. He glanced around—his men had heard those horns, too.

"Krotànya!" he cried, standing in his stirrups and lifting his sword. "Krotànya! *Legir!* For the Light! *Legir! Legir!*"

Strength returned, but strength of a natural sort, come from Lords only knew where. The whole world's power pounded in his veins, coursed through his mind and body. Hope . . . there was that, too, forgotten for so long.

He kicked his horse forward, slashing down at the milling Leishoranya—they seemed to melt before his sword as he fought on. He had brief glimpses of the enemy massed beyond the mouth of the valley. They, too, had heard the horns. He sensed their dismay, their confusion.

—*Chàrion!* he Sent. *Help's coming! Get everyone who can walk down here!*

—*Aye, Lord.*

Kahsir looked at the enemy, hunting for the Leishoran who earlier had yelled something about Dhumaric; the man must have fought in that hilltop battle a year ago where Lorhaiden had killed the Leishoranya commander. Kahsir saw enemy faces everywhere, but not the one of the man he sought. It hardly mattered: he would never forget that scarred face, or that voice.

Again the horns blew—closer this time. The Leishoranya had begun to fall back now, their commanders yelling at them, likely giving orders to regroup. Kahsir longed to be farther out of the valley so he could see what was going on. Who had come to his aid? Who had sent reinforcements?

And, most important of all, who had saved him from himself?

"Kahs!"

Iowyn's voice carried over the battle. He slashed at the Leishoran he faced, glanced over his shoulder, and saw her riding forward. He grinned at her, shouted her name, then turned to the fighting. After his mad charge to the valley's mouth, he knew nothing could have kept her away. Not that it made a difference anymore—she was here and he could hardly send her back.

He reached the edge of the valley. The Leishoranya retreated, drew their ranks together, and prepared for the charge he could not see. The horns blew again, clearer now, ringing out above the commotion. A Leishoran rode in from the left: Kahsir took a hard blow to his shield, but managed to get under the other man's guard. The warrior fell from his horse, his scream drowned in the yelling and the clash of weapons.

Kahsir broke free of the valley and looked around, momentarily confused by all the motion. And then he saw them: the Krotànya who rode to his aid. His mouth dropped open in amazement—there must have been close to six hundred of them, riding in from both ends of the road and down over the hills behind the Leishoranya.

The horns blew again, one last time before the approaching Krotànya would engage the enemy. Kahsir froze, not even daring to hope; unexpectedly, tears started in his eyes. But there it was, the last horn call—it bore the familiar signature of one he would recognize anywhere.

Lorhaiden! Lorhaiden had come!

"By all the Gods of Darkness," Tsingar cried out, "not again!"

"Tsingar!" D'Yeto's voice carried over the sound of blowing horns, of dismayed cries from the warriors who had seen the charging Krotànya. "Turn, Tsingar!" D'Yeto cried. "We've got to meet them!"

Tsingar glanced from one end of the road to the other, then to the hills behind. "Meet them with what?" he yelled. "They've got us, D'Yeto. We'll be crushed like a rotten nut!"

Again the Krotànya horns echoed over the hillsides and Tsingar heard his hundred-commanders screaming orders to regroup. *O Gods! Gods! We're done for!*

"We'll have to make a run for it," Tsingar cried, riding close to D'Yeto so he could be heard. "Spread the word . . . fight free and scatter . . . we've got to find our way back to Mehdaiy's camp."

D'Yeto nodded and turned his horse into the thick mob of warriors who were falling back into some semblance of order. A roar went up from the Krotànya trapped in the narrow valley. Tsingar reined his horse around and blundered out toward the roadway, careless of who he rode down.

Gods! Cold sweat broke out on his forehead. *What am I going to tell Mehdaiy?* He glanced over his shoulder, and for a brief moment caught sight of Kahsir. *Damn you! Damn you! One day, we'll meet again, and that time the luck will be mine!*

He heard D'Yeto and his commanders bellowing out orders for flight. The Krotànya riding down the hillside behind his men and those coming at a gallop down the road from either side drew closer now. No longer did they blow their horns: their cheers were enough to announce their coming.

And suddenly all pretense of order vanished. Tsingar was caught up in a mass of men, all intent on meeting the charging Krotànya. He looked around, frantically seeking D'Yeto. He could not let D'Yeto die—D'Yeto had seen Aduhar's body and could tell Mehdaiy what had happened. If the Krotànya killed D'Yeto, it would be only Tsingar's word against Mehdaiy's anger.

Something hissed by Tsingar's ear and the man in front of him stiffened, clawing at his back. Krotànya arrows! Tsingar bent low over his horse's neck, still looking for D'Yeto. He finally spotted his co-commander; D'Yeto was gesturing madly toward the south, his cries nearly unheard in the noise of battle. A Krotàn rode out of the fighting and Tsingar met the charge; then someone's horse bumped into his, and he was shoved up against his opponent. He slashed out blindly, felt his sword connect with flesh, and then he was free to ride on.

"D'Yeto!" he screamed. D'Yeto turned and Tsingar whipped his horse toward him. "Come with me," he called, near enough now so that he could see the sweat shine on D'Yeto's face. "We've got to escape!"

"But . . ."

"Look around you, man!" Tsingar cried. "We can't face them! We've done all we can here. Follow me!"

Glancing around to get his bearings in the surging chaos, Tsingar turned south. He kicked his horse into a trot, D'Yeto riding at his side. A few warriors grouped around them, fighting off any Krotànya who got in the way.

Tsingar craned his neck, trying to see over the confusion of men and horses. Everywhere he looked, he saw his warriors trying to fight their way free from the surrounding Krotànya. He bared his teeth, snarled, and dug his heels into his mount's flanks, angling off toward the edge of battle.

Suddenly a familiar face loomed up: silver-gray eyes,

cold as death, met his for an instant. His heart lurched: Lorhaiden! By all the Gods—it was Lorhaiden who had ridden to Kahsir's aid. Tsingar shuddered in anguish . . . to have had both Kahsir and Lorhaiden within the reach of his sword—

He lost sight of Lorhaiden in the fighting. D'Yeto yelled something and pointed forward; Tsingar looked and saw an opening in the Krotànya ranks. His heart pounding loudly in his ears, he turned his horse toward it. He would make it . . . he would survive! He burst out of the fighting, D'Yeto still at his side, and whipped his horse into an all-out run.

You're a lucky man, Tsingar, Dhumaric had said once. Tsingar laughed, a strange sound in his own ears. Lucky? He cursed in the midst of his laughter, icy tendrils of fear taking root in his heart. He would need all that luck and more when he faced Mehdaiy with news of this loss.

"Kahs!" Iowyn's voice shook, but she did not care. "They're breaking, Kahs! They're retreating!"

He turned, his face changed, its shadows gone. "It's Lorj!" he cried. "Lorhaiden's come!"

She nodded: she knew Lorhaiden's horn call, too. She followed her brother, giving chase to the fleeing Leishoranya. Krotànya arrows fell and her heart leapt. *Lords of Light! Let it be Jhada!* She looked around: in disorderly ranks, the enemy was trying to fight their way through Lorhaiden's company. And there, across the battle, she saw Jhadàvis, bowstring drawn to her ear, arrow pointed toward the enemy. Iowyn's heart sang out. Life . . . life! She had forgotten how wonderful the concept was.

A Leishoran met her charge, but she blocked his swordstroke with her own. His heavier blade knocked hers away and clanged off her shield, but she was quicker. She cut backward with her own sword and heard him cry out as her blade slashed his side. She looked forward again: the faces of the advancing Krotànya were clearer now.

Then suddenly, the world tilted and changed—her heart jerked, her breath caught in her throat.

"DREJA!"

Tears blurred the fighting as she kicked her horse into a canter, riding down any enemy who got in the way. Ahndrej had heard her voice; he turned, and his face changed in the moment his eyes met hers.

She joined him in the center of the field, and in a space his allies had swept clear, she leaned over in her saddle and touched his shoulder with her sword hand. He bent his head and kissed her hand, moving stiffly, bound and bandaged as he was. And laughed.

"Io!" he said then, voice hoarse from yelling. "Later, love . . . later!"

It hardly mattered anymore—the shadows were gone from her mind. "Let's find Kahs!" she cried.

She set her shield tightly, lifted her sword and plunged back into the battle, Ahndrej riding at her side. Her brother's tall figure was easy to spot, and she fought her way toward him. The enemy was fewer now: most of them had been killed in Lorhaiden's charge, and the rest were trying to break away from the fighting, scattering for the cover of the hills and the safety of the mind-road. Soon, there were no more enemy warriors to face, and her brother sat his horse only paces away.

"Kahs!"

He turned at the sound of her voice, his face transfigured. Their eyes met—he grinned, then called something to Ahndrej that went unheard in the noise.

"We've won!" she cried. Joy bubbled up in her heart. The sunlight . . . the sky . . . their hopes: the world set right once more. "Life, Kahs—life! It's ours again!"

*   *   *

Kahsir rose from his place, absently touched the bloodstained binding on his leg, then looked around. Lorhaiden's men filled the roadway, though several squads of them had gone off to scour the hills for Leishoranya. Lorhaiden had come north with one thousand men under his command, six hundred of whom he had brought to this battle. His mental probes of the area before he attacked had let him know of the conflict north of the valley, so he had sent the other four hundred to aid the men Nehaiden had sent out from Dramujh.

Now Lorhaiden stood close by, giving orders to the hundred-commanders who had gathered at his side. As Kahsir walked toward him, Lorhaiden turned and dismissed those men.

"If I thank you one more time, Lorj," Kahsir said, "I'll go hoarse."

"Then don't, Lord. Thank *him*." Lorhaiden nodded toward Ahndrej, who stood holding Iowyn in a loose embrace. "If he hadn't managed to reach me by the mind-road with news of what was happening, I wouldn't be here."

"And we'd likely be dead. I've talked to him, but nothing I say carries the same weight as what Io's telling him." Kahsir drew his sword-brother aside and pitched his voice low so no one could hear. "How did you get Grandfather to give you one thousand men on such short notice?"

"He knows what you've said is right—we've got to hold Dramujh as long as we can. If the enemy had opened a corridor here—" Lorhaiden shrugged.

"What's happening to the south?"

"Pohlàntyr's holding his own. A day after you left, your grandfather sent him reinforcements. Vahl's doing all right. The men your grandfather gave me for this battle are to be evenly distributed between Dramujh and the armies on the southern border whose needs are greatest."

"It's not any better then, is it?" Kahsir asked, holding Lorhaiden's gaze.

"No, it's not. But don't think about that. Now's the time to enjoy your victory. The rest can wait for tomorrow."

Kahsir nodded, glanced around at the survivors. "Lorj, Stefendhi's taking care of the wounded. See that everyone's made as comfortable as possible. And have Hairon spread the word that as soon as we've heard from the men Nehaiden sent out, we'll be riding to the city."

Lorhaiden nodded and turned away. Kahsir started toward his sister, heard her laughter, and smiled. His Dream was gone for the moment . . . his inner conflict as well. The afternoon sunlight felt warm on his face, making it easier to ignore the shadowed horizon.